Eight Worlds Must Unite...

The light that came from her was as brilliant as sunlight, and it filled cold, dark First World with golden hues and brilliant greens. For a moment, the skies lit up, bright blue and clear. Nearby animals called out; plants strained toward the source, toward Maddie herself.

How long had they been lost in this sunless, sad world? Maddie would have wept to see it, but her heart was too full of power. She was lost to it.

What Others Are Saying:

"... a lush, dreamy fable—both vintage gothic, and modern mystery ... lovingly laced with magic and darkness from start to finish."

*—Cherie Priest, author of **Boneshaker***

"Barron's book is a sexy trek through alternate worlds, with a fascinating and detailed mythology. This one is a steampunk tale that doesn't play by the rules."

*—Mur Lafferty, author and podcaster of **Heaven** and **Hell***

"A brilliant, eloquent adventure through time, space, and the human heart."

*—Jonathan Wood, author of **No Hero***

PÍLGRÍM

OF THE

SKY

Natania Barron

Candlemark & Gleam

For information, address
Candlemark & Gleam LLC,
104 Morgan Street, Bennington, VT 05201
info@candlemarkandgleam.com

ISBN: 978-1-936460-09-0
eISBN: 978-1-936460-08-3

Cover art and design by Brigid Ashwood
www.brigidashwood.com

Book design and composition by Kate Sullivan
Typeface: Berthold Baskerville

Editors: Kate Sullivan and Ellen Harvey
Proofreaders: Sarah Labelle and Matt Hydeman

www.candlemarkandgleam.com

For my sister Llana,
my first companion to worlds beyond.

1

The Last Box

ust one last box. That was Maddie's mantra. The rest of the apartment was empty, with the exception of a broom and the blinds. Five years of entrances and exits, of kisses and arguments, of conversations and pillow talk; it all became very final for Maddie Angler as she dropped the last box on the front stoop and shut the door one last time.

She felt her chest twist with the memories. Of Alvin. Of everything they'd had. Everything she'd lost.

Alvin was dead, after all. At least that's what Maddie had to believe. A year of searching for clues with the help of private investigators and half the police force of Amherst, Massachusetts, had turned up nothing. He'd gone out for a walk one day, and never come back. She'd been left to pick up the pieces.

But that wasn't all. The last box was more than just a jumble of Alvin's unfinished dissertation research. It was part of a promise Maddie had made to herself: When she moved out of their Amity Street apartment, she was going to move on, too. With everything. And that meant severing herself from Alvin's mother and his brother, Randy.

They were waiting for her down by the street. Waiting for her to say goodbye. And Maddie knew that the moment she turned around to see them, everything would get harder than it already was.

Maddie picked the box back up and turned, taking two steps before she hit an icy patch and almost went down. She righted herself at the last second, coughing on cold air.

Mrs. Roth gasped, "Oh heavens, Madeline!" She had come to help Maddie with the last few things, but really had done little more than talk incessantly and fret over Randy, who was nowhere to be seen at the moment.

Mrs. Roth was fifty-something, with a crop of short, badly dyed hair. She was fat and red-cheeked, and had a penchant for wearing sweatshirts with playful kittens on them, as well as a taste for garish handbags. To keep out the cold she wore an apple-red parka and gold-trimmed galoshes.

"I'm fine," Maddie said. "This is the last of it. Mostly papers. God, he left behind so many papers."

Mrs. Roth frowned, putting out her hands to take the box, but Maddie passed by her and went toward her car, a brown '88 Civic. The last Maddie had seen Randy, he was picking his way around it in his usual unusual manner. But now he was not in sight.

"It's hard to believe you're really leaving," Mrs. Roth said.

Maddie craned her neck. "Hey, where'd Randy go?"

"He was chasing some crows over that way," Mrs. Roth said, indicating the east-facing side of the building.

As if on cue, Randy emerged from the side of the apartment building—a converted Colonial with black and white siding—and Maddie bit down on her lip, the pain cutting through the numbness. In that first moment, Randy always looked ordinary. He was tall and slim, always more handsome than Alvin had ever been, still in his late twenties. His hat, something

Maddie had knitted for him, was pulled down over his hair, sending his rusty brown curls out in various directions and doing nothing to dissipate just how charming he could look.

Randy's eyes were downcast. But then he looked up at Maddie, and the look said it all. Just like the children's book of Madeline's namesake: *"Ms. Clavel said, 'Something is not right.'"*

With Randy, it wasn't autism. It wasn't schizophrenia. It wasn't anything a doctor could identify, though many had tried. One day, while in high school, after a bad spill on the baseball diamond, part of Randy had just shut off. Even the simplest tasks made him confused, brought him to the point of panic, made him turn inward and go silent. He was obsessive about walking certain pathways, about drumming out certain beats, about always having things in a certain order. He had good days, and bad days. Mostly good days, but the bad days were a nightmare.

Randy mistrusted most people, but he loved Maddie without pretense. He always had. And that's why she'd been his companion since Alvin died, spending at least three days a week with him. Until Alvin's disappearance, Randy was watched by a never-ending rotation of assorted professionals, but it was agreed that after the family trauma, a little routine would be good for him, and Maddie entered his life as his companion—not his nurse, or his primary caregiver, but someone to hold his hand and help make things a little more stable, a little more normal. Mrs. Roth managed Randy on her off days, but more often than not, Maddie found herself hanging around their rambling house in Sunderland even when she wasn't on the clock. And Mrs. Roth paid her well for her trouble, if that's what it could be called.

Deep down, Maddie knew that in some ways, she loved Randy more than she loved Alvin. Alvin, the older brilliant brother, the physics savant—he was hard to love; temperamental, work-obsessed, and often distant. Loving him was like stuffing her feet into a gorgeous pair of shoes two sizes too small. They looked good, but it was always punctuated by pain and numbness.

On the other hand, Randy never put on airs. He was raw emotion, and he loved Maddie, and needed her. Alvin had his moments, but as he had so clearly proved with his suicide, there was a darkness inside of him that he concealed from Maddie. Even after five years together, she was not necessary in the long equation of his life. He didn't even leave a note, despite his tendency to scrawl phrases and theorems on almost everything.

But all that time spent with the Roths meant that Alvin's ghost haunted her everywhere. In Randy's inflections, in family portraits. She loved Randy, but she was slowly drowning in the responsibility and the guilt. She couldn't look after him anymore.

And it wasn't as if she was terribly qualified in the first place. There were plenty of nurses and caretakers with actual credentials. Yes, Randy would be fine. But whether she would be okay was another matter. As painful as severing her life from the Roths was, it was necessary for her own self-preservation.

At least that's what she told herself. It wasn't selfish. It was moving on. It just hurt.

"I'm here," Randy said with a shrug. "Didn't go far." He was snapping his fingers. *Snap-a-snap; snap-a-snap-snap.*

"Hey, Randy," Maddie said. "Mind opening the door for me? My hands are full."

"Sure." Randy jogged like an excited kid over to Maddie's rundown brown Civic, bowed at the waist, and opened the door for her, always the gentleman.

"You can always get him to help," Mrs. Roth said. "You've a gift, Madeline—if you just…"

"We talked about this, Mrs. Roth," Maddie said. "I'm sorry."

Mrs. Roth pursed her lips, letting Maddie's words hang in the air. "Well, then. That's that." Her mascara was smudged, her lips quivering in an attempt to keep from sobbing.

"I won't be far, you know," Maddie said, shoving the box into the last vestige of space in the car. She kicked it with her foot, denting it just enough to allow the door to close.

The box was one among hundreds of items Alvin left when he'd disappeared and died—and while she'd sent most of the boxes away to be recycled, this one was labeled with the name of his dissertation director, Dr. Keats. And Maddie figured it was bad karma to incinerate someone else's stuff.

Even when she found out that Alvin had been cheating on her with his dissertation director's wife, she still couldn't throw out everything. A month before, she'd been cornered by one of Alvin's old classmates from UMass who'd dished the whole scandal while sobbing into her sleeve, believing Mrs. Keats was the cause of Alvin's disappearance. Finding out about the affair made Maddie realize how little of her life she'd been living since Alvin's disappearance, and how imperative it was that she do something about it. While it didn't make it any less painful to leave Mrs. Roth and Randy, it was as if fate had given her a free pass to move on.

You really didn't know him at all. You loved him, but you didn't know him.

She was tired, and mad at herself for being so naive; she'd harbored the delusion that a man like Alvin, all frenetic energy and madness and brilliance, could ever really be happy with her.

She didn't tell Mrs. Roth the sordid details, of course. That would have been beyond cruel. As far as she and Randy were concerned, Maddie was simply moving on with her life, even if Mrs. Roth refused to recognize that Alvin was dead.

To Maddie, he was already dead in a hundred ways, but as soon as she closed the door to their old apartment for the last time, a burden was lifted. Now the setting for the greatest deception of her life was gone.

Maddie pushed up her sunglasses, squinting across the

icy landscape, trying to free herself of those uncomfortable thoughts and keep from crying. The street was familiar once, but that had been when Alvin was alive. His presence, their relationship, had somehow defined how she saw things. It had been charming, with its proximity to the University and all. But now, it was a winter wasteland full of ghosts.

Time to go. February in Amherst was a wasteland to begin with, and Maddie just couldn't do with another dead winter in this place.

"All packed up," Randy declared, descending on Maddie with one of his hugs. He was taller than Maddie by almost a foot, and he smelled faintly of patchouli and wet wool, but she appreciated the sentiment. He squeezed, rocking back and forth a moment before letting go. The rocking was part of the rhythm he always had.

"Thanks, Randy. I think I needed that," Maddie said.

"And you'll be fine in the new place?" asked Mrs. Roth. A tear had fallen halfway down her cheek, resting there. "You've got everything you need?"

"I do," Maddie said. She glanced at Randy and he was still smiling at her. He was so beautiful when he smiled it almost broke her heart.

"When do you start work?" Mrs. Roth asked.

"Next Tuesday," Maddie said. At her friend Ian's instance, she'd found herself a normal job. At least it was something to while away the time. She'd be shelving books in just a few days at the Book-a-Mart in Hadley. But hopefully, in a few months, she'd get herself back into the Art History program at UMass, and resume her studies. Maybe she could even get a TA position.

"Can you get me some books?" Randy asked. "Art books, the ones with the big stones and pyramids."

"I'll see what I can do," Maddie said, rubbing his shoulder. He loved to go through her old art history textbooks, and had a particular affection for Sumerian and Egyptian art. She'd get half price on most of the books in the store, so she could likely swing something for him.

But she wouldn't be reading them to him, not like before. He had a knack for details and a thing for St. Sebastian. Still, she did love teaching, even if it was just Randy.

Mrs. Roth pursed her lips, a habit she had when she was about to say something she really shouldn't. But instead of speaking, she threw her arms around Maddie, squeezing her to the point of discomfort.

"I've always thought of you like a daughter, Madeline—and you without so much as a distant cousin to rely on," Mrs. Roth gushed. She pulled away, and touched Maddie on the cheek. "You promise me you'll take care of yourself?"

"Of course," said Maddie. She really didn't need to be reminded of her lack of family at the moment. Her parents had died when she was in her early teens, and both of them had been only children. She had a handful of second or third cousins somewhere in California, but for all intents and purposes she was an island unto herself.

"I'll see you in Boston," said Randy. He spoke with an unusual air of authority, and Maddie looked at him intently, chin down and eyes up.

"I'm just moving a few towns over—nowhere near as far as Boston," said Maddie. "I'm sure we'll see each other soon. I can make breakfast for you or something. Sunday pancakes." Sunday pancakes were one of their rituals, and though she'd promised herself she wouldn't start cracking under the guilt of leaving Randy and Mrs. Roth, she was already making concessions. Ian would laugh in her face to hear her now.

Mrs. Roth sniffled. "Of course. I'll tell you anything I hear, though, okay? If there's any sign of him."

Him. She meant Alvin, though she never spoke his name. In spite of the fact that all signs pointed toward Alvin's death, likely by suicide, Mrs. Roth refused to see reason on the matter.

But Maddie knew what February felt like in Western Massachusetts. The sorrow of it brought her down even now. And sometimes, she couldn't blame Alvin for killing himself.

Maddie walked around to the driver's side of the car. Mrs. Roth's BMW was parked a bit ahead, the engine purring contentedly; the vanity read, "CATS MAMA2". Appropriate, since her house in Sunderland held a veritable pride of Persians.

If she'd been stronger, bolder, Maddie would have told Mrs. Roth not to call her, not to tell her anything she heard. It's what Ian would have wanted her to do. He was always telling her she was too soft, too willing to yield in order to make other people happy. But Ian lived a very different life, completely unfettered. And Maddie wanted that life, too. The cost was just much higher for her.

"You know I understand if you wanted to start dating again," Mrs. Roth said, speaking through her fingers as if it would prevent the awkwardness of the statement.

Maddie cringed inwardly, and slipped into her front seat, angling the vents back toward her. Her gloves were on the passenger's seat, and she pulled them on. "It's, um," she tried to find the words for it. "Yeah."

Maddie almost laughed to think what Mrs. Roth would think of Ian and their casual relationship. She just had no desire whatsoever to share her personal life with Mrs. Roth.

Randy was peering into her window, smiling his full smile, that rare, magical smile, making him almost movie-star handsome for a moment, with those blue eyes and that strong chin. If she didn't know him better, Maddie would kiss him on the lips just for being so perfect.

"Bye, Maddie. Love you," Randy said, tapping in rhythm on her window. *Tap-a-tap, tap-a-tap-tap.*

"Bye, Randy. I'll see you around." She paused, closing her eyes and willing the tears away. "I love you, too."

"I'll see you in Boston," he said again. Randy could sound

remarkably like Alvin sometimes, and his intonation at the moment sent a shiver through Maddie, the cold sweat under her jacket and scarf sticky on her skin.

"Not today, dude. But hey, let's plan something in a few weeks, if it's cool with your mom, huh?" Maddie said, shutting the door. The window was frosty, so she rolled it down for a moment, waving to them both.

"I'll call you in a few days, to see how things are!" called Mrs. Roth as Maddie inched the car forward, then added, "We love you!"

Ian was waiting at the corner of Main Street and Pleasant Street in Northampton, smoking a crumpled cigarette and staring vacantly across the road toward the First Churches.

"Hey," he said, as Maddie approached him. "New hat?"

He was tall and thin, with black, corkscrew-curly hair and brown-black eyes. He said something once about being Greek or Armenian or Turkish, but Maddie didn't remember which. He was just vaguely Mediterranean-looking. Somehow Ian never managed a close shave, giving his face an even more sunken look than his sharp bone structure alone.

But he never missed a date, and he drank more than Maddie did, which meant that she could often leave without his notice. Not to mention, he was an artist. Hanging out with Ian was the precise opposite of being with Alvin. Instead of talking about chaos theory, they talked about chiaroscuro.

"No," she replied. "Had this a while. Found it during the move." She'd made it herself during a stint with knitting, and it was comfortable enough, though the ochre hue was a little odd.

"The apartment's all cleaned out, then?" Ian asked.

"Yup. Finally."

"Great. See? I told you that you weren't a coward."

She laughed. "Thanks for the vote of confidence."

"Here's to new beginnings." He raised his hand high with an invisible glass.

Maddie mimed in response, clinking in the air. "How about some real food and drink?"

"Sounds ideal. It's too goddamned cold out here."

They walked, neither holding hands nor making eye contact, down to Pinocchio's for pizza. They ordered—white pizza for him, vegetarian for her—then ate in the silence so common after walking in the freezing cold and being faced with warm food.

It was busy and the food was a caloric comfort to counter the cold numbness outside. The Northampton crowd was out in force: the hippie mother who reeked of pot, the suit with his tie undone, the computer repair guys from down the street. Everyone seemed to be talking too loud, gesturing too wildly. Maddie just concentrated on the cheese that had pooled on her plate to keep herself calm. She was thinking about Randy.

"You okay?" Ian asked, a surprisingly compassionate moment from him. "You're even more contemplative than usual, almost sulky. It doesn't become you."

Maddie glared up at him and Ian's thick eyebrows quirked in response. "I'm fine," she said. "Just a little pensive. Mrs. Roth came by as I was getting the last few boxes out, with Randy, and that was... interesting."

"You're free of her now, though, right? She can't keep following you if you're not taking care of Randall."

"It's *Randy*, and no, technically she can't," Maddie replied with a sigh. She twisted the cheese around a plastic fork and frowned, knowing that feeling all too well. "Randy honestly needs someone who cares about *him*, instead of seeing him as just a patient or something, and he's all alone now; we were making really good progress—better than he'd been doing with just his nurse. I just feel like such a jerk."

"But you can't be that person. That's not your job, and

you're not trained for it. Randy needs a professional to look after him. You're not a jerk."

"Yeah, really, I'm an outright humanitarian."

"Hey, you're not a home health aide. You're just a good person. And Book-a-Mart? It's just a stop along the way. You've got dreams, Maddie. It's time you at least made the attempt."

"Yeah, me and my *artistic* calling," Maddie said, laying on the sarcasm as thick as possible.

"Art history's a noble pursuit."

"*Noble*? Right. Because life depends on my ability to distinguish Rococo from late Baroque."

Ian laughed. "Shit, I hate Rococo."

Maddie had set her cell phone on the table next to her, a habit she had learned in the weeks after Alvin's disappearance, and it started vibrating. She hesitated, seeing the number and picture—Mrs. Roth—and then picked it up.

She cringed, and Ian looked disgusted.

"Speak of the devil," he muttered.

"Hey, Mrs. Roth," said Maddie into the receiver.

There was a bit of crackling on the other end, and then Mrs. Roth said, "Madeline?"

"Yeah," Maddie said, rolling her eyes at Ian who was trying to stifle a laugh. "I'm here."

"Well, I just got a phone call from someone, and I'm sorry to call you on such short notice. But I couldn't think of anyone else who could help me in a pinch."

Maddie sighed. "Sure, what's up?"

Mrs. Roth took a deep breath on the other end of the line, and from across the table Ian gestured to his pack of cigarettes, then to the door, to which Maddie nodded. She felt herself blush with embarrassment. How long had she managed to be free of Mrs. Roth? Three hours, tops.

Mrs. Roth continued. "Well, I got a call from Dr. Keats, that's Alvin's old professor, out in Boston. He called to see how

I was, and to say that Alvin had some of his books and that he needed them."

There was that last box, thought Maddie, the one that was labeled "Dr. Keats", the one that she had so unceremoniously shoved into her car, the one that had been her mantra for moving on.

Just perfect.

"Yeah, I've got them," Maddie said. She wanted to punch herself for caving so quickly. "I can send the box out to him."

Mrs. Roth paused, coughing. "Well, Randy's got this idea in his head that you're taking him to Boston. And I know it's a lot to ask, but you could take him about, show him Boston. He'd love the Science Museum. I'll pay for the trip of course, and you could return the books to Dr. Keats. He says they've very valuable."

The situation seemed far too convenient, even by Mrs. Roth's standards. Maddie took a deep breath, and twirled the ring she wore on her right hand, a garnet cabochon set in gold, which she'd been given by Alvin.

And why the hell do I still wear this? she asked herself before slapping her forehead with the palm of her hand.

Maddie tried to go the passive route, "Well, I haven't seen my schedule yet for the week after next, but–"

"Oh, please, Madeline. Randy thinks the world of you; it would mean so much to him."

Randy also "thought the world" of Pez dispensers, malt balls, and ball bearings, so the compliment was hardly as effective as it was intended to be. On his bad days, which were more frequent since Alvin's death, he'd spend hours in his room lining up his various collections in intricate patterns, staring at them for hours on end, tapping on every surface in the same rhythm over and over.

It was hard for Maddie to imagine what he must have been like before the accident. Like all of the changes in him after that day more than ten years ago, the tapping was just something he did. No reason for it. It was just Randy, now, and defied medical explanation.

"I'll see what I can do, okay?" she said, finally, her heart in her throat.

When Maddie finally hung up, she waited a few moments before standing and joining Ian outside. She hated herself for giving up so easily, and she knew Ian would be even harder on her.

"So much for overcoming cowardice," Ian said as she approached him. It didn't sound as cruel as it could, but Maddie didn't argue. Apparently it was written all over her face.

"Gimme a cigarette," she said.

He handed one over. "It never ceases to amaze me how much affection you have for the family of a man who slept around behind your back, and then offed himself. Whatever happened to you that destroyed your self-esteem so much?"

Maddie coughed as she inhaled on the cigarette, mostly from Ian's harsh words. Maddie didn't smoke often, but just enough that Ian's constant supply was welcome. "Ian. She's a woman who's lost her son," she countered, somewhat lamely.

"No," Ian corrected. "She's batshit crazy. She's got more issues than cats. And you're letting her walk over you like a fucking carpet. You should call her back and tell her you won't do whatever it is you just agreed to."

"I'm just taking Randy to Boston to return some of Alvin's old books to Dr. Keats."

"Wait. Dr. Keats's wife was the one who—"

"Yes. I *know*," Maddie said, setting her jaw. She stared down at her boots. It wasn't as if she valued Ian's opinion *that* much, and it made sense that he'd advise her to do the selfish thing; it's what he'd have done, after all. But when it came down to it, he just didn't understand. No matter how many times she tried to explain her deep-seated sense of duty to the

Roths, he never would. He just didn't connect to people like she did.

"Christ, Maddie. You're like a human pincushion," Ian said, flicking his cigarette to the ground. He crushed it with his heel. He was disappointed in her. "A glutton for punishment."

"Just call me St. Sebastian."

He sighed, rolling his eyes. "Let's go back to my place."

"Sure," Maddie said, knowing what it meant. In a few hours she'd go back to her empty new apartment wondering why she even bothered with Ian in the first place. But he was conversation, he was sex, and he was something that wasn't Alvin.

That had to count for something.

2

Boston

Two weeks passed, and Maddie started her job, where she shelved many insipid books, helped many insipid customers, and, for reasons she couldn't fathom, bought a book of Wordsworth's collected poetry.

She found the little book tucked away in the Classics section as she was tidying the store late at night. It was not a section that got trashed as sensationally as the rest of the store, and she sought it out to avoid her coworkers, who were mostly too embroiled in their own dramas to even notice her absence.

With her discount, *The Collected Works of William Wordsworth* set her back less than ten bucks. She'd stayed up that night and read the book, cover to cover, immersing herself in poem after poem. Then she'd gone to the computer and researched all she could about the poet, learning of his relatively conventional life, but large impact on the world around him. Wikipedia was surprisingly helpful on the matter.

When time came to visit Dr. Keats along with Randy, she made conversation as they drove down the Masspike, talking about the poet.

In the silence between Zeppelin and Sarah McLachlan, Maddie chatted. "I'm not typically a fan of poetry. Too much formality, you know?" she said. "But Wordsworth just works for me. I've been reciting his poems when I'm feeling super bummed about something. Which is a lot of the time lately. And it helps. I think you'd even like it."

Randy rocked slightly, his hands perched on the door right below the windows. His breath had frosted the pane so much that it was now sweating, streaking through the dew. *Tap-a-tap, tap-a-tap-tap* on the side of the door went his fingers.

"Sometimes reading books makes you feel better," he said, not looking at her. "Alvin used to read the Narnia books to me when I got scared. I always liked those."

Maddie couldn't help but smile at his response. She loved when she could get him to talk; he had the gentlest voice, low and sweet. If he sang, he'd be a baritone. But she'd never heard him sing.

"Yeah, maybe it's just a coping mechanism."

"You miss me?" he asked, tilting his head at her.

It was a good thing that she was driving, because when he was having one of his normative days, she always felt drawn to him. Physically. It was unnerving, knowing him as she did. He was so like Alvin, in some ways, and so unlike him, and so uncommonly handsome.

"Of course I do," Maddie said, clutching the steering wheel a little tighter.

"You went away, though."

"I know. It's just that I can't spend the rest of my life taking care of people, making everyone else feel better."

"Why not?" Randy asked. And when he asked it did, indeed, seem like a perfectly noble calling.

Maddie's face burned with shame.

"Because sometimes you have to take care of yourself," Maddie said.

The Turnpike was bleak, thought Maddie, and the trip no comfort. Just an endless succession of towns, each more urbanized by the next, with conveniently located rest stops all along the way gleaming fluorescent and neon. She didn't really like Boston, and had only visited a handful of times. It was a messy city, she thought, too difficult to navigate, and she never liked public transportation.

"Do you have to use the bathroom?" asked Maddie.

He shook his head. "Nah, no whizz," he said. Then: "Ethereal minstrel! Pilgrim of the sky."

Maddie felt like her stomach slipped down to her intestines. "You—you know Wordsworth?"

"Nope, not really," said Randy, sighing, and went back to looking out the window. "Just that part."

Maddie was not, as a rule, a superstitious individual. Nor was she religious, prone to wonder, or a believer in the supernatural. But there was no denying that there was something peculiar about Randy, something that often transcended his disability—or, as his mother insisted, his *ability*. Like the Boston thing, she thought. He'd been harping on about Boston even before Dr. Keats had called. Had he planted the idea, somehow? Had Mrs. Roth called Dr. Keats, knowing he was in Boston, to placate Randy, or had Randy somehow known?

But Randy's prescience was the least of Maddie's worries. Being around him was just too conflicting. Even now, she felt crawly and awkward, caught between genuine giddiness at seeing him again and the guilt of knowing this had to come to an end. Again.

God, it was hard enough the first time.

Randy was wearing the scarf she'd knitted for last Christmas, blue and yellow like a prop out of *Harry Potter*, but he had on Alvin's old parka and hat, and as he sat there in the car, she felt he was some phantom of Alvin. How many times had they made this very drive together? How many passionate lectures had he given her while she half listened?

"Anyway," Maddie said, feeling once again as if she was being stalked by Alvin, even though he was dead, "You know that after today, well, you probably won't see me much. I'm really trying to move on, Randy. And I want to start a new life."

"Maybe you'll *like* the doctor. Maybe he can help with your new life."

"Well, probably not. I'm not into old dudes. But you're lucky. You have your mom. She's your family. My parents died when I was a teenager, and I've been, I don't know, trying to replace them or something ever since. And I…"

"You'll find a family, Maddie. I know it," Randy said, squeezing her hand through his gloves.

She shivered. "Thanks, Randy. Hey, anyway. Let's get this over with, okay? We'll just drop off the books, really quick; then we can go to the Science Museum and have some real fun. I need some fun right about now."

"Good. Can we go see the mummies?" Randy asked, all seriousness. *Tap-a-tap, tap-a-tap-tap* on the window.

"Sure thing, kiddo."

Dr. Keats lived in an odd, somewhat dilapidated bungalow on Savin Hill Road in Dorchester, nestled next to a copse of pine trees. Both the house and the trees looked out of place in the neighborhood, a contrast against the neat lawns and well-preserved homes. His car, just as Maddie had remembered it from his frequent visits to the apartment, was a teal '92 Geo Metro Wagon, still pristine despite its age.

The snow picked up, sharp little ice crystals pinging off her windshield and starting to crust over. Just great; all she needed was a blizzard.

Maddie had barely come to a stop on the already slick

road when she noticed Dr. Keats sitting on a chair on his front porch, wrapped in a long, camel-colored snow jacket, red scarf, and a fedora. His long, wispy silver hair peeped out of the sides, and even from this distance Maddie recognized the dark horn-rimmed glasses.

He was a handsome man, albeit old enough to be her father, and she'd always liked him—at least, more than the other professors she'd been introduced to during Alvin's time at UMass. He seemed more comfortable around her than the others did.

She hadn't stopped to question her motives until now, as she carefully parked the car in the road. Randy was non-plussed, and continued to work at the edge of his coat, moving it back and forth between his thumb and forefinger, a hushed version of his regular beat, which didn't help. The sound alone made her nervous.

Ian was right, though. She should have fought harder to refuse Mrs. Roth's orders. This wasn't her business. And Maddie was readily able to recognize her shortcomings. She loved people too easily, saw the good in them too quickly, and never could sever ties. Even with her own parents, before they'd died, she'd simply acted, never questioned, had always done as she was told, because it was the right thing to do. She suspected, in time, she'd be happy if everyone else was happy. That's how it had to work.

But it never seemed to. She was neither the smartest, nor the prettiest. She was forever middling. And no amount of good deeds or guilt-ridden self-sacrifice could change that.

"We're here, I think," Randy said suddenly, leveling Maddie with a very Alvin-like stare. "Aren't we going to get out of the car? Look! There's Dr. Keats."

Maddie nodded and stuffed the keys into her purse along with her cell phone. There were no missed calls, because the only person on earth who really wondered where she was, knew where she was. Damn Mrs. Roth.

Dr. Keats, as of yet, had not raised his eyes from the book he was reading, and Maddie had parked far enough down the street that she doubted her presence would attract his immediate attention.

"Here, Randy. D'you think you can carry some of these books for me? We're just walking over to that gray house over there," she asked.

Randy's ensuing smile, in normal circumstances, would have cheered her up. In the past, such expressions from Randy, who was a blank canvas around most people, would have sent Maddie's heart soaring. But not now. No, now she only saw Alvin in Randy's face, the specter of his brilliant, departed, brother. And it sent an ache through her body of a kind she hadn't experienced since the first few months of his disappearance.

"I can help, I can help," Randy said, nodding a few too many times than would be considered acceptable for most people. But it meant he was listening to her, and that, at least, was a comfort. "I can carry boxes."

She loaded Randy up with one of the boxes and took the remaining box and bag. "Well, here goes nothing," she said.

They made it to the front path before Dr. Keats made any notice. And when he did, he stood straight up, dropping his book, which went skidding across the deck and off into the bushes.

"Oh dear," Dr. Keats said, righting his glasses. "It's you, Madeline, and—why, Randy, hello again. It's been some time."

"Hello, Dr. Keats," Maddie said, from behind the box she was carrying. "I didn't think you'd be here. I'm sorry for the—"

"Nonsense, nonsense. I'd called Mrs. Roth about the books, but I hadn't expected she send couriers. Goodness," said Dr. Keats, shuffling down the stairs, careful to step right to avoid slipping. He hadn't, apparently, thought of sanding or salting his stairs to clear the ice in some time. "And please, call me Geoff."

Maddie just nodded as Dr. Keats took the box from her, and stood a moment, awkwardly looking back and forth between her and Randy.

"Well, we can just leave these here, and–" she gestured to the car with her chin. Drop off the books and go–that was the plan.

"No, please. Come in for a bit of tea, would you? I haven't got much more than some bagged Lipton, but it's something warm in this bitterest cold. I'm afraid we're out of sugar, too. But–would you join me, both of you? Please, I insist."

Randy was already making his way up the stairs, and Maddie stared after him. There was no sign of another car, or any indication that a woman had lived here save for a dried wreath on the door, with the berries shriveled or fallen off.

"Make yourself at home, Randy," said Dr. Keats. "You remember where the study is. Down the hall, second door on the left, right?"

"Second door, yup," echoed Randy, as he pushed the screen door open with his boot and went in.

Maddie shivered, and not just on account of the cold. "Randy's been here before?" she asked.

"Of course. Alvin brings him by," Dr. Keats said, then corrected himself. "Brought. Before, well... how do you like your tea?"

Dr. Keats's measure of cleanliness left plenty to be desired, and his home was full of holes. What surfaces were not strewn with books, papers, and notes had been so long covered with dust that the end result was a filmy, tacky grime resembling greyed patina. The house itself smelled of mildew and burnt toast, with a hint of something sour that reminded Maddie of her of high school chemistry class. Everything was sticky.

As Maddie sat in the armchair, she noted the lack of other furniture. There was a space by the window, and gaps in the dining room where furniture should be. And pictures on the

walls that were no longer arranged right due to the absence of
their counterparts.

She wasn't the only one who had holes in her life, it
seemed.

The tea tasted as if it dated from the last century, stale and
bitter, having likely spent most of its existence in an opened
cardboard container. But it was warm, and Maddie was still
chilly, so she drank small sips. Randy had assumed a perch
on one of the larger stuffed chairs, this one done in green and
purple paisley, and was smiling like a contented hyena after
dining on an antelope.

"How have you been holding up?" Dr. Keats asked, still
awkward. He grimaced, then took a sip of tea as if to hide it. For
some reason, Maddie had the feeling he was nervous.

Maddie licked her lips. "Okay, I guess." *How's your wife?*
she wanted to ask.

"Let's go find Alvin," Randy said, with such innocent
abandon that Maddie closed her eyes and took a breath to calm
herself. He was being particularly odd, even for Randy.

"Oh, shall we?" Dr. Keats said, as if Randy's suggestion
had merit.

"You don't have to talk to him like he's an imbecile,"
Maddie said. She didn't take kindly to people overcompensat-
ing for Randy's disability. And Dr. Keats should have known
better. It was not the day to piss her off.

Dr. Keats ruffled slightly, pressing his chin down into his
chest, his eyebrows sliding down over his eyes. "I know quite
well that he's no idiot, Madeline. It just appears to me that he's
bringing up the proverbial elephant in the room, isn't he?"

"I don't want to talk about Alvin," Maddie said, as cor-
dially as she could manage. "Or your wife."

"My ex-wife," said Dr. Keats. "But you know, you're allowed to be angry. This is all very difficult."

"*Seriously*, Dr. Keats," Maddie said, standing, and brushing the front of her jacket. "You have no idea what *difficult* is. Your wife didn't kill herself! I said I don't want to talk about Alvin, and I mean it—"

"Yes, Frances and Alvin were frequently intimate," Dr. Keats said, placidly and plainly. He sipped his tea again. "Which I imagine is the source of your frustration, or at least in part. You're right in being angry with him for that transgression. But you're mistaken in thinking him dead, in thinking that he killed himself. You knew him well enough to know better, I'd think."

"Come on Randy, we're *going*," Maddie said, her anger flaring uncontrollably. Everything about Dr. Keats rubbed her the wrong way: the house, the tea, the attitude, the pedantic tone. She hadn't been this angry since she'd decided that Alvin had, in fact, killed himself, but then she'd had no one to talk to.

Dr. Keats smiled at Randy. "Why don't *you* tell her, Randy?"

A pause, and Randy nodded precisely seven times before saying: "Alvin is alive. He's just not here."

Maddie had a sudden urge to strike Randy, to knock sense into him. She imagined it in full detail, her hand arcing in the air, contacting with his cheek, the look on his face afterwards. It would break his heart, but at the moment, she felt that destruction was her only course of action. She was broken. Maybe the only way to rid herself of the past, of Alvin, of Randy was by breaking them, too.

It was rare that she lost her patience so completely, and the unfamiliar emotion made her feel sick to her stomach. Her hands were balled into fists, and if it weren't for the fingerless gloves still on her hands, she'd have bored her nails straight through her palms. Every muscle in her body strained, but she fought against the instinct to flee.

"Madeline, you should calm yourself. Anger is part of the process. But harness it, dear—use it to clear your mind, to think with more *precision*," Dr. Keats said, still not rising from his seat.

"You, like Randy and Alvin, are a *remarkable* person."

"We're *leaving*," Maddie said through clenched teeth.
"Come on, Randy."

But Randy did not move. He simply stared at her,
expectant.

"You should hear something, before you go," said Dr. Keats. "Just...just give me a moment."

Maddie felt rooted to the ground, frozen. Like the tree
in the middle of that field she always saw when she visited the
Berkshires on Route 9: knotted, gnarled with old age, covered
in ice and snow, shuddering against the bitter wind. Her life
was the bitter wind, and she was the tree. She didn't bloom in
the spring either, she just stood there, crooked and bare, waiting for the next freeze. She was stuck in unending February.

Dr. Keats walked to his side table. An old plastic phone
sat there, yellowed with age and grimy, and beside it, an answering machine dating from Reagan's inauguration. It was
grey and black with blue writing, and had a huge cassette in the
middle, as well as large, square black buttons.

Dr. Keats pressed play and Alvin's voice filled the room.

"*February Twenty-Sixth, Seven Thirty-Two.* 'Good morning, Dr. K. The trip is going well. Dropped in to see Randall.
Just...'" the message faded out, but Maddie wasn't sure if it was
the quality of the recording or the ringing that was beginning
in her ears that was causing it. Her vision swam in and out, and
she felt the nausea return again. "... 'Take care. Hopefully next
time I call I'll get you. I should need just one more trip, and
then we'll be good to go. Everything's settled from this end. See
you in March, on the second Saturday, I think."

"You see?" Dr. Keats said, clicking off the recorder.
"That's Alvin. Clear as day."

"Told you," Randy said. "Told you Alvin came to visit me."

"You're *lying*," said Maddie.

"Randy doesn't make a habit of lying to you, does he?"

said Dr. Keats.

No, Randy didn't lie. Whether it was a result of the injury to his brain, or just part of his personality, it was impossible to know, but she'd often remarked about it to Alvin. She could trust Randy with anything.

Randy sighed, and slid off his chair. He was still wearing his jacket, but had removed the hat. Now his rusty brown hair stood up in wild tufts. "Maddie. Gotta whizz!" he said.

"Jesus Christ," Maddie said. "Go, and then we're leaving. Got it?"

"Got it," echoed Randy, but he didn't move. He looked imploringly at Maddie.

"You need me to come with you." It was an observation, not a question.

Randy started wiggling. This had happened once, early in her time with him, because she hadn't believed the severity of his circumstance. Though he had never had issues going to the bathroom with Alvin, this was a mistake she didn't want to repeat. When she had refused to take him to the bathroom, he had promptly pissed himself in the middle of Big Y. It was the button-fly pants, she thought. He could master the zipper, but never the buttons. And he had buttons again today.

"Down the hall, third door to the left," Dr. Keats said, a little resigned. He sat down on his armchair. "I'll be here."

"As soon as he's done, we're leaving. So don't wait up," Maddie said, her temper slightly receding as she fretted over the bathroom situation.

The bathroom was surprisingly clean considering the state of the rest of Dr. Keats's home. Though the style of the sink and tub were significantly dated, having not been remodeled since the home was built in the 1930s, they were clean. And there was a huge, gaudy mirror above the sink. Silver and seriously out of place.

Randy had developed a habit with the bathroom routine.

He would stand at the toilet, and Maddie would turn around and sing "When the Saints Go Marching In". Then he'd relieve himself. When she finished the first verse, he'd be finished and ready to go and she'd help him with the buttons.

Maddie sang the song as slowly as possible, muttering it under her breath more than keeping the melody, but Randy didn't seem to notice.

He went ahead and did his business, as she examined the rest of the bathroom.

"Oh," she said, noting the mirror above the sink with pause. What she'd taken as a gaudy reproduction was, in fact, authentic—at second glance, anyway.

The mirror stood at two feet high and half as wide, made of silver, judging by the slight tarnish in between the details. And the design was astonishing, the metal writhing and turning in and around itself in the shape of leaves, acanthus and ivy, culminating at the top with a chubby cherub holding a lute. Maddie recognized it immediately as late Baroque, though she was surprised it was silver rather than gold. She'd done a lengthy paper on a grant about mirrors such as this, once, and published it in a respected journal of arts.

"That's got to be an antique," she said, leaning closer. Randy had his hands held out, waiting for her to turn on the water as she always did. "Gosh, it's got to be three hundred years old. I can't believe the condition. They had to have replaced the glass. It's just impossible otherwise," she said leaning forward and touching the glass.

And then, time slipped. It moved, it shuddered and shimmered. Maddie was aware of Randy's presence behind her, seeing him as she did in the mirror, moving back and forth. *Tap-a-tap, tap-a-tap-tap.* She saw his eyes, that strange blue like the rings around the moon on a winter night, saw his hands flutter up, then flutter down.

"Go find Alvin," Randy's voice implored, his hand softly

brushing the side of her face. Still gentle. Still wanting. Still waiting.

Her body responded with an overwhelming rush of energy, and then she was pulled, as if by an invisible hand, forward into the mirror. As she slipped through the glass, she felt a distinct vibration deep down inside of her, in her womb, electric and pulsing. Her breath was gone, and she was no longer falling forward, but falling down, into the floor, into the bathroom, and beyond.

3
The Haberdasher's Wife

on't scream."

It was Randy's voice, but not Randy's voice; it was sure, it was definite, but unmistakably familiar.

Maddie's world was black, and all she wanted to do was take a deep breath. Except she couldn't. She felt as if someone was squeezing her around the middle, and each attempted breath came up short. And there was a weight on her head, a tickling, strange heaviness. She was standing, that much she could sense. But all else was darkness and buzzing in her ears.

"Just take a deep breath if you can, and try not to scream. All will be quite well in just a moment," whispered Randy's voice again, his accent so crisp it almost sounded foreign. British, maybe. She felt his hands on her shoulders, skin against skin and shuddered. Had her clothes fallen off? She'd fainted in the bathroom, apparently. And now she was having delusions.

The discomfort at her waist did not let up, and she coughed. That seemed to help. Her whole body rushed back to life, numbness she didn't even notice before draining like rainwater down a window.

Vision came back in a rush of blood to her face, and she shivered with the sensation of waking from a heavy dream.

Then she opened her eyes.

The mirror before her was the same as the one she had touched in Dr. Keats's bathroom, but all else had changed dramatically: the room, even the reflection she saw, were altered. It was her face, *mostly*, but everything around it was different. She saw herself standing behind a chair, in which sat a large woman. Maddie's own hands were out, arranging the elaborate plumed hat on the lady's head, as if controlled by a will other than hers. As soon as she noticed what she was doing with her hands, she dropped them and took a step back. Except Randy stood behind her, his hands on her shoulders, a stern and somewhat concerned look on his face.

Yes. It was Randy, but it *wasn't* Randy. His hair was longer, combed and curled slightly at his shoulders. He wore a pair of glasses perched low on his nose like John Lennon used to, and was in a mauve three-piece suit that looked like a stage prop from "A Christmas Carol," except gaudier. The weskit beneath was a dizzying pattern of beadwork and embroidery, more befitting of a tapestry than an item of clothing.

Shuddering, she looked at her own reflection again; she was drawn, thinner. She reached a hand to her face, feeling her cheekbones sharper through her skin.

While the practical part of Maddie knew she ought to start panicking, she was so taken by her own clothes that she simply stared into the mirror. The costume was of such a high quality and design it was practically a work of art, composed of layers upon layers of yellow and cream-colored jacquard, finished with a feathered hat perched on her own head, offset perfectly by the high-collared lace blouse. The blouse was so sheer as to be practically invisible, falling down to the tops of her breasts, which were pushed high and together by the remarkable corset at her waist; this corset, from the look of it in the mirror, was not just steel reinforced, but plated with brass as well. No wonder she felt like she was being squeezed by a vise.

The world swayed beneath her feet, but she steadied herself.

"Where..." she started, her voice cracking as she spoke.

"Perhaps it's time for a break, dear," the other Randy said behind her.

"Oh, dear, I've overexerted you in your attempt to beautify me, Mrs. Roth," the plump woman in the chair said. In spite of her declaration, the woman looked extremely pleased with the picture she was observing in the mirror. While she clearly wore a wig, it was still rather elaborately done, plaited and then curled, streaked with red in the brown. Maddie didn't know why, but she knew the woman's name: Mrs. Dunleigh.

And before she could scream, before she could descend into utter black panic, the man who was not Randy chimed in:

"Delia, can you come here and finish Mrs. Dunleigh's fitting?" he asked. His hands squeezed Maddie's shoulders again with improper familiarity; the fabric of her blouse was so thin it felt like he was touching her naked skin. She whirled around to face him, and almost gasped. Seeing him face-to-face, so proper and perfect, made her lose her train of thought completely. Not that her thoughts were terribly ordered at the moment.

Mrs. Dunleigh looked over her shoulder as a young woman in her late teens or early twenties, wearing black from head-to-toe—but leaving very little to the imagination with the plunging neckline of her dress—swooped in.

Mrs. Dunleigh said, "Oh dear—I do hope all is well with you, Mrs. Roth. Considering all that you've been through. I hate to think I've cause any undue stress!"

"Not at all," replied the man who could not have been Randy, ending with a smile that Maddie could have sworn was stolen right from Randy's limited repertoire; just the left side lifted, and a dimple appeared on his cheek. "I'll take Mrs. Roth upstairs; I expect she's just been on her feet too long."

"Yes," Maddie said weakly.

"Do watch yourself, Matilda," said Mrs. Dunleigh softly, and then turned her head back to the mirror as Delia began arranging the plumed creation once again. "And you take care of your wife, Randall, you hear? Mrs. Roth can only handle so much."

Matilda? Mrs. Roth? *Wife?*

The process of fainting was not as glamorous or as quick as the movies had depicted it. There was no fan, no smelling salts, and no one to catch her.

Maddie felt the world fade around her, saw snatches of extreme detail—the fresco on the wall, for instance, portraying some strange Bacchanalian dance with satyrs and nymphs, the gilded chairs upholstered in green velour, the strange contraption in the corner of the room—and heard voices, voices moving farther away from her until there was nothing. All that remained was a high-pitched ringing in her ears, and the beating of her own heart.

"Ethereal minstrel; pilgrim of the sky."

In her dream, Randy was reciting the poem, through a beak like a bird.

Maddie Angler awoke, propped up in a bed so decadent and soft her first inclination was to try and fall back asleep again. Silk and fur nestled and folded precisely around her to afford her the most luxurious position possible. The room smelled slightly of camphor, and something sweet that reminded her of a lotion she'd once picked up at the mall, but more intense. The bed itself was a four poster, and directly across the large room was a fireplace, with a fire banked low, and a smattering of antiques: a writing desk, a leather chair, a screen with egrets painted across it.

Nothing was familiar, but at the same time everything was comfortable. Her feet were perfectly warm, and she'd been changed, somehow, out of whatever contraption she'd been wearing before, and was now in a long cotton nightgown like the sort her grandmother had worn.

Before she had time to think, the door opened slightly, and a ruffle-hatted head popped in. "Oh, dear me, you're awake, Mrs. Roth. Let me get Mr. Roth."

Before Maddie could assert that a) she was not Mrs. Roth and b) she wanted nothing to do with said Mr. Roth, the hatted head vanished in a blur of white, and the door shut with a heavy, solid noise.

Maddie did nothing, though. She sat. She closed her eyes, certain that in a moment she would wake up in her own bed in her crummy little apartment. This whole thing was clearly a delusion.

But the world did not melt away, and she soon got tired of sitting in the darkness behind her eyelids, so she continued to look around. Truth be told, she was too tempted by the visual elegance not to. Whatever dream this was, she was finding a strange, vague sort of joy in the detail of it, in the vivid intensity. The windows were drawn tight with thick velvety curtains cinched with clasps to keep out the cold, and they also kept out the daylight, leaving the room lit only by the flickering fire. With all the firelight and texture, it was as if she'd walked into a chiaroscuro painting. Perhaps that was her defense mechanism, descending into great artworks. Was this Carravaggio, she wondered distantly?

The door opened again and she heard low voices, though she could not make out the words.

Then, the man who was not Randy entered. He walked purposefully but slowly, so Maddie had the chance to get a better look at him.

No, he was not *exactly* like Randy. He was more filled out than Randy, his physique more toned, as if he had some regular exercise regime. And he walked with a comfortable, easy gait. And the more she looked at him, the more overwhelming the sight: the slope of his cheeks, the fullness of his lips, the brightness in his eyes. He was, in some strange way, like Randy perfected. She had a sudden urge to run into his arms and kiss him, then shuddered at the thought, clasping her elbows. What was getting into her?

"I realize this is all very confusing," the man said, sitting on the side of the bed, folding his hands one on top of the other. His nails were trimmed, picking up the light along the enamel as if they'd been polished. "And, I must say first that I'm very, *very* sorry."

"Sorry?" she asked. While Maddie knew she should be panicking, she still felt more relaxed than she had in a very long time, and the apologies did nothing to rile her. Maybe it was the bed, the comfortable sheets, or something else. But whatever the cause, she felt as if every muscle in her body had unwound and gone slack. It was a bit like being stoned. "Did you make this dream?"

Randy's eyebrows, which Maddie thought must have been plucked to attain that surprising arch, lowered over his eyes and he leaned forward. "No, no. This is no dream. I *brought* you here, you see, with Dr. Keats's help." He pressed his hands together and gave her a pleading look, then said, "Madeline, this is where Alvin is."

"Alvin." She paused, her mind slowly putting things together. "Alvin is dead."

"No. No, he isn't dead. He's here."

Maddie glanced to the closed windows. "And where is *here*?"

"Boston. Mostly."

"*Mostly.* That's comforting. And you are?"

"Well, I'm not Randy. But I'm not far from him."

"You're—*what?*" She was feeling faint again, as if the air in the room was being slowly sucked away, thinned out.

"I've seen you. Through Randy. We're... brothers of a sort. You just didn't know I was there, watching," he said. He looked almost sad when he said it.

"That's really creepy," Maddie said. "And not funny. Not at all." She squeezed her eyes shut. "You don't know a thing about me. This is just some crazy dream."

Randy took a deep breath. "You are Madeline Angler, born March 22, 1980, to Robert and Katheryne Angler, in Lenox, Massachusetts. You aspire to a career in art history, and you have a fascination for the late Baroque and, oddly enough, the Arts and Crafts Movement. You met Randy while you were working at the University of Massachusetts, Amherst, and for the last few months you've been dating a man named Ian. An artist and something of a rogue, if I may say so."

As he spoke, her entire body washed in chills; it felt like someone was rubbing cotton balls up and down the length of her skin. There were words to say, thousands of them, but none of them came to her. The words surrounded her, flitted about her, but they were quick as locusts, and so loud as to drown each other out.

"I've learned about you through Randy. It's complicated to explain," the man said. "But in *your* Boston, in *your* Massachusetts, there is *that* Randy. But here, I'm Randall. And Alvin... well, he's Alvin both places."

"Alvin is dead," was all Maddie could think to say.

Randall drew his hands down his very clean-shaven face. He looked like he was planning to break the news of her imminent death. "No. He isn't. You see, my brother and I, we're scientists of a sort," he said, wincing as he did so.

"You aren't a *scientist*," Maddie said, feeling the need to get out from under the covers, comfortable as they may have been, and leave the room altogether. Maybe if she opened the door she'd wake up. "You're a moderately functional twenty-eight-year-old man who lines up elaborate Pez dispenser displays in his room and loves listening to the Electric Light Orchestra."

"About that, well," said Randall. "There, in that world, yes. Randy is unusual; he has suffered..." He trailed off and pulled a handkerchief from his pocket. Then he took out a thick fountain pen made of hammered copper and set with a few precious stones, red and green. "Just wait a moment. I can show you."

He took a deep breath and then folded the handkerchief twice. Then he stuck the nib down into the material, in the very middle, until it bled through the fabric. He did not look into Maddie's eyes, but concentrated on what he was doing. When he was done, he opened up the handkerchief. The splotches of ink were on each of the four quadrants.

"There, you see," he said, as if that were the exact explanation Maddie was looking for. "There are versions, all of the same ink, that have bled through every layer. And two of them, especially these," he said gesturing to the two at the top which were, to Maddie's eye anyway, virtually indistinguishable. "They're almost identical—mirror images. I want you to imagine the fabric of this universe is like this handkerchief. And you—you are like the ink in this pen."

"I'm splotchy?" she asked. She ran her fingers over the edge of the blanket on the top layer of her bed, this one trimmed in fur. Thousands of tiny hairs brushed against her hand, so perfectly real, that she marveled a moment. Some dream.

"No, no. Listen to me Mat—*Maddie*," said Randall, catching himself. "These handkerchiefs, they all represent people. People who exist in separate planes, separate worlds..." he trailed off, raising his eyebrows expectantly, as if she would catch on to what he was explaining.

"You are *insane*," she said.

"You noticed your reflection when you awoke here. You are like, and slightly *unlike* yourself," Randall tried again, much more calmly and reasonably.

"So more Alice, less Dorothy," she said. Then she paused, feeling the same drowsy comfort wash over her again as panic subsided and she once again chalked this all up to a dream. Then she remembered: "No. They called me Mrs. Roth."

"You are. Here, you are Mrs. Matilda Roth, the haberdasher's wife."

"Haberdasher?"

"A hat maker. I'm the haberdasher. *Here* you are my wife. Or at least, you are borrowing her body for now. It's important that you know we've been married for three years—"

"Wait, wait, wait, wait!" Maddie said, covering her eyes as if that would somehow help her put the strange jagged pieces of the story together. "I'm borrowing somebody's body? And... you—we—are *intimate*?"

Randall did not look in the least embarrassed. He nodded his head. "Of course. Less frequently these days than before, what with your condition and all."

"Condition?"

He chewed on his lower lip. "You—or your body, I should say—is rather reliant, my dear, on the essence of *Papaver somniferum.*"

"Which in normal English is—?"

"Opium."

"Opi...*what*?!" That explained the feeling of drowsy euphoria.

"Not so loud, if you please," Randall said.

"*Not so loud?* This dream—"

"This is not a dream."

"Well, if this isn't a dream, who got my permission to move me? Why am I in someone else's body? *How* am I in someone else's body?"

Pacing back and forth beside the bed a few times, Randall ran his hands through his hair, tousling it in an unintentionally charming way. "You and your—well, we call them 'twains'; myself and Randy, you and Matilda—we're splotches, *adjacent* splotches. And sometimes, if the right trigger is achieved, we can share consciousnesses, even bodies. You see, the mirror that you saw in Dr. Keats's house was the very same mirror here, in this world. You touched it. Now your consciousness is in Matilda's body."

"First, most of that made virtually no sense. And secondly, where is Matilda? Having martinis in Bermuda?" asked Maddie.

"We can't understand exactly how it works, but you and Matilda... she's... likely just lurking." Randall, for once, didn't appear entirely sure of himself.

"Well, I'm not going to play your pretty replacement wife."

"Maddie, I understand if you're upset. But I brought you here so you can talk to Alvin."

"Well, thanks for the thought, but frankly, I'd just like to go back home. I don't want to talk about Alvin or think about Alvin, thanks. He's dead. That's that. Why does everyone keep trying to tell me different?"

Randall sat down on the side of the bed and took her hands in his. Maddie gasped, but didn't pull away. The very core of her being wanted to trust this man, wanted to believe that somewhere, somehow Randy could be perfected. Could be fixed. Even if that made no sense.

He stared intently at her, his eyes so captivating. Blue like the rings around the moon. "Suppose for a moment he isn't dead. What if you could see him?"

Maddie sighed, frowning. "I don't know."

"My understanding was that you were in love with him."

She couldn't answer. She felt nothing when she thought about Alvin. She felt no fear, either, in spite of her most bizarre circumstance. The drugs in her system were strong, slowing her thought processes and completely nullifying her emotions.

"Love? I don't know. Curiosity, maybe. If you can show me Alvin, that would be something," she said. "But I'm only saying this theoretically. And because Randy asked me to find him, just as I came through. If that's what really happened and this isn't a dream."

Randall almost smiled. "Well, our first order of business is getting the opiates out of your system. I'm hoping that you are different enough from Matilda to go without. It would be best."

"Matilda wasn't good at shaking the stuff, I gather."

Randall shook his head, looking a bit weary. "No," was all he said. He went to the door, but not before putting the handkerchief down on the ornate side table. Then he lingered a moment, staring at Maddie, one hand stuffed between his jacket and weskit.

"You really know where Alvin is?" Maddie asked, at last.

"I do," said Randall. "And Randy understands that I can help you find him. But we can talk about this at breakfast tomorrow. I will have Mrs. Fitz—that's the maid, and the one you should contact should you need anything—come by. She'll be able to help you into your clothes, and prepare you for Dr. Mitchum's visit tomorrow morning. He'll be by around the ninth hour. You should rest as you can while this body recovers. I'll be back soon."

"Not if I wake up in my Massachusetts, you won't."

He was silent a moment, watching her. She looked away from his unnerving stare just as he said: "Very well. Goodnight."

Maddie watched the door close, and did as she had been instructed: She took a deep breath and relaxed into her pillows, ready for rest. And that was the last she had left in her; she felt her body go limp, her eyes flutter shut, and she fell asleep, wrapped in the warmth of blankets and opium, ready to wake up in the real world.

Morning came, and Maddie awoke with a shattering headache. Someone was at the windows, letting in an obscene amount of light.

The pain at her temples and behind her eyes was intense, as if someone were raking needles over them. Her skin hurt. Her stomach turned. It was torture.

"It's a lovely morning, Mrs. Roth," said the shape at the window.

"Lovely?" Maddie echoed with a groan.

Darkness gave way to light, illuminating the ornate Victorian bedroom in which she had last seen Randall. And with every splinter of light came a new stab of pain.

The woman addressing Maddie was plump but moved with grace. She went from window to window with surprising ease, turning her wrist just so to snap open the curtains. As light streamed in, Maddie squinted to get a better look at her; the woman was past middle age, but her face, amidst the fleshy bits, might have once been quite pretty. She had full lips and a slightly upturned nose. Her dark red hair was tied up behind her head in a complicated swirl, pinned with a hat. She wore a yellow and red dress, corseted as well as could be for someone of her girth, so that her sizable breasts pushed up and under, almost meeting her chin.

"Mrs. Fitz?" she asked, half remembering the name, half knowing it. She rubbed her head, pressing her thumbs into her eyes until she saw stars.

Mrs. Fitz continued on as if nothing abnormal were going on. "Dr. Mitchum is about to come by, and we need to get you into something a little more appropriate. I was thinking the Japanese silk kimono, the one with the crane on it. Will that do?"

Even before Mrs. Fitz showed her the gown, Maddie knew what it looked like. The sensation of retrieving the memory, a memory that was not entirely hers, was like a jolt of electricity through her brain.

Maddie heard a voice softly whisper to her, a voice very like her own, and then she said the words aloud: "The one that Mr. Roth gave me for Michaelmas last year?" Maddie almost laughed. Michaelmas? What the hell was Michaelmas?

"The very one," said Mrs. Fitz, gliding toward the bed with the kimono slung over her arm. She had a comforting way about her that put Maddie entirely at ease. "Brought you some tea, too, dear."

Maddie didn't say anything in reply but shuffled under the sheets, willing herself to leave the perfect warmth of the bed and ignore any further whisperings. She shivered when her bare legs met the cool air, still clenching her teeth against the pain throbbing behind her eyes.

"Tea. Sure," she said, when Mrs. Fitz continued to stare at her, clearly looking for some sort of response. "My head is killing me."

Mrs. Fitz looked alarmed.

"Figuratively," corrected Maddie.

Mrs. Fitz nodded and went to fetch the tray by the door. The tea smelled strongly of mint, which didn't put Maddie of a mind to wake up. What she wanted was a good cup of coffee from Dunkin Donuts, preferably in a Styrofoam mug, with three sugars and a splash of cream. But she was surprised to find the tea to her liking when she sipped it—it was sweet, at least, and had a slightly bitter, but not unpleasant, tang to it.

"Did you have a good night's sleep, my dear?" asked Mrs. Fitz.

"I..." Maddie said, and just shook her head. No, she didn't know what to say, not to this woman, and not to the doctor. "Where is Ran—Mr. Roth?" she asked, guessing that it would be better to use the more formal title, as that appeared to be the preferred method of address. Not to mention the whole

Randy/Randall thing was entirely too confusing.

"At Mr. Bezley's, of course, buying some more felt and fabric. Looks to be a busy holiday season coming up, but you know that, of course."

A strange image of a man, around thirty or so, with a paunch about his middle and thick chops on his cheeks appeared in Maddie's mind, to her knowledge a figure she had never encountered. He was dressed in blue silk, and had a green bow tie at his throat. She had never seen the man, and yet she knew immediately that it was Mr. Bezley.

"Come now, dovey, let's get dressed," said Mrs. Fitz.

Her headache dissipated slightly after having a few sips of tea, and that was a relief. For the moment, anyway, Maddie was able to take in the full detail of the bedroom.

Everything seemed familiar, and yet completely foreign at the same time. Maddie knew she had never seen the side table, and yet she knew by some strange premonition that if she were to open the drawer, she would see a silver mirror, a hairbrush, and a small container of salve, scented with lavender. Everything was vaguely Victorian, but not quite. Brighter, in some instances; more understated in others. Maddie wanted nothing more than to take a better look, but that would undoubtedly raise the woman's suspicions.

Maddie sighed and Mrs. Fitz helped her to the floor, guiding her bare feet into a pair of ermine—*ermine, how did she know they were ermine?*—slippers. And she took a moment to look down at herself, noticed the strange narrowness at her waist, so much more trim than what she was accustomed to. She smoothed her hand down the front of her belly, felt the sharp indentation at the side. Skinny. Maddie had never been skinny.

"Mrs. Roth?" asked Mrs. Fitz, concerned.

"My apologies," Maddie said, the phrase not one of her own.

"It's *snowing*, you know," Mrs. Fitz said, holding out the

kimono. "A good omen for a good morning. Mother Mary is shining upon us."

"Indeed," said Maddie, because it felt like the right thing to say.

Mother Mary?

The kimono was comfortable, but not terribly warm; still, it smelled faintly of roses, and was soft and sumptuous on Maddie's skin. It made her skin prickle, slightly, too, feeling that rather sensual caress. It reminded her of something, and when she looked down at the golden embroidery at the cuff, she had another flash of memory: Randall clawing at her hungrily, kissing the length of her skin and breasts, promising to ravage her, to take her in a thousand ways...

She gasped, shuddering, drawing the gown up around her neck. No. Not her. Someone else. This Matilda. Wherever she was. Randall had said she might be lurking, and Maddie didn't like the sound of that word. She wouldn't take it too well if someone had taken hold of *her* body, after all.

Maybe that's where the images and words were coming from. Maybe Matilda was doing more than lurking. Maybe she was listening. Maddie tried not to shudder, but the idea was horrifying.

Just a dream. Just a dream. *Enjoy it while you can*, Maddie told herself.

"Mrs. Roth?"

"I'm fine," Maddie said, snapping out of her thoughts. She forced a smile.

"Would you sit down now, so we can do your hair a bit?" Mrs. Fitz asked. "It wouldn't do the see the doctor in such a state."

The process of having one's hair done in this place was quite the affair. After much tugging and pulling, searing and curling, pinning and fastening, both Maddie's real hair and a bit of a wig were secured atop her head in a pile of curls. It was quite the show for a simple doctor's visit.

When Mrs. Fitz pronounced her finished, Maddie dream-ily stood while the maid primped her here and there, applied powder to her face, and tucked her kimono in just right around the hips. Maddie was feeling drowsy again, as if the world had gone soft and fuzzy like her favorite pair of leopard slippers.

"Casual, but acceptable," was Mrs. Fitz's last proclama-tion as she tilted her head and stuck out her tongue slightly, measuring Maddie as if she were a piece of art.

Maddie almost giggled. This was casual?

It was during the final primping that Maddie noticed a certain painting across the room for the first time. Not another large, ornate piece—no it was a miniature portrait set above the marble mantle, leaned half to the side as if put back in a rush. She was drawn to it though she could not yet see the face clear-ly. It was almost, she reflected, as if someone were making her look, which was a very odd sensation indeed.

Maddie took the picture in her hand and examined it more closely. It depicted a tall, dark-haired gentleman with high cheekbones and a dark complexion. He almost looked Native American. And yet he bore a striking resemblance to Ian. No, more than a resemblance; they could be fraternal twins. And the eyes, they were *exactly* right.

She put the picture back and tried to hide her trembling. Her stomach turned in on itself, and then once again for good measure, threatening to spew the newly consumed tea all over the beautiful Oriental rugs.

"I miss him, too," Mrs. Fitz said, mistaking Maddie's nausea for emotion. "I was just thinking the other day, I was, about how proud he'd be of you. His beloved cousin Mattie, married to Ran-dall Roth, and working together on some of the greatest fashions this town has ever seen—putting Boston back on the map!"

Cousin?

Mrs. Fitz's babbling faded away, and Maddie heard her-self say, "He's... gone." It was a statement, not a question.

"How many years is it since the accident? Almost near to five, I'd think. You'd just started your courtship, if I recall, when we got the news," Mrs. Fitz said, her voice breaking with a sudden wave of emotion. She batted her hands in the air as if swatting an invisible fly. "But let's think on better things now, shall we? The doctor's about to arrive."

Just as Maddie was trying to put together the strange pieces of her life—how Ian could be her cousin in one world and her lover in another—someone rapped three times on the door, paused a moment, and then knocked twice again.

At this sudden noise, Mrs. Fitz reanimated and led Maddie to the wing-back silk upholstered green and gold chair, and propped her feet, still slippered,up upon a plush ottoman.

I'm like a doll, thought Maddie. And Mrs. Fitz is the puppeteer. I just need to wake up...

In the back of her mind, she heard another voice.

You won't wake up any time soon.

... *Matilda?*

Before there was an answer, other than the strange tickling sensation Maddie now had in her nose, Mrs. Fitz hurried to answer the door.

A young man entered, wearing a pale green lab coat over a vivid red and gold vest, and dusted all over with snow. Beneath the vest he wore a white shirt, and at the collar he had strung a thick black band reminiscent of what English parsons wore, except for the white bit in the middle. Though the doctor was not very tall, he was very fit. Not handsome in a conventional way, he had thick red eyebrows and tawny hair that fell to his shoulders.

"Good afternoon, Mrs. Fitz," said the doctor, Dr. Mitchum, Maddie presumed. "If you'll excuse us for the examination, Mrs. Fitz?"

"Of course, Dr. Halver," said the maid.

Dr. Halver? Maddie could have sworn Randall had said

Dr. Mitchum.

Nodding obediently, Mrs. Fitz exited the room with her hands folded in front of her, and Dr. Halver closed the door softly. He took a few breaths, as if preparing himself for delivering ominous news, and then turned to her.

He had tears in his eyes, and this immediately took Maddie aback. She had no idea what to do in such a situation, but from the small amount of experience she had with these people, they seemed to function in a weird, heightened Victorian manner. More brass, and less sense. So she gave him a serene smile.

"Dearest Matilda," said Dr. Halver, taking a few, hesitant steps toward Maddie, pressing his free hand to his breast as if it pained him. He carried a large brown leather bag in the other hand, riveted and gleaming with fresh oil. As he approached, he smelled slightly minty, like Colgate. He had a distinctly British accent, too, from Surrey. Surrey? He *was* from Surrey.

Yes. From Surrey. Very good.

Maddie felt that tickle again, as if she were going to sneeze. That voice was *inside* her head.

Can you lose your mind in a dream? I think I have, she thought.

"Dr. Halver," Maddie said, slowly. "Good morning."

He frowned deeply, the lines at the sides of his mouth giving his features an unattractive slant. "I don't spite you for having rejected my offer. I know I do not have much to give you, save for myself. And you live here in comfort, in ease, while I live out my days at the Church, dedicated to Her service. Mother Mary grants me many gifts, but a bountiful purse is not one of them. I hope you will forgive me, but I convinced Dr. Mitchum to allow me to take his post this morning. I feel there is so much more we need to say to one another."

Maddie's gaze went, as if by habit, back to his bag.

"Yes, I've brought you more tea, and that should tide you over for some time," he said. He was now close enough for her to reach out and touch, should she need to. And part of her, somewhere in the depths, fluttered at the thought.

This is the best part. He's so dramatic.

Dr. Halver swallowed hard,then fell to his knees, his head downcast. "I must tell you I do not regret breaking my vow for the nights we had together," he said, his voice scarcely more than a whisper. "I denied myself two decades of pleasure—and I had been strong, until you. The feeling of being inside of you, of feeling your most warm, precious places, was much akin to the deepest prayers, the most intense meditations I've had with Mother Mary."

Gross. Gross! Maddie was starting to fret, but again the weight of something—the tea, she now realized—was dragging her down. There was opium in the tea.

Where was Randall?

You're a big girl. You can handle this. Don't be such a prude.

Maddie's mouth was dry. Dry like she just ate a whole bag of microwave popcorn and then licked the paper clean. She forced a smile again.

Dr. Halver looked intently at Maddie, clasping his hands to his chest and pressing again, "This feeble man's heart cannot pretend to know the thoughts in your mind, and I shudder to think what mechanisms go on behind those vibrant eyes. My dear, dearest, Matilda. It is only because I cannot take the pain of such close proximity to you that I will be reassigned—inland, a bit, in Worcester, to the Cathedral of the Weeping Lady there. And not as a cleric, no... likely I will re-tonsure myself, and go through the ranks yet again."

He licked his lips, and let his hands fall down, then began to weep.

"Would that you would permit me to touch you one last time, before I depart. My body so yearns for the softer places you once gave me so willingly, and my mind... I fear I am losing my..."

The stirring occurred again, and Maddie shivered. She couldn't think what the right words would be. Clearly Matilda had led this man on, slept with him even, to the point that he was now on the brink of madness.

"I'm sorry," Maddie said at last, finding her own voice, her own words, more and more distant. "This is all just so... fa..."

She wanted to swear but she couldn't remember the word. It was a profanity, she thought, a profanity that now she couldn't summon up for the life of her. She wanted to use it, but it melted on the tip of her tongue as soon as she went to say it. It sounded like a piece of cutlery, she mused. A fork?

Having trouble, darling?

Maddie took a deep breath, ignoring the voice. Then she said, "I'm sorry, but that would not be... appropriate, I don't think." She was sweating everywhere, the silk clinging to her skin most uncomfortably.

Dr. Halver looked up at her again, imploring. "I hunger for you, but I suppose that shall be my cross to bear, these long months as I retrace my steps and search for oneness with the Lady." He sighed, a wheezing, desperate sound. "You will have to convince whomever they assign to you," said the doctor slowly, getting to his feet, "to continue your medication as I have. It has been only as a favor to you, knowing that such a prescription comforts you in times that I cannot..."

"No!" The words came from Maddie's mouth but she had not commanded them.

Time slipped forward violently, and for a dark few moments, she was not in it.

In a flash, she was now perched on the edge of her chair, her fingers digging into the armrests, one uneven nail pulling on the fabric. Her heart was pounding in her chest, thumping irregularly as if in defiance of the opiates in her bloodstream. She could feel the rise and fall of her breasts, the subtle sensuality of her nipples against the silk.

Dr. Halver was so close. How did he get so close? And why the hell was she turned on?

"No?" he asked, tenuous. No doubt the shout was unexpected.

Don't let him go. If he goes, that's it for us. Do you understand? I can't do without it. I can't do without it!

The voice was screaming, and Maddie felt a spasm of pain jolt through her, from temple to temple, paired with a sense of menace.

Gasping, Maddie tried again, "What... the..." Fork? Spoon? Knife? It was something along those lines.

Maddie closed her eyes, felt her breath coming in rasps. She tried to turn inward a moment, to gather herself.

Yes. It was Matilda. It had to be. Maddie could see her looming in the dark behind Maddie's eyelids, a thin, wan figure leaning against an invisible wall. Waiting. She was back from wherever it was she had been when Maddie crossed over, and was no longer silent.

Matilda instructed calmly, *We're going to make love to him. Once it's over, we'll have what we need, and we can deal with him later.*

"Matilda?" Dr. Halver was asking.

His name is Douglas. Call him Douglas.

"D...Douglas," Maddie said, her lips quivering as she said it, her jaws straining to resist, but unable. "I'm... I just can't.."

"You want me to go?" Dr. Halver asked.

Oh, clearly I just have to do this myself.

Maddie felt her own consciousness fade for a moment, going black and sparkly around the edges. And then the world tilted on its side. In a heartbeat, she was watching, no longer able to move the body she had just inhabited moments before.

Matilda was in control.

"No, I just want you, darling. Just like always," said Matilda.

Maddie watched from behind Matilda's eyes, the body

she now thought of as hers responding to the other woman's commands like a helpless puppet. When she rose out of the chair, she no longer had the ability to decide which way she was going to move; Matilda simply told her, and she complied.

Unable to do anything other than watch as her body moved, Maddie went to the door and latched it. She walked to each of the windows, and closed them, all with the familiarity and ease of someone who did this nearly every day of her life.

In the middle of the room, Douglas Halver watched her, his eyes hungry, his breath coming in rasps.

With a giggle that was utterly Matilda's, Maddie jumped up on the bed, so recently made pristine by the quick hands of Mrs. Fitz, and undid the silken belt at her middle, the kimono falling down and exposing her breasts and knickers. She felt the cool air of the room meet her skin, covering her in gooseflesh, and a warm feeling began down between her legs and moved, gently, like a pair of loving hands, up to her face.

But she could not stop herself. She could feel everything, but control nothing.

Though it was terror, it came with understanding. It was a familiar feeling. This was a place she knew, an addiction she could comprehend far more than opium. She was no drug addict, but she had sought out the pleasure of men many times since Alvin's disappearance. She had not necessarily found happiness there, but had discovered a well of ecstasy, a completeness that, if for only the space of a few moments, allowed her to lose herself.

But not like this.

Dr. Halver worshipped Matilda. As the first moments passed, and Maddie realized that she no longer held the power to resist, she began to lose herself in the act, as she had so many times before. She listened to their breathing, he gasping and she sighing. She concentrated as his hands explored Matilda and her both, parting, fluttering and pressing, eliciting a moan that was not utterly Matilda's.

Dr. Halver was giving himself to Matilda in a fit of passion unlike Maddie had ever seen in a man. It was almost charming if it wasn't so damned disturbing.

When it was over, Dr. Halver was crying again, babbling his thanks like an absolved sinner. He gathered his clothing and his bag and left, slightly ruffled and red in the cheeks.

Maddie struggled against Matilda, wondering if she had control again, but finding she did not. Matilda moved her hand and drained the last of the bitter tea from the cup, now very cold.

"This is my little corner of the world," said Matilda. "I would welcome you, but you're not."

Matilda, listen, I had nothing to do...

As the opium hit her bloodstream, Maddie wanted to scream, to cry. But she only fell asleep and dreamed of the day she took Randy to the zoo to look at the polar bears.

Misgivings

When Maddie next awoke, it was with the same headache but to less fanfare.

All signs of Matilda's presence were gone and Mrs. Fitz was nowhere to be seen. The drapes on the windows were still drawn tight against the light, so much so that Maddie had no perception of time. How was it that Matilda flourished in such dark places?

Part of her was disappointed that she was not home, but she had to admit, as terrifying as her first encounter with Matilda was, she was glad to be in charge again, and here. She was unsure whether it was due to the mystery of Alvin's disappearance, the strange connection she felt to Randall, or simply lingering curiosity. But part of her would have been disappointed to wake up in her bedroom back home.

Her body—Matilda's body, she reminded herself—ached everywhere. But when she explored under the covers, she found that she'd been changed into a different set of bedclothes, and from the scent of lavender and vanilla, bathed as well. She had no recollection of such an experience, however, and felt a little uncomfortable, moving down into the covers more.

No, maybe home was a better idea.

Taking a deep breath, Maddie reclined on the soft pillow and listened to the sounds of the old house. She noticed the murmur of distant voices every now and again, the chink of silverware and china, the creak of floorboards as people moved to and fro. She noticed, too, the smell of baking bread and roasting meat with sage. It was a house full of people, and a house full of mysteries.

Finally, after deciding that staying in bed would accomplish nothing, but still lingering a little longer under the warm blankets, Maddie rose and went to the large dresser and vanity set and seated herself.

There was just enough light from the gas-lamp to illuminate the face in the mirror, and Maddie turned her cheek to get a better look at Matilda's face. She had a much more intense look; her cheekbones were higher, and it made her almond-shaped brown eyes look larger, deeper. The hair was longer than hers, but the same color brown, unremarkable, but nothing that required much in the way of coloring. She had the same full bottom lip, the same rounded eyebrows. Familiar, and yet strange; off enough to be mesmerizing.

When she'd had enough of the reflection, Maddie turned to examine the antique vanity itself. It was a marvelous piece of furniture with a Victorian elegance, but its beauty was dulled due to the magnificent objects upon it: a silver grooming set, an inlaid copper jewelry box, a hurricane lamp with brilliant stained glass roses, and more. She ran her fingers over the multitude of beautiful pieces.

The priceless objects made her yearn for the library. She wanted to know their history, their make, and provenance.

Three pieces in particular held her attention, though. She could swear she had seen them before: one was a silver pocketwatch engraved with the initials "MAR," another was a pin with a Japanese beetle done entirely in minuscule mosaic, and the last was a copper mirror with turquoise inlay in the shape of a fleur de lis. Were they things her grandmother had owned? Or had she seen them in a museum? She couldn't recall.

Maddie took a silver ring out of one of the drawers and slipped it on her finger. A perfect fit. She looked down at her hands and sighed. As much as she wanted, she could no longer trust her own body, and she could no longer believe this was simply a dream. There was too much mounting evidence to the contrary. Randall would likely visit her again, and she could hopefully get more answers.

No, not hopefully. She *would* get more answers. She deserved them. Who did he think he was, anyway?

But the thought was discomforting. She knew that she trusted Randall on impulse because she trusted Randy. But what was to say Randall was any less devious and cruel than Matilda?

A polite knock on the door brought her out of the dark and into the present.

"It's Randall," a voice announced.

"Um, come in," she said, turning slightly. There was a shawl over the back of the chair, and she grabbed it, wrapping it around her shoulders. Modesty was likely not something with which Matilda was familiar, but for the moment Maddie was in control and she found comfort in doing things her way.

She did not want Matilda to visit again, yet knew there was no hope of that. Her nose was already beginning to tickle, and she had a crawling sensation at her throat.

Randall entered and shut the door softly behind him. He had changed out of his other attire, and was now wearing a green velvet brocade embroidered vest under a black jacket. The chain of a pocketwatch caught the light as he moved toward her, glimmering remarkably.

Gorgeous, Maddie thought. She meant all of him.

"I'd like to go home," she announced as Randall approached her. "You can do that, right? I mean, you did orchestrate my whole arrival here, and after the last day or so, I'm ready to get back to the way things were, crappy as it might have been."

When he didn't answer immediately, she continued, "This is an interesting place from, you know, an aesthetic perspective, but I really miss gas station coffee, and Twinkies."

Randall looked grim, his brows so far down over his eyes he almost looked as if he were scowling. She stopped talking.

"In time," he said, after a moment's pause. He rubbed his hands together as if he was cold, but it wasn't cold in the room at all. As he approached, she noted the rosy color on his cheeks and the distinctly outdoors smell he brought with him.

"I came as soon as I could," said Randall, clearing his throat. "I..." He faltered, shaking his head, and tried again. "I had no idea Halver had... that Matilda would be so difficult. We thought it would work as a complete switch, or at least, as a replacement. But I didn't know she could surface, that she would take you over. It had to be terrifying, to say the least."

"How did you know?" Maddie asked, half ashamed.

"Halver always leaves his tea in the kitchen after... after they...." Randall looked a little embarrassed. "I didn't think you would have gone through with something like that of your own volition."

Randall gave her a pained, and yet hopeful look.

"I'm glad you don't think I'm that much of a slut," Maddie said. "But I still had to go along with the whole thing. She's very forceful when she wants to be, it seems."

"You weren't maligned in any way?"

"I had to watch," Maddie blurted, and found she was on the verge of tears. "I had to *do* things. I felt everything but couldn't control it. That was *really* messed up."

Randall looked genuinely horrified, pressing his fingers

into the bridge of his nose. It looked as if he might even cry. "I am so sorry, Madeline. I never wanted you to experience such a test, not ever. Matilda, for as much as she is like you, is *not* you. I hoped you'd have a more gentle initiation."

"There is a bright side. Sort of," Maddie said, turning and wiping her eyes.

"Oh?" asked Randall.

"I'm at least accepting this can't be a dream. But whatever this is, whatever this other reality is, I'm definitely *over* it. I want to go home."

Randall chewed at his bottom lip, waiting an uncomfortable moment before replying. "Madeline," he said, softly, "I assure you that if I could send you back, you would go back. But the touchstone only works one way..."

"Touchstone?" Maddie said.

"The mirror," said Randall. "You see, the mirror was years of work on my part. It was very difficult to arrange for Dr. Keats to purchase it, considering the lineage of such a piece, and to pinpoint it in your world in the first place."

"So, that mirror is the same here as in the future?" asked Maddie, trying to assemble what Randall had described.

"Not the *future*. This is not the past. Not *your* past, I should say," Randall said, firmly. "This is a very separate, unique world. Connected in many ways to yours, but not yours."

"Of course," Maddie said, feeling very weary. She closed her eyes, longer than one would with just a blink, and stared at the back of her eyelids.

"Are you quite alright?" he asked. "The stress, it's getting to you—"

"No, it's just a little overwhelming to absorb at once," Maddie said, tossing her hands up in resignation. "I have no idea what you're talking about, or what kind of weird warped 'present' this is. And I really just want to get home. But apparently that's too much to ask after I was brought here against my will."

Randall tried again. "The mirror is the touchstone, a gateway. A portal between worlds. Though this Boston is, as I mentioned, as much the present as your home is. We are mostly in sync, though at times there are unpredictable hiccups. But sometimes travel is possible."

Maddie considered, pulling at a long curl, straightening it out and the letting it bounce back. "That can't be easy to account for."

"Some rare twains, like Alvin, can travel between worlds without such objects. We call them wanderers. But the touchstones are an alternate method, particularly useful for the uninitiated to travel between worlds."

"Worlds. Plural?"

"Yes. There are eight Worlds."

"Right... and eight Maddies running around." Maddie tried not to laugh. Looking at Randall's sincere, sober, face helped a great deal in that respect.

"More or less, yes. Though currently there are only three, we think. At any rate, if you can work with Matilda, you may be able to get home on your own, moving between the worlds as Randy and I are able to do. You could simply jump back to your world, and free yourself of our sordid problems, never to consider Alvin again for the rest of your life."

"Okay. Easy enough. So tell me how you switch with Randy."

"Randy and I are... different. I have moved back and forth many times, and though it is often a significant challenge to work with him, as I cannot permeate his somewhat complicated disability..." Randall used the word awkwardly, as if he had searched for another term but could not locate a more accurate replacement. "He has never left your world."

"Great." Maddie said, folding her arms across her chest. "You brought me here, into this body that I can't control because *you* thought that I wanted answers about Alvin. Now you're telling me the only way back is to work with my crazed opium-addicted evil twin? That's not exactly fair."

"It's not a matter of simply returning you, or telling you how to do it with Matilda. It's... it's more—"

Maddie's patience disintegrated. Her head throbbed with every heartbeat and what she really wanted was more opium. "Really, what is *wrong* with you? I just spent the last year of my life trying to forget Alvin, trying to mourn, to make sense of my own life. And just when I've finally reconciled all that, you take me here and tell me Alvin's alive. That's a special kind of cruel."

Whatever feeling of trust she had toward him was quickly dissipating and being replaced by searing hatred and all-out ire.

Randall spread his hands out as if in some sort of peace offering, and then shrugged. "But I thought you would want to see Alvin."

"Well, I don't."

"You really don't want to know where he is?" he asked. He raised his eyebrows, pleading one moment, then turning impish the next. "Tell me you aren't the least bit curious. In spite of his infidelity—you loved him once."

"I did. Once," Maddie said. "Meanwhile, I'm stuck here. Wherever the hell *this* is."

"This is Second World," Randall said. He held up two fingers. "And this world is not so reprehensible or backward as you might deduce from meeting Halver, Matilda, and myself."

"I haven't seen more than the inside of this room. It gets better out there?" asked Maddie, admittedly intrigued. She gestured to the drawn drapes. "I gathered it's winter."

"Yes. It's been snowing. It's lovely. If you'd permit me, I'd like to show you around the city a little. I'd like to take you to my office, as well."

Randall had a way about him, she had to admit that; he was beyond convincing. His smile was so familiar—so Randy—

that try as she might otherwise, her resistance waned. She desperately needed to trust someone.

Maddie was trying to come up with a reason to refuse him, but all she could think about were the aesthetic possibilities. If this Boston truly was its own entity, yet related to her own, the possibilities were tantalizing. She couldn't resist the opportunity to explore an alternate world, akin to her own and yet entirely set apart. While she knew she'd never manage to publish a paper on it without becoming the laughingstock of academia, it was an opportunity she couldn't pass up.

Randall smiled, "For an art historian, I can't stress how remarkable it will be for you to experience this Boston. It truly is a marvel, rivaling Paris and Londinium."

He knew her too damned well.

"Londinium?" She was about to say more, when she was hit by a wave of pain in her head. She bent over, wincing against it.

"Ah, yes, the withdrawal," Randall said, shaking his head.

"Or Matilda. It's hard to tell the difference," Maddie said.

Randall winced, reaching into his weskit pocket and retrieving a small packet with marked handwritten script in blue ink. He placed it on the dresser. "It's not a cure-all, but it will alleviate the worst of it. For a few hours, perhaps."

"What's this?" she asked.

"A combination of herbs. Similar to what you'd call aspirin, I think, but with an extra kick. It'll help take the edge off, and is safe enough for short periods of time."

"Comforting." She picked up the packet, and turned it around. She couldn't read the writing—it had blurred slightly as if exposed to too much moisture. Under the paper she could feel soft capsules.

"Sweets to the sweet," she said with a sigh.

"I'll send Mrs. Fitz in to help you into your clothing, and then we can go for a walk."

"Might as well," she said. "Let's just hope Matilda doesn't come along for the ride."

Randall sobered, pausing at the door. "Yes, let us hope."

The words were intended to be comforting, but Maddie felt a sense of dread as Randall shut the door.

After Mrs. Fitz was done dressing her, and even with the admitted allayment of her headache by the medicine Randall gave her, Maddie wondered how on earth she would manage to walk for more than fifteen feet without keeling over again on account of her outfit.

The dress she wore was no doubt a most fetching cut, even she couldn't deny that; but the discomfort of the corset at her waist, cinching the living daylights out of her, was practically intolerable.

The torturous corset was the centerpiece of the whole affair, made of hammered silver metal, its frame stitched with a backing of muslin dyed deepest crimson, so that the red shone through gaps in the metal panels. As a result, her small breasts were pushed up and covered again with a white sheer material that went all the way to her neck, fastened with tiny pearl buttons. The blouse flared slightly at the shoulders–though nothing as extraordinary as she'd seen in some late-Victorian examples–and then tapered to her wrists.

Beneath the corset fell layers of red and grey fabric, embroidered elegantly with interlocking leaf patterns. The hem was silver, too, offsetting the design of the corset; all in all, a tremendous effort, mercilessly squeezing in her middle and bearing down on her body.

Over the entire dress, Mrs. Fitz put a short, cropped jacket, embroidered with *millefleur*, that dizzying floral pattern of the Unicorn tapestries. As over-the-top as it was, it was still per-

fect in combination with the rest of the ensemble. She stepped
into a pair of boots buttoned down the side with silver buttons, soft as kid, and lined with mink. A simple, single plume
adorned her little black hat, with a short veil that fell just above
her eyes—really, all display and no utility there.

"The cameo or the flower brooch?" Mrs. Fitz asked, holding out two pieces of jewelry.

The cameo depicted a woman at three-quarters pose, with
a laurel garland in her hair, the detail striking even in duotone;
Maddie could swear the woman was looking at her and shook
her head. The flower brooch, on the other hand, was cut red
glass, fashioned in such a manner as to make the petals look
remarkably lifelike.

"The flower brooch," said Maddie, without hesitating. As
beautiful as the cameo was, something about it unsettled her. It
reminded her a little too much of Matilda, lingering and looking.

Mrs. Fitz nodded and then pinned it to her lapel with her
deft fingers.

"There we are now," she pronounced at last. "A right
lovely lady."

Maddie had not ventured—to her knowledge, at least—any
further than the expansive bedroom in which she'd awoken.
She vaguely recalled the shop that she'd seen upon first arriving, staring into that strange mirror, and assumed that the
house would be situated in such a way that that the boutique
was adjacent to the house. Memories from Matilda, no doubt.
Even when she was hiding, Matilda had a way of being present.

On shaky feet and with her head throbbing again, Maddie followed Mrs. Fitz out of the large oak door and into the
hallway. It was bathed in warm sunlight, provided by a series
of themed stained-glass sun windows that ran the length of the
ceiling, depicting scenes from the *Song of Roland*. Except Roland was a woman.

Everything was carved of dark wood, or else wallpapered

with extravagant designs that spoke of influence from Morris and the Arts and Crafts Movement, yet with a persistent Victorian note. Intricate brass lighting fixtures lined the hallways, and even simple objects, like doorknobs and crown molding, took on a life of their own when rendered with artistic, naturalistic flair.

Maddie was so taken aback by the art that she stopped walking to stare.

"Madam–" said Mrs. Fitz behind her, clearing her throat.

"Yes?"

"Don't you want to take the lift?" she asked, giving her a curious glance and pointing behind them.

"Oh, yes," said Maddie. "Of course."

Mrs. Fitz gestured to her left with a wide sweep of her hands and Maddie viewed the so-called lift for the first time.

To call it an elevator would insult the sheer artistry of it, so elegant it was. The first set of doors revealed a filigree of floral flourishes and intertwining vines, etched in such detail as to make the two-dimensional metal look as if it were carved in relief. When these doors pulled away, the inner doors–polished so deftly they were smooth as mirrors–parted to reveal the intricate inner sanctum, a combination of dark mahogany wood and mirrors, set between with oil paintings and crystal sconces; in the middle was an immense chandelier dripping crystal drops as real as rain.

There was a crank to the side, the shaft bright burnished bronze and shaped like a unicorn's horn, but set with a round knob on the top. It was Baroque-organic perfection with a Victorian accent. Baffling, but beautiful.

Gaping still, trying to rein in her wonder, Maddie walked into the lift and folded her hands one over the other. Mrs. Fitz pressed a series of buttons inside, pulled an ivory-adorned knob in the middle, then pushed it down with a twist of her pudgy hand. There followed a low grinding sound from somewhere below them, then a steamy hiss.

The doors closed, and they began their descent.

Three bells chimed, and the lift came to a stop—softer, Maddie reflected, than even some of the elevators she'd ridden in before, in her other life—and opened up into another hallway, much like that she had seen with the Roland windows.

While the design and decoration of the Roth home was by no means as elaborate as a place like Versailles, it still held a certain whimsical similarity, albeit with more unity throughout. The Roths fancied mirrors and used them to generate a feeling of space within the home, which was already quite spacious, and combined the cozy colors of green and red with dark mahogany and gold. Many walls were adorned with artwork, sculptures, paintings; others held volumes and volumes of books, their straight spines in a rainbow of colors adding their own beauty to the overall design.

Randall was waiting in the foyer, dressed in yet another outfit, one that complimented Maddie's frock precisely. He wore a long maroon wool jacket, cut tight around his trim middle, set with a sash over the shoulder in silver. His russet-brown hair was tied back and he wore what could only be described as a low top hat, set with a silk band. He carried a brass cane, which he turned over in his hands nervously.

"A vision, as always," Randall said. He squeezed Maddie's arm lightly, and it comforted her. She could feel the warmth of his body so close to hers, reassuring and undeniably real.

It felt like being with Randy, in spite of how different they were. She couldn't shake her comfort, which both annoyed her and enticed her.

She wanted to know more of him. And she hated herself for even thinking that. Did she want to love him because he wasn't… unusual, like Randy?

"You'll have a chance to see a little more of the house later, but for now, I want you to experience the aesthetic wonder that is our great city," Randy said, quietly so Mrs. Fitz could not hear. He leaned over to her ear. "Boston is a center of fashion, and we are fashion's center."

"I can see that," Matilda said. "So much for sweatpants."

Randall chuckled. "How are you feeling?" he asked as they made their way down a few stairs and into a long hallway that led to a pair of towering wooden doors. Stained glass here depicted two coats of arms, but both so elaborate that Maddie could not tell what they represented. Light and a little noise from outside reverberated down the hallway.

"Headache's a bit better, but this corset's a piece of work," she said with a wince.

"Indeed," said Randall. "I do not envy women for their adherence to fashion. But if you are to be Matilda for the time being, you should play the part. People would pass out in the streets should they see you public without a corset."

"God forbid," Maddie replied.

"Here we are. Our carriage awaits," Randall said as the doors were cast open.

A blond boy stood on the other side of the door, dressed in blue from head to toe, gesturing down a flight of marble stairs and to a carriage guided not by horses, but by a marvelous golden wheel affixed to a track. The wheel glimmered in the cold morning light, and as stately and elegant and mysterious as it was, Maddie stared at it for only a moment, for the world around her opened up like a vast, incredible dream.

The across the cobblestone street read "Beacon Hill Dist." and they were, in fact, on an actual hill. From where Maddie stood, she could see all of Boston sprawled out before her, a Boston so different from the one she'd known in her other life that she felt her head swim with the view.

The sky was smoggy as she remembered it, but dotted with hundreds of air balloons, many of which were so complex and colorful they looked like floating bouquets of flowers.

There were no skyscrapers that she could see immediately, but there were many tall buildings all the same, with spires, both of the church and civic variety.

And the city was *alive*. Carriages, all with similar golden guiding wheels, maneuvered through the streets while people bustled about, mostly too busy in their daily activities to notice Maddie and Randall exiting the house.

Music was coming from somewhere; someone laughed. There were trees, shrubs, and plants everywhere, mostly evergreen. What snow had fallen recently had been moved out of the street, or melted altogether, but some still hung on eaves. Ice glinted off every iron grate.

"Your fur, madam," said Mrs. Fitz, behind her. Maddie felt the warm embrace of a stole around her shoulders. "And your purse." She took it, and Randall continued to help her down the stairs and into the carriage as she complied in a most dazed manner.

The carriage was painted bright green on the outside, with a series of scrolling numbers on a brass plate affixed to it. Inside it was much warmer; the seats smooth velvet, and the glass-paned windows of double thickness. Maddie situated herself, sitting a little awkwardly with the bustle, and Randall smiled.

"You are unusually mute," he said.

"I honestly don't know what to say."

"Then keep your eyes open, and enjoy yourself."

Randall tapped his cane on a brass panel before them and the carriage car hissed and began rolling forward. It was surprisingly smooth and built up speed at an impressive pace. Heat emanated from a vent in front of them, but in spite of it, Maddie shivered.

"How does this thing work?" she asked Randall. "I mean, considering no one is driving."

"Well, this functions by virtue of rudimentary programming. Instead of a motor, propulsion is achieved by a series of impressive magnets run in a vast network throughout the city." He pointed to a panel in the side of the carriage where series of sliding knobs were arranged, much like a brass-plated soundboard in music studio. "It's altogether not that complicated, and far safer than your self-propelled cars. Dangerous lots, those are. Especially that tin can you rattle around in."

The memory of the Civic, the smell of the heat in the winter when she first turned it on, came rushing back to Maddie, and she felt a little dizzy with the recollection. Her own memories were starting to feel less and less trustworthy. Her car had been brown, right? Or was it blue?

She decided to think of something else.

"I've been meaning to ask," she said, staring out the window as they passed a group of schoolchildren, all dressed in yellow and black like little bumblebees, "if my body—I mean, if this is Matilda's body, and she's here too, what's going on with my body? Could she skip over to my side and take my body for a ride?"

"Well, Matilda has never had a desire for transcorporeal travel, as far as I know. It's unlikely she'll go to your world."

"You know, that's almost comforting."

"As to your body—you are likely still staring at the mirror, in suspended animation. At least, Alvin used to say I nodded off when I traveled, and he would often prop me up in the library with a book; no one really took notice. But I always go somewhere safe."

"And Dr. Keats's house is safe?"

"He has been given instructions," Randall said, somewhat cryptically. "Randy knows what to expect, as well. As I said before, he understands."

The thought of her body, standing frozen in front of the mirror like Lot's wife, made her shudder.

"And it's a second-to-second comparison? I mean, time is exactly the same?"

"Mostly."

"There you go with the 'mostly' again."

As uncomfortable as the course of their conversation was, Maddie found herself utterly distracted by the landscape. In fact, Randall was talking at length about transcorporeal travel, but what she saw in the streets of this Boston distracted her from his words entirely.

This was a brand-new chapter in her love of design, and she was trying to put her finger on the aesthetics she observed; yes, there was certainly a Victorian influence, with a splash of Edwardian. Yet everywhere she turned, she saw hints of the Pre-Raphaelites and of Morris; the buildings, the fashion, the wrought iron.

But nothing was quite as she remembered it from her own world. It was as if someone had presented a visual representation of a memory of an aesthetic, rather than built one from scratch. A bit like drawing a picture of an elephant without ever seeing one before, only reading about it. Though for all that, it was no less elegant or beautiful.

She felt Randall's eyes on her but continued to look out the window. He'd gone quiet.

More of Boston came into view, and Maddie got a clearer look at one of the hot air balloons far above the skyline. They were tiered balloons, she now saw, with what had to be buildings below them, suspended, unbelievably, in air. Could that possibly be?

Randall smiled, noting her expression. "As I said, we do well for ourselves in the Beacon Hill District," he said with a quirk of his lips. "But, there are those in town who take extravagance to a new level."

"Those are *houses*? Up there? All the way up there?" she asked. It was like seeing the Breakers suspended five hundred feet into the sky. She couldn't quite make out the details of the homes, but there had to be close to two hundred of them; other flying contraptions, smaller ones, darted to and fro between the buildings in the air.

"Assuredly," he said, softly. "It's not the land that's important, but rather the grandeur and scope of the whole business. You can imagine the cost of refueling those. Some even produce their own gasses inside." He shook his head disapprovingly. "It's a beautiful sight, to be sure—but every now and again one of them erupts into flames. Quite a few million pounds have been spent researching other methods for elevation, but none have been found yet. Would you like to see them? We have an invitation to call on Count Gascon, one of the inhabitants, tomorrow. It's a gala event."

"*Count* Gascon?"

"A middling noble. The monarchy is very important here, as small as it is. Boston, though you'd never believe it, is surrounded by wilderness to the West. These United States comprise mostly the eastern seaboard and little else, along what you might call the Megalopolis. At any rate, we never did away with the monarchy here. I suppose they give everyone a feeling of comfort, of order. It's been at least five years since the last scuffle with the Wilds, but there is always a possibility."

"Wilds?" Maddie squinted at Randall. "Like the Wild West?"

"Not exactly. You see, we never quite managed to make our way past the hardier tribes of the Appalachians."

"I'd love to get my hands on some of their art," Maddie said, almost breathless with the possibility. "Native tribes out there, flourishing for hundreds of years without disruption."

"Oh, I'm afraid that will have to wait some time, hostilities being as they are. And I didn't say it was without disruption."

Maddie's head was hurting again, helped in no small part by squinting and craning her neck toward the floating mansions in the sky. How peculiar. Why would anyone, she thought, risk so much to make that kind of statement? Though, she had to admit, cities in her world were built almost as precariously, destined to be wiped away in the wake of a hurricane or an earthquake. Maybe Randall was right: People weren't so different after all, even worlds apart.

She rubbed at her temple, staring now at the brown row houses on either side of the road. They were mostly familiar, except less stark than she was used to. They were as much a part of her Boston as this one, but here there was a more defined personality to each house; different topiaries, various wrought iron gates, elaborate gardens, custom paint. Still, seeing the buildings was enough to be almost—almost—a comfort.

"So what's caused the difference between our two worlds?" asked Maddie, looking sidelong at Randall. "Was it one large event that sent this world into its direction, and ours into another?"

The haberdasher looked surprised at the question, and rubbed his chin. "I have often wondered the same, having not been around quite long enough to know for certain."

"Not quite long enough?"

Randall shook his head. "Just a turn of phrase. But first and foremost, this country here was built not on the principles of God Himself, but on Mary Herself—with the belief that, as the Mother of God, she literally was—and is—the Mother of All. So you can imagine immediately how much of an impact that made. Like ripples in a pool."

"That explains the Marian slant I noticed earlier with Halver."

"Precisely. Medicine, as you likely saw upon meeting Douglas, is controlled by Her Church, as are the banks. The rest—law and criminal justice and science—are in the hands of the S.O.F., the Society of Friends, a long branch of the Quakers."

"I can see how that would change the course of the world. I mean, we have Quakers, but most people don't know them outside of the oatmeal thing."

Randall laughed, getting the joke. He seemed very much a part of this world, and yet he knew some of her old life. Maddie found her mood brightened; she wiggled a little deeper into her stole, marveling in the properties of fur–something she had never had the chance, the lack of conscience, or the money, to wear before.

"But it goes far beyond practiced religion," Randall said, somewhat less enthusiastically. He cleared his throat, and looked down at his hands. He was delaying.

"Beyond how?" asked Maddie. "I've got the monarchy thing down. The Wilds, whatever that means. Seems like enough to make a difference."

Randall mumbled something that sounded like "argon."

"What?"

"Dragons," he said, not meeting her eye.

"Like, *dragon* dragons? Like *rahr*! dragons, spitting fire?"

"No, no. Not quite like you think. Most of them don't walk around as dragons. That would be quite difficult to manage, I'd think."

"I'm losing you again."

"The word is somewhat loaded, hence my hesitance to use it. But from the Greek, a dragon simply means 'that which sees'. Certainly, a few of them over time have preferred a scales and teeth approach, but that is far from normal."

"Normal. Right. Because there are *normal* dragons."

"Yes, here our dragons are like gods. We have a much more intimate connection with them. They live among us, recognized in many instances. Your world is known for its remoteness, its resilience to such things. Which is why it was so difficult to get you here."

"It was difficult to get me here because there aren't any dragons in my world?"

"I didn't say there weren't *any* dragons in your world. On the contrary, it's only that they often go about unnoticed, recognized only as prophets or seers or saviors."

"Like Jesus? Wait. Are you telling me Jesus was a dragon?"

"Jesus was not a dragon. Not... clearly this isn't the time for such a conversation. We're almost at my office." He pointed out the window to a Tudor style townhouse, stretching down half a block. A variety of signs hung from posts, denoting an assortment of archaic-sounding businesses, including an inn called, of course, The Red Dragon.

They got out of the carriage at a little docking station designed for just such a purpose, and Maddie followed Randall into the building and up a narrow flight of stairs, two doors down from the inn and tavern, to the third story. No lifts in this building, and it seemed almost medieval by contrast to the Roths' home. When they came to a green glass door, he pointed to the stenciled letters there: Mssrs. R. A. Roth and J. G. Iosheka. No further elaboration.

Maddie's second sense, which she attributed to Matilda's lingering memories, gave her no clues as to where she was or what she should feel. As she walked into the room, for the first time since coming to Second World, she felt no connection to the place whatsoever.

It was part laboratory and part library, half of the room being taken up by a wide assortment of Bunsen burners and beakers–all long empty and cleaned out–and the other with books stacked up to the ceiling. It smelled of lingering chemicals and a hint of mildew. Two desks sat on opposite sides of the room, one cleared completely and another in a state of utter chaos.

"This is where Alvin and I spend most of our time," Randall said.

Wanting to skirt the subject of Alvin, Maddie asked: "Who's J. G. Iosheka?" She shivered into her stole. It was alarmingly cold in the office. And while there was a fireplace, buried behind a chest of drawers, she figured there wasn't much of a chance that it was in working condition.

"Well, that's who I've brought you here to talk to. Before we talk about Alvin," Randall said, going over to the cluttered desk. He removed a ring of keys from his pocket, and after a few tries—no doubt due to the decidedly dim light—he got the drawer open.

"This Iosheka guy is not in your desk, I hope," Maddie said. She noticed a row of pickled specimens on the other side of the room and backed away. "Or over there."

Randall laughed. "Dear me, no. But those *are* his. He's a bit of a biologist. But it's been some time since we shared the office, though I keep his things here as a matter of sentiment, I suppose."

"He's not here and you want me to talk to him?" Maddie asked. Perhaps Randall was more addled than she had been led to believe.

Randall pulled out a small silver compact from the desk and held it out to her. It looked like a woman's makeup compact, the sort that she had seen at the Victoria and Albert Museum; it was finely made, and glittered, even in the dark room.

"It works better in darker places," Randall said, flipping it open. "Or else I would turn the light on. Come over here. Take a look. Don't look at me so suspiciously."

Maddie took a few steps closer, and Randall held out his arm so they were both looking at the compact. This close up, she was aware that it was thrumming slightly, like a tiny purring motor.

As she turned to see it better, she noticed that where the mirror would be was a piece of iridescent cloth, and instead of powder there was smooth brass with a large, red stone in the middle, looking much like the one in the cabochon ring Alvin had given her.

"Take it," Randall said.

"It's not going to electrocute me, is it?"

He chuckled. "No, it won't. Here, press your thumb on

top of the red stone. Then watch. And listen."

The compact was warm in her hands, far warmer than it should have been from being held such a short time. And it vibrated in concert with the purring noise.

She looked sidelong at Randall, who looked as excited as a parent on Christmas morning, and then pressed her thumb into the stone.

At first, nothing happened. Then she felt her thumb ache a moment, as if bruised. Before she had time to question it, however, the cloth at the top began changing color, bleeding into a variety of shades until a face appeared. Then the face began to move. It was like a miniature television, rendered in fabric.

And while she knew she ought to wonder more fully at the mechanism in her hand, Maddie found her attention elsewhere.

For she was looking at Ian's face.

"You did it!" said the man who looked like Ian on the other side of the compact. He was older than Ian, and more fit. Maddie remembered the painting in her room.

"John..." she murmured.

"Wait. This isn't Matilda, is it?" John asked, squinting through the transmission.

Maddie looked over at Randall, unsure what to say; he gestured for her to speak.

"No... no, this is Maddie. Madeline," she said. She was nervous. "Well, mostly. Randall said something about trans-corporeal travel."

John laughed. "I thought so! Excellent. Good on you, Randall. And welcome to Second World, Madeline."

"You can just call me Maddie," she said.

Randall came up behind her, putting a hand on her shoulder. She drew a breath at the touch, but tried to keep her face still. "It wasn't easy, but it worked," he said. "And I wouldn't trust this with Matilda. You know how she is."

"Indeed, indeed. Well, Madeline, are you faring well with

this scoundrel?" John asked, quirking his lip just like Ian.

"Scoundrel?" she asked.

John chuckled again. "Figuratively. He's a good person, Maddie. No need to worry. You're in good hands."

"I didn't have much of a choice in the matter," Maddie said.

John raised his eyebrows, the picture becoming less precise for a moment before resolving again. "None of us have the choice to be what we are. Sooner or later I would have figured out a way to get you here through Ian, you know. Randall's approach was gentler and quicker."

There was a threat there that made Maddie shiver. "You know about Ian?" she asked.

"And he knows about me. But don't worry. We're on good terms. He's been keeping an eye on you since Alvin left your world. And in a way, I've been keeping an eye on you, too.

"Of course, Alvin will be furious if he finds out I've helped you. Not to mention Mary," John pointed out, flicking his eyes to Randall.

"I know," Randall said. "But you've got the best capabilities, even if you are out there in the Wilds."

"It's not as wild as you think, Randall. I believe you'd quite enjoy it," John said with a knowing grin.

Randall chuckled. "I know. I'm afraid I'd never return."

"You act like that's a bad thing," John said.

"I'm not ready yet," Randall replied. He fell very quiet, and his hand slipped off from Maddie's shoulder. But rather than continue in the line of conversation or respond to Maddie's inquiring eyes, he asked, "One more thing. Ah, you haven't happened to have seen Alvin in the last few days, have you?"

John frowned. "Afraid not. He doesn't typically come to me unless he's truly desperate."

"Keep an eye out for him, will you?"

John nodded. "I will. Take care."

Randall took the compact from Maddie, snapped it shut,

and stowed it in his weskit pocket. "We've an appointment to keep with the Hildebrandts," he said, not making eye contact.

"Wait, wait... what?" she asked. "We have an appointment? It's all a lot to swallow."

"Indeed. And I'm sorry. But I thought you'd be glad to see–"

"Glad to find out this creep's been spying on me? That... that... he's apparently my cousin or something, according to Mrs. Fitz, when in another world I slept with him?"

"He's not really your cousin. Or, at least, no more than I'm–"

"And what was that about *losing* Alvin? I thought you told me you knew where he was. Wasn't that the whole reason you brought me here? To see Alvin?"

"Maddie, I... you just said you didn't really want to see him. So I didn't press the issue. And then he rather vanished."

"Fantastic," Maddie said. "Let's just go. I want to get back home and go to sleep."

Randall looked crestfallen, but Maddie stomped out of the office nonetheless and waited for him to catch up, tapping her foot in the hallway.

It was going to be a quiet ride to the Hildebrandts', whoever the hell they were.

5
The Three

An hour later and Maddie was sitting next to Randall in the exorbitant parlor of one Mrs. Hildebrandt, listening to a rather boring account of his recent run-in with Countess de Borasi, drinking a cup of bitter tea.

Bitter tea? Maddie rolled her eyes and peered into the cup suspiciously. She tried to convince herself that drinking opium tea couldn't possibly be common to all women in Second World, but she put the cup and saucer down nonetheless, just in case. For the time being, she concentrated on the woman with whom they had their appointment, Mrs. Hildebrandt, named Deborah—after the saint, she insisted.

Mrs. Hildebrandt was a longtime friend of the Roths, known for her ability to start a trend in Boston with nothing more than an angled feather in her hat. But this was more than just a fashion consult; Randall suspected she might have some inkling of where Alvin might be, since she moved in a variety of intriguing circles. When Maddie asked what "intriguing" meant in that context, he clarified with "readers and thinkers and painters and the like," which didn't sound like the sort of people Alvin would hang around with.

Mrs. Hildebrandt was middle-aged and painted with makeup. Her lips were cherry red, her face porcelain pink, her eyes rimmed in kohl then smudged with blue and green. She was a gilded rose, though, for her figure was voluptuous in all the right places, and she wore an elaborate taffeta dress—in three shades of pink set with hemmed lace about the cuffs—with an air of authority.

Clothing aside, Maddie found her rather vapid. If the woman suspected Maddie was anyone other than Matilda Roth, she gave no clue. Randall answered what few questions she addressed to Maddie, mostly related to pricing and current trends, and they all sipped tea and listened to Mrs. Hildebrandt chatter away.

Well, fancy seeing you here again. Delicious tea, isn't it?

Tea. She'd been right; that was the problem. Maddie had been overwhelmed by the house and the company, both of which were remarkably ornate, and had paid very little attention to the drink she'd been handed. Even though she'd stopped after a few sips, she noticed the gradual heaviness of her eyelids, the way her tension and muted anger melted away deliciously and was replaced by something warm and sensuous.

I really didn't think you were quite **that** oblivious.

Maddie had no voice. She also had no sight. The world had gone black in the middle of the conversation between Randall and Mrs. Hildebrandt.

I'll take the deafening silence as affirmation, said Matilda.

Matilda's voice came not to Maddie in sound, but *feeling*; it was some base vibration that she couldn't pinpoint in source or composition, but could understand as well as the beating of her own heart.

I'm stronger than Randall thinks. He and Alvin always thought they were the geniuses. Twains. **Twains**! Matilda laughed, the derisive noise slicing through what was left of Maddie's consciousness with precision.

Where am I? Where are we?

The thought was Maddie's but it, too, had no sound, only feeling. The words were formed oddly, the concepts distorted and skewed, but she successfully changed the course of Matilda's comment.

What are we, don't you mean? It's a much more intriguing question.

I just want to get home.

There was a tremble in the blackness, and Maddie sensed Matilda was irritated. Well, then. Expect to see me much more frequently. I can work with you to get you back to your body, but that's providing you treat mine well. Continue to take the tea, and continue to do as I instruct. Randall's absolutely infatuated with you, likely because he no longer knows what to do with me. He will tell you many things, but temper everything that he says with the knowledge that he is as crooked as he is conniving. And he's a coward.

Maddie was afraid to ask about Alvin. She didn't like the way Matilda spoke to her, so venomous and demanding. But she seemed to be knowledgeable at very least, and that was something. *Randall keeps telling me that Alvin is alive...*

Yes. He is alive. And you'll find him, I suspect. But by that time you'll have other things to worry about. Like what to do once you have him in your arms again. And what to do with Randall, who so adores you.

What if I don't cooperate with you?

There was a shimmer in the dark. Laughter.

You can't get back without me. Don't—what's that word you're so fond of?—ah yes, don't **fuck** with me. And I won't fuck with you. It's that easy.

Then, with a rush of air and her senses tingling, Maddie was back in Mrs. Hildebrandt's parlor again, sitting on a soft cushioned sofa, coughing tea out of her nose. Randall sat beside her fussing with a handkerchief and muttering apologies to Mrs. Hildebrandt, who only looked mildly upset. One of her perfectly arched eyebrows lifted in surprise.

"She's not been well," said Randall, doing his best to smooth over the situation.

Calm yourself. He doesn't like a fussy woman. Just say the ride here was rather difficult, and that the cold weather this time of year is bothersome.

Matilda had not left. Rather, she was sitting in the back of Maddie's mind like an unwanted spectator. It was a most uncomfortable sensation, a dull pressure between her eyes that made Maddie's nose tickle.

However, Maddie said the words as she was instructed, still gasping for air, and this seemed to placate both the hostess and the husband. After Deborah gave her most sincere well wishes, the Roths were on their way.

As they left the mansion arm in arm, Maddie still coughed every now and again. The restrictive corset was preventing her from a normal recovery.

See, I can be of great help to you, if you let me.

I can manage on my own.

Can you, now? Well, I'll be quiet as a mouse. You know where I'll be.

"Maddie?" Randall asked, leaning toward her, searching her face. Maddie felt Matilda's presence pull back as soon as Randall spoke her name, as if a curtain were drawn somewhere in her mind.

The opium made it difficult for Maddie to pinpoint any particular emotion, but she suspected something like fear was nibbling at the back of her mind. If she brought up the subject of Matilda's little interruption, or the presence of the opium in her tea, Randall would indeed be angry. And he'd force her off the stuff. And honestly, even Maddie had to admit that the calm of opium was welcome in this strange place.

Plus, Maddie didn't like walking around on the verge of a panic attack, and Matilda had a point. She might even be helpful.

"Maddie?" Randall asked again, this time more firmly. "Are you listening to me?"

"I'm sorry," she said, squeezing his arm with her gloved fingers. "I'm tired. I told you that already."

"Would you like to go home for a bit of a rest?"

"Yes, I think that'd be lovely," she said. "Honestly, all I want to do is get out of this getup entirely and roll around in the bed naked..." Then she stopped, realizing how provocative the statement sounded. She smirked.

He cleared his throat, and like a gentlemen, let the issue hang in the air until she corrected herself.

"The... corset. It's really restrictive. I sort of feel like my organs have been rearranged, you know?" she asked, then stopped. "No, I suppose you don't, considering you don't wear one."

By now they had arrived at the black carriage, the single golden wheel at the front recently cleaned by one of Mrs. Hildebrandt's servants, and it caught the chilly winter light. It was beautiful in its simplicity, that perfect circle, and Maddie stared at it a moment before letting Randall help her into the carriage.

"I'll be happy to take you home," said Randall, swooping up beside her, and closing the door in one swift movement. He did move well, she thought. So unlike Randy, so deliberate, almost as if he'd had instruction as a dancer. "But would you permit me just one detour? It's something I think you'd really find fascinating, and it might be surprisingly restorative."

"Restorative?" she asked.

"I know your love of cathedrals, and we have our own, something you simply cannot miss. It's called the Cathedral of the Weeping Lady, and it takes up two entire blocks downtown. You can see some of the domes and spirals from here."

"I don't know..." said Maddie. She felt Matilda there, suddenly, like someone peeking over her shoulder, except from within her. But Matilda was silent. Maddie had the impression that her twain was just listening, waiting.

"It's the gem of our city," he continued. "Designed by William Morris himself, if you'll believe it."

"William Morris? I had no idea he'd have designed a church. I always thought he was just one of those Pre-Raphaelite socialist types with thoughts bent on saving the world one hand-pressed tile at a time," Maddie said, thinking herself quite clever for the mini-lecture she'd delivered in the space of a sentence, especially considering the opium. But she did give herself away; Randall had piqued her interest, and she couldn't hide it.

Randall nodded, and she thought he looked amused as well, "Indeed, that's Morris in your world. In this world, Morris was one of the most devoted Marian priests—and his talent, well, I say it flourished here even more than it did in your world. There is a certain indelible well of inspiration for some when it comes to the Great Mother."

"Great Mother?" asked Maddie. "You sound like a neo-pagan."

He shrugged. "Not much of a difference in some things, I suppose."

When it came to describing the Cathedral of the Weeping Lady in academic terms, Maddie couldn't get it right no matter how hard she tried. It was as if... as if... as if nothing she could put into practical terms. God knew she'd studied William Morris enough, but the Morris that was woven into the fabric of the Cathedral of the Weeping Lady was so much more realized in comparison.

Everything was sculpted Morris. Trees grew from the columns, their strong limbs reaching out and skyward, detailed leaves and fruits painted with vibrant colors and ready to pluck and eat at the peak of ripeness. It was Morris in relief; Morris in three dimensions. It was like nothing she had ever imagined. To her knowledge, no one in her world had built a cathedral that looked like the Garden of Eden on the inside; everything was organic, everything was circular.

"Circular like the womb of Mary rather than the cross of Christ," Randall explained. "An entirely separate aesthetic."

"It's marvelous," breathed Maddie. "I can't get over it. I just want to crawl into the corner and stare at the ceiling for the rest of my life."

Randall could not suppress his smile, in spite of his decidedly reverent expression since entering the cathedral. "That's a marked change of opinion toward this place."

"Hah, well, you did play to my weaknesses: William Morris and redheads. I'm defenseless." Maddie grinned and glanced at Randall, who was walking in front of a torch, which sent shots of bright red through his usually more subtle russet hair.

"Good to know," he said, rubbing his chin thoughtfully. Then he paused, and pointed up as they passed into another part of the sanctuary. "Here's where the ceiling gets even more wondrous."

The ceiling was comprised of exposed wooden beams, and painted between the eaves were more designs—dizzying leaves, interlacing petals, stamens and more fruits. Chapel after chapel, circle after circle, Maddie and Randall continued to walk through the remarkable cathedral until they finally reached the central space, which truly felt like a womb, it was so deep and dark. The dome above rose skyward, carved of stone and wood and gilded over, the colors as brilliant as if God Himself had painted them moments ago.

Thousands of candles lit the sanctuary, reflected in shallow pools of water rimmed with black and white stones. The ground was littered with low pillows, upon which many men and women sat, their heads down, muttering prayers. Some of the women stood by the wells, dipping their hands in, splashing water over their shoulders.

They passed a row of statues, all women in various poses. The tallest was hooded, with her face completely obscured, but right beside her was a face familiar enough that Maddie took a step back and gasped in recognition.

"Oh," Randall said, concern on his face. "You recognize this?"

"Can I touch her?" Maddie asked, tears springing to her eyes. It wasn't just a likeness; the statue was virtually identical, down to the curl of hair by her ear, one stray curl amidst those remarkable, silky blonde locks.

"Of course," Randall said. "You can see that many have given their homage to her."

"Who is she?" Maddie asked. "She looks like... so much like someone I knew."

"She is Saint Therasia, Mother Mary's youngest sister and the patroness of writers and knowledge. She looks familiar?"

"I had a friend." *Girlfriend.* "Agnes. At home. She was taller than this, but... she died. Not long ago. I miss her."

"I'm so sorry, Maddie. I had no idea," Randall said, putting his hand gently on her shoulder.

Maddie traced the lines of the statue's face with her fingers, remembering the feeling of her skin, the touch of her lips. Agnes had been one of the loves of her life, someone who forever left an imprint on Maddie's heart. But Maddie had, in turn, broken Agnes's heart. And Agnes...

"Let's move on, if you don't mind," Maddie said, wiping tears from her eyes.

"Maddie? Are you—"

"Please. I want to see the rest."

They left Saint Therasia in the shadows behind them and Randall directed Maddie toward the center of the sanctuary, where a circular altar, almost like a baptistery, stood, low to the ground. A woman sat on the edge of it, her legs dangling, her hair draped like a curtain over her face, bent over praying. She wore saffron-colored robes that gave no clear indication to her gender, cinched about the middle with maroon. Almost like a Tibetan monk, Maddie thought, except with hair.

"That's Priestess Orella," Randy whispered. "She's as high up in the church as you can get without being Mary Herself."

Matilda was strangely absent, and had been since Maddie had set foot in the church. Again, it was like visiting Randall's office: All trace of Matilda, or her memory, was absent. Maddie relished experiencing this strange, lovely part of Second World without Matilda's interference, but the statue of Saint Therasia had left her somber.

"So the highest positions in the church are held by women," she observed quietly.

Randall nodded, and gestured to a pair of large purple cushions. "Let's sit, and I can tell you a little more."

Maddie complied, trying not to stare at Randall, trying not to fall into that intense gaze. The way he pulled on his ear, as he was doing now, when he was about to lecture on something was the precise gesture Randy used to use when he was lining up his Pez dispensers and contemplating their proper placement.

She missed Randy. She ached with missing him, and her life.

"You think Randy's okay?" Maddie asked, before Randall began with the explanations.

"Well, yes, I should think so. He was prepared, as was Dr. Keats. Are you worried?"

"Of course I'm worried. I always worry about Randy," she said, looking down at her hands. *Not* her hands–Matilda's hands. She shivered. "I guess it makes a little more sense, now. How we were all drawn together. Alvin and Randy and me, I mean. And you and Matilda, John and the rest..."

"Maddie, listen, about the statue–"

"I don't want to talk about the statue. Tell me about this rich Marian society of yours. I definitely have respect for a world built around the worship of a woman," she said with a grin.

Randall folded his hands so that his index finger and

middle finger were separated; it was something all the praying people did. He continued. "It is believed that the Mother of God speaks particularly to her daughters, and as such, has entrusted them with significant benefits in understanding spiritual matters. The priestesses don't just practice their religion, they *are* the religion. Though that's not to say there are no priests. It is still quite common."

Two priestesses walked by in their saffron robes and long, long hair, likely grown since childhood. As one turned to acknowledge the two of them, Maddie noticed that she was pregnant.

Randall noticed her eyes widening. "Some take vows of celibacy, especially the men. But it is believed that the children born of a priest and priestess hold with them the innocence of the Christ himself, a kind of purity found only through coupling done without sin."

"Without sin?"

"Yes. It is part of their vows, to do so only with uttered prayers."

"Yeah, I'm sure they *all* keep their vows," Maddie muttered, remembering her recent acquaintance with Douglas Halver.

"As I said, some things are not so different between our two worlds," Randall replied.

Maddie looked down at the ornate purple pillow beneath her. Her corset was still digging into her ribs, but the tea from earlier had allayed a bit of the discomfort.

"And Matilda. How is she with this sort of thing?" Maddie asked, genuinely curious, though she likely knew the answer. "Churches and religion, I mean."

"She hasn't told you herself?"

"We don't chat often," Maddie said, biting down on her lip.

He sighed. "Well, yes. I suspect she was rather furious with me, wasn't she?"

Randall turned to look at Maddie sideways, and as he did so, she felt her heart skip inexplicably. It was a trick of the light, or the opium, or the incense–or all of it, perhaps. But in that moment she saw three faces: Randy, Alvin, and Randall, all looking at her at once, all looking into her. She saw the lines of the faces she loved, the eyes both light and dark, and something swam in her chest, a longing, a need that was so sudden it almost brought tears to her eyes.

Randy, I'm sorry. I'm sorry, she thought.

"No, no," Randall was saying, oblivious to Maddie's moment of epiphany. "I am of a mind that Matilda is a devotee to only one religion: her own," he said. "And I am not so different, I suppose. As to the mythology of it, I do not necessarily follow it. But I come here to admire the artwork." He looked away, and for a moment, Maddie thought he was blushing a bit.

"It really is splendid," said Maddie. "Thank you for bringing me."

Randall looked taken aback. He straightened a bit, brushing the front of his lapel. "You are most welcome."

Maddie slipped her hand into his, and simply enjoyed the view for a while, hoping the stillness would calm her mind and still her soul.

After the restorative visit to the cathedral, it was time to go home. The incense was so strong that the whole carriage smelled of it on the way home as Randall and Maddie sat in comfortable silence. As they pulled up to the Roths' Beacon Hill home, which she noticed for the first time was called Farleigh. Randall had appointments to keep, and Maddie was exhausted–and elated–from their outing. But she regretted that he had to go. Her exhaustion overwhelmed her desire to be with Randall, and Matilda's warning had made her second-guess his motives.

She needed to talk to Matilda again.

"Please send Frank if you need me for anything," Randall said before dropping her off at the door.

"Of course," Maddie said. "But really, I'm just going to take a nap. You don't have anything to worry about."

Randall did not look convinced. He took Maddie's hand and kissed it gently. "Just promise you won't suffer needlessly."

"I promise I'll holler," she said, blushing at the kiss. "Thank you, again."

"You are always welcome," Randall said.

Thankfully, Mrs. Fitz was waiting, almost magically, by the front entryway, with a fresh kimono and a basket of warm scones. If she hadn't been, Maddie might have lost her resolve and gone back with Randall. He was the only true place of comfort she'd found here, even if it was imagined.

Once back up in her salon, Mrs. Fitz helped Maddie out of the corset, to which she uttered restrained thanks in spite of wanting to burst into tears of gratitude.

For the time being, Matilda was still quiet, but Mrs. Fitz had left a platter of tea.

When the maid left, Maddie walked the length of the room a few times, eyeing the tea and scones. The scones were still warm, studded with currants and ginger and baked with a hint of cardamom by the smell of them. Maddie's stomach churned. She'd not eaten in a while, and pastries were tempting.

As she nibbled on a scone, unable to resist any longer, Maddie reflected on her twain. Yes, Matilda had been very convincing with her threats—but she also offered a ray of hope. If Matilda really was smarter and more connected than Randall, perhaps she could help Maddie get back home more quickly. Perhaps she was the *only* way home. Home to regular televisions schedules and sorting books and wishing she'd been more persistent about her graduate studies. Home to Randy, who she could never truly know; home to responsibility; home to a world with no answers and no comfort.

But, no, Maddie didn't want to think like that. Those were crazy thoughts, she reminded herself. Her life, not this borrowed one, was far better. She had electricity, for instance, and didn't have to walk around wearing a metal torture device.

Drink it. Matilda's voice was coming through thinly, as if she were on the far end of a bad connection on the phone.

I'm not so sure I trust you.

Of course you don't. You have no reason to. Which is why I'm here right now. To prove to you that I can get you valuable information about Alvin, which is, I think, what you want.

Maddie thought about that. She ran her hands over the smooth fur coverlet on the bed. She could see the tea out of the corner of her eye.

It isn't as simple as that.

Well, let me put it this way: What has Randall done to prove to you he has any inkling what's going on with Alvin? After all, he didn't even tell you he was missing, did he?

Maddie didn't want to think of the compact, of her talk with John. She had no idea to what extent Matilda could read her thoughts, but since she hadn't mentioned the incident in the office, Maddie assumed it was a true blind spot.

So Maddie thought of Randall as hard as she could. *He tried to get clues from Mrs. Hildebrandt, but your interruption threw us off course.*

Maddie waited to see if Matilda picked up on her obscuring of the facts. The silence between them stretched for too long.

Then Matilda scoffed. Randall doesn't know anything. I can get you the information you need. You just need to drink the tea and let me loose for a few hours.

The house had grown very quiet. Matilda was there in her mind, that thin, familiar shadow at the back of her eyes, wait-

ing, wanting. Always wanting. She was like one of the horse-
men of the Apocalypse: Famine, likely.

When Maddie didn't answer, Matilda pressed. Let me tell
you what. If I don't get you more information than Randall has given you, you're
free to do what you want. Kick the habit, have a jolly old time. Just know it can't
last forever. Trust me, darling, I'm a far better ally than nemesis,

I don't know...

Heavens. You're such a coward.

Don't call me that.

I'm calling it as I see it, darling. You don't want to risk another peek into
my sordid life, I know. You're afraid that you'll see a repeat of what happened
with Dr. Halver, and I can understand your temerity on the situation. But I
promise you this: What I have in mind is nothing like the Dr. Halver business. In
fact, it's an entirely opposite experience.

I don't–

Come, sister. Make up your mind while you still have it.

It was the use of the word "sister" that decided it for her.
Because Maddie felt, deep down, that as Matilda's twain she
should feel closer to her, should trust her more. They *were* like
sisters, as close as Maddie would ever come to having a sibling.
That had to count for something, right?

And Maddie was tired. Tired of being told what to do,
tired of depending on other people. Matilda was her, was at
least a part of her. So trusting her felt far more natural than
trusting Randall. Or at least that's what she told herself. She
convinced herself that any lingering doubts about Matilda were
simply because she didn't understand her.

With a sigh, Maddie drank the tea.

There, she said. *You win.*

Maddie waited as the world dimmed around her. She expected control to some extent, that Matilda would let her come
along, let her at least see. But the world went to utter blackness,
instead, and Maddie fell into what felt like a pool of water.

She was drowning. She was sleeping. She was lost.

But, not entirely. Someone, something pulled at her middle, yanked.

Maddie opened her eyes again, the taste of the tea still bitter in her mouth, and was no longer sitting in Matilda's room. She didn't even think she was in Matilda's world.

And it was quite possible she was in her own body.

Maddie was surrounded by green trees. Green trunks with green moss, green grass at her feet, a green canopy above her head. Every green she'd ever seen in her lifetime, and then some she hadn't, enveloped her; greens that were almost black, greens nearly yellow, greens like lichen on boulders–the green of life.

Though it wasn't cold, Maddie shivered. For some bizarre reason, she was wearing one of her own hand-knit sweaters, by all accounts a disaster. She'd knit it out of wool for Alvin years ago, and it had not only been a little too small for him, but far too itchy to wear. He'd broken out into hives when she'd made him try it on.

"Well, there you are," someone said. An old voice, crackled with age.

And then, before Maddie could answer, a bright laugh:

"Turn around, child. Let me see you."

Maddie spun, still shivering in her damp wool sweater, not knowing what to expect. There was a breeze, and the leaves and trees shifted around her as she turned, providing a natural accompaniment to her movements.

Behind Maddie stood an old black woman of middling height, leaning on a stick, her long hair streaked through with silver. Her clothing was brown, and homespun, almost the same rich color as her skin. The woman's face was familiar, but she couldn't place it. Another statue, perhaps?

"I'm M'ora, by the way. Good to finally meet you, Madeline," the woman said.

Again, Maddie couldn't speak. Thoughts came more easily to her. *Where am I?*

"Some place," said the woman, casually. "It's an in-between place that isn't any particular place, because it's the safest place to be when she's got the reins. Better than her little dark corners. Shame, shame on Matilda for throwing you out when you're so young and vulnerable."

You know Matilda?

"Of course I do! She's *me*. And I'm *you*. And you're *me*. Sisters. Twains. You're the lark, she's the nightingale. I suppose I must be the albatross if we're using the Romantics."

I thought I was confused before...

M'ora smiled, and clapped her pruned hands together twice, still holding onto her cane. The ground before her swirled, shimmered, and then opened, revealing a green marble well, deep with water. Maddie's eyes were drawn to it, and she was reminded of the similar altars at the Cathedral of the Weeping Lady.

M'ora spoke, waving her hands over the water. "You see, Madeline: We are pinpricks of possibilities, scattered across universes, and yet connected... here, here, and here..."

The old woman dipped her cane into the mirror-smooth water—and it did not stir. But where the wooden cane touched the silvery water, three lights came to life: one green, one red, and one white.

"That's you—the green one. I always think of green when I think of you," M'ora admitted. "Now. Our worlds, and our twains, are connected like beads on a string. Connected for the time that we all exist in our own worlds. You're the maid to her mother, and to my, well, crone."

She said it with no self-deprecation, but with a certain note of humor.

I'm no maid.

M'ora chuckled. "It's a figure of speech. Age-wise, you could say. You're still a baby. And Matilda, for all her misinformation and mischief, is right about one thing. We are stronger together. I know it to be true. But whether or not we can get by without snuffing each other out, I don't know."

I don't think that Matilda wants to kill me... Panic prickled at Maddie's senses, again.

"I should hope not. But Matilda knows about you and thinks she's stronger than you–she knows about me, too, but she is afraid of me and so she's always stayed away. But more than anything she craves power, lives on it. Do not trust her, and do not tell her about me if you can help it. Have you been able to keep things from her so far?"

A few things. But it's hard. I don't know when she's listening.

"Be on your guard at all times. Especially when she's at her strongest. Otherwise you'll not only fail in your quest to get home, but in finding your love."

You mean Alvin.

M'ora laughed again, like dry leaves over concrete. "Perhaps. Love is... curious. Many-faceted. Deep and strong like a current, overwhelming as a downpour, and as hard to hold in your hands as melting snow... That love of yours is out there somewhere, but if you find him, I'm not sure it will be what you are searching for."

I just want to go home.

"Do you? Well, Matilda and I, we can help you–if you let us. But you must find your strength. You are letting the world– both worlds–walk right over you, and scuff their feet in your hair. That's hardly befitting of one of your stature."

I'm afraid. I'm lost.

Maddie wanted to weep, to bury her face in her hands. But Matilda was pulling, pulling at Maddie's very soul, pulling her back to Second World. She could feel the beautiful green world fading. The vivid greens cooled to blue, to yellow, and then evaporated into blinding white mist.

She heard M'ora's voice in the distance as she tried in

vain to stay with her: "Try not to fret, my dear. We're all parts
of Her, you know. You have a *true* heart, and true strength—it's
only that you've forgotten how to use it. You've taken up the
armor of sadness and fear instead. And while it works for a
time, it's bound to shatter. The smiths of that sort don't make
anything that lasts."

6

Nothing To Do
With Dragons

ood to see you back. You're here just in time for the fun.

There was an edge of cruelty in Matilda's voice when Maddie returned to Second World, the kind of cruelty that comes from practice. Maddie braced herself as well as she could; she was already feeling perilously insubstantial.

Deborah and I were just beginning to enjoy our evening.

Maddie tried to shroud her memories in darkness, and for the moment it seemed to be working. If Matilda had any concern about where she had gone, she did not let it change her focus. And she was indeed focused.

"Just a moment, darling," Matilda said aloud, tossing her hair back. Maddie felt Matilda controlling their shared body again, and her arms rose up, unpinning the curls from her head so they fell down her back in soft ringlets.

Here, have a look.

Maddie's view swam into color and texture again, and she saw Deborah Hildebrandt sprawled in front of her on an enormous four-poster bed, her corset already half undone. Her lipstick was smudged, making an untidy smear across her cheek, and her golden hair fell down over her shoulders. She had a hungry, vibrant look in her eyes. Yes, she was a lotus-eater, as well. But she burned with more than opium.

You and Deborah are... a thing?

I told you we're more alike than you think.

Agnes and I were complicated, not...

Don't tell me you didn't care for her.

Agnes, poor Agnes. Maddie tried not to think about her again, about what she had meant, about the promises broken. But Matilda had a way of making her contemplate the macabre.

"Come darling, you left me waiting earlier," Deborah pleaded.

"Of course, of course, my sweet," replied Matilda.

Matilda's heart was thumping slowly on account of the drugs, but Maddie's own sensations stirred inside of her. Deborah was gorgeous, a Venus. Where Matilda was bone and skin, Deborah was round and soft, plump and perfect; her skin was like carved ivory, her lips full and round. She had not been on opium long, then, or else did not suffer some of its more cruel effects.

Yes, yes, Matilda said with a tremble of a laugh. She is rather gorgeous. Are you jealous? You should be. She's delicious.

Maddie felt longing, desire; she wasn't sure if it was Matilda's body responding, or something else, but it felt good. It felt comfortable, it felt right. There was lightness, even in the darkness Matilda wore about her like a cloak. Something more.

You love her, Maddie said.

Maddie could feel Matilda's presence squirm, wriggling like a worm at the edge of a hook.

No. Just lust.

I know what love feels like. I can feel it through you; you love her. You absolutely do.

Then, Maddie felt a mental shove. Matilda's presence rose

like a wave, pushing Maddie further back in their collective consciousness. She could only feel distantly, and could watch. Voices were low; she had to strain to listen.

So Matilda was capable of love. And now Maddie *knew*, and that was something—that was power. It was a power that Matilda would have used against her had she been in the same position. A weakness—or strength, depending on the way she looked at it.

Matilda and Deborah continued their dance, their hands twining together, delicate and yet strong, knowing. Their lips brushed, teased, fluttered, and then, when the pleasure was too much to put off any longer, they crushed together, hungry and wanting. Flesh to flesh, skin to skin, they continued, as corsets were pulled open with practiced hands, skin caressed, words of endearment uttered.

Maddie found she was able to fade into herself, what remained of her within Matilda, and close the eye of seeing like a door. She could hear the muffled cries of pleasure and pain behind the door, could feel the pressure of bodies in motion every now and again, but for the most part she left Matilda to it and all else faded in the distance like waves crashing on the shore.

She had beaten Matilda at her own game. Twice, now.

Maddie's memory of M'ora and her bizarre dream still lingered, but she willed herself not to think about it. So she thought of Alvin and of love. Of the way they had once loved each other. Sure, as the years had passed, their love lost much of that initial spark, that seemingly endless desire that once caused her butterflies at the merest thought. But at one point, she remembered thinking it was the most beautiful, most pure thing she'd ever experienced—and she had believed, when she looked in his eyes, that he felt it, too.

But who *was* Alvin, really?

Even if he had hidden things from her, she desperately wanted to know the truth; she deserved closure, even if he hadn't offered it. If Alvin *were* alive, then she would find him. Not for his sake but for her own. Maybe Randy knew the answers, and he was trying to help her all along. It was far more than delivering a box for Mrs. Roth, but Maddie relaxed a little thinking that finding Alvin would help Randy, in some way.

The opium only would last so long, and Maddie felt a continual thinning of her own self the more she retreated from Matilda. For the first time, she wondered what Matilda must feel since Maddie's appearance in her own body, if she felt as strangled and slowly suffocated as Maddie was feeling.

And then she thought of Agnes. Agnes and her long blonde hair and hawkish nose; Agnes with her shy smile and reading glasses. Agnes in the moonlight, as if carved of stone.

When Maddie returned again from memory, she was behind Matilda's eyes in the carriage heading home, and it was raining. As always, the experience of surfacing was disorienting and she clutched the side of the carriage with a jolt.

Once more, she could see and feel, but Matilda was preventing her from control. Sensations flooded in all around her, and Maddie gasped as the world came into view.

It was nighttime. Gas-lamps reflected on the long cobblestone streets, wobbly strands of light streaming through the water and oil. Matilda had dressed in a long wool embroidered mantle that covered her head and reached down to her toes. She was shivering, and her shivers became Maddie's.

Matilda felt tired to Maddie. She couldn't explain it any more than that. She didn't hear the sigh from the other woman, but she felt it. They shared a certain world-weariness together, mingled in loss and memory.

Maddie initated conversation, since Matilda was clearly not in the mood. *Listen, Matilda. I promise when this is over, you can have it all back. I'm sorry that it had to be this way. I don't know Randall well enough to judge him, but it was wrong for this to happen, for me to hijack you. But it wasn't my choice, you know.*

Silence. Then:

I have information about Alvin. Do you want it?

I... guess I do. Maddie found it strange that Matilda ignored her heart-to-heart, but she tried not to let it bother her too much. She did not want an enemy.

Alvin was last spotted in Charleston, two nights ago, by Mr. Hildebrandt. I think Randall was after the same information, but Deborah was reluctant to trust him. At any rate, there's a very popular gambling house in Charleston, right on the river—it's a steamship, called the **Faust**. I don't know if he's still there, or what he was doing there. But that is the most recent information.

Matilda was fading, sorrowfully. Maddie knew the feeling; it was separation, that deep, bone ache that remained when one's lover was gone.

It hurts. I know.

Yes. It does. A pause. I'll tell you what. Press Randall a little more; he is likely withholding information so that he can spend some time with you, besotted as he is. I wouldn't recommend going to Charleston alone if I were you and I want to be certain Alvin's in Charleston before we have to make a trip.

Maddie tried to ask another question, but she felt Matilda's presence slip away, and landed more fully in the body, as if someone had taken a sheet out from underneath her. Then, simple as that, she had the reins again, and Matilda was, for all she knew, completely absent. Not even a shadow remained in her mind.

Maddie sighed, and leaned out the rain-streaked window, watching the Boston night, wondering what it was she'd stumbled into, and remembering the look of Agnes's face in the candlelight.

Maddie left a note for Randall when she arrived back at Farleigh, and retired to her room and the bath. She treated herself to a lavender-scented soak in the huge copper tub, helped along by Mrs. Fitz, and then had a full body massage by Lola, one of the other servants in the house, who had come from the Kingdom of Norway and spoke no English. Then she crawled into bed, her skin smooth and soft and clean, and promptly fell asleep, vowing to get more answers from Randall and put herself in better control of the situation after some good, old-fashioned rest.

The next morning, after Maddie had been primped and dressed—today it was a copper corset, atop an emerald green bodice and bustle, a most striking combination—she met Randall two floors down in the breakfast room. Maddie had woken up to another dose of pills with a handwritten note from Randall, expressing his desire for her comfort.

The breakfast room itself was octagonal in shape, and as far as Maddie could tell, served the sole purpose of serving the day's first meal. Extravagant to say the least, especially considering she didn't even own a kitchen table back home.

But, as she entered the room more fully, she had to admit it held a certain charm. It was so bright and fresh, the walls bedecked in lemon and white, the curtains trimmed in gold satin. The breakfast glassware was cobalt blue, the dinnerware silver with scrollwork about the stems, and bouquets of flowers—bright red orchids and velvety violets—presided over the rest. She noticed a wrought-iron rack full of newspapers, though none of the familiar titles were there. There was instead the *Boston Courier*, the *New Amsterdam Chronicle*, two days old, and the *Athens Herald.*

Randall had not noticed her yet. He was sitting, one leg crossed over the other, in a smoking jacket, reading a small pamphlet with great focus; the front of the pamphlet depicted a vessel that looked vaguely like an airplane, except more el-

egant than the Wrights'. It made use of the principles of aero-
dynamics a little more thoughtfully—the body curved like a fish,
and the wings wider and smoother. A glass dome fit over the
top of it, and it reminded Maddie slightly of a stage prop from
20,000 Leagues Under the Sea.

"Good morning, dear," she said, feeling a little giddy in
his presence again. She made a clumsy curtsey as Frank and a
serving maid entered the room with lemon-scented towels and
a platter of crullers.

"Why, hello there," Randall said, getting up from his
chair. He looked pleased enough to burst, and bowed at the
waist, as if remembering proper decorum. "How lovely. You...
you look lovely."

"Of course, Mr. Roth," she said, as one of the manser-
vants helped lower her into the high-backed Chippendale style
chair at the table.

Frank offered her towels, which she took, washing her face
and hands like they used to do on flights and still did at some
Chinese restaurants in her own world. Breakfast was brought
out in short order; Maddie declined the tea and asked for milk,
instead.

Once served, Maddie poked at a fantastic take on eggs
Benedict, with smoked white fish instead of ham, paired with
saffron fried potatoes, and white, pearly beans heaped over the
Hollandaise sauce. As delicious as the food was, her stomach
was already swimming without the opium tea, and she opted
for some soft cheese and fruit rather than more of the rich meal.

"Thank you, Frank. We'll ring when you're required
again," Randall said, dismissing the servants.

Once the servants departed, Randall smiled at Maddie,
his eyes intent. "You are a vision, as ever." Alvin hadn't complimented her in years, and never so eloquently.

"Thank you," Maddie said, feeling her cheeks burn with
the compliment. She leaned over and whispered, "You can tell

I'm not... you know..."

Randall made an attempt not to laugh. "You requested milk. A dead giveaway."

"Fair enough."

"Breakfast suffices?"

"More than suffices. I just wish I had the appetite for it," Maddie said. She pushed some of the eggs to the side, avoiding Randall's bright blue gaze. She wanted to chastise herself for feeling so flirty, but she was enjoying it. So she pointed her fork at the pamphlet. "Flying machines, huh?"

"*Aerocars*," corrected Randall. "Prototypes. We've got larger, commercial-style planes, of course, with Stirling engines. But most travel between the continents is done by steamship—remarkable vessels. The aerocars are quite an accomplishment on our part, but they're reserved mainly for Her Majesty's Service."

"Her Majesty?"

"Queen Victoria the Sixth," Randall said, quickly, as one of the servants came back in. "God save the Queen of America."

The Queen of America.

"Letter for you, sir," said the servant.

"Put it in my office please," Randall said.

Maddie had swallowed her toast, and it scraped its way down her throat like a bolus of sawdust. Randall then dismissed the manservant, who clicked his heels and made a swift departure, requesting to be called upon should anything be required.

"In Second World, there are many things that are not how you might imagine. I mentioned the monarchy, I thought."

"So—no president, then."

"Not for the last century or so; the last was a man by the name of Wilson. After that point, the monarchy re-established itself, helped in no small way by the wars at that juncture, happening in every direction at once. Much like your World Wars, but not quite as catastrophic. Thank Mother Mary, that sort of thing has been... underdeveloped."

"Nuclear weapons, you mean," Maddie said. "Couldn't a twain, like myself, bring back information like that?" She shuddered at the thought.

Randall pushed some of the potatoes around his plate with a fork. "It had never been a concern, as most twains do not concern themselves in such matters. Plus, things like that can't physically transfer, like Alvin can. But with him, and his mind..." He gnawed on his bottom lip, then began stroking the side of his face thoughtfully.

"You don't trust him."

"I don't know what to think at the moment."

"Matilda thinks Alvin was abducted," said Maddie a little reluctantly.

"Matilda thinks—oh, I see. You've been speaking with her. I surmised as much happened when you went out..." His face fell a little, but he continued talking anyway. "My intuition tells me no. Alvin is a complicated man, and a dedicated scientist. It's why we sent him to your Boston, to learn, to become invested in the learning tradition that has so shaped your world. But mathematical science: physics, time-travel, the like."

"More multiverse theory?" she tried.

"Yes. I'm a bit of a natural scientist, and he is perhaps more traditional. We've worked together for a long time, in concert, to great success. And I've always trusted him implicitly."

"But something changed your mind?" Maddie asked.

The windows in the breakfast room faced a central courtyard, and though the season was still in the chill of winter, the topiaries had been done up with ribbons and lace, with both glass and real icicles hanging delicately from them. A cardinal alighted on a branch, down below, and Maddie watched it for a moment as it fluttered its wings nervously, twitching its little black-beaked head from side to side. Maddie wished there was less talk of Alvin and more enjoying the outdoors.

"John suspected it years ago, but I didn't listen. More re-

cently Alvin's been... erratic," said Randall. "He used to keep
a log of all his travels, here, so I could read about where he'd
been. I've only been able to get to the Sixth World–that's
yours–"

"Right," Maddie said, trying not to sound sarcastic or
rude. She smiled a little as she sipped her milk. "The Sixth
World."

"I'm only able to travel to and from Randy, so I was curious as to Alvin's adventures. But over the last few years, he's
been going places without my knowledge, and being more se-
cretive. No time more frequently than when he was with you."
He cleared his throat. "I was relieved when he finally returned.
Initially."

"Initially?"

"He was supposed to return, to your Boston. But he didn't.
And I..."

"You saw what we went through. Via Randy."

He nodded. "Then I discovered he'd been visiting Sixth
World, but neglecting you entirely."

Maddie felt her stomach go cold. Her eyes swam with
tears, and she grabbed the table napkin.

"I tried to confront him on the matter a few times, but
he refused to listen to me. The only way to resolve the matter
was to get you here, I reasoned. Then he couldn't avoid you. I
brought you here without his knowledge, but three days ago he
found out, and vanished."

Randall reached out to touch her hand, but she drew it
back. Maddie tried to keep a brave face.

"So let me get this straight: You brought me here, and
told me I could see Alvin again, except he's *missing* because *he*
doesn't want to see *me* at all? *And* you have no idea where he
is or how to get me home? You know, I was almost starting to
like you, Randall..."

Randall winced at Maddie's hard words as if they pained

him. "It is all very bad timing."

"What did you think bringing me here would help accomplish?" asked Maddie. "Clearly you didn't do this just for Alvin, because he doesn't even want anything to do with me. And you knew it."

Randall fell silent, and turned the pamphlet around in his hands, now that he had given up fiddling with the fork and knife.

"You seemed to enjoy the cathedral," Randall said.

"That was a fluke."

"You're not curious?" he asked. "There's nothing you'd like to say to Alvin?"

Maddie picked up one of the elaborate silver spoons and twirled it between her fingers. It was wonderfully unladylike.

"He doesn't want to see me. And I'd like to kick him in the junk, honestly."

"He's afraid of seeing you again. Because of how he feels for you," Randall said. "You're the only one who can get through to him."

They fell silent as the manservant came in again with more newspapers and a pile of old books, boldly bound and leafed in gold.

"From the library, sir," the servant said.

"Thank you, Frank," Randall said. "This will be most helpful in my research."

Frank departed, and Maddie had to ask. "Your research, huh? You said you are a scientist, and your office definitely shows it. What is it you study, exactly?"

"Why," Randall said, surprised, "the arcane."

"The arcane," Maddie repeated, trying to be polite again, but dropping the spoon with a clatter. One of the servants came to the door at the sound, and Randall shooed him away.

"Magic, to use a more colloquial term," Randall clarified. Seeing Maddie's dubious look, he continued, "All things are part of magic: every religion, every philosophy, every hope, and every world."

"And there's millions of worlds, right?" Maddie asked. "I mean according to you here in Bizarro Boston." She grinned cutely.

"There are eight connected worlds, which we can access to varying degrees of success, immediately. But there are infinite worlds beyond that."

"Okay, so all I need is a magic wand and you can call me Glinda. I'll be the good witch, and Matilda can be the bad witch. Or maybe I'm not a witch at all. You don't suppose there's a pair of silver slippers around here, somewhere?" She tried to make light of the situation, but Randall frowned at the mention of his wife.

He ran his hands over his hair and slumped over in his chair. Randall's intensity was discomfiting, and she could not bring herself to ask him the thousands of questions on her mind. He was so damned convinced of what he was saying. That she and Matilda had switched, as it were, was more likely to her a manifestation of science and physics than magic. But where did the lines blur?

When he didn't reply, she said, "It's all a lot to take in. And I think now that you have me here, you have no idea what to do with me."

He rose and came round to her side of the table, and held out his hand to her. Maddie took it, as if she hadn't a choice. His skin was very warm to the touch, but extremely dry. His long fingers curled around hers, encircling them, squeezing with just enough pressure to indicate the emotion he was trying to get across.

"I loved Matilda, once," Randall said, not letting go of Maddie's hand. His voice shook, so he cleared his throat and tried again. "I loved her with *everything* I had in me. I bared my soul to her, and she opened me bare. She nearly ruined me."

"Why don't you divorce her?" Maddie asked, laughing

nervously. Having Randall this close, actually touching her, sent her whole body into flux.

Maddie waited a breath; no, Matilda was silent still.

"That is not an option."

"But you're *miserable.*"

"An unfortunate truth," he replied, hanging his head.

Maddie rose to her feet, but she did not let go of Randall's hand. Instead, she clasped it harder, a gesture of comfort, of understanding. She stood very close to him now, her eyes at the level of his chin. He was in pain. Not just about what he'd done to Maddie, but what he had already lost with Matilda and the continual difficulties she presented. And she could feel the pain emanating from him, like heat rising from blacktop.

"And while she's been out on her affairs—what have you been up to?" Maddie asked.

"Work," Randall said, a little too quickly.

"So she finds comfort, why not you?" God, she wanted him. Maddie tried to rein herself in, but she was having a difficult time controlling the overwhelming giddiness. It must be the memories housed in Matilda's body, she tried to convince herself. Or else her dormant feelings about Randy surfacing.

Randall's hands were shaking, but Maddie squeezed harder, looking at the familiar face, feeling her heart flutter in her chest. *Not Alvin, not Alvin, not Randy,* she said to herself. *Not now... not here...*

Randall's breathing became more labored. "I do not wish to stoop to that level," he said, honestly. She caught his shoulder twitch, as if restraining himself from something. "I do not wish to commit *adultery.*"

"You mean you won't. You *wish* to," Maddie said, pressing closer to him, feeling a little dizzy. She could feel little through the clothing she wore, the metal corset and the reams of cloth. But it made what she *could* feel—his fingers, and then the side of his face as she lifted up her hand to touch him—remarkably intense.

And then his lips were on hers. The initial sensation surprised her, as if the nerves on her lips were more alive than
ever before. Like she'd just bitten into a chili pepper. The depth
of the kiss was more complete than any other kiss she'd had in
recent memory, and she worried vaguely if that was still the
lingering effects of opium. But–no, that couldn't be right. This
was like the fluttering of a thousand wings, around her and inside of her.

Desire rose in her, and she was unable to control it. She
grabbed him, feeling the strength in his arms, feeding off what
she knew his body was capable of. Her only thought was of taking him, right on the breakfast table if she had to. She grasped
his fingers, and then went on to explore–

"No," Randall said, almost a whisper. Then, stronger:
"No... Maddie... *Madeline Angler.*"

Hearing her full name was as jarring as a glass of cold water down her back, and she staggered back. Randall stood some
distance from her, steadying himself on a chair.

"It wouldn't be–" she tried to say "wrong."

"You are *not* my wife," Randall said, the words sharp, cruel. He seemed aware of his tone, and shook his head, his back
still to her, and said much more gently, "As much as... as much
as I admire you, Maddie–you are not of this world. Once, perhaps, I entertained the notion that somehow... but now–"

"Why the hell not?"

"Because I do not think you love me," he said, turning to
look at her now. His eyes were red-rimmed, but she did not see
any tears. "I have seen you, watched you. Lady above, but I
have suffered watching you through Randy's eyes."

"You don't have to love someone to find comfort."

The words were far more terrible than she'd intended,
and Randall nodded as if she proved her point well enough.
"Since you've lost Alvin, you've been seeking *comfort* in such
companionship. And I do not wish to be part of that."

She bristled. "I'd really hate to think you're calling me a slut, because I was starting to really like you, Randall."

"We all seek comfort in different ways, we all look to dull the pain of loss; some seek the bottle, other seek attention, pleasure," he said. "And in that way you and Matilda are more alike than you think."

"I am nothing like her! *Fuck* you!" There it was! The profanity she had been searching for. Her discovery was not without a feeling of triumph either, even amidst the sinking feeling of rejection.

"You were with *Alvin.* Perhaps he'll be ready for a fuck when you see him," he said, not without his own share of venom. He handed her a slip of paper. "Start here. I'd advise you not to go alone. Take the compact, if you wish. John will be happy to help any way he can."

"You're *abandoning* me? Again?"

"I have work to do. You're the one in such a sodding rush. Stay. Go. I don't care."

"You are a model of gentlemanly behavior, Mr. Roth," she said.

"You wouldn't have any idea what that is, would you? Considering you actually prefer that depraved little world of yours," he said, turning from her. "Regardless. I'll see you this evening for the gala at Count Gascon's. I *do* expect you to be there. Or send Matilda. Whatever you prefer."

He turned on his heel, and left Maddie staring at the note in the middle of the breakfast nook, unable to read the words for the tears in her eyes.

It took Maddie a while to compose herself again. Her head was ringing with the continual headache, and now her stomach was cramping from the withdrawal as well. With Randall upset at her and gone, the burden of her loneliness was overwhelming. So she decided to ramble from room to unfamiliar room for a time, absorbing the details, to take her mind off the argument and the difficult decisions in front of her.

She wanted to stay angry—at Alvin, at Randall, and Matilda, too—but the design of the house itself lifted her spirits. And it proved a point. Maddie loved the decor, finding Matilda's tastes were remarkably like her own. The design was eccentric, but colorful and with an impressive overall sense of harmony and purpose. Each room was, in its own way, a work of art, inspiring to Maddie's aesthetic sensibilities.

The library was musty and quiet, bedecked in greens and reds and golds, with real Persian rugs in a multiplicity of warm colors and patterns; the salon was whimsical and airy, brought together by a series of Baroque nude sculptures and curtains of blue-black silk; the drawing room was open and friendly, crimson and mustard shades set off with dark mahogany furniture and a hammered copper ceiling.

The loveliest room by far, however, was the gallery. It housed a collection of oil paintings and sculptures rivaling the quality of the best museum exhibits Maddie had ever seen. Few of the artists' names were ones she recognized, but she could see their influences: Carravaggio, Titian, Turner. Every painting was a masterpiece, and led Maddie to wonder just how well-to-do the Roths were and how many artists lived in such a world to provide such an impressive display of talent.

Once she was finished her tour—which took the better part of the morning— Maddie decided it was time to talk to Matilda again, if only to pick her brain a bit. Maddie was feeling useless, helpless, and far too tired to go out alone. If she was going to find Alvin, and if she was to get home, she would have to work with Matilda. Even M'ora agreed on that point, whoever the strange old woman really was.

Maddie found Mrs. Fitz in the kitchens and requested

some tea; the maid was perplexed that Maddie was there in the first place, but went about making the tea as her mistress admired the tidy kitchen. It smelled of drying herbs, baked bread, and spices, the mingled aroma resulting in perfect comfort.

When she had her opium tea in hand, Maddie then wandered to one of the sitting parlors, feeling a little guilty. She had just ordered up a drug, after all.

This particular parlor was her favorite, as it housed a library of romantic novels and poetry. She felt it must be one of Matilda's places, especially judging from the specific decor; nothing had been spared in workmanship or material. No clock was out of place, no single candlestick extraneous. The gilded marble mantelpiece depicted eight cherubs chasing each other playfully.

Maddie realized the irony in those cherubs. There were no children at Farleigh. And yet, in her own parlor, Matilda made herself look upon them every time she retired to read.

Maddie found a familiar volume, though far older and with superior binding to her own copy: the collected works of William Wordsworth. She took the book and sat down in a silk striped chair, then rifled through looking for *her* poem, as she liked to think of it, while she sipped her tea. And indeed, there it was: "To the Skylark."

"Ethereal minstrel, pilgrim of the sky," Maddie began reading aloud. "It's just the same here. The poem's no different..."

It does have quite an allure, doesn't it?

Hello, Matilda.

Matilda materialized behind Maddie's eyes, waif-like as always, but less substantial than before. The opium had not yet given her enough strength.

Though, I always preferred Coleridge.

Of course you do. You both like the same stuff.

My greatest gowns and designs, they are all created under the influence. Just as the great Kubla Khan.

Maddie wasn't interested in hearing self-justification, and tried to change the subject. *I'm not here to talk about the drugs. Just here to talk to you. Randall's given me a name; someone he thinks might give us more information about Alvin's whereabouts.*

Oh, that's delightful, said the other woman. Whose name is that?

Maddie glanced at the note again, said the name softly, "Georgiana D'Arc."

Matilda giggled, and Maddie felt her gaining strength. Her muscles relaxed and then felt the curious sensation of Matilda slipping back into their shared skin, pushing her sideways, using her voice as Maddie faded away.

"That's his mistress," said Matilda, smiling brightly. "Alvin's."

Mistress, eh? Randall said he wasn't too pleased about me being here.

"Yes, that might have something to do with it."

Maybe I shouldn't see him. Maybe... maybe you should do it.

Matilda sighed, bored. "He needs to see you. That is one point on which I agree with Randall. And I will make sure that happens."

I don't know.

"You deserve the chance to give him a piece of your mind."

It was more than convincing. Maddie felt Matilda's surety, her strength and her power. Yes, damnit. She *deserved* answers from Alvin, and so did Randy. If he didn't want to see her, then that was his problem. He couldn't hide from her forever.

When you put it that way...

Matilda smiled. "*Georgiana*, though. She's fun. She's *French*, and a countess in exile. Most of the French live in exile, but you'd not know that," Matilda said, half to herself. "At any rate, I've been working on a dress for her; though be warned, she is in mourning. Her husband died not more than a few months ago, so she may not be as forthright with information as Randall hopes."

You're actually helping me?

Matilda stretched out her legs and smoothed the front of the corset, running her fingers down her thighs. "I just want my body back, sister," she said, almost gently. "And my life. And the sooner I get you to Alvin, the sooner you'll leave. Alvin is a meddling fool, and he deserves to come face to face with the people he's hurt." She spoke as if she had experience on the matter.

When Maddie did not reply, Matilda continued speaking, lowering her voice. "If you feel yourself fading too much," said Matilda, rising from the chair, then draining the last of her tea, "just recite 'To the Skylark' over and over. I find it helps. And if you get tired of Wordsworth, you can always try Shelley's. Oh! And don't forget there's an event this evening, a dinner at Count Gascon's house. I have no desire to be there, myself, but I think you'll find it amusing, to say the least."

Matilda—

"No, fret not. I heard what went on with Randall earlier, and as endearing as his loyalty is to me, it is, however, quite unnecessary," she said, opening the door to the parlor, and looking up at the skylight, a marvel that went up all four floors. "If you tempt him again, he won't be able to resist. He's just not capable."

He loves you.

"He, my dear, is a bigger idiot than his brother."

Trysts and Trials

On the way, Matilda explained that Georgiana D'Arc de Montpre was spending the week at one of her many homes, a Colonial marvel overlooking the bay, and since she never went out of her own accord, they had to drop by.

Maddie was amazed to see what a transformation the bay area had undergone in this Boston. It was as residential as could be imagined; industry was reserved for further north, Matilda informed her. The builders of Second World had done a rather impressive job re-routing some of the waters that way, and constructing elaborate underground lochs for such business. Despite the occasional smokestack and airship, this Boston seemed to shun the visible representation of its technologies.

But, supposed Maddie, in a world with magic—a concept she was still trying to wrap her head around—technology might not be so necessary.

"It really isn't like that," said Matilda, tugging on her gloves and flexing her fingers. Maddie had been thinking, sulking again, in the corner of the woman's mind, and was surprised that she was even being addressed. Throughout the ride to this part of Boston, Matilda had all but ignored her.

Isn't like what? she asked.

"*Magic.* Not like what you think it is," said Matilda. "Not fairies and sprites and unicorns."

But dragons, I hear.

"Dragon is just a word," Matilda said. "Use whatever one you prefer: prophet, godling, avatar." As no one was driving the carriage, and one of the countess's servants would be greeting Matilda upon her arrival, there was no worry about talking aloud, at least for present time. "If you stop thinking of green, scaly things, that might help you. Magic is... well, it's *people.* It's human beings, doing extraordinary things. It's traveling in time and space, ascending to unfathomable truths, or in some cases, descending to unimaginable depravity."

So, where do we fit? I mean, how does magic work with twains?

"It's a curious question," said Matilda. "You know, we have gifts, you and I. We can do things some men only dream of, the ability to travel between dimensions being the least of..."

What do you mean?

"Have you ever stopped to consider your ability to woo men—and women come to think on it—when you're single-minded about it?"

Uh... like, sexually?

"Sexually, or otherwise; your ability to communicate, to seduce. You're very good; Randall was almost unable to resist. Tell me: Have you ever failed to get someone into bed with you if you really, really wanted them?"

Had she? She'd never really thought about it. When she was younger, she'd been shy. But later, once she'd realized her own sexuality, that had changed. Not her first boyfriends, not Agnes... No, come to think of it, she'd never even been *dumped.* Not counting Alvin, of course, but that was its own unique situation.

"And clearly, I'm *very* good. Better than you even imagine."

And brazen.

"Why shouldn't I be?" asked Matilda. "Randall knew what I was when I married him. My abilities are a celebration of all that I am, all that we women are."

I thought that was what having children was supposed to be.

Matilda fell silent, her lecture interrupted. She folded her hands primly, resting them in her lap. "How positively *medieval* of you, Madeline. Well, that's not the point," she said. "Sensuality is a gift, if used correctly. I'm only asking you to look at yourself with a different pair of eyes; embrace what you have."

Right. Well, forgive me if I don't join up with a brothel.

But Maddie knew what Matilda meant, harsh words aside, and recognized that she was right, too. There was an undeniable power in sexuality and sensuality, and Randall had helped to awaken that. The incident in the kitchen was overwhelming. And she shouldn't be ashamed of it, she realized. It was an ancient power. Any glance through an art history text, even the basic ones, would demonstrate the influence of the female form, all across cultures, religions, and traditions, not to mention acts of love.

Though she would have liked to think on it more, Matilda had other ideas: It was time to tend to Georgiana D'Arc. The carriage came to a stop aside one of the palatial "cottages" by the bay, this one numbered 879, and Matilda wearily lifted herself from the seat. It was just beginning to rain, and a red-clothed butler helped her down from the carriage, an umbrella already in his hand.

"The swatches are in the trunk," Matilda said, taking the umbrella. "And be careful with them. Those pieces of cloth are worth more than your life."

The butler goggled at her, and then retrieved the leather suitcase.

Georgiana is not a Marian, said Matilda, internally, as they moved through the countess's home, toward the sitting room. *Just so you are aware.*

Though the home was certainly grand, it was as simple as Farleigh was elegant. Everything was smooth, straight, Colonial, as if the home had not changed from the late 18th century; which was impossible, since the house was a recent construction. It still smelled of planed wood and fresh paint. But clearly architects here were more than happy to provide houses designed in a historical, straightforward manner. Everything looked authentic, hand-milled, and far from fabricated.

The home was characterized by dark wooden floors accented with periwinkle blue walls and spartan crown molding, clean and crisp but decidedly boring carpets, and minimal wall decoration. Everything was antique, or a high-quality reproduction, but nothing moved with the vibrancy of the Roth home, or the Hildebrandts'.

Looks like she hasn't moved past the Colonial period, Maddie said.

She's a Quaker.

An adulteress with a pious side. Intriguing.

She grows on you, I promise.

Maddie turned with Matilda and saw Georgiana D'Arc de Montpre, sitting on a ladder-back chair, engrossed in some extraordinary crochet, delicate and as intricate as a spiderweb.

"Madame Roth," announced a voice, and Georgiana looked up. It took Maddie a moment to register where she'd seen the face, what with all the black lace and velvet hanging about her. She looked as if she were dressed for a mortician's funeral.

But Georgiana's face was nearly identical to that of Mrs. Frances Keats, like enough to be a sister. A stab of fear and shame coursed through her, but Maddie was not in enough control to do anything about it.

Matilda had the reins.

"Georgiana, darling," Matilda said, coming up to the woman and taking her hand gently when it was offered. The woman's hands were frigid despite the roaring fire in the hearth, and very fragile, as if the bones beneath would crunch like twigs should Maddie exert enough pressure.

The woman looked far from depressed, her eyes all but twinkling, though her smile did not last long. Her eyes were not like Frances's, thought Maddie—no, Frances had vibrant blue eyes, and Georgiana's were brown, almost black in the dim light. No, perhaps not a twain...

No, not a twain, said Matilda. But close. She's just unusually similar to another. Which explains Alvin's infatuation.

How do you know she's not a twain?

Matilda did not answer; instead she turned her attention to Georgiana.

"How are you managing?" asked Matilda.

It was then, as Maddie struggled to let go of the anger brought on by Alvin's infidelity, that she realized Georgiana was entirely blind. When the countess was asked the question, she tilted her head to the side, but her eyes did not follow.

"I'm well," Georgiana said, "I didn't know you were paying me a visit today, and in this weather of all things."

"It's no trouble, and it's just a little snow. The carriage is well-equipped," said Matilda, breezily. She clicked open the suitcase with her thumbs, and then set it on the table, rifling through the pieces of fabric quickly, searching for one in particular. Maddie was waiting, still and silent, trying to piece together the rather sordid background of her once fiancé. The first two times she'd been under Matilda's control, she'd had to endure sex with strangers. Though this was nowhere near as disconcerting, she wasn't sure if it was less painful, or cruel.

"New samples," said Matilda. "We've some beautiful brocaded velvet I was thinking would complement the last gown rather well. Just in from Jamaica."

"Excellent, I'd love to feel it," said Georgiana, extending her fingers and placing her crochet down.

As Georgiana explored the various panels, a butler arrived with tea and scones. Matilda dismissed him and took it upon herself to make the tea for Georgiana. She knew precisely how she took her tea and, if Maddie hadn't have known better, she'd almost have thought the two women were having another affair. But... no. There was no sense of lust coming from Matilda, simply love and respect and even a little appreciation.

You admire her, Maddie said.

A bit, yes. She's a good woman.

And Alvin?

He admires her, too, but in a different way; I think he might pity her, as well. The two have a bond, and a special one.

Apparently one that outshines the bonds of, well, you know. Marriage. Or engagement.

It isn't just about sex. You realize, Georgiana was married to Montpre when she was sixteen; she suffered through the best years of her life with a man old enough to be her grandfather. That he's died has set her free.

"I like this one," said Georgiana, holding up dark red swatch, so deep it was nearly black. A damask pattern was pressed into the velvet. "Do you think you might be able to put this into the lining of the sleeves?"

"Oh, come now," Matilda said. "Lining? We can put it on the bodice—it would set the whole city astir."

Georgiana giggled into her hand, shaking her head. "Oh, no. That's the last thing I want, dear Mattie."

"As you will," said Matilda with a laugh. "I'll put aside a little extra for you, though, with the next order Randall makes—just to make sure we have enough if you happen to change your mind."

"How *is* your husband?" asked Georgiana, moving the material again back and forth between her fingers. A single line now appeared between her brows, turning her round and placid face more severe. She looked concerned.

Matilda took her seat again, inhaling the soft floral tones of Earl Grey tea before answering: "Yes, he's been under a little stress as of late, what with Alvin's return from abroad and his sudden disappearance. I swear, we cannot keep the man down."

"Alvin is missing?" asked Georgiana, her voice soft, unsure.

Setting her teacup–a surprisingly vibrant bone china pattern with interlacing sweat-pea motif–back down on her saucer, Matilda nodded, "Three days; gone without a trace."

A moment passed between the two women, and some sort of understanding was made, though Maddie couldn't guess how. It couldn't have been the eye contact.

"Alvin visited me briefly, three days ago," said Georgiana, sitting straighter in her chair. She cut a surprisingly buxom shape, thrusting out her chest as she did so; she was not quite so slight as Matilda, but the sharpness of her chin and thinness of her fingers and wrists had given Maddie that illusion. "He seemed... distracted."

"He's *always* distracted," said Matilda.

Maddie was pulled slightly forward, feeling herself get a better grip of the situation. It had been a while since Matilda's last bit of special tea, and it wouldn't be long before Maddie was in control again. But not now–she needed Matilda; she needed the details. She needed to know, even if it cut a hole in her heart. Both she and Randy were owed answers, and damned if she wasn't going to go down without a fight.

Georgiana smiled, a little too knowingly. "He is always, though, isn't he? But this time he sounded more fretful than before. He mentioned something about a meeting with some of the priestesses, and settling a debt of his in Charleston; but he's always talking like that and..." she paused, taking a sip of tea before adding, "We hadn't seen each other for quite some time and we didn't spend much time in conversation."

It was as blatant as Maddie could stand. She wanted to reach over and slap the woman, both for what she'd learned in her own world and what she was experiencing here. For someone with purported powers of seduction, they seemed to fail her the moment Alvin walked out of the door and into the arms of other women.

Decorum, darling, Matilda warned and Maddie complied.

Georgiana leaned forward, conspiratorially, but her eyes hit the wrong mark; the motion came off as wooden, awkward; it made her pretty, round face seem like a doll's. "Truth be told, and not a word of this to Randall, if you please?" Georgiana said.

"On my *honor*," Matilda said, very quickly.

"I just think that he's in over his head. He's a brilliant mind, to be sure, perhaps the greatest of his generation–the greatest in the last *dozen* generations. But the nature of his work is delicate, and he takes too much upon himself. He seemed suspicious, to me. Of everything...

"So, I gave him some money; he tried to refuse, but I insisted. What am I going to do with it all now that Edgar is gone? Our debts are settled, his last being the final nail in his coffin, so to speak," she said. She bristled a little at the mention of her husband, then shivered. "Quite honestly, I want to see as much of the money done away with as possible. I don't fancy I'll want to be involved with the family much longer... just long enough, and then I'll fade away into obscurity."

"Oh, dearest. Don't speak like that. You can marry again; you're still young," encouraged Matilda. Maddie thought it sounded painfully fake.

"And barren, and jaded, and *blind.* I've no interest in playing such games."

"You know that hasn't stopped you before–"

Georgiana almost smiled, and then shook her head. "If he's gone to anyone, it's Joss Raddick."

"Raddick? The captain of the River Guard?" Though

Matilda said the name as if she'd heard it only but once or
twice, Maddie caught a glimpse of the man in her mind: naked
as a jay-bird, and rippled with muscle and scarred in a thousand places from head to foot. Mustachioed, blond, eyes like
jet. Yes, he was quite the presence.

"Alvin mentioned a particular debt that he hoped Joss
could help him with; I gave him enough to settle it. I hoped he
would make the trip and return within the day," she paused,
frowning a little guiltily. "Please let me know if you find him."

"Of course, dear," Matilda said, touching her friend on
the cheek. "Of course."

They chatted for some time after, but Maddie remained
quiet and just listened. She was feeling sorry for herself. She
wanted to hate Georgiana, but she was a sweet woman who had
clearly lived a more difficult life than Maddie had. The hardest
part was that she liked her, admired her, even, and felt sorry to
leave her all alone in that cavernous home. She might have had
Alvin's attention, but she had little else in the world.

When they reached the carriage again, Maddie asked: *So,
what can you tell me about Joss Raddick?*

Matilda laughed aloud. Not yet, darling. First, you've a ball to
attend.

They returned at last to Farleigh, and Matilda acquired
a bottle of wine from California she claimed to be of world-
famous vintage. Maddie didn't recognize it, but barely got a
taste in as Matilda drank it down quickly, using her last strength
to concentrate on the alcohol.

As Matilda informed her, they were already running late
for the gala event that evening at Count Gascon's mansion,
and Maddie required some lessons before gallivanting around
in public as Matilda Roth. As they bustled about the house,

Matilda lectured. She explained how close James, Count Gascon, was to the queen, and that there was always a possibility that Victoria herself might make an appearance. As it was, not even Matilda had met the queen in person yet, but James had sworn up and down that she was planning to attend one of his events soon. He couldn't confirm when, due to the delicate matter of the situation, but it was a way to ensure plenty of positive replies from the elite.

Due to the importance of the event, Matilda chose their clothing very carefully. James's favorite color was green, something she knew from her rather intimate involvements with the quite eligible bachelor.

So, with Mrs. Fitz's help, Matilda assembled her costume—it was so elaborate it could be called nothing but—out of silk and taffeta, lace and satin, all green as the sea in the summer. Set with a copper corset, the contrast was stunning. Mrs. Fitz combed Matilda's hair until it shone, and then curled it up delicately along her neck, the twists kissing the length of it to her shoulder. Peacock feathers, both the green and albino variety, were then placed along the ringlets. Makeup was thick, but lasting: powder, blush, liner, lipstick. Her features, though hollowed by her prolonged use of opium, were beautifully enhanced. She almost looked healthy.

Then came the jewelry: the garnets, the opals, the necklace set with amber and emeralds. They had a light of their own against Matilda's alabaster skin. Then one more detail: a spray of perfume, somewhere between lilacs and vanilla, misted about her shoulders.

Beautiful. Admittedly, Maddie said.

We clean up rather well, 1 suppose. Not as fetching as in my day, when 1 was your age. 1 was a little fuller then, closer to the ideal. As you'll see when we arrive, the current fashion is... well, you remember Rubens?

Yes, the Master of Butterfat.

Rubens would be well at home with our ladies, shall 1 say. The rounder, the better, in the eyes of society. But, as in your culture, some take the ideal to the extreme. It would be almost comical if it weren't so sad.

I haven't seen many women that seemed abnormal—

My darling, you've yet to see the truly elite. In your world, they risk their deaths to look like bags full of antlers; here, they do the opposite. It isn't all so different, is it? Regardless. The coach will take you to the landing, and you will meet Randall there. Then you can see for yourself.

I'm still pissed at him.

Oh, I'm sure you'll be rutting like rabbits before the evening is over.

We will not!

As if in punctuation to her comment, Matilda ran her hands down her breasts and shivered. Maddie felt every thrill, and their shared body flushed magnificently.

Maddie was about to protest further when she noticed she'd been granted the reins again. It felt so marvelous, breathing of her own volition and seeing the world as she wanted, that she forgot her indignation entirely. She swished her dress from side to side and giggled. She had never worn such a beautiful ensemble and she was certainly more used to Matilda's clothing by now.

I abhor this sort of thing, and could certainly use the evening off. Consider it a gift from my side. The wine did the trick...

"Matilda—" said Maddie, unexpectedly through Matilda's lips. She put her hand over her mouth.

"What's that, dear?" asked Mrs. Fitz.

"Nothing; thank you, Mrs. Fitz," sighed Maddie, and shrugged at the visage in the mirror, wondering just where it was Matilda went when she was gone.

Randall was running late, as the note from Frank said. So, when they finally finished the preparations for the evening, Maddie dismissed Mrs. Fitz and sat in Matilda's bedroom, watching flurries out the window. The flakes swirled and danced, and coupled with the bit of wine still in her veins and the thrill of having control of this body once more, Maddie watched for quite some time, simply reveling in the serene moment.

The clock chimed the hour, six o'clock. The gala began in at seven, and still no further word from Randall. She was starting to wonder if she'd at last be stood up.

Walking over to the vanity, Maddie rifled the drawers. To her surprise, she found the compact that Randall had given her, the one she'd used to speak to John Iosheka, Ian's twain. Yes, she had stowed it there for safekeeping, before welcoming Matilda back.

Without much more than a thought, she opened it up and pressed her finger to the stone as Randall had shown her, half curious and half doubtful that anything would happen.

At first, nothing did happen, and she was quite ready to have done with it. Then the fabric began to bleed colors again and John's face appeared.

"Why, Madeline," he said. "I didn't expect to see you again so soon."

"Wait. How do you know I'm not Matilda?" she asked.

"Matilda despises me soundly. She would not contact even if her life depended on it. Would you like to come visit?" he asked.

Maddie could make out details behind him, vaguely brown and black walls, like a log cabin.

"I'm not sure I can get to where you are. Besides. I have somewhere to be in an hour or so..."

"You'll be fashionably late, as always, if it's the gala at Count Gascon's that's held every Marymas. And we can keep an eye out on your room just in case you're called away."

It *was* tempting.

"I promise it'll be short. And you won't regret it," John pressed.

Taking one look behind her, Maddie brought the compact up closer to her face. "How... how will I get there? From what Randall said you're quite far away."

"Use the compact," John said. "Just press your lips to my portrait, and I will do the rest."

"All things considered, that's not the strangest set of instructions I've received since arriving here," Maddie said. She took a deep breath. Randall had given her no warnings about John, and seemed to trust him with details about Alvin. And if Matilda took issue, she was not speaking up.

"It's simply the best mechanism. Come now. There's nothing to worry about."

He was as convincing as Ian.

Maddie leaned forward and put her lips on the fabric inside the compact. It was rough, like burlap or coarse linen, and she tried to pull away. But she couldn't. The sensation was much like being stung by a thistle; her lips erupted in pins and needles, followed by her tongue and the roof of her mouth; next, her face and neck. In a few heartbeats, her entire body was prickling—painful, tickling, itching—and then she slipped.

The world turned on its head, and she went with it.

Maddie's whole body went freezing cold and she was plummeted into the dark. Then, with a whoosh of air in her lungs, light returned.

In a flash, she was sitting in a wooden chair wrapped in furs: thick, golden furs. The room itself was lit by fire and little else; it was quite dark. A log cabin, yes, but rustic and far from the sort she'd seen advertised in magazines at home.

She was also quite naked under the furs.

John knelt before her, staring into her face as if they had indeed just kissed. He was older than Ian, by at least two decades, his long, black hair shot with silver. And he looked decidedly native, not least because of the feathers and beads in his hair. But he wore a white linen shirt, like the ones worn by gentlemen in town, a little threadbare about the collar, and trousers and boots.

"There we go," John pronounced.

Maddie shivered. Her goosebumps had goosebumps. "Why are my clothes gone?"

"You will be returned to them, if that's what you're wondering, when you get back. Things just don't quite translate the same across the Border," John said. "But the fur should be quite comfortable. It's a lion pelt."

"A lion?" Maddie asked. She was divided over thrusting it away in horror and snuggling into it more for warmth. It was delightfully comfortable. And it smelled strangely familiar.

"I could have brought you back as a dove," John said cryptically, standing and going to the window. He opened a crude leather shade and peered out, then looked back at her.

"Thanks. I think," Maddie said. "Never thought of myself as much of a dove."

John gave her a knowing smile. "You've a dove's heart."

For some reason, Maddie blushed and looked away. It was dark outside the cabin, but she noticed the play of light behind the shade. "Is someone else here?" she asked.

"My wife," John said. "She'd like to meet you."

Maddie looked down at her hands; she was still holding the compact. For the first time, she noticed the device etched into the top: an eight-pointed star.

"We all used to have those," John said, indicating the compact, and then walking to the fireplace. He poked the smoldering logs, and they hissed and popped in reply. "But there's only one left. And technically, it should be Matilda's. But she's not proven herself worthy of it."

"Yeah, she's a bit of a spitfire," said Maddie, cringing momentarily, waiting for her twain to surface. But there was no response. "When she's of a mind to do something, she's virtually unstoppable."

"We are not on good terms, she and I. Her current incarnation is more vile than I can recall in a very long time."

"Incarnation?" Maddie asked.

It was starting to make sense to Maddie; something beyond twains and transcorporeal travel. What was it that M'ora had said? You are a part of *Her*. But at the time she had supposed that meant Maddie herself. Or M'ora. They were twains, all a part of each other... and yet John had a casual sincerity to him on the subject.

Maddie recalled a few Eastern philosophies about reincarnation, how some believed in the continual rebirth of groups of people. In one life, one's best friend might be one person, but in another life that very same soul might be born into a sister or a mother or an uncle. But they clustered.

Hadn't Randall mentioned clusters?

John was about to answer Maddie when the door opened, clattering on its hinges, and a woman wrapped in furs entered. Her eyes were slanted, her hair jet-black and braided. Her lips were thick, almost pursed, and her cheekbones stood out prominently against her olive skin.

Across her shoulders she carried a day's worth of kills: two long white foxes, a beaver, and a clutch of birds. There was a bow slung on her back, too, wrapped with cord on one side and strung with gut on the other. And though Maddie couldn't see them, she had a feeling the woman carried with her a great many knives and strange hunting wares.

The wind blew the door open, and the woman turned to close it again.

"Pinga, there you are," John said. His face softened to see her, a look of true affection. But Pinga was steel-faced.

"This is the one?" Pinga asked. "Where on earth did she get the lion fur?"

Reflexively, Maddie had expected Pinga to have some strange accent. But her English was impeccable.

"She came with it," said John. "But she isn't here for long. I hoped we could discuss things a bit, together. It seems Madeline here is beginning to figure things out."

"You mean no one's told her?" Pinga asked, tossing down her kills on a long table. It was stained in a variety of places, no doubt from continual use in skinning and de-boning.

The huntress took off some of her layers of clothing, mostly made of skin and fur, until she was in a wool tunic and high boots, then began to skin the foxes as if it were the most normal thing to be doing in the world.

"I think Randall has tried, a few times," Maddie said, feeling uncomfortable as Pinga's knife came down on the fox and slipped its skin from muscle. The smell wasn't too great, either. If Boston felt like a Victorian nightmare, this was the Dark Ages. "He gets a little distracted with his philosophies and all his research."

Pinga snorted. "He's in love with you. He doesn't want to hurt you or confuse you more than he already has."

"He... he loves *Matilda*," corrected Maddie.

Pinga stopped slicing and smirked at Maddie. "Eh, same thing. Still. He's been watching *you* for the last five years."

"I'm more confused than when I started," Maddie said. "I feel like I'm missing something."

"You are," said Pinga, going back to her work. "But you're practically a baby."

"So I've been told," said Maddie, with a touch of bitterness.

"That compact you hold is very old, my dear," John said. "And it represents the very essence of who and what you are. You made it once. Another version of you, I should say. Along with another version of me."

"So, in addition to this whole twain thing, we're also reincarnated," Maddie said. It sounded a lot less crazy when vocalized, somehow.

John hoisted an iron cauldron and positioned it over the

fire. "Indeed. And we can live a very long time. Eight worlds. Eight sets of twains, each with similar characteristics and ruling passions, you might say. Rarely do eight exist across worlds at the same moment. It makes things more complicated," John said. "Miriam here in Second World, whom you've not met, is one such instance: She currently shares twains across all eight worlds, simultaneously. But we are not on speaking terms, she and I, so I do not know for sure what the effects may be."

"You fight?" Maddie asked.

"Don't all siblings?" Pinga asked.

"Do we all look alike?" Maddie asked, remembering M'ora, who said she was part of Maddie, who said she was a twain, but looked as different as possible. "I mean, Matilda and I are just different enough. But you're both...well, you look like you're Native Americans."

Pinga replied, "With practice, many twains can alter their visages as much as they want, until race and creed mean nothing."

"Think of the eight worlds like points on an eight-pronged star, like the etching on your compact. Second and Sixth are nearly mirrors of one another, are they not?" John explained.

As if the compact was aware of its discussion, it began to shake in Maddie's hands. Then she heard a voice from inside, soft and tentative. "Mrs. Roth? Mr. Roth has sent you word to meet him at the landing—I've sent the carriage for you whenever you're ready."

"Mrs. Fitz," said Maddie, flipping open the compact. The room was dark beyond, lit by the suggestion of firelight.

"You don't want to keep him waiting," Pinga said. She made her way to the birds, now, and feathers fell at her feet, sticky with blood.

"But I had more questions. About Alvin, about Matilda..." Maddie protested. But she felt herself slipping already. Whatever magic—she hated using the term but it was the only one that fit—had brought her here was dwindling. "About magic and transcorporeal travel..."

John went to her and knelt again, putting his hands on her shoulders. He looked so much like Ian and yet so much more wild. It did him a great deal of good.

"Try not to worry too much. You'll have enough time for that come tomorrow. Matilda is your key to Alvin—but don't trust her too much. You'll find help. And answers. I promise."

His words were comforting, but they spoke nothing of her own world. "I just want to go home," Maddie said.

"Do you?" John asked.

Then he pressed his lips to hers, and she fell back into Matilda's room, the now-familiar sensation of the corset pressing at her ribs.

"Mrs. Roth?" asked Mrs. Fitz, still at the door. "Are you all right? Mr. Roth has sent a carriage..."

"Coming," Maddie said, checking Matilda's reflection one last time. She'd come back without so much as a feather out of place. "Sorry to keep you waiting."

Count Gascon's mansion floated some thousand feet above Boston, and reaching it required a short trip via air balloon Maddie learned. First, she was taken by carriage to a special docking station made just for the journey.

She could only describe the landing and connected structure as a Victorian ski lift, except rather than being hung with swings, it was bedecked with scarlet and gold-tasseled balloons. The length of it, all the way up to the mansion, was lit with strings of lights that could not quite have been flames, but must have been something like phosphorus, for they cast a green glow on the metal framework.

The door to the carriage opened, and Maddie spied Randall, a few steps up, leaning on the brass rail, waiting for her.

He saw her immediately and descended the stairs, his tails flapping behind him. He was dressed as flawlessly as she, his outfit the same pale green, the weskit shot with copper; Maddie didn't know how he had managed it, since Matilda hadn't mentioned her dressing plans to him. Perhaps Mrs. Fitz had coordinated. His hair had been combed and tied back with a gold ribbon, his glasses polished and catching the light; his eyes moved behind them, cautious, full of emotion. They had not left on the best of terms.

"You look beautiful," he said softly, holding out his hand to hers.

Maddie reached out to grab his hands, feeling the warmth of them even through her kid gloves. It was snowing again, and Randall ushered her toward the awning below the dock.

"Thank you, Mr. Roth," said Maddie, gently. "You look like quite the picture, yourself."

He sniffed. "You smell like a fire."

She grinned in spite of herself. "I visited John, briefly."

"Physically?" Randall asked, his mouth agape.

"Yes. Mostly. I mean, my clothes didn't translate, but I–"

"What... what did you speak of?" he asked. He looked worried.

Maddie shrugged. "He mentioned that twains were reincarnated, and told me a little about the Eight Worlds and their structure. It made a surprising amount of sense. I mean, inasmuch as anything makes sense these days."

"Maddie, I–"

"Look, it's our turn," Maddie said, pointing up to the servant arranging the seats. "Don't want to miss the flight. We can talk about this later, okay? For some reason, I'm really excited about attending this party."

"I hope you're not afraid of heights," he whispered, as they walked side by side, inclining their heads as people greeted them.

Lords and ladies—many of them, as Matilda had mentioned, leaning toward more robust dimensions—made their way up the landing to the air balloons along with them.

From this distance, Maddie could see the full balloon structure, including a car at the bottom of it, capable of holding a few people at a time. Maddie looked up and saw a half-dozen other balloons all rising along a thick rope running the length between them and the floating mansion.

"Listen, about earlier—" Maddie tried.

"Apologies and discussions of your adventures while I was gone can wait for a while, don't you think? You said it yourself. For now, I just want you to enjoy the view."

"Oh?" Maddie asked, as he helped her into the car below the balloon. It was theirs alone, and cold though it was, Maddie felt quite cozy with Randall nearby.

"Yes, my dear," he said. "Prepare yourself for a feast of the eyes and a famine of the soul."

As the balloon took flight, Maddie caught her breath in amazement. All of Boston fell away beneath them, cloaked in the light of the setting sun, the snow cast in glittering gold. The river flashed silver; carriages wound back and forth about their business. The buildings, some looking as if they had grown out of the harbor, looked like dollhouses from so high up.

"I don't tire of the view," said Randall, pointing toward the harbor.

"I thought, what a stupid idea to have a home up here. But now I see. It's like strings of pearls and light," Maddie replied, softly. "I had no idea."

The balloon stopped at the front of the manor, where a carriage house might be. As they exited, Maddie continued to stare higher up. The balloons holding the home up floated far above them, like smooth clouds in the distance; but every now and again, a plane would zigzag by, as Randall informed Maddie, to check on their current status. While no palace had fallen yet, it was still a possibility. And an event at the count's was no time to let the guard down.

They passed through a stone arch, which Randall explained was not stone at all, but a kind of plaster resin. Cutting corners to reduce the weight of the building was necessary in such a situation, but Maddie was amazed at how much attention to detail had been given. No single block was the same, and the arch was weathered to look like something from an English gatehouse.

And the theme continued, as the entire palace was reminiscent of an English castle, except brighter and cleaner. All the windows in the expansive manse were lit from within, glass paned in a multitude of colors.

The grounds were covered in a blanket of snow, the pine trees and topiaries decorated with red and gold candles, baubles, and silver icicles. Holly, ivy, and a few hardy trees with red berries adorned the walkways, winding around in garlands when they approached the staircase, which was carpeted in thick, red velvet.

"Gives new meaning to 'deck the halls,'" Maddie muttered as she nodded to the butlers on either side of the door, and stepped into the mahogany-inlaid entrance hall. "I've never seen such an elaborate party."

"It's our favorite festival, of course. Marymas. When Mary's divinity was realized, when she was brought into the greatest mystery of all," said Randall softly, squeezing her arm almost affectionately. "The count spares no expense; he holds three balls, this being the second, during the season."

"John said he's not on good terms with Mary," Maddie said, recalling the conversation. "And that there were eight of her twains across the worlds."

"Yes, that is the case. Mary and John are locked in a bit of an impasse…"

But there was no time for more conversation, as the crowd

soon swallowed them up. There were seemingly a thousand faces amidst the swirling of skirts and the bobbing of heads. Between the powder makeup and cleavage, Maddie had a difficult time orienting herself, and keeping the names straight. So, she continued to smile, continued to nod knowingly, and laugh when it seemed appropriate.

There was no hint of Matilda. Not lurking, not waiting. No, Maddie felt as if she was truly in control again and she was giddy with it. The mental strain alone of dealing with Matilda was almost too much to bear.

After making their way through the entrance hall, Maddie and Randall were ushered down through a sitting room and into the ballroom. Instead of marble, everything was inlaid wood; the flooring was a dizzying pattern of rosettes and ivy leaves, the carved columns painted like oaks. The twenty-foot ceilings were brilliant in gold leaf and white, hung with mirrors, and touched along the length with chandeliers dripping with crystals.

Someone was playing harp, and another violin; Maddie thought she could hear the sounds of other instruments, but couldn't quite pick them out. It was warm in the room, and she gave her stole to a butler, who took it away for her while a server offered her a glass of mulled wine.

Randall's arm was a constant comfort amidst the throng.

"I must admit, Mrs. Roth, the gown you're wearing tonight is extraordinary," said a corpulent gentleman to her right. He had a white mustache and the complexion of a boiled lobster. The woman on his arm—his wife, presumably—was half his age, but twice his size. Her breasts were proudly hoisted, and nearly exposed to the nipples due to the magnificent silver corset at her waist, and Maddie tried not to stare. She was dressed in layers of custard-yellow chiffon, her red hair pinned up with a thousand tiny pearls. She wore an amber-colored gemstone around her neck as big as Maddie's fist.

The fat, red-faced man continued when Maddie stared at him a little dumbly. "What say you make one for my Annette here? I think green would suit her wonderfully."

"Of course," Maddie said. She decided that Annette looked like a late-life Henry VIII–except without the beard. She had a blank expression on her face, but smiled very sweetly.

"Mrs. Roth can, of course, come by for a fitting in your home," said Randall, suddenly all business. "You know where to reach us. We're happy to accommodate."

A horn blared, and Randall pointed to the front of the room, squeezing Maddie's hand as he did so. "And there's the count."

8

Dance

At the front of the hall stood the man of the hour, Count Gascon. He was in black tails, like most of the men, but wore a sash of darkest emerald, set with a series of bows and medals. Some looked military, she thought, ropes and the like; but such things were far from her expertise in this world, and Matilda was of no help.

Count Gascon was handsome, if a little flabby about the middle. He had an open, friendly face with wide-set blue eyes, and dark hair oiled at his forehead in three precise locks. The rest of his hair was tied back, and what was on his chin had been combed to a point. When he raised his voice to speak, it was a lilting baritone.

"My most honored guests!" he said as the room began to fall silent. Hushed whispers followed.

"Dinner will be served in twenty minutes; until then the orchestra will be taking requests. And then–*then*, my friends, we shall *dance*! God save the Queen of America!"

"God save the Queen!" cried the crowd.

"Mary bless us all!" finished the count.

More conversations followed, many of which were exactly like the exchange with the red-faced man whose name
Maddie could not recall, and his Annette. She could see why
Randall had insisted on being present at such an occasion; it
was good business. And he was good at making appointments,
even when Maddie did scarcely more than smile and nod.

Not to mention that Matilda showed remarkable genius
in her clothing selection. Not a single soul was wearing green,
save for the Roths and the count; they stood out resplendently,
even in the elegantly dressed throng.

When dinner came, Maddie and Randall were seated one
table over from the count. The count spent a great deal of time
watching her. Maddie smiled courteously as she could, and
concentrated on eating her food; though as more and more
courses came, she found she was able to eat less and less. The
corset was preventing her from breathing, let alone eating.

The sheer scale of the food was astonishing to Maddie, let
alone its creative presentation. Much looked too good to eat,
with flowers carved out of everything from radishes to haunch-
es of meat, and gold paste mixed in with various dishes to create marbling, buttons, or whatever whimsical design the cooks
desired. By the time the third course, lamb–at least a flock was
fed to the seventy-odd guests–had arrived, Maddie was feeling
a little ill.

"Eat a little something off of every plate," said Randall.
"Or move it around to make it look like you have. That's the
trick." He had been pushing food around more than actually
eating, and gave her a charming grin and a wink.

Maddie did her best, continuing through the vegetable
platter that came next, the roast beef with leeks and wine sauce,
then the potage. She nibbled, and pushed her food around, taking sips of her wine every now and again.

Finally came dessert. Chocolate–the finest she'd ever eat-
en–was baked into a thick custard and put inside a pastry, then

frozen. Yet the plate was warm, so the chocolate melted and pooled as she ate it. It was like melting chocolate cake, only far better, and she surprised herself by nearly finishing it.

"Now! For the dancing!" called the count, standing from his seat.

Randall put his arm around her shoulders, and whispered, "Come. Join me for one dance, at least."

"Randall–I can't," whispered Maddie. "I'm so full I can't..."

"You'll do fine. Just follow me. You took dance classes at some point in your life, didn't you?" he whispered into her ear, tickling her neck. "Or are you so uncivilized as to shun such ordered elegance?" His breath smelled of punch.

She tried not to giggle, but the wine had gone straight to her head. "I'm not uncivilized. I took two years of ballet, and dancing in junior high, thank you very much. But I don't know anything fancy."

"Then give me the honor of a single dance. After, we can take a walk, just the two of us," Randall promised, looking at her over his golden spectacles, his blue eyes glinting. "There are some things I'd like to talk to you about."

"Fine," she said. "But just one dance." She felt a silly smile spread on her face. She remembered Matilda's promise–*Oh, I'm sure you'll be rutting like rabbits before the evening is over*—and part of her truly hoped that would be the case.

The feast was cleared away, but there was still plenty of available food should the guests desire, set up alongside the dance floor on long tables. Liquor flowed freely, far more than just wine: brandy, smoky whisky, and plenty of sickeningly sweet punch. Maddie had been offered the latter it twice, and found that after the first cloying sip, she was enjoying it.

Randall whisked her onto the dance floor, taking her quickly into position; she could tell by the lines of his body, even before he began to dance, that he was good. He had his hand firmly on her waist, pressing inward so that their bodies touched and gave her a quick kiss on the cheek.

"Thank you," he said.

"For what?"

But then the orchestra struck up in earnest, and dance began again. The music was surprisingly complex, not what she had expected. It was music with an Eastern influence, part Ravel, part bhangra. She tried to keep up with the strange hand movements and various changes in partners.

So soon after eating, Maddie worried she'd be sluggish, but the alcohol had the opposite effect. All she wanted to do was dance, in spite of the fear that she'd make a complete idiot of herself.

"What do I do?" she whispered in his ear as the women made a line on one side of the room, and the men on the other.

Randall just smiled. "Just hold up until the waltz. You can do that, right?"

"I think so," she said, just as she hit herself in the head with her hand. Maddie and Randall both burst out into fits of laughter, but continued on, breathless.

She caught the gist of the dance, but missed quite a few steps, even stepping on Randall's toes once. But he did not seem to mind. He was enjoying himself, and couldn't stop smiling. When they did come together, in between reels and changes, he was sure-footed, practiced, and always had a smile for her, reassuring and kind.

She wasn't supposed to trust him. But she trusted Matilda less. And it felt good, for the first time since Alvin had left, to have her heart soar.

Then came the waltz. The lights dimmed down, the music returned to a softer, sweeter pace. Other dancers surrounded them, but through the haze of nerves and wine, Maddie felt like it was just the two of them now.

Maddie was acutely aware of him. Randall's whole body blazed hot beneath her touch, and her heart was pounding out of control. Not her heart; Matilda's heart. But, still, the emotions were her own, more than they had been since she'd arrived.

"You did well," Randall assured her.

She giggled into his lapel. "You might as well have brought a dolled-up monkey. I knocked that poor woman's hat off—"

He giggled, trying very hard to keep a straight face during the somber, serious dance. "No, you're just inexperienced. Not the same thing."

"I'm terrible. Admit it."

"Well, you aren't exactly elegant out there. But you looked like you were having fun, and that's what matters."

Maddie laughed. "Yes, I did enjoy myself. More than I have in a very long time."

They made a turn around the ballroom floor, and Maddie peeked over Randall's shoulder at the expansive flowers that were the majority of the other women at court. Some were more slender, but by and large, the richer they looked, the more copious their rolls of fat.

One reminded her of Mrs. Roth, dressed in an apple-red dress with fur about the collar.

"So tell me," Maddie said in Randall's ear. "What about Mrs. Roth? Randy's mother. How does she fit into the picture?"

"You mean—"

"You said there was only one Alvin between our two worlds, and that he split time between this world and that one. That he figured out a way to travel unlike the way you and I do. Was she not his mother?"

Randall went quiet a moment, and Maddie thought she'd made him nervous. He finally cleared his throat and said, "Well, he had a twain. There, in Sixth. But that twain was killed. And he was able to staunch Mrs. Roth's suffering—you might say prevent it—by, for all intents and purposes, replacing him when the event happened. As I said, he knows how to predict certain phenomena in space, time, and dimension; it was a particularly fortuitous switch."

"Good lord," Maddie said. "So Mrs. Roth has nothing to do with all this?"

"Nothing aside from being the vessel from which our twains in that world were born. She looks a bit like our mother here, bless her departed soul," he said softly. But he was no longer looking at her. Instead, he was focused elsewhere. "But not entirely. Genetics are but one part of the puzzle."

"So far, you all look very much alike," said Maddie; still, she thought of M'ora and Pinga.

"Sometimes it depends on how you see, that's all," he replied with a grin.

"Depending on how I look at it? Like one of those Magic Eye pictures?"

"Though I have only met Randy, I have spoken to other twains who have reported very different versions of themselves. Not even of the same gender."

The song was over before Randall could expound on the revelation, and they were approached by an as of yet unattached woman in a purple frock with a stuffed squirrel hat.

"May I have this dance with Mr. Roth?" she asked.

Maddie wanted to say no. But if she danced too much she'd likely make a scene—or injure herself.

"Of course," Maddie replied, feeling how forced her smile was. "I'll take a rest. This is tiring." She sounded just like Matilda, and Randall gave her a perplexed look.

"Are you certain?" he asked, grasping her hand as she started to walk away.

"Absolutely. Have fun," she said, squeezing his hand gently.

Clearly Randall was regarded as a particularly prized dancing partner, for as soon as the first dance was over with the squirrel-hatted woman, and Randall tried to take his seat by Maddie, he was whisked away by a certain Mrs. Teague, and off they went.

Maddie sat for a while, rubbing her thumbs together as she watched the scene. She wished she hadn't asked Randall a question about Alvin and Mrs. Roth; it had put a damper on the nice moment.

Ah, well. From the looks of things, he was still enjoying himself. He danced with absolute flair and abandon. She didn't think she could recall him smiling this much since she'd met him.

Maddie closed her eyes and listened. She wondered at the many voices around her, and then noticed that if she listened just right, the words became unfamiliar. Oh, there were some words she recognized. But plenty of others that were foreign, bits of languages she knew only a few phrases of.

She suspected language, among other things, was different here. But Matilda's body must help her process it. It had to be.

She was fiddling with the cuff of her sleeve when she caught a whiff of a familiar perfume, though no clear memory came to mind. Glancing up, she realized who it was: Deborah Hildebrandt. Her heart did a little syncopated beat, somewhere between nerves and excitement, and she busied herself by staring at Mr. Hildebrandt, who looked washed out and horrifyingly old next to his lovely wife. He couldn't have been more than sixty, but he was very thin and palsied already. Though he was wearing the best clothes money could buy—likely a number done by the Roths themselves, in crushed dark blue velvet— there was something bedraggled about his appearance.

Deborah was radiant, her golden hair in ringlets, and her makeup elegant. Her shoulders looked bare on first glance, but Maddie saw that she was in fact wearing sheer lace of a weave so thin it was like spider silk; it was studded with tiny pearls, and gave the illusion that she had been sprinkled with snow. A silver corset offset the dark blue of the dress and picked up the glitter about her shoulders. The crowning piece was a sapphire about her neck, surrounded in opals.

"Good evening, Mrs. Roth," said Mr. Hildebrandt, pausing by her table, and reaching for her hand. Maddie gave it
reflexively, smiling as keenly as she could. She wanted to look
at Mr. Hildebrandt, but Deborah commanded attention. She
was easily the most beautiful creature in the room.

It made sense that both she and Matilda desired beautiful
things.

"Mr. Hildebrandt, Mrs. Hildebrandt," she said, as he
stooped to kiss her hand.

"She looks so remarkable in that dress of yours, Matilda,"
Mr. Hildebrandt said, referring to his wife.

"Indeed," agreed Maddie, smiling as she thought Matilda
would. "It is a unique piece, and one of the best I've yet to
design."

"After tonight, I suspect half the court will be after you
for a copy," he replied with a wheeze of a laugh. "I think your
husband is making appointments on the dance floor."

"It is his strength," replied Maddie.

"You don't mind if Deborah sits with you a while, do you?"
he asked. "I've got to make the rounds, and I'm afraid she's feeling a bit poorly this evening. I wouldn't like to leave her to the
other sharks." He may have been old, but he was sharp; he had
a glimmer in his rheumy eyes, and when Deborah looked to
him, she gave him a smile of remarkable compassion.

"Of course I don't mind," said Maddie, attempting to be
as cool as Matilda would have been.

Mr. Hildebrandt deposited his wife aside Maddie, though
not without pausing to give her a kiss on the cheek.

The two women sat in silence for some time, listening to
the music and watching the dancers. Maddie felt nervous; she
shouldn't blow her cover, but she also had no idea how she
should act. Should she be flirtatious? Should she bring up their
meeting yesterday? Had Deborah any idea what was going on?

"Randall seems to be enjoying himself," Deborah said,

her voice low, smooth. Her white hands lingered at the edge of the table, a huge faceted opal showing on her ring finger. "I always love seeing him dance. It brings out a side of him that's unexpected."

"It does," Maddie said, quietly. "He lets himself go a little, I think."

Deborah smiled sweetly, batting her dark lashes toward the dancers. "It's good for him. Mary and all the dragons know he takes himself too seriously. I dare say taking myself less seriously has contributed significantly to my overall happiness. We are only so important as the next person in line. And unless we're Queen Victoria, there's always someone higher up."

"Most certainly," said Maddie. The song had changed now to a slow waltz, and it was not without a little regret that Maddie watched as Randall went to dance with yet another partner.

"He hasn't asked you to dance in a few turns," said Deborah.

"There is only so much we can share."

"Not too much, I hope," said Deborah. Most eyes were on the dancers, but Maddie could feel Deborah's gaze. It was exhilarating, strange as it was. Maddie had been and had *not* been with this woman, and yet she could see why Matilda was so besotted with her. Deborah was the ideal: sensual, voluptuous, intelligent, witty. She sighed and added, "I miss you."

Maddie turned and said, "You—"

Deborah put her hand upon Maddie's and squeezed. "If only I could make you smile the way Randall does out there on the dance floor. Some day yet, love. Some day yet."

There was no time to respond, for Mr. Hildebrandt was back, and he indicated that he had to introduce Deborah to a colleague of his; Deborah smiled a little wistfully, and accompanied her husband away, and Maddie stared after her, dumbstruck.

A few dances later, and Mr. Roth returned, sweating and smiling, declining yet another offer from Mrs. Teague. Yes, if Randall desired, there were easily two-dozen women more than happy to tend to his needs.

"I must see to my wife, you know," he said, bowing from the middle. "She'll think I've forgotten her. But how could I? She is a vision."

Mrs. Teague laughed and went in search of another partner, and Randall sat down beside Maddie, taking her hand absently.

"You know, Matilda's never danced with me," he said, soft enough for only her to hear. "You don't know how glad you made me tonight."

"I'm glad to have done it," said Maddie. She was breathing a little faster now that Randall was near, or perhaps it was leftover tension from Deborah's appearance.

Everything was made brighter, more crisp and clean, just by Randall's presence, and his hand. The world seemed to revolve around it; she had removed her gloves, and they were now entwined, skin to skin.

"Shall we take that walk now?" he asked.

"Certainly, Mr. Roth. If you would be so inclined." Maddie was feeling lightheaded again. She'd indulged in a little too much punch waiting for Randall to stop dancing, and the noticed the floor swayed slightly as she got to her feet and followed him outside.

Though there were plenty of walking grounds at Count Gascon's manor, it was chilly, and few of the guests were interested in seeing the count's premises without the warmth of a fire and the comfort of food.

As Maddie and Randall took a turn about the cloister, they were by and large alone. Their boots crunched atop the snow, and they walked side by side. The butler could not be located, and so Maddie had Randall's velvet coat draped across her shoulders instead of her stole.

"You'll freeze to death," Maddie protested yet again.

They passed through an archway hung with shimmering garlands at the back of the mansion, the sounds of the dance quieting as they walked farther away. The wind was too much to bear in the open, but the cloister worked well to buffet it.

"I'll be fine. I'm always warm," he said, though the rattling of his teeth belied his true condition.

Maddie closed her eyes for a moment and looked again for Matilda, but she was still gone.

Shivering into the warmth of the jacket, which was, in all truth, welcome, she sighed contentedly. It was good to be in the quiet after the craziness of the feast. The air, cold as it was, was crisp and clean up here, and helped clear the alcohol haze.

"I'm sorry if I upset you this morning," Maddie said. "I was out of line. This whole thing," she waved her hands in the air to try and indicate all of Second World, "hasn't made it easier."

"No, no. I should apologize. I was more curt with you than I ought to be... but Maddie, I've got to start being a little more honest with you," he said. "I mean, about Alvin, about–"

"More honest? It kind of sounds like you've been lying when you say it that way."

"I haven't told you everything up front," Randall said. "Knowing he's alive is enough of a burden in the first place, and I just didn't want to burden you with too much information."

"That's almost gallant of you. But I think I can handle myself. I did find out some information on my own. Well, with a little help from Matilda."

Randall tried to look composed but failed. "Oh?"

They settled against the side of a column, watching each other in the golden glow of the swaying lamplight above them.

Gargoyles and winged gryphons, delicate carved birds and gamboling goblins twisted up the stonework, every little detail crusted in snow.

"Yes," Maddie said. "He seems to be accruing some extensive debt, according to Georgiana D'Arc, if that's what you mean. I know about *their* affair, too." She told him what she had heard at the countess's house, thanks to Matilda.

Now Randall looked absolutely crestfallen. "We have a bit in common, don't we? But I'm glad, I suppose, that you're making peace with her inasmuch as you can. She... she isn't here right now, is she?"

"Not a trace. And it's a relief."

"I can imagine," he murmured, his thoughts clearly elsewhere. "She would not be happy with me about now, I don't think."

"Hey, let's talk about something else, though, huh?" She turned to face him, putting her hands on her hips. His jacket flared out and she looked like a green bird in the snow. "She's not here, and I want to make use of my time. I want to ask some questions."

"Go right ahead, madam," he said with an affected bow that ended in a wobble and a grin. He had been drinking a bit, too. When he laughed, the steam coming from his mouth was tinged with whisky.

"How much of Randy do you remember? I mean, the times we shared together. The trips, the hot dogs, the endless Wendy's spicy chicken sandwiches. He once told me about someone he called 'the other me'. Was that...?"

The question set Randall to smiling again and he reached out and touched her cheek with the tips of his fingers. "Sometimes it was me. Randy lets me in, at times, but never completely. Still, I remember many, many instances together. I remember the details, the places, the expressions on your face, the things Randy never could understand.

"Sometimes I thought I was on the verge of breaking through, of comforting you when he could not. But I never could. It baffled and amazed me how you found the strength to continue to care for Randy, especially after Alvin's disappearance. And while you were with Alvin, I never understood how you could cope with him, either. He was never the most compassionate partner."

"It wasn't easy," she said. "Sometimes I think I was crazy to do it in the first place. But I wanted to be good enough for him."

"You were *too* good for him. You have a remarkable heart, Maddie. Far more than he ever deserved."

"Up until a few months ago, I'd have argued that point."

Randall reached out and skimmed a finger full of snow from the open paws of a fat carved sphinx above Maddie's head, then brought it to his lips, tasting it, grinning like a child seeing his first flurry. "Delicious," he said. "Like the finest spring water, I say." He skimmed some more, this time from the head of a gargoyle, and ate it again.

"You're crazy," said Maddie.

"No, there's something about snow here. It's sweet. Like sugar."

Maddie laughed a little nervously in reply.

"Try some," he said, coming up to her with his finger covered anew. It was beginning to flurry again, and Maddie could see flakes on her eyelashes as she blinked. They melted quickly, making her eyes water.

"No thanks," she said, pushing his hand away.

He pressed closer, waving his finger back and forth. "You'll thank me," he said. "It's like manna from heaven."

Maddie could have blamed the cold, but she knew that the shaking she was experiencing had little to do with it. She could smell him, a combination of his cologne and his sweat mingling with the snow and liquor. It was sweet and spicy, intoxicating. And it spurred her on, despite her better judgment.

She leaned over, cautiously, and lapped at the melting snow on his finger like a cat tasting milk. A refreshing blast of cool sweetness melted onto her tongue, and she gasped in surprise.

"See? What did I tell you?" he asked.

"Mmm..." she said.

But she would not let it rest there; she couldn't. He was too close, and she had made her choice. Even Matilda had said couldn't resist her a second time. Flush with the power of that knowledge, and drunk on wine and merriment, she took his hand and brought the finger to her lips, carefully sucking the remainder of snow from it. She caressed the length of his finger with her tongue, lapping up every last drop of moisture. His finger was chilly when she took it, but was warm when he withdrew.

She did not let go of his hand.

He was breathing shallowly.

Maddie pressed closer to him, looking into his face and marveling at the beauty of it. Light from the nearby lamp shot copper streaks into his hair, traced the lines of his jaw, and set the slight hairs left since his last shave flashing like amber.

"There is no shame in it," she said, the words sounding hauntingly like Matilda's.

"It is—"

"*Natural*," she replied, pushing him back, step by step. They were now in an indentation in the wall of the cloister, where once there might have been a statue, but which now fit two people just perfectly. "It's natural for me to feel this way, so I've been told. And for you, too. I can't help but feel as if... if things were different in my world, Randy and I..."

"Maddie—"

"It feels inevitable, doesn't it?" she said with a wry smirk, pressing even closer.

He only moaned in response, his shoulders dropping, letting go. He could not refuse her, not even if he wanted to. She felt her own heat rising, blazing; it was power. Matilda was right. It was strength, it was beauty, that realization—it was near perfection.

It was epiphany.

"What... what about Alvin?" he asked with a great deal of effort.

"What about him?"

"What if you find him? What if you love him? What if you—"

She kissed him, interrupting him, and leaving the questions unanswered. In that moment, she did not care. The kiss said everything she needed, filled her up to bursting with joy. At first Randall resisted, but soon gave up. Surely he could feel it, too. He kissed back, his hands roaming hungrily over her body, lifting up the layers of her skirt, seeking warmth and comfort there.

Randall pulled away, taking a deep breath. "Dragons above. We'll freeze out here," he said, almost giggling. Yes, he'd had a lot of whisky. Randall looked around for a proper exit.

"We can't just *leave* the party," Maddie pointed out, shivering through the heat within her.

"We have chambers to retire to," he said. He slipped his hand into his pocket and pulled out a silver key on a red ribbon. "Count Gascon knows what his company is capable of. See, I am prepared."

"You scoundrel," she said. "You *were* prepared."

Fumbling, kissing, nearly tripping over one another, they made their way to their designated room. It was in one of the turrets, looking out over the city, and lit with candles, as if someone had been expecting them.

The door was not shut three seconds when Randall was on her again, and she on him. Kissing alone was a revelation. On some level, Maddie knew this body was not her own, the responses were biologically not hers. And yet she felt entirely

in charge and shockingly comfortable. She wanted to laugh until she cried. It had never felt like this before.

"Damn the corset," said Maddie, reaching for the laces
and finding them nearly impossible to loosen.

"We have time," said Randall, as they sat together now on
the edge of a large, fur-draped bed. The fire at the hearth cast
moving shadows into the room, turning skin to gold, eyes afire.

Maddie pulled Randall's hair out of its ribbon, and it fell
into his face. She reached up for his glasses, removing them as
well, as he took the pins from her hair one by one, tracing the
line of her neck first with his fingers, and then with his lips.

"There you are," he said, kissing her cheek.

"I don't know who I am, but I'm yours to take," Maddie
said. The words were particularly profound to her, somehow.

It was all the encouragement he needed. He tore at the
corset, the strings at the back finally loosening, and with a
whoosh of air, she was free of it. The feeling of the air, chilly
drafts amidst warm currents, on her skin and down the cleft of
her breasts and belly sent chills down her spine, but it was just
the beginning.

He leaned over her, leading her gently to the bed.

"So beautiful," he said, slipping his fingers under the collar of her chemise, and tugging so it fell down over her shoulders. He took one breast in his hand, smoothing his thumb over
the erect nipple, caressing it longingly, then bent to the other
and took it softly between his lips and teeth.

Maddie arched her back in response, the sensation rippling through her, pleasure like falling rain over her skin. She
gasped, moaned, as she felt his hot breath on her skin, moving
down to her stomach, kissing her navel. Randall's fingers found
the band of her bloomers and undid the lace, then pulled. Finally, she was revealed to him in full.

Randall simply admired her, then, running his hands
along the length of her, before realizing his current state: he

was still quite dressed. Maddie rose to her knees on the bed, and pulled him to her, removing his shirt and vest, smoothing her hands over his chest, the golden hairs there soft against the palms of her hand. Then, button by excruciating button, she released him from his trousers.

Then, the world fell silent. All was touch and sight, light and darkness, as they came together in bliss. He was an ardent lover, careful and yet wracked by moments of sheer passion. He played her body as a well-tuned instrument, knowing each and every tender, aching inch of her.

Maddie knew him, too. She had once been close to Alvin, and his brother was not so different. Except here there was more. Even after years with Alvin, this one time with Randall was utterly different.

She had never been so lost before with Alvin. There had always been something else to distract her; the room was too cold, she was self-conscious. But here, how could she be? She was not even in her own body, even if she could feel every caress and every thrust.

Knowing his desire bolstered her own. Maddie slid up atop him, as he reached up for her again. She felt beautiful, there, watching him watch her. She felt as if she were beauty embodied, perfect in spite of her flaws. Matilda was right: It was power.

But it was more than that. It was connection. It was love. It was magic.

And for the first time since crossing into Second World, things we starting to make sense for Madeline Angler.

Morning found them tangled together like hawthorn and hazel; Maddie awoke first, and spent a few minutes just watching Randall sleep. His lashes were very dark against his fair skin, a detail she'd not noticed before, especially through the glasses. He had freckles just under his eyes.

"Good morning," she said as his eyes fluttered open. His irises were black against the sapphire blue, so striking an artist could not have done it better.

"Maddie," Randall said, reaching up and running his hand through her hair. "You look... ethereal."

"I can't take the credit for that, I don't think," she said. "I'm a bit chubbier." She poked her stomach.

"No, no. When you're in charge, everything is different. You glow. It's remarkable."

"Alvin used to tell me I looked like Frankenstein's bride in the morning," she said, remembering his requirement that she brush her hair before they were intimate.

Randall frowned. "I still don't understand what it was you saw in him."

"Wit. Intelligence. Charisma. A certain chaotic brilliance. Frenetic energy, in a good way..." She tried to put it into words. "I always felt like we got each other, even though we were so different."

"You still love him."

"It's funny," Maddie said in reply, finding herself less frightened by the question than she might have been earlier. "You might not know this, but I saw Randy first. It was by the Lichtenstein, at the Fine Arts Center at school. I was a tour guide, and I noticed that every Thursday this gorgeous guy with a terrible taste in fashion came wandering around, staring at the Lichtenstein. One day, I mustered the strength to go ask him out. But I didn't make it to him.

"Alvin appeared, not three steps from Randy, and introduced himself. He was all smiles and energy, and quite handsome in his own way—though never so much as Randy. Alvin told me Randy was *compromised*; I think that's the word he used. And I could see it, the way Randy looked at things, the way he saw the world. But..."

"But?" asked Randall, rubbing her back gently.

"Alvin was confident. He was *brilliant*. He had this odd way of speaking, sometimes so formal, you know? Which makes sense now, I guess. I was attracted to him just so intensely, I drove myself crazy with it."

"And Randy?"

"I stayed with Alvin in the end because I loved Randy. And I even loved Mrs. Roth. I honestly don't think I'd have ever left Alvin if he hadn't disappeared. But after a while, I was lost without him. I was tired of chasing his shadow, the shadow of him that I loved... and I guess I still love that shadow. I never had closure, I never had—"

Maddie felt her head explode with a stab of pain and she gasped, turning to the side, unable to complete her sentence.

We have go to Charleston, unless you forgot, Matilda said, from within.

Shit. You're here. I don't remember drinking any opium.

"What is it?" Randall asked, concerned. He slipped his hands around her shoulder.

Matilda was angry, Maddie could feel the emotion seeping into her own consciousness. It's not just a matter of the right drugs. I said I was going away, didn't I? I'm glad you enjoyed yourself. But there isn't time. We need to get to Joss Raddick and find your Alvin.

Maddie winced, hating the way Matilda had said that. *My Alvin. Hardly. He's half this city's Alvin.*

I've let you have my body and my husband. I think you owe me one at this point.

Randall frowned when she did not answer, and Maddie slipped out his grasp and out of the bed. There was a green satin robe set out for her and she pulled it around her shoulders.

"Maddie?" Randall asked, squinting in the morning light. "Please. Did I say something?"

She sighed in reply. "I'm *sorry*. It's hard to concentrate

when she's harping on me."

"Oh. It's Matilda, then." He winced.

"Yes."

"You're going?"

"I am."

"To find him."

Him. It was just the way Mrs. Roth used to say it.

Maddie shivered with the memories. "Matilda knows where to go and—it's what you brought me here for, Randall, isn't it?"

Tell him he's a flaccid coward, Matilda hissed.

Randall looked doubtful. "She *knows* where Alvin is?"

"She knows where to start, yes. With a fellow named Joss Raddick. And so far, Matilda seems to be the most helpful in the situation. Don't look at me like that. You're the one that said I should try and work with her. And there's a chance that Alvin could help, too. He's the expert."

Randall sighed, turning to face her more fully. He shivered, gooseflesh appearing and then vanishing on his arms. "I suppose he is."

"You could come," she tried.

"I… don't know if I can cope with that scene right now. And I know I can't cope with Matilda."

"She frightens you?"

He nodded.

Matilda cackled from behind Maddie's eyelids, and she shuddered, wondering if this was the right decision.

Randall sat up in bed, and then walked to her, naked still. He reached out his hand and drew it through her hair, taking the ends and curling them around his fingertips. "Would that I could keep you here."

"Would you?" she asked, closing her eyes. "Would you keep me, or Matilda?"

We're going now. Matilda insisted, sounding like a persistent child.

"You don't have to leave me," Maddie pressed.

"I..." he trailed off, nestling his head on her shoulder. Then he gave her a sweet kiss on the lips, and that was all. "Be careful."

Maddie, for once, didn't know what to say. She took his hand, and squeezed it, then gave him a sad smile.

"Just don't forget yourself," Randall added. "I couldn't bear to lose you."

"You might have already," she said, kissing him on the cheek, doing everything in her power to keep from breaking into tears.

She had trusted him. But he was a coward. In the moment that she needed him, when she was most afraid, he ran. When she had asked, he had refused. All his words and charm and smiles were nothing in the face of his fears.

Matilda was right.

9

Charleston

It took some time to reach the street again, but no sooner had the door slammed on the carriage than Maddie was thrown aside.

With a violent shove, Maddie was thrust back out of control; she had never been pushed away so easily before, especially without opium, and the effect was dizzying. She could still see Randall lingering at the docking area, staring after the carriage they had taken. Had she chosen wrong?

What's going on? Maddie tried to ask. But Matilda wasn't answering.

Another push, and Maddie was shoved out of Matilda's body entirely, unable to feel or see for quite some time.

Amidst the blackness she had a few flashes: Matilda settling a few things at the house, drinking a cup of opium tea, changing into a riding gown, slipping a knife and a derringer into her boot. None of it boded well.

Once they were in the carriage again, and westward bound, Maddie was at least granted sight again. Matilda couldn't keep her strangle hold on her forever, it seemed. From her own experience, utter control was hard work, and exhausting. Maddie sensed Matilda was keeping her strength for something.

Yet she could not stay silent forever. As Maddie let memories and regrets wash over her, Matilda had to taunt her.

Poor little lovebird. But Randall? Really? He's such a bore.

It's not Randall. It's everything, it's—

Oh, you're so dramatic. It really is pathetic.

Can we just get this over with? I want to go home.

Charleston was a two-hour journey in a vaguely northwest direction, and after that, Maddie waited quietly at the back of Matilda's mind while she watched the landscape change around them.

The world may have still been blanketed in snow, but after scarcely an hour of driving, it bore no resemblance to the Victorian elegance of Farleigh and the floating mansions of Boston. The palatial homes and buildings gave way to more rudimentary storage houses and abodes, and the streets were bumpier. Then came more factories, plants, and even a smattering of farms. Even deeper, and the bridges were painfully unattended to, as well, jolting the carriage back and forth as they traveled over rough, icy water below.

Then came trees and little else.

Why would anyone want to live out here?

It's not a matter of wanting. They're stationed out here. They're the River Guard. The Charles River. Charleston, Matilda explained.

I get that, said Maddie.

Ahead loomed huge garrison rising out of the horizon, abutted by a fortified bridge. It was at least a hundred feet tall and constructed of dull stone and wrought iron, crenellated around the tops. It was still light out, but blue fire burned at the top of each of the four turrets. The garrison stretched in both directions as far as the eye could see: a wall of impenetrable rock.

"Mary guards this place," said Matilda, muttering to herself. "The fires still burn."

As in the Mother Mary, I'm guessing. Maddie was still trying to keep up. When she started losing the present, she could
feel her own consciousness slipping away. Matilda was strong,
stronger than she'd ever been. But Maddie did not want to
keep her guard down, did not want to let Matilda know how
frightened she felt.

The priestesses of Mary come here, and keep her fires burning. It's one of
her things, you know, the blue fire. And, as of yet, an unexplained phenomenon.
Though chances are, if Alvin or Randall had the time and the inclination, they
could explain it in terms of science. Regardless, the good news is that if it's blue,
it means we're safe. There are no enemies within sight.

And who might these enemies be?

Matilda left the question unanswered, but Maddie saw an
image in her mind: John Iosheka. Filing that away for further
reference, Maddie continued to listen to Matilda speak.

Charleston is on the other side of the garrison, said Matilda. And it's the
last bastion of civilization for quite some time. The Wilds start about ten miles
west, and the world beyond is untouched until California—but as you keep re-
minding me, you just want to get home, and the last thing I need to do is burden
you with the details of the state of my particular world.

They passed through the gate with little pomp or circumstance, and the carriage was then changed; the wheel was replaced with a bay mare that looked worse for wear and de-
spondent about her task. Matilda explained that the method by
which the roads worked in town were by no means capable of
functioning this far out.

It couldn't have been more than six miles, but the journey felt longer now that they were in such unfamiliar territory.
Maddie felt naked and scared out in the open, as if the sky were
too high, the trees too dense. The forest was old here, the trees
covered in moss and lichen, their limbs often barely hanging on.
These forests were unattended, probably since the dawn of time.

And Randall was gone. He was back in Boston, likely
warm in his parlor, smoking a pipe and reading a volume of

poetry. He had chosen to stay behind. Matilda was right; he had been a coward. When it came down to it, he was too afraid of Matilda to stand up to her.

So much for chivalry. But the Roth brothers never really did adhere to such backwards beliefs, teased Matilda, picking up on Maddie's thoughts.

Why would Alvin be out here? Maddie tried to change the subject.

He would have been brought here.

And how will this Raddick person help us?

Joss Raddick knows everything that happens in Charleston. Georgiana is right. Joss also happens to have a hand in the steamship **Faust**, the one that docks in the river, and if there's anything unsavory going on, he'll be alerted to it. He's a remarkable fellow, and an old friend to Alvin. Most of the time. And look. Here we are.

What then came into view was somewhere between an old western ghost town and Old Deerfield, thought Maddie. The homes were dated and shoved close together, but not well kept in the least. Everything was snow covered, muted brown and practically rotting in the snow. A half-dozen carriages convened together, lined up in a row by the longest and cleanest of the buildings.

And this is Charleston. The large building there is the inn, the Green Lion, said Matilda. Most of the carriages are for whores and the like, or visiting friends.

I see. Sounds like this place is right up your alley.

My dear, once you cross the garrison, the laws just don't apply.

"Look, it's Mrs. Roth!" called a boisterous voice outside the carriage. A bearded man carrying an axe over one shoulder and wearing a combination of leather and plaid appeared at the window of the carriage, smiling from ear to pockmarked ear. "Good to see you again! Been a while. Here for some more trading? I hear we've got a new silk store in from Jamaica just yesterday—"

"No, no—personal matters today, I fear, and no business.

Though if it's a particularly good lot, I'll be happy to take a look," Matilda said with a smirk. "It's good to see you, Gared."

Gared opened the door for Matilda and helped her down, continuing to ramble, "Much of the town's gone, as the herd's on the move. I came by to fell a tree for the Green Lion, so I did, and skipped out on the hunt altogether. Bad knee makes hunting more painful than I'd like, so it was no loss on my part."

"I presume Captain Raddick is unavailable, then?" Matilda asked.

"Not in the least," said Gared, pointing with his bearded chin toward the largest of the buildings, a low-lying inn with a faded green sign. "He's been entertaining some visitors from the South, you see, and he's been at the cards for almost three straight days. It's a good thing the flames are blue, you know. Likely he'll find the imprint of the chair on his rear if he doesn't move."

"Yes. Our dear captain has a soft spot for the cards. Last time I paid him a visit, I made out like a bandit," said Matilda, dismissing him with a wave. "Good to see you again, Gared. Send my regards to Gertrude."

"Of course, Mrs. Roth. Thank you, Mrs. Roth," Gared said.

You're quite the regular here, aren't you? Maddie asked.

I go to impressive lengths to get business done. No risk, no reward. Matilda was clearly losing her patience.

I wouldn't wander around here alone. Gared seems okay, but it's kind of rough and tumble.

You think I need protection. Dragons above. I can take care of myself.

So I see...

As soon as they set foot in the inn, the temperature rose to the point of discomfort. The fire was warm enough, but in combination with the presence of about two dozen men embattled in a game of cards, smoking, and stinking of drink, it was barely tolerable. It smelled like piss and bad grain alcohol, and the room had likely not been swept in months, if not years.

The building that housed the inn might once have been magnificent, but now was disheveled. It was characterized by peeling wallpaper, broken lamps, and further punctuated by a dull and uncared-for copper bar-top, stained and oxidized. A piano, its paint chipped and keys pulled of ivory, sat despondently across the room; judging by the dust, no one even bothered playing it anymore. The carpet had holes throughout, like some giant moth had worried its way into the fabric. Even the windows were smeared with the accumulation of so much dust and sweat.

And to add to the overall ambiance, the whores were out in force. The painted ladies looked like burlesque dancers to Maddie, their skirts short, their hair in ringlets, their faces a dazzle of white, blue, and red. One had her arms draped around a big soldier, clad in grey and gold, her head leaning against his. She looked like a lovesick teenager. Maybe she *was* a teenager.

When the door shut behind Matilda, all eyes turned to her immediately. Most looked back at their games pretty quickly; about half looked to be soldiers, while the other half Maddie couldn't place. A few looked like extras from a spaghetti Western, their features not entirely native or quite European. She remembered Matilda saying something about natives, earlier. Maddie had assumed they were the people in the Wilds, considering how Pinga and John looked. But she'd been wrong before.

Then she saw Joss Raddick. He was undoubtedly handsome, but as rugged as they come. He had a scar down the left side of his cheek that went up into his hair, ragged and deep enough to speak of a brush with death. But his dark eyes were clear, odd in contrast to his golden hair; his jaw was sharp, his nose broad. He reminded Maddie of pictures she'd seen of Wild Bill Hickock, but more brawny and a little more conventionally handsome with his thick lips and high cheekbones.

"There you are, you lout," called Matilda.

Joss Raddick gave a boisterous laugh, then excused himself from the group. Maddie watched and experienced everything as Matilda giggled and ran into the man's arms. He picked her up and swung her around, then kissed her fully, wetly on the mouth. He did not smell of alcohol or cigarettes; no, he tasted faintly of lemons, his beard scuffing against her cheek and leaving a scent of cinnamon.

"Matilda," he said, setting her down, stroking her cheek with his hand. "The nightingale returns."

"Joss," Matilda said, all airs gone. "Joss Raddick. *There* you are. I hear the herd's on the move, but you've been sitting on your arse, is that right?"

Joss laughed, his smile exposing his wide-set white teeth. "Someone's got to stay behind. And besides nothing's so boring as hunting elk, not this time of year. Might as well pick apples for the ease of it." He pretended to shoot something with a gun, then laughed again.

"You know there's more to it than that," said Matilda, removing her cloak and handing it to him. Joss took it, then offered her a seat.

"Can I get you something?" he asked. "Clem's made some decent elk patties, and we've got sandwiches. Pudding, too. And a whole new cask of rum from the Indies, just got in yesterday."

"Whisky," she said, without hesitation. "Straight."

Who is this new Matilda? asked Maddie, desperate to understand.

The old Matilda, Matilda corrected.

While the captain went to get Matilda a drink, she surveyed the room, Maddie watching along with her. Rather than stay silent, Matilda narrated what she saw.

There are about a dozen other River Guard here, mostly poor men who've worked their way up the ranks of society, finally finding the highest position possible. Some are married, but most choose not to. They don't last long out there.

What's the danger? Maddie asked.

Everything. The Wild, darling, is out there. The gate we passed through runs the length of Boston, and its suburbs, as well as some of the smaller towns. Mary protects us, with the flames, with her soldiers. The River Guard pledge their lives to her. But... other forces are at work, too.

So Boston is like... a cultural oasis. Nothing out here ever got civilized?

Oh, there's civilization in the Wilds. But it's not anything like here. As I said, there are other powers. As Randall mentioned to you, other... dragons, gods, what-have-you. Mary and her brothers and sisters are ever quarreling here, and after the last war, a bargain was struck. Mary was promised the cities along the coast would lie in peace, and her brother, a very powerful and very terrible individual, was given the lands in between. That's why we build our floating palaces, you see. There's no place to grow but up.

What was it John had said about a twain who existed in eight instances? At the time, Maddie had thought he was talking about a twain named Miriam. But Miriam was Hebrew for Mary...

You still haven't figured it out.

Figured what out?

What we are, you ninny.

What do you mean, what we are?

But Joss was back, and Matilda had the reins again, and was no longer responding. Joss slid into the chair across from Matilda, and grinned, placing the whisky, which was presented in a surprisingly pristine glass considering the caliber of the inn, before her.

"Saints alive, but it's good to see you," he said, lowering his voice. "You look as ever lovely."

"Ah, all the nature of the beast," Matilda said, coolly, brushing her hair with the back of her hand.

For a brief flash, Maddie saw a glimpse of Matilda's mind. When she said the word "beast," Maddie saw white, needle-sharp teeth, and wings flecked with blood. If Matilda noticed she'd shared the thought, she gave no indication.

But Maddie was growing warier, afraid.

Matilda sipped the whisky, and it burned on the way down. It was so smoky it was almost effervescent. "And you, you look hale as ever. How many years is it that you've been out here?"

Joss dropped his voice, "Thirty, here in the River Guard. So, I'll likely be returning to Philadelphia in a year or two; start over. People are starting to get suspicious, of course. They always do. At least here, men don't last as long as in many of the places I've been posted. It's been nice to set down roots for a bit."

He rubbed the side of his face, taking a sip of his own drink—something that was certainly not alcohol, but smelled faintly of sarsaparilla. He looked suddenly ill at ease. Maddie found it odd that he would have been with the River Guard so many years, when he himself looked scarcely out of his forties. But perhaps he was just well preserved.

"I never thought I'd hear you say that," Matilda replied. "Set down roots? Why, don't tell me you're getting soft. There isn't a woman here satisfying you? Or a young lad?"

"No, no. Of course not," Joss said, waving Matilda's suggestions away. "It's just a good gig. But it's coming to a close. You know how it is, feeling a part of something can be good for us."

"Yes. Yes it can."

Joss frowned, but without losing the glint of merriment in his eye. "You don't just come here unannounced. So what've you got up your pretty little sleeves?"

"I've brought one for Alvin," Matilda said, lightly, taking another sip of whisky. Her voice was full of mirth, and her body trembled as she said it, nearly aroused.

"Matilda..."

She tapped her forehead. "Here. Right here. She's *listening.*"

Joss's eyes went wide, and he bristled. "Matilda–" He looked wildly around over his shoulder then lowered his voice. "You–you can't just do that. It's not a game."

"It was Alvin who *started* the whole game, and I am just having my turn. Why is it that he gets to have all the fun?"

Joss did not respond immediately. He looked behind him, then at Matilda again. "Which is she from?" he asked in a whisper.

"Six. She's one of Alvin's. Of particular interest to him, I think. Randall brought her here, and neither of them have any idea how convenient that is."

Six? One of Alvin's? Maddie was trying to hold on to consciousness as hard as she could, but Matilda was pushing her to the edges.

No answer from Matilda.

Maddie felt strangled, breathless. Usually she could just cling to Matilda's breathing patterns, and scarcely think about it. But now, it was as if she were breathing through a straw. She probably didn't need to worry about breathing, considering it was her consciousness and not her physical body at risk, here. But it was comforting to breathe.

Joss didn't miss a beat, but his shoulders slumped. "And that's why you're here, of course. Trying to find Alvin. You know I'd expected that. But... well, it's a mighty delicate situation, if you understand, Mattie. Alvin's gone a bit rogue on me, and I'm not sure I can trust him."

"None of us can trust Alvin, but then again, none of us can help what we are," said Matilda, softly.

"Oh, that right? Alvin can't help being a murderer and Randall can't help but being a flaky coward, is that it?" Joss said, slapping his hand down on the table, making the whisky spill all over his hands and the grimy tablecloth. The men behind them were too engrossed in their game to take much notice. "I'm sure it takes a lot of convincing on that account for even you, Matilda."

"That's not exactly what I mean," she replied.

Joss didn't buy it, and sipped his drink again. "Well, care to try again, then?"

"Alvin is the maelstrom, and you are the sea. Can't you calm him down?"

"Sometimes the sea just feeds the storm. You know that. He's losing it. I don't know why but he's... even more chaotic than usual. Like something's snapping. Or snapped."

"Surely you can take me to him," she said. "For my twain's sake, at least. I did promise her closure."

Joss shook his head. "I don't know. You bring out the worst in Alvin, sometimes."

Matilda laughed.

"Besides," Joss continued, "what if you're just lying? You do have a history–"

"*Listen.* She's from Six; you understand. You know what it's like there. She still doesn't believe half of what Randall or I have told her, so I'm trying to make the transition as smooth as possible."

Joss smirked. "Ah, I see how things are now."

"You do?" asked Matilda.

"You have no desire to school her. You just want her out. Or done away with. Seems to me she was brought here against her own volition. I've never heard of someone coming from Sixth of their own will. Not since the Magdalene."

Before Matilda could reply, Joss barreled over her. Maddie liked him just for that. "My guess is it was one of Randall's experiments. Except he can't get her back. And she can't get herself back. And you can't get rid of her. So you need Alvin."

Matilda froze. "I want my life back. And yes. Alvin can help."

Lies. Matilda was lying. Maddie could feel it, but she

couldn't find the truth between the words. Matilda's mind was a fortress. And that worried her. A great deal. Everything was closing in. Teeth like needles... blood-flecked wings... something lurked inside Matilda, ready to devour her whole.

Joss snorted. "You've got a way, Matilda. Always have. What I don't understand is why in hell you'd want to give this lass a second chance, considering you're probably just planning to dispose of her in the end."

Shock etched itself across Matilda's face.

Joss sighed. "Yes. He's told me what he's been up to. That's Alvin's philosophy, isn't it? And he's done well by it, or so he swears. He keeps trying to get me to do the same, but I don't want that kind of blood on my hands."

Maddie struggled as sight was cut off from her. She could hear, but the world faded around her into a black mist.

"You have plenty of blood there already; what's a little more?" Matilda asked. "And you enable him. It's hardly different."

"So you're undecided," Joss said. "Not sure if you should kill her or keep her?"

Kill me? Matilda!

Matilda continued, giving no sign she'd heard Maddie. "She's not strong enough, nor is she clever enough. The worlds would not weep for her loss. And she's so ignorant as to think she's got the upper hand."

Joss laughed. "And what makes you so sure she doesn't?"

"Really, Joss. You insult me. It's simple. I take her to Alvin, explain the situation, and see what he thinks. Randall wanted her here to make up for whatever it is he feels he must, as some insipid gesture of kindness regarding Alvin's departure from her world. And he still trusts me enough to look after her. And as if this annoyance of sharing a body, my body, were not inconvenient enough, I think she may have been speaking to M'ora."

"Fine," Joss said. "But if there's any killing involved, I'm going to cut out."

"Oh, come now, Joss. The only death I'm interested in right now is the little one."

Then Maddie felt a great pressure at the very center of her being, and the next moment, she was thrown from Matilda's body and hurtled through darkness, falling without end, her own consciousness melting away into oblivion and nothingness.

Then one, last, desperate thought:

I'm sorry, Randy. It was the last thought Maddie had for quite a long time.

"There you are. Wake up, child."

M'ora.

Maddie stirred, moving her face toward the source of light. There was snow, just at the edge of her vision, expanding into darkness. She moaned and turned around, looking up into the doorway of a small cottage; its open door was painted bright red and golden light spilled onto the snow over the doorjamb. The smell of stew emanated from within, and her stomach growled in response. She immediately thought of lamb and turnips, something she'd never cooked nor, to her memory, eaten.

The figure at the door was black against the light from behind, but as Maddie's eyes adjusted, it became clear: It was M'ora. She stood straight, but still leaned on a cane. Her eyes twinkled with something between merriment and amusement. It was the kind of look Maddie's grandmother gave her when she learned she'd done something wonderfully rebellious in her teen years.

"I can only leave the door open so long before the drafts get too bad," M'ora said, softly. She chuckled. "Unless you're enjoying yourself out there. But I can't imagine you would."

Maddie sat up slowly, her joints stiff from being in the cold so long. She brushed snow from her face, her chest, her pants. She was wearing the old sweater she'd made for Alvin again, but this time she also had mittens and a hat.

And it was very much *her* body. She felt flabby and soft, like a boiled egg. Her ankle ached as she stood, the remnants of an injury from softball when she was a teenager.

"There we are. Come now. The table's set," said M'ora, holding the door open wider.

M'ora turned and entered the cottage. Maddie looked over her shoulder into the dark surrounding the cottage, and the hair rose on the back of her neck; *her* hair, on *her* neck. But that was less important than what she saw: wolves. She could see their outlines there in the dark, see their eyes glitter hungrily. It was enough for her to nearly break into a run.

"You know that there's—" she began, glad to find her voice this time.

"Wolves. Yes. But they're here to protect me, not to hurt me. Oh, I don't think they'd think twice of making a meal out of me if I should stumble toward them, but they do a very good job of preventing anyone from getting here. Which is a comfort," M'ora said with a smile.

The table, as it turned out, was set in the middle of the one-room cottage, and laid with dinner for three. But as it was, so far Maddie saw only M'ora. Charming clay bowls were the order of the day, and the napkins had to be hand-embroidered, delicate like something out of the Biltmore, the height of Victorian elegance. Odd, considering M'ora's world was a dim medieval place. A fire roared in the hearth, and three cats switched their tails nearby, every once and again opening their eyes. The ceiling was hung with herbs dangling from the rafters.

"Simple, but it's home," M'ora said.

"It's lovely," Maddie said, going to the fire as if drawn to it.

"I told you that you could come if you wanted," M'ora

said. "And you did. I'm guessing Matilda gave you the boot?"

Maddie nodded. Her skin felt raw everywhere, even under the leggings she was wearing.

M'ora continued, "This is my world, my place, my real home. Last time we spoke we were in an in-between place, neither yours nor mine. Hard to find, those are."

"How did I get here?" Maddie asked. "I don't remember trying. Matilda just snuffed me out. I thought I was dying."

"It'd be a lot harder to kill you than that," M'ora said. "You likely couldn't get back to your own world, so you came to the closest. Mine."

Maddie found the chair surprisingly comfortable, loath as she was to leave the fire, and she signed contentedly. All of Matilda's presence was gone, not even a shadow remaining. No teeth, no wings, nothing but the peace of a crackling fire and the promise of a meal.

"Am I here in my own body?" she asked, looking at her hands. It felt right.

"Could be. But that, at the moment, is the least of our troubles." M'ora tapped her cane on the floor, then proceeded to set out tea. "There's a bad wind in the air."

Maddie took a cup of tea as it was given to her, and inhaled the soft notes of chamomile and lemon. It didn't smell like opium tea, which was a start. "Thank you, M'ora. I'm sorry—I don't know the first thing about any of this."

"You know more than you give yourself credit for. But in time… if you *have* time… I must admit I'm a little concerned," said the older woman, taking the seat opposite Maddie. "But first…"

M'ora heaved a sigh, then shook her head, her long white locks turning to curly black, the lines of her face filling and then vanishing altogether, until Maddie was looking at a reflection like her in every way save for the length of her hair and color of her skin. M'ora was beautiful, ripe as one grown in the fields themselves, and smiling. "Much better."

"You...you lied to me," Maddie said, feeling the betrayal like a kick in the chest.

"Well, age and wrinkles don't have to go hand in hand. Not if you don't want them to. Not if you're like us. In fact, none of what we are born with we have to keep. Many of us change our faces as effortlessly as some change their shoes."

"Like *us*?" Maddie rolled her eyes.

"Twains. Sisters. Cousins, relations. However you'd think of us." M'ora took Maddie's hand in hers, gently. "I must say it's absolutely cruel what Randall and Alvin have done to you."

Maddie nodded, trying to hold back tears.

"I'm assuming they haven't told you much more. And here I am, doing no better, shrouding myself in a glamour to pretend I'm something other than my own self. I suppose, at the heart, I'm just worried and... I want to trust you, Madeline. I want us both to trust each other. But I fear it isn't so easy."

Maddie frowned. "Matilda shoved me out, after she'd given me the impression we were going to be able to work it all out together..." Anger flared and she tightened her fists, then let them go. Holding on to the teacup was a better strategy. The clay felt so right, so earthly, so real. "I want to go home but–"

"You want to know about Alvin."

Taking a sip of tea, Maddie nodded, knowing how stupid it sounded. "Every sign points to the fact that he's a colossal ass-hole. But I can't let go until I know for sure. Randall was right about that, at least. I'm just not sure his methods were entirely ethical. But Randy... he's probably the only person in all the worlds I still trust, and he gave me his blessing to find Alvin. I just don't understand."

"You need closure, of course."

"And I thought Matilda was my key to that. But she kicked me out. I don't *understand.*"

"It's because you're growing more powerful. And Matilda

is frightened of you."

"Frightened of *me*?" Maddie tried not to laugh.

"There are only three of us right now, all across the Eight Worlds," M'ora said. "And Matilda has been working, with Alvin's help, to swiftly do away with us now that she knows of us. I have been hidden from her here, but I'm beginning to think she suspects."

"I *know* she does," Maddie said, shaking her head. "I'm getting the feeling that even when she's away, she's listening; I tried not to think about you, like you said, but–"

"Don't worry yourself, child. It was just a matter of time." In spite of her words, M'ora looked rather worried.

"I want to believe you. But it's like you said. Trust isn't easy," Maddie said.

M'ora sipped her tea, almost at the same moment that Maddie did, but she smiled behind her cup. Her lips were so very red that Maddie expected lipstick to stay behind.

"I have no doubt that Randall, bless his yellow little soul, has tried to tell you, as well. Matilda has, too, in her way, I'm sure. But she likes to see you squirm, likes to see you thrash about like a hooked fish."

"That's what I felt like when she was talking to Joss Raddick."

"You met Joss Raddick and she still didn't tell you?" M'ora asked, clearly shocked.

"Tell me what?"

"Why, that we're *dragons*, dear. Facets of the goddess."

"Dragons?" was all that Maddie could say.

M'ora pursed her lips, thinking. "Consider the gods, all the gods you've heard of. Gods of life and death, destruction and rebirth. So many, so similar–some strange and cruel and terrible, true. But there are threads, connecting them all. You know there are stories in every language and culture about individuals with power beyond human capabilities. Sometimes they're saints, like your St. Mary and St. Paul; sometimes they're gods, like Hephaestus, like Athena. Yes?"

"Yes..."

"Doesn't it make more sense now? The reincarnation, the twains, the sheer intelligence and capabilities of the people you've met? Your inability to connect fully with friends, your limited family? Your connections to other twains like Ian and Agnes."

Maddie wanted to dispute it, but she felt a strange flush wash over her body with the realization. It shouldn't make sense. But it did.

"God, I feel so stupid not figuring this out sooner," gasped Maddie. "And how do we die? *Do* we die? Matilda acts like she's immortal."

"No, not entirely. And that's the problem. You see, we can't be killed by usual means. We may age as we wish, past our forties, and plenty choose to; some fade, sail to strange islands in between our worlds. Other dragons may hurt us, wound us, bruise us and make us bleed. But we cannot die in the ordinary way. John hurt Miriam, there in Second, most grievously, and that is at the heart of their discord.

"No, the only way we can truly die is to be killed by one of our twains, or take our own lives. Most often, we simply diminish."

Maddie swallowed on a dry throat, then took another sip of tea. Her heart was thumping in her chest, and she was frightened. Suddenly M'ora was far more terrifying to her than before.

And Alvin. Was that what had become of his twain in her own world? It had not been an accident, after all. "So Alvin's figured it out. How to kill his twains. That's why he doesn't want to see me."

"Alvin believes that by eliminating his twains, he can be more powerful. That he can achieve full enlightenment; that he can ascend. It is rumored among us that when all other twains are eliminated in a particular set, the remaining individual would be the complete embodiment of the original god—not fragmented and cast about the worlds, as we are now. That individual could move from one world to the other, a true god in every sense, rather than merely a dragon. And with this power, not only could they kill other twains, but they would prevent any others from arising in their stead. It's a tempting fate, but it was not tried until Alvin."

"He used physics to figure out how to travel," Maddie said. "To predict certain events in time, that's what Randall said." She paused, "But he's clearly not yet a god—so he can't have done it yet, can he?"

"He has not succeeded. But throughout the ages he has tried. Alvin, Loki, Coyote, Puck, Gwydion. Many have been born and revered by mankind. He has not always been this ruthless, so our stories say, but more often than not he stirs dissent among us for his own needs."

"Someone's got to stop him," Maddie said. "But how the hell can we stop him if we can only maim him?"

"At the moment, he suspects but does not yet know where his last twain resides. But he is pressed for time. He consults his equations and knows that soon, one of those he's killed will be reborn again, and then he'll have to start all over again."

"How do you know all this?"

"I have never been reborn; I am now as I was first made, unlike you. But within you are memories of hundreds of lifetimes, and in that is a great deal of power... should you be able to access it. You are gifted, that way. Alvin would want to use it, if he could. Or else destroy you and prevent you from using that information. I suspect part of his interest in you is seeded in that knowledge; or rather, his desire for it."

Maddie could scarcely believe there was something she knew—or had the potential to know—that Alvin didn't. She would have laughed were it not for the somber atmosphere.

"That son of a bitch," said Maddie. Her tea had gone cold through the conversation, and she set it on the table. "And he was *with* me just to keep tabs on me. To test me. You don't think Randall knows, do you? About the memories?"

M'ora rose and went to the fire, rubbing her hands together. She adjusted the shawl around her shoulders and stared at Maddie. "I do not know Randall as you do, but I know his twain in this world, a man named Ravel. In my experience, his kind is not so devious, but often rather self-absorbed."

"That's not terribly heartening. I've heard him called a coward and selfish now. I sure can pick them."

"You love him?"

"I don't think I can help myself," Maddie said, feeling the weight of misery and simultaneous excitement from admitting it. "It all feels so inevitable. I would have. With Randy... but..."

"But what, child? Love is love. There is no shame in it. We are made for it, after all."

"We? And who are you suggesting *we* are?"

Maddie thought a moment, remembering what Matilda had told her before. Then it dawned on her: "Aphrodite. Matilda...she tried to tell me. She was talking about love, sex, and power. And John said I have the heart of a dove."

"Yes. Love and beauty have has many faces, my dear. You and your art, Matilda and her fashion, me and my weaving," M'ora said, gesturing to the table where the embroidered napkins were still folded. "But it's simply our ruling passion, not the one that defines us. So understand that; it is not *all* that we are. We are much more."

"And the others. Pinga was a huntress, like Artemis. But Inuit, or something close. I suppose there are plenty of parallels."

"Indeed."

"Ian. John? No idea."

"Though he is often given the name of All-Father, or Father of the Gods, he is no more than a god with the ability to create, and the honor of being the first."

Maddie bit down on her lip to keep from giggling. "Zeus? He's *Zeus*?"

"More or less. Mostly less." M'ora grinned back in response.

"And Randall. I can't quite place him."

"I called him yellow earlier. But golden is more like it. He is an avatar of knowledge and light. Of healing. He has helped to heal your heart, indeed," M'ora said. "And he is a golden child, beauty embodied. It is no surprise we are so often drawn to him."

"Apollo? Really?"

"To use your Greeks as an analogy, yes. It is said as such. You might call him Thoth, as well, or Utu, or another of the golden children."

Maddie had to stand. She was felt like crawling out of her skin; it felt too tight, too itchy, too bumpy. She wanted out, but there was nowhere to go. So she paced the floor of M'ora's cottage, wrapping her arms around her, trying to put the pieces together, excited and terrified.

"God, this is so much to absorb. So, forgive me for being so bold, but why the hell are you helping me? You're not interested in the kind of power Alvin seeks?" Maddie asked.

The other woman frowned, shaking her head, then biting down on her lower lip. "I believe that the key to healing the rifts among us has nothing to do with killing others off, and has everything to do with leaving us all to our own worlds. To preservation."

"Separate but equal, you mean?"

M'ora sighed again, and Maddie wondered if she was frustrated with her. But no sooner had she thought it than the woman smiled. "Ever since the twains began traveling between worlds, we have lost our golden age. Once, we were able to have children... now it is so rare. But now all is chaos; we are out of balance. Alvin and Matilda and their ilk are pushing us all further apart, tempting the powerful with even more power. Science and magic; together it's a horrifying business. But... not all of us have lost hope."

"It sounds hopeless."

"Well, there's one other thing, you see," said M'ora, gesturing to the empty seat beside them.

Taking another minute to compose herself, M'ora smoothed the front of her smock and went to the door that stood between a bookshelf and the fireplace. She called something softly into it, and then stood to the side.

"Coming," said a young man's voice, followed by hasty footsteps.

Then, there was Alvin; Alvin at sixteen, with moppy hair and a gawky gait, and nut-brown skin, the same impossibly dark eyes and easy smile. Seeing that face, as young as it was, still caused Maddie's stomach to drop out from beneath her. She felt like her insides had gone to liquid.

She had not believed until that moment. Not truly. The concept of Alvin living still felt intangible in spite of the wondrous things she had seen in the last few days. Now, seeing his twain before her with her own eyes—so young and innocent and new—shocked her into the true realization.

"This is my son. Arthur," said M'ora. "Arthur's predecessor is many millennia gone, and we have waited for his return. I have tried to protect him, to shield him from Alvin. But I believe Alvin will be coming for him. Soon."

Maddie bit her tongue, wanting to make a quip about the shallow gene pool, but Arthur was too sweet and sincere for her to be so cruel.

"Good day," said Arthur, his expression slightly suspicious. He looked from Maddie to M'ora and back again. "Who's this, mother? Is she your—"

"Sister," said Maddie quickly. "I'm your mother's sister,

Madeline."

"Magdalen?" asked Arthur.

"Madeline. But you can call me Maddie," said Maddie.

"Aunt Maddie, okay," he replied, grinning.

M'ora drew closer to Maddie and clasped her hands in her own, squeezing tight. Her touch was painful, burning, but Maddie endured it. "I risked a great deal in letting you through here. I put a hole in our defenses, defenses that took thousands of years to build. Alvin may now be able to breach the First World if they discover Arthur is here. So you must convince Matilda to spare you. If Alvin manages to come here, he will find us. And I have little help save the wolves."

Maddie felt the urge to cry, to sob, to gather M'ora up into her arms and cradle her there, and weep until the tears were gone and a sea had risen up around them. She did not doubt that was a possibility, considering what they were. "I just don't know how to get back. Matilda threw me out."

"Look into yourself. You have done it before. For ages you have traveled, wandered. Now should be no different," said M'ora. "Think on your greatest gift; pull it around you like a mantle, and follow the strand where you want to go."

"I can't... I..."

"Just still your soul, and follow the strand. Hold these, if it helps. Sometimes all we need is a little reminder," M'ora said, reaching down the front of her shirt. She pulled out a string of eight pearls, large as muscadine grapes, and pressed them into Maddie's hands.

Sitting down, Maddie set her jaw.

Then she closed her eyes, tears falling down her cheeks.

"Now, you must return to Matilda. You must save yourself. Only then do we have hope of redeeming Alvin, and saving Arthur. I believe it is what Randy wanted."

"I'll try," Maddie said, clutching the string of pearls. One was darker than the rest; instinctively, she knew it was First

World, where she was. To the right, Second. She pressed the second pearl to her lips and breathed deep.

At first, nothing happened. She could hear M'ora's fire, sense the sturdy chair beneath. She almost sobbed for the feeling of failure. Then she tried to remember the stillness of meditation. She imagined that the seat sank away from her, and she went down through the floor, feeling her limbs fly out from her sides, suspended in air as if gravity had given up.

And she thought of Randy, the first time she had seen him, standing to the side of the Lichtenstein at the Fine Arts Center and it felt as if she was exploding from within as a huge expression of energy and light filled up the darkness entirely.

Out of the blinding white light, she saw eight spheres emerge, brilliant as polished opal. She guided herself toward the brightest one, pressing forward what was left of her being. She had a sudden, violent image of herself in Dr. Keats's bathroom, Randy towering over her with a concerned look on his face. She was slumped on the black and white tile floor, bleeding from the nose. Her home world called her.

But if Matilda didn't manage to kill her off now, she would find her later. And the last thing she wanted to unleash on her world was the venom of one such as her. Maddie was tired of running away, tired of turning tail. She was done with it.

So she turned toward the opal spheres and followed one of the strands—the polar opposite, as in her own compact. Her compass. Second World. She could feel it. The sphere of Second World was a million colors, refracting and moving in light and time, but as she approached it, the surface shifted, became smooth and shiny. It was a mirror, a window, a portal. And there, the side of Matilda's face, bent closely over another: Joss Raddick.

She continued on, and followed the strand, a bolt of white energy projecting from the heart of her into the next world.

A Considerable Distance

nce again you're interrupting, Matilda said as soon as Maddie was joined with her again. I didn't expect you to get back so soon.

Maddie was blazing with anger, and it felt good.

We're nearly finished... give me just a moment... For all her airs, Maddie could tell Matilda was indeed frightened.

Matilda was tangled—predictably—with Joss Raddick between soft, satin sheets in the captain's own chambers. He was positively ravaging Matilda, bent over behind her, grasping her and pounding her, grunting and grumbling in a most unattractive manner.

We need to talk.

I'm a bit occupied at the moment.

Too. Bad. Maddie snarled.

For the entire time that Maddie had been part of Matilda, she had been thinking of the body they shared as a horse. There were reins, though they had no physical presence, and sometimes they were relinquished to her. When opium was involved, Matilda always had the upper hand.

This time, it was quite beyond the opium. Now it was just a battle of wills.

Maddie concentrated, stilled herself. She reached down deep into the center of her—into whatever essence of her there truly was left. She filled her mind with her fury; she stoked her thoughts with anger. Anger over Alvin abandoning her and Randy, about Matilda and Randall betraying her. It stoked the flames, gave her focus and strength.

And inch by inch, she was gaining on Matilda. Maddie first started by falling in rhythm with Matilda, familiar with the push and pull of lovemaking and anticipating Matilda would be somewhat distracted.

The thighs; *yes,* she had control. She leaned slightly to the left and Matilda didn't even break stride. This was good. Very good.

Enjoy the void, Matilda, Maddie said, and with all her might pressed through. It felt like she was being squeezed through a rabbit hole far too small for her body, but she managed to come out on the other side, casting Matilda aside utterly.

Then, with a rush of musky air, Maddie realized she had complete control. She felt a protest from Matilda, but ever so vaguely, and then pushed back against the tide with all her physical strength, so that Joss fell off the side of the bed, completely off balance.

"Agh!" he cried, grasping his side. He flew into the side table and the lovely blue hurricane lamp crashed down behind him, its shade shattering into a hundred shards of green and gold. "Good hells, Mattie!"

Still disoriented—and yet again completely naked and in the presence of a stranger—Maddie scurried to the side of the bed and searched for Matilda's boots. There they were, propped up against the bedpost of the ramshackle bed. The derringer. She took it in both hands and stood, stark naked and shivering, leveling it at Joss.

"I knew you were fickle, but this is ridiculous," the captain said, looking quite genuinely wounded. "I swear every time this is going to be the last, and then you get me to change my damned mind with your big brown eyes."

"Shut up for a sec, okay?" Maddie said. "Keep it down." The humor was not lost on her, though, and she almost laughed.

"Ma—oh, I see," Joss said, slinking up against the wall, breathing hard. His blond hair was plastered across one side of his face, and much of him had flushed a most uncomely red. He had to be embarrassed. "Pushed the old lady aside, then, have you? Finally figured it all out?"

"You could say that. Nice to meet you, Captain Raddick," Maddie said. "Officially."

"She's going to be hopping mad when she gets back, you know," he said, raising his hands in the air. "Matilda Roth doesn't like people meddling with her affairs."

"Well, I don't like people trying to *murder* me. So, let's consider it a draw."

Joss rubbed the back of his head like a scolded child. "Sorry how this looks, I just…"

"Can't resist, I know," Maddie said. "It's our thing."

"Well, it's more than that. I don't… I don't get to see many others like me."

"Wait. You're one, too?" Maddie asked. "How can you possibly stand her?"

"Ah, well. She wasn't always so terrible."

"How would you know?" spat Maddie. Her anger still pulsed around her, great and terrible and comforting.

Joss looked genuinely sad, his hard features softening. He looked older, more careworn, as he experienced this new depth of emotion. "I remember them in their last life, Randall and Matilda. I know what they went through to get here, and it's a damn shame it worked out this way this time around." He frowned, narrowing his dark eyes, measuring her. "Trust me.

You don't know what you're in for, I'll tell you that."

"Then *enlighten* me." Now Maddie had the thrill of the hunt in her. She was facing down Joss Raddick and he had fear in his eyes. She liked the feeling.

Joss rubbed his nose on the back of his hand. Clearly he wasn't getting up from where he was; which was a relief, seeing as that the gun was not going to do her much good if he did. "Back up a bit," he said. "Put the gun down. *You* can't kill me, at least not with the gun. Let's start this over again."

Maddie lowered the gun, however hesitantly. She had half a mind to shoot him, just to see if it was going to work. He was still breathing hard, sweat beading on his chest, but he looked sincere. And she was exhausted. Going back and forth like that, then pushing Matilda out of the picture, had sapped her of most of her energy.

"Fine," she said, and reached to put a robe around her. Sure, it wasn't her body, but it was still cold in the room.

"I'm Joseph Raddick," he said. "Captain of the River Guard. Captain of... well, the rivers, oceans, lakes, and other such bodies of water. And believe it or not, you and I have often been friends."

"Poseidon?"

"Once, in another world, perhaps. Here, I just prefer to stay near the water."

Maddie nodded. "Madeline Angler. From the Sixth World. Apparently I'm the mighty Aphrodite."

Before Maddie could say more, the door in the room next door banged against the wall, shocking both of them into silence, and derailing Maddie's train of thought entirely. The wall thundered three times, the windowpanes shaking with the effort.

And someone was shouting. More than one person.

The timbre was familiar. A voice Maddie had not heard in over a year.

"Is that... Alvin?" she whispered to Joss.

Joss frowned. "Sounds like his particular brand of arrogant and furious. He was supposed to stay on the *Faust*. I promised I'd wring his neck if he didn't..."

Maddie tried to brace herself. She knew she should. But there wasn't time for it.

Apparently discovering that the adjacent room was the incorrect address, the door to their room flew open on its hinges, and Alvin Roth stood there, swaying drunkenly on his legs. He'd lost weight, his face was bloody and bruised, and he reeked of whisky.

But it wasn't long before the source of the noise followed, and Randall Roth barreled into him from behind and began punching him.

Maddie shrieked, half out of surprise and relief at seeing Randall and half because she simply had no words to express her current emotional state.

Alvin. It really was Alvin.

Randall held nothing back. He was far more fit than his brother, and nowhere near as drunk. His hair had come undone from its lace and was unkempt about his shoulders, and his riding attire was torn in half a dozen places. His jaw was bruised, but he'd taken far less of a beating from his brother.

But there was no mistaking the look in Randall Roth's eyes. Maddie had seen so much goodness, kindness, in him before, that seeing the rage behind his eyes actually made her a bit afraid. He blazed with it.

"Get up, you *coward!*" shouted Randall, shaking Alvin, who had apparently given up the fight. "I'm not done with you!"

Alvin had passed out, but Randall didn't care. So Maddie jumped into the fray, trying to get Randall off of Alvin, moved by some strange, almost maternal reflex. This was not the way her reunion with Alvin was supposed to be!

But Randall was too far gone, too furious. There was noth-

ing she could do; he didn't even seem to recognize her as she
called his name and tried in vain to grab his arms.

Then Joss thundered. He stood, naked and terrible and
unmoving, and let out a sound that made the ground tremble. It was the thrumming of the ocean, the deep tones of the
depths, and Randall shuddered, stopped, and slowly backed
away from his brother.

"I'm sorry... I..." Randall tried to get the words out failing.

"Just what the hell is going on here?" Maddie demanded.
"I thought you were staying behind?"

"Maddie?" Randall asked, blue eyes searching hers.

"Yup."

"Thank heavens. Get me a drink," Randall said. "And I
can explain."

"Here, kid," Joss said to Randall. "Help me get Alvin up
into the bed, and then I'll get dressed and get you as much
whisky as you want."

After being moved, Alvin was still out cold. Whether it
was from alcohol or trauma, or both, Maddie couldn't guess.
Apparently twains were still capable of passing out from pain.
But she brought some ice and water, and they put him in the
bed, just the same.

As she waited, she dressed again, but she was terribly nervous, and kept stealing glances at Alvin.

Alvin looked just as always, save for the attire, which was
drab and rather pitiful, especially considering this world and
its remarkably high sense of fashion. But the rest of him was
the same. His hair was longer, grown just over his ears, and it
curled familiarly at the nape of his neck. How many times had
she kissed him there? Drawn her fingers through the hair? She'd
known every inch of his body, once, every freckle and crease.

But the more that she looked at him, the more she saw a
stranger. It wasn't just the bruises or the swelling; it was as if
something inside of him were different. As if some light inside

of him was extinguished, making him unrecognizable, the way certain light brought out a painting just right. Or wrong.

Maddie didn't know what to say to Randall. She was angry with him for being so cautious with her, for doling out the details of what exactly it meant to be a twain so slowly.

"I could have handled it, you know," she said to him, while they waited for Joss to return with the whisky. She handed him a scrap of cloth to hold over his bleeding cheek. "The whole godling thing. The *dragons.*"

Randall winced, cradling his cheek with the cloth. "Joss told you?"

"I... I figured it out," Maddie lied, not yet willing to share about M'ora. "Matilda tried to tell me. She toyed with me about it. But eventually I figured it out," she said. No, that wasn't entirely the truth, but it made her feel good to have one-upped Randall a little.

"I'm sorry."

"You say that a lot."

"I know," Randall said, shaking his head. "I've a penchant for self-preservation, you might say."

"Still, you came back. Thank you," she said. Maddie wanted to go to him, to envelop him in kisses and stroke his hair. But she held on to the bedpost, instead, staring at Alvin.

Randall watched her and they sat in silence until Joss returned.

"So start from the beginning," Joss said to Randall, as the latter sat nursing a generous glass of whisky. "I've never seen you two boys at it like that before, and I can only guess what the problem is." He looked pointedly at Maddie. "Now I know Alvin's breaking. I can see that. But pummeling his head ain't gonna help."

Randall frowned. "When Maddie left with Matilda, I went back to my office. I started rifling around Alvin's old things. Thinking, a great deal, about what Maddie had said to me before she left. That I saw too much good in Alvin to judge him correctly."

"Don't we all," Maddie said.

"I never spent too much time with his papers. They were disorganized and, frankly, not my strength. So I trusted him in his part; John did not. John told me, repeatedly, that he suspected Alvin was up to more than simply wandering. But I never imagined that he was capable of something so terrible."

"Killing off his twains, you mean?" Maddie asked. She angled up her chin and folded her arms across her chest.

Randall and Joss both stared at her. The silence was satisfying.

"Apparently he's schooled Matilda, too," Joss added. "Maddie's been back from what sounds like something of a harrowing experience."

"Matilda?"

It was Alvin.

Maddie startled, and felt her throat tighten. She'd almost forgotten about him. It was much more comfortable thinking he was sleeping than awake. That scheming brain of his was a danger, even if he was losing his mind.

Randall was already out of his seat, ready for another round, but Joss shot him a warning glance, and they simply watched as Alvin roused more fully.

Alvin blinked, then lifted himself up on the bed. Then he fixed his eyes on Maddie, and his expression went from puzzlement to surprise.

"Maddie..." he said with a long sigh.

"Hi," was all Maddie managed.

She didn't want to cry. It would ruin everything. It would make her look weak and fragile, it would make her vulnerable. The men in the room—two of them, at least—had a newfound respect for her. But now she was risking that all with tears because she still loved Alvin. Because she had mourned for him for so long in the dark, in anger and frustration, and now she saw him again. The raw, wounded part of her from the months after his disappearance had not healed.

"Oh, don't cry," Alvin said, a note of true pity piercing through.

"It's so easy to think you're just a monster," Maddie said, drawing back toward the window. She wiped her face with her sleeve. "Except, here you are. God, Alvin. Here you are."

Randall took a few steps closer, and kept his arms crossed. "I told you, I couldn't stand by and watch her suffer on account of you."

Alvin blinked, wiped his hands over his eyes. "Maddie, I can explain."

Maddie tried again. How could she ever get it right? She didn't have enough words to tell Alvin what she felt. So she said, "You have no idea what you put me through."

"I put you through exactly what you needed," Alvin said, sitting up abruptly. He was gaining in strength again, that same arrogance changing his features, hardening him. "You are far more fully realized than when you were in your home world. That it took Randall's meddling is a little unfortunate, considering you really could find better company."

"What do you mean? Randall has been nothing but a gentleman. Mostly," Maddie said.

Alvin laughed, bitter and derisive. "A gentleman? Really?"

"Alvin," Randall warned. "Now is not the time for this discussion."

"Oh, I think now is exactly the time for this discussion, my dear brother," Alvin said with a bitter laugh. "Or were you hoping she'd never find out? That you'd remain her knight in shining armor, protecting her from me and giving her the love Randy never could."

Randall went a most unusual shade of pale, blanching his usually handsome features like sun-bleached parchment.

"Alvin, please," Randall said through clenched teeth.

"Oh, I see. You haven't *told* her about Randy," Alvin said with a triumphant grin.

Maddie looked at Randall. "What *about* Randy?" Her ears started ringing, and she felt her blood pressure rise. Up until that moment she had believed Randall to be the most forthright with her, the single person she could truly trust in this godforsaken—*gods*-forsaken—world. He was the closest to Randy; he had to be good at heart.

Randall didn't respond. He didn't even look at her. He just buried his head in his hands.

"Randall." Maddie said his name in a whisper, tears returning again even before she could stop them. "Tell me."

"I was waiting until the right time," Randall said, lamely.

Maddie stared at him, searching his eyes for clues; but Randall was fixed on Alvin. "What's he talking about, Randall?" she asked again. "You didn't hurt Randy. Tell me you didn't hurt him…"

"So prescient, my dear," Alvin said. He folded his hands on his stomach, like he did when he lectured.

With a drawn-out sigh, Randall closed his eyes. "I made a miscalculation. Something happened during the first switch, the first time I visited Randy."

"He got scared, and he panicked," corrected Alvin. "Magic, unchecked, is a mighty dangerous thing. And he was like a flailing fish out of water, poking holes all throughout Randy's consciousness. A bit like Swiss cheese. Or Lorraine, come to think of it."

Maddie sunk down into the bed, the springs creaking and helping her keep a grasp on reality. A normal sound in what was feeling more and more like an entirely abnormal universe. "His accident. You caused his accident."

"Not all of us are as talented as you and Matilda, let alone Alvin," murmured Joss, who had been standing quietly by the

window. "Sometimes the switch is far more difficult than anticipated–especially going into Sixth World. Most of us don't
even try."

Maddie gasped, trying to breathe. She had the sensation
that someone had kicked her in the gut, and she wanted to cry,
but the tears were reluctant through the shock. "You made him
that way? You broke him, Randall? *You* hurt Randy? And you
didn't tell me?"

"I tried to tell you," Randall said. "Yesterday, after the gala."

"I do enjoy a lover's quarrel," Alvin intoned from the bed.

"How many did *you* break, Alvin? How many did you
kill?" Randall asked, his voice rising with such intensity that
Maddie startled. He was blazing again, his hands balled into
fists. "At least I made peace with Randy. Made friends with
him, as much as I could. How many have you destroyed in the
name of your 'research'?"

Alvin was staring at Randall, challenging him. Maddie felt
something flicker inside her breast, painful and hot as a cinder. She watched as Alvin's eyes went black, the brown vanishing and the pupil completely taking over. He may have been
bruised and bent, but he was not powerless.

They all felt the threat.

But what could they do? None of them had the power
to kill one another; they could duke it out, and Maddie had a
feeling that Alvin's capabilities were quite beyond anything she
could imagine, but it would leave them nowhere. She couldn't
risk being wounded; none of them could.

"Did you figure it out all on your own, Randall?" Alvin
asked. "Or did my self-righteous little dove over here help you
out?"

"We came to separate conclusions," Randall replied.

"Well, as much as I'd like to continue this conversation, I
think it's time I left," Alvin said. "I am close to finding my last
twain, and when I do..."

"You're cracking, man," Joss said. "Give it up. You'll be doing everyone a favor."

Alvin didn't even seem to hear Joss. "And technically Matilda's problem, even though my dear brother set all of this into motion," Alvin said. "So I think I'll leave it to her."

When a coal popped in the hearth, Maddie jumped. Her vision was going sparkly around the edges, the harbinger of a fainting spell. A harbinger of Matilda. She stared down at her feet, the tapered ends of her boots peeking out from beneath her dress.

She didn't have much time, and she wouldn't be safe for long. Chances were when Matilda came for her, she was dead.

So, the way Maddie saw it, she didn't have too much to lose. She might as well try.

"Alvin, this isn't you," Maddie said, at last. She approached him, put her hands on his shoulders. He let her.

Then she held out her hands, and he put his in them automatically. It was the most familiar and yet discomfiting feeling she had yet in this Second World. The ground felt insubstantial around her feet as she held him, and though she smiled through it, she wanted to vomit.

"Alvin," Maddie said, gentle as she could, breathing evenly to calm herself. She thought of the power she'd used on Randall, her ability to blaze with love and affection, with lust and temptation.

She wanted to envelop him in her magic, ensure that he could never leave—if that's what she had to do. It might mean losing Randall, but if Alvin really was as mad as M'ora believed him to be, then it would also mean saving Randall's life. And potentially many more, considering no one knew what Alvin would be capable of, were he to achieve full godhood.

"Come home with me," Maddie said. Part of her was still mourning him, she realized—not still, but again. He was dying before her, though he was very much alive. This was not a death of the body but of the spirit. She could sense the fault lines in him, like Joss had said: He was cracking, no doubt from killing himself across the eight worlds. "Alvin, let's go back home. Together. We can start again. We were happy once, what says we can't be again?"

He let go of Maddie's hands, and she could tell by the look in his eyes that he was completely immune to whatever magic she was trying to use. She might as well have been trying to woo a redwood. "There isn't any going back. You know nothing of this; there is no choice. This is how it always works."

"What do you mean, how it always works? You can make a different choice, Alvin," said Maddie. She was clenching her teeth, and her chest felt tight as a fist.

"This is how it's always been," said Alvin. "It's survival of the fittest, as simple as that. Some of us can rise to the call, and others shy away. I was made for this purpose and this purpose alone. I am the bravest of my twains in two thousand years, and I'm not about to give up now. Who am I to question what I am?"

She choked back a sob. "You think you're a god, but you're nothing more than a murderer."

Alvin chuckled. "I'm not a god yet. But I'm very close. And I'll be damned if you'll interrupt what's taken me over a hundred years to plan."

"A *hundred* years?" she echoed, looking at Randall and then to Joss. "That long?"

Alvin looked over at his brother and nodded. "Yes, at least that long. Randall's helped me considerably, though he's never known the full extent of it. I knew he wouldn't exactly approve."

"You damned fool. You're killing yourself, can't you see? Your body is wasting away," Randall said. "You're hardly more than a shell."

"What does it matter? Soon, I won't need it. And as to

promises? I convinced Randall to help me with promises. But what are oaths to me?" Alvin said with a shrug. He started walking toward the door, but Joss Raddick walked into his path. "Just words, words, words..."

"How can you be so selfish?" asked Maddie. "You've got nothing left but yourself."

Alvin pulled out a ring of keys from his pocket, for the moment ignoring Joss's presence at the door, and checked their order. Then he said, "Well, yes. That is precisely the hope. But it isn't just my desire for power. It's *science*. It's study. It's multiverses and fractals and quantum theory, and a host of other concepts you'll find far too boring to even bother with. That's how you've always been."

"Consider me ripe for a new lesson," Maddie said through gritted teeth.

Alvin laughed again, high-pitched and manic. "You really think that our five years together means anything to me? It's but the flap of a butterfly wing in this vast universe. I tried to give you lessons, Maddie, but you've always proved too dull and caring." He paused to acknowledge his brother with a wink. "In that way, you two make an excellent match. But then again, you always have. In Sixth World, I was just given a leg up, considering Randy's condition—courtesy of my darling brother, ironically enough. I'd never have had a chance, otherwise."

"At least Randall's not a murderer," Maddie said, which, all things considered, was not that much of an accolade.

"I really don't have time for any more discussion with you, Maddie. Now Randall, Joss, you're more than welcome to come along. No hard feelings, I hope."

Then he raised his voice and closed his eyes. "Matilda—I beg you, send this little dove back where she belongs, and join me. I've had enough of her."

Alvin started for the door and Maddie could feel Matilda pulling at her consciousness, dragging her down with as much power as she possessed. Her skin felt slack, her bowels clenching, as she struggled against the pull.

And for a brief moment she was in control again.

Words were not working. So Maddie lunged at him. She tried to strike him, but he caught her wrist, his hands clammy and familiar. Then she screamed, "I stayed here to find you, damnit, because I loved you!"

Alvin sighed, lowering her arm. "No, you stayed here because you have some bizarre sense of duty to Randy. You can't save me. I've saved *myself.*" Alvin grinned wider, his eyes narrowing as a realization struck him. She'd seen the look a thousand times when he achieved some great advance working on his theorems. "But something isn't right. You know too much. I can feel Matilda trying to break through and yet you're keeping her at bay."

"Let go of me," Maddie protested.

"Don't you dare touch her!" Randall said as he moved forward, helping Maddie out of Alvin's grasp. She didn't let him hold her long, either, and sent him a look that could have melted ice. Joss was ready to come to her defense, as well, strange as it was. Maybe the fickle man of the sea was not as self-serving as he'd appeared before.

You won't last long. Matilda predicted. You might as well give up now.

Maddie was exhausted. Her grasp on Second World was slowly dissipating.

Alvin closed his eyes and smiled serenely. "Of course. It makes sense now. She's been to First World. How could we have been so blind!" He laughed. "At last!"

"No–no–" Maddie argued, trying still to keep consciousness. "I don't know what you're talking about."

"Methinks the lady doth protest too much," Alvin quoted Shakespeare, looking greedily at her. "Well, isn't that an unexpected felicity! You've opened up a beacon into the First World.

How astonishing. You succeeded where Matilda could not."

Alvin began to laugh, and he clapped his hands together. There was a whooshing sound, and then he said: "Come, Matilda. Let's get this over with."

Maddie struggled desperately hold the reins, to keep a finger-hold on Matilda's body. But she was too tired and too sad; she didn't even have the strength to speak.

Her vision swam and the world shimmered, moved. Colors ran together like pastels on the sidewalk in the rain. Her grasp on the body was wrenched away, like someone wresting her fingers with a crowbar. She bent over, trying to keep concentration on her perspective, but she was longer able to. Matilda overcame her, laughing triumphantly.

The game had changed.

"I'm here, Alvin," Matilda said, through the lips Maddie was using just moments ago. Maddie could barely hear what was going on; all sound was bent and moving as if she were under water. "Just waiting for the right moment to appear; it was quite dramatic there for a moment, wasn't it?"

"As always, a flawless entrance. Very good, then," said Alvin.

"Shall I do away with her now?" Matilda asked. Her tone was greedy.

Alvin paused, considering. "We don't have time for that, especially considering she'd be your first. For now, send her home. But be sure she knows if she attempts to leave Sixth, she's dead."

"I can make sure of that," Matilda said. She sounded disappointed to be denied destruction. "At the very least we know how to get to First World, now."

Maddie sensed Randall's presence dimly, and thought about what Alvin had said about Randy.

So this was it.

The sorrow of her knowledge of Randall's lies was all-encompassing, sending her into complete darkness. She had loved him. She had loved so many, and been broken by them all. Why should she fight anymore? The darkness in her mind was worse than the one pressing around what remained of her being.

The First World. She had foolishly led them there. Likely Matilda had used her, this entire time, for just such a purpose. M'ora would never have welcomed Matilda, but she had welcomed Maddie unquestioningly. And now Arthur would die, so innocent and young and perfect.

This time, fading was worse than death. Maddie was enveloped in complete numbness. The blackness that surrounded her was paralyzing, the kind of thing she feared as a child—an impermeable darkness so pervasive that it was like being drowned in tar. She was nothing; she was nowhere. But she could tell. She knew. There was no sleep here, no dreams, no escape...

She hit the floor, hard.

When Maddie opened her eyes it was not to the glow of gas lamps or candles, but to cool fluorescent light.

"Madeline?" asked a voice, distant and distinctly British. "Randy, would you please get that towel for me?"

"Dr. Keats?" asked Maddie, opening her eyes slowly. Her eyelids felt like lead. "Randy?"

She was on the floor of Dr. Keats's bathroom, what felt like just moments after she had touched the mirror. She smelled the singed scent of the oil heater, the bleach cleaner in the toilet bowl, a hint of ammonia. There was blood in between the black and white tile, which explained the stuffy feeling in her nose, and the warm, pulsing pain.

"I'm sorry to have upset you—" Dr. Keats was saying. "I

may need to call the ambulance."

Maddie tried to sit up. "I think I just slipped and fell. I was..."

Dreaming?

When she sat up, there was pain, but welcome pain. With the pain came the familiarity of her own body—her true body. She looked at her hands—definitely her own: plumper, the nails pared down and painted sparkly red. There was a chip on the right index finger; she'd done that playing guitar, a few days ago, in a lame attempt to remember the chords she used to know.

"Madeline?" asked Dr. Keats again.

"I'm fine," said Maddie. "I totally spaced out and had a really wacky dream and—"

Randy's voice came unexpectedly from behind her. "I've got the towel, Dr. Keats. Maddie? You okay?"

Maddie turned around, her body awash in gooseflesh. There was Randy, looking concerned, handing her the towel in his elegant hands. He was as she'd left him, hair tousled. Innocent. Beautiful.

But in a totally different outfit.

She burst into tears.

"Dear Lord," Dr. Keats said. "I'm sorry, I should have told you about this from the beginning, but I admit to thinking you might be beyond your realm of understanding..."

"Oh, you have no idea what I'm capable of understanding," she said, sniffling. Her eyes were puffy and red, and she had to pee something fierce. "Have I been standing here the whole time?"

"You... phased," Dr. Keats said. "You flickered. You were partially transparent, at times, and at other times entirely gone. It was not as I expected. But I am immensely glad to see you. Did you find Alvin?"

Her whole body ached, especially at her ribs. She grabbed a fistful of toilet paper and started wiping her face with one hand while searching for the cause of her pain with the other.

There was something in her sweater pocket.

Her fingers touched something cold, etched, circular. She pulled it out.

In the bright light of the bathroom, the compact looked ethereal. The eight-pronged star's design was so delicate as to be laid upon the silver with frost. But Maddie didn't open it. She let the realization sink in, licked her lips, took deep, greedy breaths of bathroom air.

"Shit," she said at last. "Just... *shit.*"

Dr. Keats was blinking at the compact. "That's the symbol of Ishtar. The top of that is clearly an artifact from considerably before the Christian period–Sumerian, I think–though it's been attached to a curious Victorian contraption–"

"Sounds about right," Maddie muttered.

Maddie steadied herself on the sink, giving a sidelong glance to the mirror. "You fucking bitch," she hissed, wishing Matilda were there so she could slap her across the face. "I can't believe I trusted you!"

"Pardon?" asked Dr. Keats.

No, Maddie had enough regrets. "Listen, Dr. Keats. I need to talk to Randy. Alone. And preferably not in the bathroom," she said.

Who knew how much time she had? It was imperative that she reach First World and warn M'ora, if she could. She had the compact, and that was a start–but who would she contact, and would it even work?

Dr. Keats began to argue, but Maddie shot him a look so venomous, he backed up and relented. "Of course. There's a sitting room, two doors to the left. It used to be my wife's–"

"Good enough. Come on, Randy. Let's talk," she said.

She took his hand and he squeezed back. Just holding him grounded her. Kept her from flying off the handle. There was so much to process; just concentrating on the simple act of getting him to the sitting room was enough.

The sitting room was a graveyard of books, and Maddie had to throw half a dozen volumes to the ground before she found a decent place to sit. Randy looked perplexed, but he seemed more concerned about her than anything. He sat when she asked him to.

Closing the door Maddie took a deep breath, trying to steady herself. Her body felt like she'd just run a marathon and she was ridiculously hungry. And she still had to pee.

"Randy, this is very important. I need you to listen to me," she said. "Can you do that?"

"Of course," Randy said. "I love you, Maddie."

"I love you too, Randy. Which is why you need to listen very carefully." She knelt in front of him, placing his hands on her heart. "I found Alvin, but... he's broken, Randy. The only way I can get back to him is if I try and talk to the other you. Can you do that for me?"

Randy stiffened, his face going blank. "He always asks to talk to you, but I tell him no."

She knew she couldn't simply argue with him, so she asked him a question instead. Sometimes that helped. "Why do you tell him no?"

"Because he loves you. And..." Randy looked away, tugging at his ear.

"I know he loves me, Randy. And it's okay."

"But *you* love me. And you love *Alvin*," Randy argued. "If you love him, you can't love the rest of us."

It was a valid point. But only to a degree. "Sweetie, I love you the same. I will never stop loving you. My love for you is as big as the universe." Universes.

Randy didn't look back at her, but started pulling at the edge of his shirt.

"Randy," she said. "You told me to find Alvin, and I have. But there are a lot of people who are going to suffer if I can't

talk to the other you. Alvin has made some bad choices, and
the only way we can stop him from getting into more trouble
is if I talk to—"

"To Randall. Yeah. I just don't want him to hurt me
again," Randy said. "It's okay when he watches. But if he comes
through more, it hurts."

He had tears in his eyes.

"I know it hurts, but he'll be careful. I know he will." She
was half saying it to convince herself. Deep down, she believed
Randall had kept the secret of hurting Randy from her so she
would trust him. Now the realization was raw in her chest, and
she bit her lip to cast away tears. "You can visit him and bring
him here. Do you know how to do that?"

Randy nodded reluctantly.

"If you can't let him through, then at least give him a message. Tell him that I'm trying my best to get to First. That Alvin's twain is there. *That I have the compact.* Can you do that?" It
was worth a shot.

"You have to give me something," Randy said.

"Sure, whatever you want, whatever I can give," Maddie said.

"A kiss."

There was no hesitation. He said it and gave her a very
pointed look. No joking—not that Randy was a joker by any
stretch of the imagination—and his blue eyes stayed steady and
unblinking.

"What?" Maddie flushed immediately, drawing back.

She had gotten very close to him, having knelt down in
the process of begging him to contact Randall. Now she saw
the unfairness of it. Randy's entire adult life had been compromised because of Randall, and Maddie had then gone and slept
with him, mostly because Randall reminded her of Randy in
the first place.

"It's a good idea," Randy said. He reached out to touch

the side of her face.

"Randy..."

"Please. Just kiss me," he implored, as normal and as rational-sounding as any man in a similar situation.

She took a deep breath and put her own hand on his cheek, stroking the fine stubble there. Without the glasses, he didn't look quite so much like Randall, but it didn't make it any easier. Maddie tried to separate the two men in her mind, but they blurred. Her heart loved them both, and it seemed there was nothing she could do about that. As much as she despised Randall at the moment, she needed to speak to him.

"I'm going to have to leave, Randy. To see the other me," she said, gently in his ear. He sighed like a bellows and nuzzled his cheek to hers. She felt desire rise in her like a tide and swallowed. "I'll be back if I can, but I want you to stay here and take care of your mom; take care of yourself."

"Kiss," Randy reminded her.

Maddie nodded and brought her lips to his. She sensed instantly that her assumption of his sexual innocence was wrong; after a heartbeat of gentle kissing, he became more forward. Randy's mouth was as expert as her own, and she tried to pull away, breathless, only by virtue of her own will and knowledge that her time was short.

But the kiss deepened, became something more. There were memories there, memories of a thousand lifetimes. Maddie as a woman, as a man; Randy as a man, as a woman. A hundred cycles reborn and reunited. A perfect union of friendship; a perfect storm of dissonance. She saw it all rise and fall before her eyes, connecting her on an unfathomable level to this man who had so found his way to her heart and in that moment, she knew what she was giving up. She and Randy were meant for each other in a way she would never have with Randall. With anyone, for that matter.

She had to tell him. She had to let him know. "Randy,"

she whispered, pulling away.

But when she looked into his eyes, Randy was gone.

Those were Randall's eyes.

"You!" she shouted, stumbling back. The memories had disoriented her. "I wasn't finished talking to Randy."

Randall started to say something, stood up, and vomited.

"Great. You just barfed all over Sartre," she said, gesturing to the offended volume.

"This is extremely disorienting," Randall said, his accent clearer now than it had been in Second World. Had Matilda's ears distorted her hearing? Now he sounded almost British. Upper crust, absolutely. But the tones of his voice were the same. "It's surprisingly like moving a puppet. And the language! This is fascinating. You can understand me?"

"Yeah, clear as day," she said, recalling how odd the language of Second World sounded to her if she tuned her ear just right.

Maddie wanted to kick him in the knees, but she restrained herself. He was not feeling well, and heaved again.

"Welcome to Sixth World. Come for the inter-world intrigue and murder, stay for the Twinkies and Coke," she said.

"We have to get Dr. Keats," Randall said, coming up for air.

"Where's Randy? You didn't hurt him, did you?"

"No, gods, no. Maddie—he's here," Randall said, tapping his temple. He noticed the shorter hair and pulled at it, thoughtfully. "I came as quickly as I could, but time is running out. You have the compact?"

Maddie nodded, patting her sweater pocket. He reached out to touch her and she flinched away from him.

"I'm sorry," he tried.

"Later," insisted Maddie. "Right now we have to deal with Dr. Crankypants out there."

"We need his aid. He's the one that helped Alvin travel. With his assistance, I can figure out a way to get you to First

World. If that's what you want."

"Alvin's final twain is there."

"I know," Randall said, taking her by the shoulder. Maddie picked up his hand by the wrist and moved it off since he clearly wasn't getting the message.

"Not right now, buddy," she said. "You seriously have no idea how mad I am at you, do you?"

"I just want you to be certain of this. You *do* know that Matilda will try and kill you..."

"Randall, I can't let Alvin get away with this."

"I know. It's only that I didn't have a chance to tell you–"

"I said *later.*"

11

Journey

D r. Keats was right outside the door, and Maddie wasn't in the mood for playing games. So she pointed to Randall.

"Randall's here," she announced, looking at Dr. Keats. "I'm guessing you've met."

Dr. Keats's eyes went wide, and he looked back at Randall, then to Maddie. "Ah, more or less..."

Maddie took a breath and gave the doctor the most cordial smile she could muster. "Okay. So, Alvin's going to First World, where we think he's going to kill someone. And Randall here seems to think you can get me there."

The professor's face drained of all color, and he was backing up into the hallway. "This is all highly improbable. Alvin said—"

"I don't care what Alvin said," Maddie said, "if you don't do this, we're all screwed."

She took a step toward Dr. Keats, who was now bracing himself on the wall opposite the bathroom door. Maddie felt that same sense of power flood over her that she'd experienced in Second World. But this time the source was not passion and love, but flowing from protection, from anger. All that was standing between Alvin and the ruin of his own twains was her and Randall. If Dr. Keats couldn't help her, the ramifications for her world—and every world that Alvin had touched—would be quite beyond their reach.

"You know what I'm talking about," Maddie said. "Alvin had theories. Dangerous theories. And now, there's just one more death between him and total chaos.

"Oh, Alvin, you *didn't...*" sighed Dr. Keats. He pressed his fingers to his eyes and shivered. "Yes. There are ways. But the First World is difficult. Third and Fifth would be easy, but First?"

"*How* difficult?" Maddie said.

"I can bring you to the door, but the traveling... you have to do that on your own. And there is great risk," Dr. Keats said. "You're not trained; it's a procedure that, to the uninitiated, may result in—"

"What? *Death*? I think I'm beyond that at his point," Maddie said.

Dr. Keats shook his head. "I have no idea what could happen to you; the result could be worse than death. And we have no idea what might happen if we attempt to send Randall through in Randy's body. What happened to Randy in the first place—the damage that was done during the event—there's no telling what may happen with this attempt."

"We'll figure it out," Randall said. "We haven't got a choice."

What followed could not be described as exact science, or as magical art. Maddie observed, with Randall watching silently, as Dr. Keats cleared a space in his bedroom, moving books and papers aside to reveal a series of arches and diagrams etched into the dark mahogany of the floorboards.

Eight points on a star, like a great compass.

Indications of other substances remained behind on the

wood: wax, burn marks, and a variety of stains that Maddie had no desire to inquire after. It looked like something out of a turn of the century séance scene, and yet it made sense to her. She'd seen it before, smelled it before. Something in her mind triggered.

"I'm going to call John," Maddie said to Randall, as Dr. Keats continued setting things up. "Do you think this thing gets reception from here?"

"I have no idea," Randall admitted.

Maddie took a deep breath and opened the compact. It looked as it had in Second World, save that the metal inside looked a bit corroded, as if it had oxidized on the trip over.

She pressed her finger onto the stone and waited, tapping her foot in anticipation. Doing something was better than standing around staring like an idiot.

The compact shuddered, and when she looked at it, she noticed that the fabric's colors shifted, swirled. For a moment she thought there was a clear picture, but nothing recognizable surfaced.

Then a woman's voice came through, crackled: "Yes?"

It was Pinga.

"Pinga, it's Madeline. I need to speak to John," Maddie said.

A high-pitched whine followed, calling the attention of Dr. Keats. Maddie shook her head at him and pointed to the task at hand.

"Pinga? You there?" she asked.

"...not here..." The voice wavered, low tones emerging amidst higher ones. "...Miriam... something happened when you left, Joss Raddick is gone and... no sign... flames went out... troops from the East..."

"Gods, no," Randall said.

"I don't understand, I can hardly hear–" Maddie said into the compact.

"Joss must have gone with Alvin. He was all that was preventing John and his troops from advancing," Randall said.

"Great. So we left to prevent a holocaust and they started a war," Maddie said, flipping the compact closed. She wanted to throw it across the room.

"They've always fought. It's their way," Randall said. "Especially in Second."

"Why am I helping you people out again?" Maddie demanded.

Dr. Keats stood up and announced, "It's almost ready. There isn't much of a window where this will work, so I advise you to say your goodbyes here."

"Goodbyes?" asked Maddie.

"Randall–you can't possibly be willing to risk your life and Randy's," said Dr. Keats. Put that way, Maddie couldn't very well argue. She had wanted Randall along, if for moral support more than anything, but now she saw little valiant about him risking their lives.

"Maddie, there's no telling what would happen," Randall said.

Dr. Keats continued, "I have no idea what the ramifications could be if Randy *and* Randall go through. It could be catastrophic."

"What do you mean, exactly?" she asked.

"If I told you exactly what I mean, you wouldn't understand a word of it. Art historians are generally poorly suited to the ways of physics," he said, his tone acidic.

"What about Alvin?" she asked Dr. Keats. "Won't he need to get here to get to First World?"

"He no longer needs this portal, it seems. If a beacon has opened up–a sort of alleyway between the worlds–he could exploit it," Dr. Keats said.

"I guess that would be Matilda, considering I led her straight to M'ora."

Randall looked pained, an expression that Maddie had never seen on Randy. It made her heart twist, made her hate him for coming to find her and pushing Randy aside—even though she had been the one to ask him to. "Maddie. I just can't. You've got to understand," Randall said. "I don't want to risk Randy."

"What does Randy say?" she asked.

"Nothing," he replied after an uncomfortable pause.

"I get it. I'll go in first," she said. She found an elastic in her pocket and tied back her hair. Then she thrust her finger at Randall. "He can go in if he wants to, but I won't force him. How's that?"

Dr. Keats was concentrating now on aligning a series of black, polished stones. He glanced up at Maddie and said, "However you like." He stood, then, stretching his back, and continued: "I'm bringing you into the only way I know; I've no idea how time moves on First, as it's always been obscured. So you'll have to consider that. Alvin may be right in front of you, or two years away by then."

"I'll risk it."

"Suit yourself."

Maddie looked at Randall. "Tell Randy I love him."

Randall nodded solemnly; he was crying through Randy's eyes. Before she let herself give in to the sadness, she approached Dr. Keats. "Okay. Here we go."

The air in the bedroom felt charged, like the air after a storm. There was also a subtle, but growing, vibration that began at the center of the room where Dr. Keats was working. Before long, even Maddie's ears itched with it.

"First, you must open the door," Dr. Keats said.

"What door?"

But Maddie saw it before she could finish her thought. Where the diagrams and drawings were a moment ago, there was now a trap door, set with a pristine brass handle in the middle. There was a faint blue glow around its the edges, spilling out between the cracks in the wood.

And she felt drawn to it.

Considering everything she'd experienced in the last few days, she didn't question the sensation. She just proceeded toward it.

"How do I know it's right? Can I peek or something?" she asked. Her voice seemed drowned out. "I mean, what if you're tossing me into Cthulhu's loving tentacles or something?"

Dr. Keats backed up toward the door to his room. "It's blind faith, Madeline. Either you've got the bravado or you don't; and if you don't, you've wasted my time."

He frowned, shaking his head, tufts of his semi-combover rising and falling in the breeze. The breeze?

"You don't have to go," Dr. Keats said. "You are putting yourself in harm's way—"

"I'll be in harm's way, permanently, if something isn't done. And I have the compact. Compass. Whatever it is. I think it can help."

Bending down, Maddie grabbed the brass handle on the door and pulled. It swung open immediately, as if it were made of balsa wood and papier-mâché. What lay beyond was utter darkness, dotted with a few stars, all of them unfamiliar. It was like jumping down into the night sky, and Maddie felt her orientation shift, like she'd been caught in the undertow of a wave.

The door wanted her to enter.

"It's a freefall," she said, shivering, staring at Dr. Keats across the chasm.

"I can't see anything," Dr. Keats shouted. The wind was whistling; chilly, flower-scented air wafted up through the door. "You've got to jump. It won't be open for long—"

"You coming?" she asked Randall, catching his gaze over her shoulder.

Randall looked away. "I'm sorry," he said.

So she jumped.

Stars. Far up above. Green, red, yellow, swirling in swaths of pearly matter. A very different firmament.

Maddie was laying face-up, in soft, dewy grass a few inches tall. It brushed against her cheek, gentle and welcome, fine as fur. A feeling like childhood, like home, like spring.

Slowly she stood up, cautious. The First World–she hoped that's what it was, anyway–was silent but for the blowing of the wind and the whisper of the grass, all in the cool dark of night. She glanced up at the stars, wishing for a moment that she could stay and count them, draw them in her mind, remember them. So beautiful.

So she'd made it. She felt good, strong, as if she'd had a long night of sleep. She stretched, enjoying the feel of her own limbs. Her whole body–the one she was born into–had transferred. No more seeing the world through Matilda's eyes or being slave to her whims and sordid affairs.

Maddie was alone. Randall hadn't come. She felt unexpected pressure behind her eyes, and blinked away tears. Enough crying. After the debacle with Alvin and the heart-wrenching affair with Randy, she just didn't have it in her for more sorrow. She had to go on.

The moon was gone, or else there was no moon, so Maddie had to see by starlight. From what she could see, she was in a field bordered by tall, long-limbed trees, the gentle breeze rustling their leaves and causing their branches to sway. If there was a door somewhere, like the one she'd come through, it had vanished, or else was so high in the sky that she could not see it.

Maddie looked up again to the sky, watching the captivating stars, lulled by their mysteries. This was a truly different world and she felt she deserved a moment's quiet here, among the trees and the stars, before she sought out Alvin again, before she faced Matilda. Before she faced the unknown.

She was still staring up, trying to decide which way was the best way to start walking, when she noticed a spot of darkness in the sky. There was something flying high above her, a bird or a bat, perhaps. Some of the stars vanished beneath its wings as it circled lower.

She squinted, and it grew larger, until she made out the silhouette. A keen terror jolted through her, where before she had only felt peace—in the First World, who could say if birds could eat people? About to duck down entirely, Maddie threw her hands over her head, when she heard her name.

"Madeline." It was Randall's voice.

She peered through her fingers, her heart skipping at least three beats, then starting up again with greater alacrity.

The bird with Randall's voice was sleek and black as the night and had alighted on the grass, where it now stood tilting its head from side to side. It was a few feet in front of her, a dark spot on the blue-black grass.

"Get up. Please," he implored.

"Randall?" she asked, getting to her knees, and then standing fully. Her jeans were soaked through from the dew, and she'd not noticed until now.

The raven opened its mouth again, experimentally, its eyes glittering in the starlight. Then he said: "Yes. It's me."

"But you... you're a..." She squinted, watching the bird twitch its head as it spoke. Maddie thought it looked almost painful.

"Raven. One of the symbols of Apollo. But yes, that's *problematic*, isn't it? Do you mind if I sit on your shoulder? You are unseemly tall from this particular vantage point."

Maddie said, "Sure, I guess..." and he took flight, landing gently on her right shoulder, testing his perch with one foot and then the other. "But, um... why are you a bird, exactly?"

"There's a twain of me, here. His name is Ravel," Randall said, shaking his head as if to dispel water. "What you are witnessing is a protective curse. You see he's a far more experienced magician than I, and I've no idea how to change back."

"And you knew this when you jumped in? And Randy gave you permission to hijack his body?" She was terrified that Randy would be in danger, even if she was afforded the relief of Randall's presence.

"It's only my consciousness that's trapped. I attempted to break through through Ravel, as I do with Randy. But he captured my entire consciousness in this confounded bird," Randall said. The raven that was once Randall Roth squawked. "The twains of First World are powerful and paranoid, but I couldn't let you in here by yourself. Would't be very gentlemanly of me."

"Gentlemanly," she repeated, taking a few paces in one direction, looking around, and then stopping, wrapping her arms around herself. It was colder than before. "What about Randy?"

"I traveled with his help," Randall said. "I assure you he's fine."

"Says the man who ruined him," Maddie responded, biting down on her tongue as she said it.

"I made a *mistake*," said Randall. "I've been torn apart over it, but what can I do? There are still mysteries in what we do, and mistakes can happen. You'll learn to make them yourself, too. It's not an easy life, being what we are. It's magic and science and wonder and a great, terrible burden. And most of the time, it's oppressing loneliness. Except when you find someone you can share that emptiness with, someone who makes you happy."

"Yeah, well, don't expect a welcome party. I'm sick to death of all of you at this point. I just want some peace and quiet."

"I didn't mean for you to become so tangled in these affairs. I love you, Madeline," he said. "I do."

"It's a common occurrence, I'm learning," she said. "Comes with the territory. So forgive me if I don't necessarily reciprocate."

"That isn't what I mean," Randall said, but Maddie shushed him with the palm of her hand, up. He stiffened on her shoulder, digging his talons into her sweater just slightly. Had he had hands, it would have been a light squeeze.

In the distance, a horn blew.

"I hope that doesn't mean Alvin's succeeded," Maddie observed.

"If he had killed his final twain I suppose we'd know. The worlds themselves could be thrown into chaos. Alvin thinks he can resurrect the pure essence of his god by killing off his twains entirely."

"At least, providing a new one isn't born in time," Maddie said.

"Yes, precisely. Which is why he's moving so fast now. I swear to you, Maddie, I didn't know the depth of his treachery. I only learned later."

She walked a few paces, then stopped.

"So why *didn't* you tell me about the whole dragon thing, anyway?" Maddie asked. "And about Randy?"

Randall was crouched very low on her shoulder, his beak right by her ear, the raven equivalent of a dog with its tail between his legs. "I wanted to explain it to you scientifically."

"Scientifically?"

"It's complex, but I thought I could show you," he said.

"You mean like the handkerchief?"

He clicked a laugh. "I had other visual aids in mind. But there never was to be enough time. I was certain you still loved Alvin, and I didn't want to demonize him, either. I didn't think that was fair of me."

"Gallant," she said.

"Not to mention Matilda had her tines in you so deep; I worried that if I told you about Randy, that you'd think..."

"You're a horrible person?"

"Something along those lines."

"Well, in comparison to the rest of the people in our little pantheon, you're practically a saint. At least you appear to have a conscience."

"The guilt is immense."

"And Randy. Does he know about this?"

"He does. He is more clever than you think."

"He's more than clever. He's remarkable."

Randall went quiet for a moment. Then he said: "He is."

"He doesn't deserve what you've brought upon him."

"I know."

She shivered. "Jesus, Randall. It's good to have you here."

"You're not angry?"

It was hard to be angry when Maddie felt so alive. The air of First World was clear and clean, by far the purest air she'd breathed in ages. It was moist, and almost sweet on the tongue. Maddie wondered if the snow here tasted as good as it did in Second World, and almost smiled.

Then she laughed, starting off toward the trees, and a particular birch that she had pinpointed. "I'm furious. But not just at you." She poked him. "And you came through after me. You didn't have to do that. For a second, I thought you'd stayed behind, but then..." she took a deep breath, getting choked up again.

"We always find each other. Somehow."

"So I hear."

First World was full of nothing but sleepy squirrels and trilling birds, and no matter how much time passed, the sun never rose. It was perpetual dusk. Not that it was boring. No, there was something curiously alluring about the everlasting twilight. Maddie found it wasn't that she missed the sun–on the contrary, her eyes became rather used to the minimal light–just that she found it difficult to navigate. She'd never realized how much she relied on the sun to move about her life. Now it felt as if part of her had gone missing entirely.

It became clear, as well, that contacting M'ora was far more difficult than Maddie had imagined. Every time she closed her eyes and tried to concentrate, she was met with more darkness, nothingness. Whatever connection she had forged with M'ora was gone. Yet she knew Matilda was not far.

It was like the opposite of the sun, a lingering darkness that was just over her shoulder. The strength of that impulse led her to worry that Matilda had killed M'ora already, that they had already run out of time. It was a special kind of failure to go belly-up even before a journey started.

And there was the issue of time. Second World and Sixth World seemed to move at approximately the same pace. She didn't have to worry about slipping through some wormhole and ending up fifty years in the future. But if time was the same on First World, it didn't feel like it. In fact, time didn't seem to exist at all.

Feeling panic flitting around her, Maddie stopped in her endless wandering and took some deep breaths, stretching. It was good to be in her own body, but she was out of shape.

She couldn't be lost. Not with what she was, the power she had. Every time she attempted to orient herself, she kept seeing the string of pearls M'ora had shown her, kept imagining the strand that kept them together. And then she thought of Matilda, and of Alvin, and something in her refused to accept they were too late. It was as if Maddie could *feel* them in spite of their distance.

Randall kept to himself, and finally she had to ask: "So, is this world really slow, or is it just me?"

"Not sure. There is so little we know about this world."

"Yeah. I know. I think I'm the resident expert on the matter, and that's a scary thought."

"What do you mean?" Randall asked.

"Well, first off, I let everyone in. I put a hole in the celestial Hoover Dam." She sighed. "And then there's Alvin's twain."

Randall chirped. "I'm guessing it's not as cut and dried as he and Matilda think?"

"Alvin's twain is M'ora's son. I met him."

"Heavens," exclaimed Randall.

She ducked under a low-hanging limb, and ran her hands over its soft, moss-covered surface. Randall was looking down at her now from another branch, his glossy black feathers catching in the light from the stars; it looked almost as if he was streaked in oil. She felt very fond of him in that moment, very protective. For the first time since watching Randy, she felt as if she had something to care for, to keep safe. A raven could fly, but he was so fragile and small. Looking at him, hearing his voice through the strange animal's mouth, made her realize how much she would miss him if he were gone.

Yes, Maddie did love Randall. But she still loved Randy, too. It was confusing. Every time she thought of them, they blurred together like a reflection in a funhouse mirror. Where did one start and the other end?

To make no mention of Alvin.

Randall said, "What if we do save him? What then?"

Maddie sighed. "I don't know, Randall. I just have to believe there is some goodness left in him."

"And if there isn't?"

She didn't reply. Maddie didn't want to think about it. The darkness that was Matilda seemed to rise and fall just out of the corner of her eye, pressing and nagging, always watching. Yes, she was near.

As she walked on, Maddie convinced herself that Matilda couldn't possibly know where she was, or else was far enough away that she didn't consider her a threat.

They continued in the dark, Randall perching on Maddie's shoulder, and whispering to her every now and again. She thought she caught a glimpse of brighter grey at the horizon, but it only vanished again, as if a trick of her eyes. No, no sun. Just an illusion.

She had a sudden craving for a huge, 32-ounce Mountain Dew, from one of those machines at Dairy Mart that would mix it up with ice. God, those were good. She could do with the caffeine. In Matilda's body, she never had such memories, such cravings. But now it was almost unbearable. She could taste the chemical sweetness on her tongue, and she longed for the satisfaction of bubbles making their way down her throat.

"Oh, Maddie, look!" Randall said, turning his beak to the skies.

Taken out of her junk food fantasies, Maddie obeyed. Above, meteors streaked across the sky, vibrant orange against black, followed by a shower of more—sparkling, magnificent. Maddie had, on occasion, seen a meteor shower back home. The Perseids, for instance, she remembered seeing one evening with Agnes. But it had never been like this. These little meteors looked like colored, luminescent rain, as varied as the Northern Lights. Streaks of dappled, rainbow light coloring the night sky nearly as brilliantly as fireworks on the Fourth of July.

"Beautiful," Maddie whispered when it stopped.

She had stopped to watch the display in the sky, but picked up the pace again, heading vaguely toward where the majority of the meteors had fallen. It was something to go on. In the oppressive twilight, there were few clues to go by, and even though Maddie felt as if every step only got her more lost, she continued.

"Maddie?" Randall asked.

"What is it now?" she said, coming to another abrupt stop.

"You've forgotten to use your compass."

"I... you're right. I totally forgot."

She reached into her jeans pocket and worried out the silver compact, still cold. She was about to open it up when Randall pecked her shoulder.

"Ow!" Maddie cried. "What's that for?"

"Don't open it. I wouldn't broadcast. Turn it so the etching is facing you."

Maddie complied, staring down at the silver, eight-pronged star. She closed her eyes and concentrated, feeling the cold metal on her hands and shivering. Nothing happened.

"No dice," she said.

"Well, chances are it's confused. This is a new world after all. I'd say you need a True North."

"A what?"

Randall said. "It may need to be recalibrated. There's a hole, in the very center..."

Maddie looked down into it. Indeed, there was a well in the center. It looked like it coursed through all the prongs of the star. Something dripped there would flow through the entire design. A drop of liquid...

"Blood. Or spit..." she murmured.

"Blood magic is powerful," Randall replied. "And it's likely our last hope. Unless you want to keep wandering in circles." When she didn't reply, he pressed on: "Just try it. Please."

"You just want to bite my finger," she retorted.

He clicked. "Maybe a little."

"Here." She put her finger up to his beak. First, Randall rubbed his head on her finger like a cat might, then he nipped it gently. When that failed to draw blood, he gave it a mighty peck.

In the dark, her blood looked black. Wincing, she dropped some into the center of the compass. Once her finger made contact with the metal, she felt her whole body tense, as if someone had pulled her spine like a string. She felt, rather than saw, her blood seep along the etching on the compact, slowly making its way around the eight points from the center.

But when the show was over and Maddie relaxed again, the compass showed no sign of change. She shook it, turned it around in her hand and gave up.

"Oh well. Let's walk this way," she said, stuffing the compass into her pocket again.

Maddie turned around, taking a few paces to her left, and the compact went frigid in her pocket, as cold as if it were made of ice, right through her jeans.

She slid her fingers down into her pocket to touch it, but the metal stuck to her fingers. Then she had to pry it off, along with some of her skin, leaving behind cold burns. "Wow," she said. "It's covered in frost."

"Fascinating," Randall said.

Backing up, Maddie then stood in the center of the clearing, where she had been when the compass went cold. Just as quickly, the compact went warm, comfortable, and the sensation spread up her arm into her chest. It was not unlike the feeling of opium being dumped in her bloodstream. It was a feeling that spoke of home, of familiarity. Of welcome.

"There's currents of warmer air that the compass is picking up," she said. "When I move out of them, it goes cold. Really cold."

"It might not be a perfect science, but I'm willing to go with it," Randall said.

"Then let's go," Maddie said, and continued onward through the wood, past the trees, and into the darkness before them.

The sun did not rise. Maddie found herself fantasizing about food again. In the Second World, food had been so replete and imaginative that she'd never found herself pining for the sorts of things she used to eat at home. But now, even ramen sounded good. Or a Twinkie. Or a Nutty Buddy Cone. Or take-out Chinese—greasy pork on fried rice smothered with plastic packets of duck sauce.

Her fantasies, however, were unrealized. They had yet to see anything that resembled human civilization, but had at least found water, and trees growing apples. At least, they tasted like apples; Maddie had the suspicion that if she had held the fruits up to ordinary light, their skins would be black, or purple. Something wholly un-apple-like. Randall, for his part, hunted for worms, some distance away, embarrassed to be doing such a thing, but unable to do much about biting into the apples.

Just as they had finished taking a drink in a shallow stream, Randall, without warning, flew up into the canopy above, his talons breaking through the skin on Maddie's shoulder on liftoff.

"What the—"

"Get in the tree!" Randall half-squawked from above. "Climb!"

But Maddie couldn't. She heard the command, saw the tree, knew her capability. She wasn't exactly athletic, but tree climbing wouldn't be too tough. Yet she was rooted to the ground, not by fear but by something else. Curiosity.

She sensed it before it arrived, and there was something comforting, familiar about it. The sounds it made, the way it breathed.

The trees rustled, and the darkness deepened. What approached was dark, hulking, overgrown with lichen and leaves. It lumbered toward her; stared at her, raised its hoary arms above his head and screamed. A green man, leaves and moss and brambles all twisted together in some magnificent creation, sprung from the deepest magic of the earth.

"Maddie!" begged Randall.

She had no weapons, so she stowed away the compass and held out her hands. "Come here, viney guy," she said, gently, like she used to do with horses. "I'm not going to hurt you."

It was stupid, of course. She knew it as she said the words. But Maddie felt a kinship with this creature, as alien as it was. It pulsed with magic, and for the first time since crossing over to Second World, she found herself hungering for it. If only she could tap into it, drink its sap and take it for her own, she would know something, taste knowledge and make it hers.

The green man's eyes blazed in its leafy face, unearthly purple in this blue-black world. Then it opened its mouth, which wriggled with maggots and beetles, and let out a cry that stood Maddie's hair on end. If a plant could scream, it would have made such a sound, coupled with the fluttering of a thousand wings.

But she was not afraid. She should be. She knew it. And yet she was strangely calm. If she could convince it to be hers...

"Who are you?" Maddie asked, bending her knees and holding out her hands.

It screamed again, thrusting its insectile tongues in the air and shaking its head from side to side.

It considered, sniffed the air. Then it started coming for her.

Maddie gasped as the first vine sliced across her forearm, cutting through her sweater and through her skin without trouble. It stung right away, like nettles, and the pain brought clarity.

She had been here before. In another life. Another Maddie. It was the first time such a memory came to her—she was fairer then, with light hair and bright blue eyes. But the face was similar, and most importantly, she simply felt the same. The woman in her memory was her, she knew it.

But as exciting as the revelation was, Maddie knew she was in trouble. In her memory, the verdant creature had pounced upon her, trying to smother her, rape her, torture her into the forest floor.

Maddie backed up, but there was a vine wrapped around her middle now.

The heart. Look to the heart.

The words were not Matilda's, not M'ora's. Some other woman, some other memory.

"But where the hell is the heart?" she muttered, gasping as the vines pulled tighter around her waist. She recalled the cor-

sets of Second World and would have laughed at the similarity
if she'd had the air.

Randall swooped down and started pecking ineffectually
at the creature.

Vines tightened around her; Maddie could feel them in
her hair, smell their loamy leaves gathering around her, whispering to her. She shoved her hand in front of her, snaking her
way through slick vines. But she came up with nothing, just
more sinewy plant matter dragging against her skin. Its heart?
She couldn't very well get to its heart.

Then the ground began to shake.

Maddie was now suspended a few feet off the ground, her
legs twisted up above her head like an upside-down rag doll.
Maddie closed her eyes, fighting the urge to faint. But just as she
was about to tap into something great and terrible, some deep
well of power in the very center of her, the creature shrieked
and dropped her. Her head collided with a log, and she rolled
sideways into a shallow stream, completely dazed now.

The green man slunk back into the woods, hissing at her.

But now she was staring at a set of boots. She looked up.

"Good ever-evening, Maddie Angler," Joss Raddick said,
charming and smooth. He had a longbow, and was standing
straddling the stream, one leg on either bank.

"What... the hell... was that?" panted Maddie.

Joss offered her his hand and, while she wasn't entirely
sure what to make of his presence in the first place, she took it.

"That was a spirit of the forest," Joss said as casually as
if he were mentioning squirrels. "Crazy buggers. But we have
an agreement. It's a good thing I got here in time or you might
have been later than you already are."

"I was doing fine," Maddie said, picking leaves and brambles out of her hair. Her sweater was so covered in burrs that
she took it off altogether, shivering into her long-sleeved t-shirt.
"Well. I'm bleeding."

"Not for long you won't be," Joss said. "Allow me?" He held out his hands.

Randall chirped from above. "I'd let him do it."

Maddie pulled up her sweater to her elbow. Even in the twilight of First World the wound looked raw and ragged, throbbing beneath the skin.

Joss took a deep breath and put one of his huge hands on either side of Maddie's forearm, then closed his eyes. Deep breaths followed, and slowly, slowly, little black flecks of moisture began escaping the wound. They hovered in midair a moment before falling to the ground, and as each left, Maddie felt herself relax and unwind a little more.

"Poison," Joss explained. "Nothing a little water can't cleanse. I can't heal you entirely, but this will help."

Maddie pulled her arm away. The skin was tighter and the wound was crusted, but it didn't hurt like it had before. Now it felt more like a deep scratch. "Well, thanks, Joss. But I wasn't expecting to see you here. Or else I thought you were going with Alvin. You said you stay put, after all."

"Doesn't mean I can't do otherwise if I choose," he said. "It's always been easier for me. All waters come from the same source. Sort of like my own personal road between worlds. Just jump in, and find the right current."

Maddie took a step across the water, her Chuck Taylors squelching, and Randall flew down to her shoulder and bobbed his head at Joss.

"Randall?" Joss asked. "Oh my."

"Yes. It's hilarious," said Randall.

"A raven? Of all the things." Joss said with a laugh.

"Ravens are clever creatures," Randall tried to defend himself.

"Whatever Randall is or isn't," Maddie interrupted, "he's been helpful. But we're pressed for time. So if you don't mind..."

"Wait," said Joss. He took a step toward her, and the

ground rose up with the motion, water dripping from his boots. When he put his foot down again, her feet were dry. In fact, all of her was completely dry.

"Wow. Thanks," she said.

"I can be of help to you," Joss pointed out, gesturing to the ground.

"Can you?" asked Randall, whose head was down near Maddie's ear, listening very carefully. Although Maddie knew it was ridiculous to think that a raven could growl, she swore Randall just had.

Joss shrugged, as if Randall's approval was the least of his concerns. "Yes. I can help you find your way."

"I found my way back from Sixth World just fine," Maddie said. She hadn't called it home.

"And you didn't just stay there?" he asked.

"Clearly not." She wanted to say "duh," but the sentiment might not be appreciated in present company.

"Maddie, you had a chance to get away." Joss's eyes looked like pools of moonlit water, unearthly and inhuman.

"But for how long?" asked Maddie. "These people want me dead and they're coming after me. What's to say they won't do away with me in a few weeks, anyway, in my own world? I want this on my own terms."

"Brave of you." He meant it. Joss sighed.

"How can we trust you?" Maddie asked. "You were more than willing to screw Matilda, before. More than willing to stand by while Alvin plotted the end of the world."

"You can trust me because I have spent the better part of the last hundred years protecting Randall and Matilda," Joss said, frowning as he admitted it.

Randall clicked. "What are you talking about?"

Joss sighed. "I knew you. Last time."

Randall was fidgeting again.

"Except it fell apart," finished Maddie. She didn't have

Matilda's memories, even connected as they had been, but she had a strange sympathy for her. "So it's more than just Alvin. We're all capable of destruction."

"Sometimes. It's the same with humans," Joss said, wiping his eyes with the back of his hands. "But you, Madeline. You remind me of the old dragons. The ones with spirit. And Matilda has tired me out. I could never refuse her or deny her, but now... now I feel like I can."

"We could use the help," Maddie said to Randall.

Randall bobbed his head. "We could. Especially someone handy with weapons, considering I've got naught but feathers and flight. Still, I'll keep two eyes on him."

"Very well," Maddie said. "Come along, boys, we've got miles to go. I think."

"The catch is I can't stray far from the water like this." He gestured to his body. "But I can try and transform myself. And I may even be more helpful that way."

Randall laughed, a repetitive *ka-ka-ka*. "You're not practiced enough for it, Joss. You're as out of shape as the rest of us."

"You'd be wrong on that count, Randall. Wrong indeed," Joss said.

Joss Raddick took two steps closer to Maddie and Randall, and then held his hands up over his head, much in the way a diver would before plunging into the water. He took a deep breath and bowed until his hands entered the wet earth below him. His hair fell free from its tie and grew, shimmering white in the light of the stars. His neck elongated, growing thicker and developing an elegant arch as his face slanted downward, his nose becoming a snout, his eyes moving to the sides. The whole of him grew, shedding his clothes like dry husks, as the center of him rose higher and higher—flanks, tail, powerful legs.

When he was done, he was a horse, black as the night sky, but his pale mane shone brightly and was soft to the touch; Maddie couldn't help but reach out and stroke him.

"So do you want to keep walking?" Joss asked. "I'm a free ride."

"Never look a gift horse in the—" the bird began.

"Randall!" scolded Maddie.

"Sorry," Randall said, though he was still chuckling to himself in a most birdlike manner.

"A black horse and a black crow—are you sure I'm not the harbinger of death?" Maddie asked.

"Beauty can be a dark lady," said Randall. "But for future reference, I'm a *raven*, not a crow."

"Semantics," said Joss.

Maddie mounted Joss by grabbing fistfuls of his mane, then swinging herself upward. He was a very wide horse, not the sort pretty girls with rich parents stabled, and Maddie winced as her legs accommodated for the girth. Randall flew up and landed on her shoulder again.

"I can go much faster than a typical steed," said Joss, tossing his mane a little. He was damp all over, like he'd just jumped in the river.

"I didn't know horses could swim," she with a laugh.

"I'm not much of a swimmer, honestly," Joss admitted. "Odd as that is."

"Great, because I'm not much of a rider," she said.

"It's just like riding a bike," said Randall. "A big, hairy, heavy-breathing bike, through a creepy old forest in the middle of perpetual night."

"Thanks for the help, honey," Maddie said, swatting at him gently. "Well. Here goes nothing. Let's go, Joss. Tcha."

12
A Considerable Dissonance

It was *not* like riding a bike. It was holding on for dear life and doing her best to coax Joss in the right direction. He often had a different idea of where they should go, most often lured by oats growing near riverbanks, but Maddie's compass was continually guiding them in one direction. Thankfully, it didn't take them too long to get reoriented when Joss led them astray.

The going wasn't always smooth, as the forest was thick, and more than once they had to dismount and lead Joss through brambles and over rocks.

But as they continued, with no change in landscape to speak of, Maddie felt her spirits darken. Sure, she had quite the entourage. Part of her couldn't wait to see the look on Alvin's face when she rode in on a black water-horse with a talking raven on her shoulder.

Still, that was just the problem, wasn't it? What was she going to do to do if she caught up with Alvin? Or, even more terrifying, what was she going to do if she was too late? In her heart, Maddie didn't want to believe Alvin was beyond sav-

ing, but she had already failed once, so miserably. Maybe seeing her—as her true self, and not peeking from under Matilda's
skin—would make a difference.

Maddie couldn't help but lose herself to memory as they
rode, remembering how Alvin was with her, once. Those first
few years they shared together, how careful and considerate
he had been of her. How magnetically they connected. She
had never experienced such a feeling with anyone, and when
it went away, when the passion and the enthusiasm vanished,
she thought it was just part of a normal long-term relationship.
She'd never managed to hold on to any others for longer than a
year or so, and as every year passed with Alvin, she felt more accomplished, like she had achieved some invisible, unsaid goal.

"You're quite pensive, my dear," Randall said at her ear.

"Yeah," she said. They were going slowly now, picking
their way through low-lying vines. Flies buzzed around Joss's
head, and he continually flicked his ears to discourage them,
but to little avail.

"You can talk to me if you like," Randall pressed.

"Don't know what to say," she admitted with a shrug.
"Not that it matters much, anyway. My problems seem pretty
insignificant in the grand scheme of things."

"Don't sell yourself short," Joss said. "I'd hardly met you
before I decided you were the side worth allying with. Right
now, you're the only one who's had the pluck to stick up to
Matilda and Alvin. Up until your appearance, none of us really
knew how deep the two of them had gone."

Joss's voice was much more gentle in horse form, and his
laugh was a soft rumble. From what Maddie could tell, it wasn't
so much that Joss and Randall were speaking in animal form
than she could simply understand them. If she listened really
hard, it didn't even sound like English.

Joss stopped abruptly, lowering his head; he made a warning noise somewhere between a snort and a sigh, staring a few

meters before them. Maddie felt the muscles in his neck tense, and she scanned the forest before her for a sign of what he saw, stroking him gently. Joss's ears went back.

Where he stared was a pack of wolves clustered around the base of the larger trees ahead of them. They stood between Maddie and a clearing, the largest they'd seen since first arriving in the middle of the field.

Maddie knew the woods around M'ora's cottage had been patrolled by wolves, as protection, but she had little faith they could keep her safe against what was coming.

But the wolves didn't know that.

She cursed. They were so close to M'ora's cottage now, and there were wolves in the way!

Maddie tried to reach M'ora, squinting and concentrating. But there was no response.

"We might be able to use you back like you were before," she said to Joss, as quietly as she could. "With the bow..."

"No!" it was Randall. He took off into the air, and flew forward toward the pack, his beak clacking in nervous rhythm. They were snowy white wolves, and stood out vividly in the darkness, their unblinking eyes like yellow amber.

Maddie's heart leapt into her throat as she watched Randall fly circles above the wolves' heads, crying out in a language that was somewhere between bird and man's: *sqrwark raaah–raaagh swrak.* She couldn't catch a single word of it, and she was positive that the wolves were going to reach up and snap Randall in their jaws, chew him to bloody bits. It looked like he was teasing them, even. And as soon as they made a quick snack of the pesky bird, they'd get horse and human.

She made a motion to dart forward, but Joss stayed firm.

"Just watch," he said, so quietly it could have been missed among the shaking leaves.

Maddie tried to argue, but thought better of it. Joss was eerily reassuring. Instead, she looked again, and for the first time, she saw that the wolves seemed to be listening to Randall's manic chatter. The pack was made up of at least a dozen wolves, one of which was larger, with a black streak down its side. As Randall continued to talk, the wolves' hackles went down, and they sat, their heads poking up like expectant little children, watching the raven fly back and forth.

Then, they rose and dispersed, striding away on lanky legs. They turned their heads every now and again to get a last glance at the strange visitors.

"Why, that was thrilling!" said Randall, coming back and standing on top of Joss's head; the great horse stood perfectly still, though he had been watching the whole thing. Maddie had the suspicion he was terrified of the wolves, as any good horse ought to be.

"What the hell did you just do? Direct them to the nearest steakhouse?" asked Maddie, giggling with nervous relief. "God—they just walked away."

"It's one of my—our—things," said Randall. "Wolves. One of our forms. I had no idea what to say to them, but it just rather came to me then. They're M'ora's protectors; her cottage is just ahead there."

"Have they seen anyone else at the cottage?" asked Maddie. "Because if they say Alvin—"

"No, they said they were unaware of anything unusual happening at the cottage," replied Randall.

"Then we beat them here?" she said, astonished. "We beat Alvin here?"

"Not entirely," said a woman's voice, familiar and icy.

Maddie had been so intent on Randall's safety, she had missed the presence of two women sneaking up behind them. One was of middling height, with long, curly dark hair and dusky skin; she carried a bow and arrows, and was dressed as the medieval equivalent of a forester—a green tunic, with matching boots, skirt, and cape. Pinga, but in another world.

Artemis. Ninhursag. Diana.

Beside her stood a woman with Agnes's face, just like the statue of Saint Therasia. Her eyes burned blue in a face as dark as M'ora's had been, and she was resplendent in a white sari. Her hair was nearly as pale as the dress, and opals shone about her neck. She also carried an elegant spear, silver-tipped.

It made sense, for the first time.

"Agnes," Maddie whispered, tears coming to her again. "Athena..."

"Amela suffices, here," the woman who was not Agnes replied. "This is Daena." She indicated Pinga's twain.

"Sisters," said Joss, bowing his head low. His muscles twitched; he was nervous.

"You're to come with us," Daena said, staring

"It's probably best that we assent," Joss said. "There is power here. I can feel springs under our feet whispering it. The very air–"

"Not you," Amela said. She swept a long arm toward Maddie. "Just her."

Maddie stood a little straighter on top of Joss, winding her fingers into his soft mane. "I'm just here to speak to M'ora."

Joss tensed under her. No, Maddie had not taken the time to explain the details, and more likely than not the man was shocked at her casual use of the elder godling's name. Things were happening too fast for her to keep track, and at least for once, Maddie felt a thrill at keeping someone other than her in the dark.

Daena laughed. "She's here to talk to M'ora," she chortled, looking over at her sister, Amela. When she looked again at Maddie, her eyes were pools of starlight, furious and proud.

"You aren't allowed to simply speak to M'ora," Amela said. "That isn't how it works."

"But I'm her twain," Maddie said, almost adding that they'd spoken before–that she'd managed to get to First World herself. She bit down on her tongue.

"It doesn't matter," Daena said. "You are untested. You are foreign. If you wish to come into contact with M'ora, you must prove yourself."

"Prove myself how, exactly?" Maddie said. She didn't want to get down off of Joss, as being mounted gave her a false sense of height. She couldn't tell if it was a trick of the light, but these women just looked bigger than they should have–if she were down on the ground, chances were she'd only rise to their chests.

Randall's claws were tensing rhythmically on her shoulder. "Be careful," he whispered. "We ought not separate."

"Oh, but you'll have to," Amela said, lowering her spear at Maddie's heart. "Or we'll send her back home. We cannot harm her, but we can wound her. Our magic is far stronger than you'd imagine."

"Oh, I can imagine," Randall replied. "That's the problem."

Daena held up her hand and snapped her fingers shut. Maddie felt the air go cold around her feet, and then Randall chirped. He tried, clearly quite hard, to communicate, but nothing came from him but bird chatter.

Joss's head went down, and he pawed the ground, shaking his coat. He, too, had been struck dumb.

"As I was saying," Amela said, "You, young brightling," she indicated Maddie, "have two choices. You may leave, or you may be tested."

"I don't think you understand," Maddie said, "I have important information for M'ora. About Alvin. About the murder of twains."

Though Daena did not laugh, her luminous, terrifying eyes flashed. Amela, brought her spear closer to Maddie's middle.

"But don't you see?" said the huntress. "We already have Alvin. You helped us set the trap. The decision has been made."

"That doesn't make any sense," Maddie said.

She was shaking, terrified, as if some great barrier had been keeping her horror at bay. Randall was right: These were old, powerful gods, greater and more destructive than the twains she had met before. Randall, John, Pinga, even Alvin—all now seemed but children in the shadow of these creatures, these immortals who had lived in darkness for time out of mind.

Maddie was outnumbered. And for once, she wasn't the only one out of her league.

"But M'ora... she came to me," Maddie tried, willing her voice to comply. But she sounded even more scared than she felt. "I wanted to help her, I came here... to help her."

"Help her? *Help her?*"

Maddie could hardly hear herself speak. It felt as if her ears were filled with water. The dim, strange forest began to darken in earnest. Was it truly night, or was she slipping from reality? If she was cast from her own body, something that could be only done by M'ora, who had apparently betrayed her, would she truly die?

"Leave, or be tested," Daena said, in a voice like wind and fire, a voice that shook the earth and twisted the branches of the trees.

I can't leave. I have too many questions, Maddie thought.

"Then so be it." It was M'ora's voice that came to her, and then all was void.

Out of darkness came light, dim and dull, but light still. It was the light of morning, hazy and hot. New England blue, smoky. The smell was enough to bring Maddie firmly back. The water alone smelled so unusual, tangy and sweet and sour at the same time that it could only be one place. Home.

She was standing on familiar ground, the Bridge of Flowers in Shelburne Falls. How many times had she visited it with

Alvin? It was one of her favorite places in the world. Until Agnes changed that.

The waters churned below but did not fade into the greenery. No, in this strange world the bridge and the river rose out of nothing and then transitioned to sand.

"You could have stopped this," said Agnes, appearing like a phantom on the railing. She wore the same blue dress Maddie had met her in, the same bangles and hoop earrings. Agnes Nelsson was like a Viking princess of old, statuesque and brilliant and terrible and lovely. She loved too hard, she fought too hard.

Maddie felt her heart twist. She remembered reading about her death in the paper, not long after Alvin appeared. She had jumped. She had drowned.

But before that, for one beautiful summer, she and Agnes had been lovers and friends; they had shared dreams and desires. But Maddie let her go. She broke her heart, telling her that she had no long-term commitments in mind. That she was dedicated to her schoolwork. That she didn't need distractions and, thought this whole thing might be a phase.

Most of it was lies. Maddie was afraid of being pigeonholed, treated differently. And Agnes's mood swings unsettled her. For weeks, Agnes would be placid and lovely, and in the space of a day, she would become inconsolable, violent, angry, sorrowful.

"Agnes, I never knew... you could have told me," Maddie pleaded. She took a step toward the ghostly vision of Agnes, but she moved just out of her grasp.

Agnes sighed like the wind. "I told you. You were my goddess. I told you I couldn't live without you."

"And I couldn't live with you. I couldn't... be what you needed me to be."

Agnes turned to Maddie, her hair blowing across her stony features. "I waited for you for two hundred years. And when you came back, you were so weak, so unfamiliar. I thought I could break through you. I tried."

"I'm so sorry, Agnes. I'm so sorry..."

"Then come with me," Agnes said, striding closer. She held out her hands, so long-fingered and flawless. "Jump with me, and we will start anew. In another life, we can have each other again."

The water churned below, welcoming and cold. Maddie knew it would take just one step, and together... they could plunge together. She would be rid of Alvin and Randall, free of her burden to Randy and Mrs. Roth. She could start over without a care in the world, a new twain scrubbed free...

Agnes took another step closer.

The temptation was strong. But not strong enough. Those she loved were waiting for her: Randall could be in danger, and she needed to confront Alvin one last time. She wasn't even sure if the twains of First World were truly aware of the threat he posed, not to mention Matilda's scheming. She could not leave this world because her job wasn't over yet.

The thought steadied her feet.

"I love you, Agnes. I always will. But I can't help you now. This is your choice. It was always your choice..."

Agnes nodded, and turned away from Maddie. She took one long leg and cast it over the stone bannister, then the other. With her arms wide, she jumped.

Maddie forced herself to look. But just as Agnes made contact with the frothy water below, she turned into a snowy owl and flew away.

The sands began to blow, consuming the river, blinding Maddie to the scene. She felt the rough wind blowing against her skin, rubbing her raw, blowing away the remnants of her clothes, tangling her hair and taking away her breath. She felt herself lifted bodily, caught in a cyclone of dust and darkness.

And then she was deposited on a beach. Face down in the

sand, to be exact. Abrasive rocks and shells dug into the side of her face, and these were what caused her to turn about open her eyes, coughing and clutching her side. There was sand in her mouth, between her teeth, crammed in her ears and along her scalp.

Not to mention she was utterly naked.

Sitting and wiping the sand from seemingly everywhere, Maddie took in the lay of the land. It was a fairly straightforward beach, akin to the sort she'd visited in North Carolina during her childhood. Dunes, sea grass, orange flowers, green-blue waves. It was a peaceful place, a welcome place, in spite of the lingering memory of loss and love. Agnes might never forgive her, even after a few times.

No, Maddie didn't want to linger on thoughts of Agnes. It hurt too much, and she had Arthur to think about, Arthur who was innocent of all this and who stood to lose the most if she couldn't stop Alvin.

But why had she been tossed out? What use was she in the middle of a beach?

She took in the landscape but found no houses, no boats. No sign of human life. Not even footprints. And while it was brighter than it had been in the woods where she'd met the green man, there was still no sign of the sun. All was washed out blue and white, the sea and the sky melding into one at the horizon.

Maddie closed her eyes, tried to sense Matilda or M'ora, or anyone for that matter. But nothing came to her, no feeling as she'd had before with the compact or when she was within Matilda.

"For once, I'm completely alone," she said to the sea.

"Not exactly," came a booming voice from behind her.

Maddie swiveled around, covering her breasts. As if it mattered. She was beginning to think propriety wasn't a priority to these people.

Standing behind her was Ian. John. One of their ilk. It was their face behind dark skin and curly hair, but nearly fifty feet tall. His feet were like canoes, and he stood behind her arrayed in simple white linen, the angles of his face so familiar, but his size utterly unreal. Just looking at him gave her a headache.

"Now that's what I call a god," she said in awe.

"We are *not* gods," he replied. "We are parts of gods. We are shattered fragments of the source, spread across eight worlds, destined to live and die and be reborn."

"This is still First World?" Maddie asked, squinting up at him. The sun was behind his head, giving him a halo.

"It is."

"Huh. Wherever I was before was all... *dim* and stuff."

He paused at her pitiable description. "Our fair earth has many faces. As do we all."

"Well, that's well and good. And while I'd love a lecture on the particular idiosyncracies of this particular world, I've got to get back and find Randall. And Alvin. But I'm guessing I've got to get through you, first."

He laughed. The rumbling began somewhere down near his feet, then trembled up like thunder, magnificent and terrifying and somehow joyful. "That is not my test," he said.

Maddie stood up, figuring her shyness really had no place in the face of a fifty-foot high quasi-god standing like some living statue on the seashore, and held out her hands. "Then what the hell am I supposed to do?" she asked.

"Be what you are."

"Great. First you people break my heart, then you tell me to be myself," she said.

"Your actions reverberate across the worlds. Do you understand that now?"

"Crystal clear," Maddie muttered.

"It is a good first lesson. I am Dyas, by the way," he said. "Though you have met my twains, I am not much like them."

"You're a hell of a lot bigger," she said.

"We diminish as we are reborn, every time closer to our human children, it is true. But some of us prefer a more diminutive stature regardless. Personally I do not; being close to humanity is not important to me, as there are none here in First World."

"Fantastic. I suppose you just forgot to make them?" she offered.

"No, we *destroyed* them."

Throwing her lot in with M'ora and the First World was starting to look like a really stupid choice, even worse than trusting Matilda. In fact, Matilda's trysts and generally ornery nature paled in comparison to this monolith of a creature calling himself Dyas.

And why were they bothering with Maddie in the first place? Why hadn't M'ora just outright killed her? Clearly she'd had an ulterior motive.

"M'ora needs you because you're useful," Dyas replied to her thoughts. "But right now you are green."

"Hey! You're not supposed to be in my head!" Maddie snapped, shaking a finger at him.

Dyas growled. Or laughed. It was so damn hard to tell.

Suddenly, Maddie figured out just what was meant by this "test." If, and it was a big if, Matilda had found some way to get to First World, by some trick of Alvin's so-called science, there was a chance M'ora *couldn't* get to her. What was it she had said? There was a block between them. A *rift*.

Yet Maddie had lived inside of Matilda. She knew her likely better than any other twain in existence. She had sensed memories and emotions Matilda had not been able to conceal. Yes, perhaps there was a chance Maddie was stronger than she felt.

Dyas said, "I am the First of the Eight. And I am closer to All. I can hear your thoughts. Except for Matilda; she is a darkling. You understand?"

"Not really. But I get that you want me to find her, because you can't."

Dyas nodded. He held out his hands, thicker than tree-trunks, his fingers like gnarled limbs. The skies swiveled overhead, unnaturally, lightening almost to the point of sunrise and then going out. Maddie sank back down in the sand, shivering; it was night again, except now Dyas was holding the moon between his hands. He'd plucked it from the sky and was cradling it like a child.

Then he knelt, his knees pushing up hills of sand, and Maddie was face to face with the moon.

"M'ora is the bright side of the moon. Matilda is the dark," Dyas said, turning the moon to face her. Instead of keeping its glow, it was dark. And etched into the craters was Matilda's face, pitted and grooved, but very much her own. It was a startling, surreal sight to see, her face as tall as Maddie's entire body.

"You are neither," Dyas said, turning the moon so it was at half–precisely half. "You are *balance.* M'ora can reach you, Matilda can reach you. But you separate them. Matilda is hiding in our world. We have taken the one you call Alvin, and he will pay the price. But Matilda must be at the trial."

"Now there's to be a trial. How remarkably civilized," Maddie said, aware of how much like Matilda she sounded. "And you got Alvin? That means he can't harm anyone?"

"That is left to be determined." Dyas frowned. "Will you find Matilda?"

"I don't know if I can. I can't sense her here at all."

"You are not trying hard enough," Dyas said, rising again. He did not so much stand as he grew, a completely vertical motion up to the stars. His head was crowned with a coronet filled with starlight and comets tracking across the skies. King of the gods, indeed. Maddie was not afraid of him so much as she was cautious, wary. Maybe he was right: The more times a twain was reborn, the closer they were to humanity. Because he certainly seemed generations removed from her.

Maddie stood, too, feeling sand in most uncomfortable places. For once, she truly wished she had Matilda's clothing. Even a metal corset would be welcome.

"I need my guide. My bird," Maddie said.

"You may find him, if you need him," Dyas said.

"How?" she asked. "I'm buck naked on a beach without a boat. How the hell am I going to find anyone, let alone a particular raven, in a world I know nothing of?"

"You already have the power. You have only forgotten."

"How can you be so sure?" Maddie asked. She had only blinked, but it had been long enough. Dyas was gone. Two vast footprints remained in the sand, the wind blowing them away with each passing moment.

"Perfect," Maddie muttered. "Wait! Maybe he means the compass."

It had translated with her between worlds; maybe it had come along on this latest journey. Maddie started rooting around for it in the dunes and beneath the sea grass, hoping to turn up something useful. But all she found were rocks, hard and unrelenting beneath her hands. Dyas had manipulated the entire world around him, but she was at its mercy. What the hell was she going to do?

She took a deep breath and tried to remember what happened when she used the compass.

"If I had a compass, I'd hold it out like this and look... that way," she said, turning to her left. The moon was gone, and she shivered, wondering if Dyas really had taken it out of the sky. Trippy.

"I'd think of Randall, first. As helpful as Joss is, I... I just... ow!"

Her hand had ignited. She jumped back, cradling her fingers. Had there been a spark, there? Some fire? Her pointer finger and thumb still stung, feeling blistered. She sucked on it ruefully a moment.

But curiosity outweighed Maddie's alarm. She was alone, after all, and if she was ever to get through this alive, she was going to have to find Matilda again, whether or not she wanted to. So far this was the only progress she had made.

Steeling herself for pain, she held out her hand again as if holding the compass. She flicked her fingers experimentally, then stared down at the center of her palm, concentrating on the very middle as the waves lapped against the shore.

Was it just her, or was the tide rising?

No, that was a distraction. She would have to start walking, and presuming the compass worked because of some strange, innate power, perhaps she could use it to her own advantage, even if it wasn't physically present.

As she concentrated, the sting in her hands came again, this time less severe. It started in her middle finger, then pulsated toward her thumb and pinky. Then, to a lesser extent, spread to her other fingers, connecting everything in a dull, humming kind of pressure.

Maddie was about to give up when light began pulsing from her hand. It started in the middle, then reached out: the middle finger connected to the pinky and thumb, then elongated on the axis—four points. Then another four points, within those.

The compass.

It was radiant, green light. In her own hands. It wasn't the compass itself that held the power; she had only channeled her own.

She remembered M'ora's words: "That's you. The green one. I always think of green when I think of you."

"Well, hell. I'm hoping you work the same as the pretty compact," Maddie said to her hand, and almost laughed. "Let's find Randall."

Maddie closed her eyes and concentrated. She thought of Randall's smile; of Randy's smile. She thought of Randall's clever eyes; of Randy's innocent eyes. She thought of their smell. Of the feeling of their lips...

The light went out.

"No! Come back, come back!" Maddie shouted at her hands.

She tried again. Joss, this time. Surely he would be easier to find. She didn't have him all muddled up with someone else. Hadn't he said the roads between his world and this one were rivers? Something to that effect. Surely if she was in the middle of the ocean, he'd be somewhere nearby.

Maddie was ready for utter failure when the compass began to glow again in her hand, this time keeping steady. It pulsed a few times, as if considering her thoughts; she tried to draw Joss in her mind as clearly as possible, remembering the lines of his face, the color of his hair.

And sure enough, a new light appeared in the center of her hands, swirling steadily amidst the ethereal compass, bright blue and constant.

And pointing directly out to sea.

Rather than give up, Maddie stopped and considered. All she needed was a big scallop shell and a breeze, and she'd be a living diorama of *The Birth of Venus.*

She laughed at that.

Who was it in the picture with Venus? One of the Horae, which would be helpful if she could scare one up. And winds. Zephyrs. Sure, *The Birth of Venus* was one of those cliché paintings, one that even non-art history students knew. And yet, Maddie felt thinking about it wasn't out of place at all. If Randall and John and the rest were right, then Maddie herself had some universal, metaphysical connection to Venus, as she truly was. It was just a painting from the 15th century. But who was to say it was useless? A little imagination could go a long way, especially in a place like this.

The wind picked up, blowing steadily out to sea. With it

came a deep, murky smell, sulfurous but not entirely unpleasant.

Maddie kept the compass going with one hand, and knelt down at the shore, where there was more rubble and rock. She didn't expect to find a scallop shell as big as a boat, exactly, but she felt there was a clue there. She only had to find it.

As if in response to her thoughts, the compass thrummed in her hand, beating like the heart of a star.

Still, after digging for a while, she came up with nothing but shards of rock and shells. Her fingertips were raw and sore.

Frustrated, and hoping she didn't have to simply go to Matilda alone—dreading that was the truth of it, and fearing she wouldn't survive the encounter—Maddie walked into the frothing tide, letting the water swirl around her legs, tickling her skin.

The tide's pull was surprising, and the sand around her feet sifted away quickly, so her feet began to sink.

Just as she was about to pull her feet out, Maddie felt her heel strike something hard. Something buried, awaiting discovery.

She extinguished the compass a moment and pulled at the mass at her foot. It was stuck well, and the cold seawater rose up past her elbows as she worked at it, churning and resisting her. But she gritted her teeth and dug her heels in, until she fell back on her bare bottom to the sand, winded, but with her prize. Whatever it was.

Looking down between her legs, she saw the perfect outline of a very large quahog still stuck with sand. But unlike the quahogs she was familiar with in her own world, it was mouthing at her, opening and closing its hinged lid with the rhythm of the waves.

Grabbing it with both hands, she immediately started prying it open. Surely the secret must be inside. But it resisted heartily, the muscles clamping down with intense strength, nearly catching her fingers in the process.

"Maybe it's like the compass," she said, turning it over in her hands. "Gotta figure I'm kind of a one-trick pony at this point."

So she held it out in her hands and concentrated. She thought of Joss, out there somewhere in the rough, churning sea, and begged the stupid quahog for guidance. It jumped in her hand, popping as if it were a baked potato in the microwave, then shuddered.

Then it opened, almost like the compass itself. Two strings of pearls fell out on each side of the half of the shell, like shoelaces. The pearls were so small, they were hardly more than pebbles, but they reminded Maddie of M'ora's lesson. If that lesson was accurate at all. But rather than think of her First World twain's treachery, she focused on the task at hand.

"Huh," she said. "Shoes are better than no shoes, I guess." Maddie laughed through her nose. "I've clearly gone crazy."

There was still a good amount of flesh within the quahog, evenly dispersed between two halves. As she slid her foot in the first one, she winced; it was warm and slimy. But in a moment, it was actually reassuring. The tacky substance inside melted around her feet, and before she knew it, she was quite comfortable. Not exactly Birkenstocks, but she'd take it.

"Just like the *Birth of Venus*," Maddie said to herself as she stepped out toward the water again. She did not want to be taken by the waves, but something told her she didn't need to worry.

One step, cautious. Her foot bobbed a moment, but then, as the tide rose again, she found she had a surprisingly firm foothold. A step with the other foot; yes, that was it. She was on top of the water, skimming the surface like waterbug, the pearl laces twisting up her calves of their own volition. The strands emitted a soft glow in the moonlight, tracing beautiful shapes around her legs and stopping just below her knees.

And the shells were no longer shaped as they had been. No, she was indeed wearing a pair of slippers, tapered against her toes and fine as any ballet shoe. The outsides glimmered with mother of pearl. Even Matilda would be impressed.

She took a deep breath, trying not to think of the depth of the water. As a rule, she hated swimming in the ocean. And naked and cold as she was, the prospect of any dog-paddling any distance was rather disheartening.

Summoning what was left of her courage and shaking off her fatigue, Maddie slid one hand out, her arms flailing to keep balance, and proceeded. It was worse than ice skating, since the water actually moved beneath her.

"Gotta do better than this if I want to keep the compass up," she muttered.

She managed another few feet, and finally was able to keep her balance with a single arm up.

Maddie turned about to spy the shore. Dyas's footprints still remained, and the moonless sky spoke of her own insignificance.

Now was the time to move. She was free. So she slid upon the surface, gliding like a cross-country skier, holding out her hand and moving toward the blue blip on her compass.

"There we go," she said, laughing in the wind. "Just me and the great big sea."

Time undulated; the sun rose, set, rose again. It felt too fast, and Maddie should have worried about getting a sunburn, what with being buck-naked on an immense plain of water. But she was thinking of Joss, and the faster she got to him, the faster she could get to Alvin, to Randall, and to answers.

Sure, she was playing with the big dogs. They made that clear. And they weren't going to let her just traipse into their world without a challenge. But they wouldn't start the trial without Matilda, and if Matilda was hiding somewhere in First World, well, Maddie was the only one who could find her.

At the second twilight, Maddie spotted land. An island, to be exact. And on the shore twinkled a small, blue-flamed fire.

Joss.

She called out to him, but her voice was so dry from dis-use that she hardly made a sound.

This wasn't good.

As she approached, she saw him standing with a spear, poised to strike. No, not a spear: a trident.

What must she look like, slinking across the water in the dark? Naked and sunburned, her hair a tousled mess, her legs entwined in glowing pearls?

She tried to call out again, but nothing more than a croak came from her throat. The sun slipped away over the horizon, and she put down her compass, the bright light extinguishing.

Too late.

He had thrown the trident.

At least I know he can't kill me, she thought, just as the tri-dent made contact with her thigh.

She flipped, head over heels, and skidded across the water, crashing into a wave at least six feet tall. Maddie felt her head make contact with rocks, tasted water in her mouth, salty and full of minerals. Her thigh radiated with pain, and she impul-sively went to touch it, then reeled with the threat of passing out.

The trident was firmly embedded in her leg.

13

Breaking

 nly by luck did Maddie Angler manage to wash up on shore. But without her shoes.

"Oh, damn!" she heard Joss call in the distance.

Was he really that far away? Or was she just losing consciousness again?

"Maddie... you didn't even... oh damn," Joss said again. She felt his hands on her chest, pressing to feel if she had a heartbeat.

"Do twains even need hearts?" she asked, feeling drowsy and a little giddy. "You can't kill me... I..."

"I can hurt you, though," Joss whispered. "I can wound you."

"Ow," Maddie gasped as Joss started poking around at her wound. He was still too blurry to make out, but she could tell it was him just by virtue of his presence. "What's the point of being a twain if you can bleed?"

"You've been reborn many times," Joss said. "Your body's not as strong as mine. Or theirs. But you found me, and that's miraculous. I'm sorry—I shouldn't have speared you."

"What an enlightening opinion," Maddie replied. She had

closed her eyes at some point, but now she opened them and giggled.

Joss's face was but a breath from hers. He'd gotten bedraggled since the last time she'd seen him, his beard strewn with seaweed and his skin darker. He was clothed, at least. Which was something, considering how often she'd seen the man nude.

"Looks like I'm the naked one this time," she said, baring her teeth. The pain in her leg moved from searing and gutwrenching to throbbing and mind-shattering.

"I'm not much help," Joss said, finally moving his face away.

Maddie was resisting the urge to kiss him, and wanted to slap herself for even thinking it. She was just as bad as Matilda! What was she thinking? It was shameful.

"I've got to find Matilda," she said, trying to sit up.

Joss forced her back down, his warm, dry hands firm on her shoulders. She felt the sand relent slightly beneath her head, and she sighed as the pain continued.

"First, you have to be able to walk again. I still can't believe that was you, skating across the water like that. I figured it was some horror out to get me..." he said, his voice trailing off. Joss stood and walked around past Maddie's field of vision. "It's been difficult as of late, and I'm sorry. I'm jumpy."

"You? Jumpy? That green man didn't worry you... ow..." She gasped as the pain started crawling up her leg, tears springing to her eyes.

"I have been marooned out here," he said.

"Can't you swim?" she asked.

The waves had been treacherous until Maddie figured out their puzzle. But there was something else in Joss's eye when she glimpsed him before screeching in pain again. He stood, then knelt again. She reached up to touch the side of his face, needing to make contact for some strange reason, but he turned away.

"Maddie..." Joss said.

She steeled herself to speak, gasping and crying a moment before managing another coherent phrase. "You don't know how to help me."

He was silent a moment. Maddie looked over his head and swore the moon rose and fell. Stars swirled. She could blame it on the pain, but she had a feeling it was more than that. Something ethereal, impossible to pin down. He put his hand into hers. Touching him felt good on many levels.

"No idea," he said. "I could bring water, but... this is not a poison I can heal."

"Kiss me," she said, unable to fight the urge. She would have laughed if she could have, but the tears and the pain were a force impossible to reckon with. "Kiss me just for a minute."

"Madeline..."

"Joss!" Maddie pleaded. The pain was mounting, surrounding her. She could feel and hear the worlds in the distance calling to her, especially her own. If she gave in to the pain, she would leave this world–so close to Alvin!–and end up having to explain to the ER doctor why there was an antique trident stuck in her leg. If such things transferred across the worlds.

But that didn't matter.

Her thoughts were getting jumbled up.

"If I don't figure something out..." she attempted, "I'll be sucked back home. And I won't be able to get back. Not in this much pain. Please. Just kiss me."

"I can try to sew up the wound," he offered, balking at her affection. There was fear in his eyes.

"If I was... Matilda... you wouldn't think twice, you bastard," Maddie shouted. "I'm losing my mind with the pain and the only thing this strange twain body is telling me to do is kiss you."

"Maddie..."

"Please, Joss."

With a sigh like breaking waves, he knelt down and smoothed his hand down her cheek. Then he leaned over and kissed her on the lips.

It was not a kiss of passion, but Maddie felt better as soon as his lips touched hers. His beard tickled at first. She couldn't explain how she knew what to do, but as soon as he kissed her, she began breathing in. Maddie opened up her lungs, stretched out her arms, and took in as much radiant energy as she could from the marooned godling of the sea. The kiss felt as if it opened up his entire soul to her.

Maddie saw his memories, his lifetimes, strung together. Joss Raddick as a king, as a pauper; a fisherman. She saw the faces of those he loved, some familiar like Agnes and Matilda, and others foreign. Maddie saw the faces of children, heard their laughter—felt his sadness, his loss. What he had given up to live so long.

The memories dissolved, and Maddie's body tingled, starting at the top of her head, then flushing downward. The tingling sensation stopped a moment at her thigh, where the trident was still stuck firm. But the pain eased considerably.

Then she began to laugh. She pulled away from Joss, who fell down beside her, and reached for the trident. Eyes wide open, Maddie saw how insubstantial she really was, how insignificant her mortal body was. The power, the kiss, had allowed her to cut through her base understanding of her own being. Now she understood that she was more than flesh and bone. She was spirit, and karma, and magic, and love, and lust.

Looking at her thigh, she noted how lines of light pulsed around it, twisting like delicate fish line.

"That's one hell of a knot," she said, wiping her eyes with the back of her hand.

Joss stared at her leg, jaw hanging open.

"Now that I can see it, I can untie it," he said, somber. She had never seen him so mirthless.

"Please, go ahead," Maddie said.

Joss winced. "How's the pain?"

"Right now, not so bad... I didn't hurt you, did I? With the kissing?"

Then he smiled. "On the contrary. I feel quite revived."

The way he said that reminded her of Randall, and Maddie felt a stab of guilt in her stomach. Not now. It would have to wait.

"Please, before I pass out again," Maddie said.

Joss took a deep breath and then put his hand over his heart, as if making a silent prayer. Maddie didn't press him about it; the pain was slowly returning, the lines of energy radiating down her leg starting to dim.

But Joss was deft. Maybe it was because he had thrown the trident, and it was a part of him, too. Or maybe it was simply that knots made sense to him. Maddie had never seen someone so confidently approach a knot, nor so skillfully untie it.

He didn't even use his fingers.

He merely waved his hands above the wound, and the knotwork complied, rising and falling with an invisible tide between them. She felt every twist and turn, like invisible cords beneath her skin. And when the last knot released, her muscles all relaxed, and she fell back on the sand.

"It's out," Joss said, the trident hitting the ground with a dull thud.

Maddie's body still tingled, and she sighed. "Good. Give me a second to rest, then we've got to figure out a way to get out of here."

When Maddie was strong enough to walk, she and Joss traced the periphery of the island together. It was twilight again, and Maddie gave up trying to tell the time by the moon and stars. Apparently, the basics of astronomy just didn't apply here in First World.

Joss looked tense. He only spoke when Maddie addressed

him, and continually looked out to sea, longingly.

When they found no more quahogs, or anything useful other than palm fronds and some driftwood, they sat together by the fire in silence, scanning the horizon. There was little to eat other than a handful of berries Joss determined weren't poisonous. But it was a sparse meal.

The island was perilously small. And Maddie was exhausted. Whatever she had accomplished by kissing Joss was done, but now something hung between them like Damocles's sword.

"So," she said at last, "no dice."

"No dice, indeed," Joss agreed. He drew a circle in the sand with a stick and looked over to her.

"You've got nothing?"

"Nothing to what?"

"To suggest. You're older than me by a few centuries, I'm pretty sure. But you're glum. Can't you turn into an albatross, or a whale? Sail us on out of here?"

"As I mentioned, Posis, my twain here, has marooned me. If I set foot in the water, I'm declaring war with him. And to be quite honest with you, kid, I'd really prefer to stay out of this business."

"You want to go home?"

He nodded. "I made no promises; I followed you, thinking it would be straightforward. But now..."

"I frighten you." Maddie shrugged when she said it.

"You are more powerful than I thought. And I'm worried that the twains here are seeking to press you to power, rather than to simply test you. I worry they want to use you."

"Use me? Because I can kiss people and get all glowy?" She smoothed her hand over her thigh, all unscathed, as if she'd never been struck there.

Joss shook his head. "It's more than that. The First World has never reached out to us before. I don't trust them."

Maddie stood up, finding herself rather agitated with Joss's attitude, and brushed the dirt from her bottom. She had Joss's shirt tied around her waist, but it did little in the way of hiding anything. For a moment she was almost embarrassed; then she thought better of it. Even the concept of her own body was feeling less and less substantial since her last few translations, not to mention what had happened after kissing Joss.

"What are you doing?" Joss asked.

She had closed her eyes and held out her hands. "Yoga," she said. "I need to center myself. I'm feeling all wound up."

"Yoga?" he asked.

"Oh! My compass!" Maddie said, falling out of mountain pose and scrambling over to Joss. "I forgot to show you."

"Your compass?" Joss's expression indicated he believed Maddie had completely lost her mind.

Maddie nodded, holding out her hand. She smiled as her fingers kindled almost immediately, the lines joining and clarifying in the space of a few heartbeats. And it didn't hurt like it had before. So she was getting the hang of it, after all.

"Stars above," Joss said. The blue light reflected in his eyes, casting shadows on his noble face.

"It's my compass. It's not just... I mean, in Second World, I have a physical compass. A compact. It came with me to Sixth, but then it disappeared. Anyway, I figured out how to use the power without the object. That's how I found you. But the last time I tried to think of Randall, I was zapped," Maddie said with a frown. When she said his name, the center of the compass went from blue to orange for just a moment. "I got a pair of shoes from this quahog..."

Joss raised an eyebrow.

"I know, it sounds really weird. But that's how I got here. The shoes were these slippers, and I skated across the water to you. I'm sure I can figure out a way to skate us both to where we need to be. To stop Matilda and Alvin and M'ora, or whoever we're stopping at this point."

Joss sighed in response to her ebullient courage. "Maddie, I'm tired. I never meant to get involved in this."

"But you *are* involved. You fucked Matilda, and she's fucking all of us. And you're right, we *can't* trust the twains of First World." She paused, looking him over, fixing him with her gaze. She could sense there was something honest about Joss, in spite of his curious association with Matilda from before. He was a twain with no connections, not really. But he was developing something like affection for her. She read it in every line of his face. "But I think we can trust each other."

"You think so?"

"Yes," Maddie said. "I saw... when you kissed me, I saw the things that mean something to you. The faces, the friends. That's why you were hesitant to do it, right?" she asked.

He nodded. "I've been kissed like that before. I know what it means."

"Joss, don't you see? We have love in common. We love people. Whether or not it's against our better judgment. And that means we have a hell of a lot more to fight for than anyone else here," she said.

"I don't know. I've fought wars, and lost, and love never mattered."

"But it's worth a shot, isn't it? For all the people we love?" Maddie sighed, taking in the sea air.

Joss nodded reluctantly.

The wind picked up, and Maddie shivered. Something was happening to her, deep on a level she was just starting to understand. Even though she was no longer glowing from the inside, as she had after she kissed Joss, her whole body was sensitive, flowing, almost liquid-feeling beneath her skin. It was sensual, but somewhat unsettling.

She walked to the water's edge, and dipped her toe in,

smiling as the cool currents caressed the soles of her feet. The water went on forever, reaching to the horizon, curving at the edges like the oceans of her world. But everything smelled saltier, cleaner. The skies, when they were of a mind to be anything other than twilight, achieved a most astonishing blue at the apex. Azure.

Joss was standing some paces behind her.

Maddie continued with her half-baked plan. "So, I can locate Matilda. That's the good part. The complicated part is that we can't get to her. At least, since your horse-changing magic stuff doesn't work here. Because if you fall into the water, you end up fodder for your twain, is that right?"

"That about explains it," Joss said.

"If only I could..." Maddie wondered aloud.

"Could what?" Joss asked.

"Change into a horse," she said. "How'd you figure that out, anyway?"

Joss smiled. "It first happened when I was thirty or so, I think... in this life, at least. I was on the run from a man who swore I was stealing from him, back when the Frontier was still in dispute. I got to the Mississippi River, flanked by half a tribe, and then... well, I thought to myself that if I didn't figure out a way across the water, I was going to end up dead. I wanted to be swift as a horse. Fleet-footed. That term, precisely, is what I thought."

"Interesting," Maddie said, looking back over the water. "And can you turn into anything that flies?"

"Here? No. That would be too much of a threat."

"You think I could do it?"

"Do what?"

"Turn into a horse. Or my equivalent."

"You could try. We *are* in dire straits."

"There you go with the water puns again," Maddie said with a wry grin. "But I'm going to try."

For the first time in a while, Joss actually looked excited about something. He had a glimmer in his eye, that characteristic spark of someone passing knowledge on. "First you must relax. Open your mind. Let things flow through you; that's about the best advice I can give," he said. "I don't know if it'll work for you... I've certainly never seen Matilda do it. But considering what you've accomplished in so little time, I wouldn't be surprised if you could turn into a dragon—the scaly kind, not the sort we already are—and cart us both off."

"Sure. Easy-peasy, right?"

So she tried. And she failed. Again and again and again. To her knowledge, and despite a most concerted effort, absolutely nothing happened. Not even a hint. Maddie started scolding herself inwardly for ever thinking she could manage magic of the same magnitude as Joss. Joss demonstrated how he was able to transform back and forth into a horse, always on the sands, of course, and it looked absolutely second-nature. Like a bird unfurling its wings.

She watched Joss undergo the transformation to his horse over and over, noted how the lines of his body rearranged. It was like he possessed a second skeleton under his skin, something entirely ethereal and unrelated to his human form. He had complete control over it, and could rearrange at his desire. This curious framework, she believed, had to be the key to transformation. It folded up or stretched out depending on how he commanded himself.

Yet despite her ability to mimic process, whenever she tried herself, was useless. There were no sparks, no hints of magic happening in any capacity at all. She simply did nothing.

"Yeah, this is totally not happening," she said, plopping down on the sand. Her head pounded with the strain of concentration, and she was growing thirstier by the minute. If they didn't find a way to get off the damned island soon enough, what physical material her body was comprised of was going to wither and die. She was fairly sure that was a possibility. It might take longer than it would for the average human being, but it was certainly plausible.

For all his encouragement, Joss was little help. He couldn't explain how he did what he did, and Maddie was growing more and more frustrated with him by the moment. In fact, he was starting to get rather forlorn about the whole matter of their marooning.

The sky had a second sunset, and but the sun never quite rose. Time in First World slipped and slid like currents in a tide pool.

"I keep wondering why I keep hoping for the sun," she said to Joss. "Then I remembered. Randall. It's like I'm waiting for him."

Maddie was lying prostrate on the sand, staring up into the weird blue sky, when she heard lapping at the shore. At first she figured it was just a change in the tide, but then she remembered that there hadn't even been one since she arrived. The tides were oddly nonexistent here on Joss's island. Maybe the moon really was gone.

She turned her head to see Joss standing at the edge of the water, dipping his toes in.

"Joss!" she called, scrambling to her feet. "What the hell are you doing?"

Joss gave her a look—a strange, eerily detached look. His face was steely, his eyes almost dead. He looked remote, god-like, harder than iron.

"Joss," Maddie said again, more cautiously. "You can't go into the water. That would cause way too much trouble. The last thing we want is another twain on our tails. You said it yourself, you didn't want to come along for any of this."

"You're right," he said. Then he smiled, and it melted his cold veneer. He was radiant. "But you need a little danger right about now, Madeline. And I think this just might do the trick."

Joss plunged into the waves, and immediately they began surging around him. The water turned from blue-grey to an unforgiving purple and brown, churning up the sand and silt below, twisting around Joss's ankles and crashing up to his stomach.

There was no fear in his eyes. There was release. Welcome.

"Shit, shit, shit, shit!" Maddie cried as she started off toward him.

Whatever power Joss's twain held, it was great. Maddie could feel it all around her. Not just in the power of the waves, but in the sound of the wind, the spray of foam building all around them. It thrummed in her ears, filling the center of her with pressure, fear, longing.

Water continued to swirl about Joss, pulling him down into the darkening surge. His hair came unbound, falling long and pale down his shoulders and back. The veins in Joss's neck and chest became more pronounced, and there was a flicker of pain in his expression.

That was it.

Maddie sprang forward to rescue him, somehow.

She was halfway into the air, clutching Joss somehow, before she fully realized what had happened. As soon as she noticed what she was doing–flying–she banked unexpectedly to the left. Pressure below, and laughter followed, but she took a deep breath and focused in front of her her, staring straight ahead and toward the horizon.

"I knew it!" Joss said from somewhere below her. He was laughing like a maniac.

Maddie hurt all over, and after finally achieving a comfortable altitude, she ventured a reply. "What... what happened? What..."

She glanced to the side. Wings. Wide, brown wings with long, silky feathers. But she distinctly felt hair atop her head and over the rest of her body, all rustling in the wind. And she smelled just like the lion's pelt John had given her to wear when she'd transported to his cabin.

Yet she spoke normally. If she had transformed into some creature, it was far easier to speak than she had expected.

"You're a bloody sphinx," Joss replied. "Now, let go a little, please. Your talons are digging into my side."

Thankfully, there was another island nearby, and there Joss was able to take up a more comfortable spot between Maddie's lovely wings. She was rather vain about them, fretting unexpectedly about whether or not the salt air would damage their plumage. It was strange to be in this form, but exhilarating, too. And she was aware that she ought to be a little more disoriented, and rather confused by it all.

But it felt right. There was no other way to explain it. It was no different than her own, human body, she reflected. At the core, she felt the very same. The framework had shifted and that was all.

"You're beside yourself with pride," Joss said, adjusting himself on her back.

"I should be. This is awesome," Maddie replied, pawing the sand with her talons and shaking her back legs.

"Yes, it is. But we might want to use that compass of yours again."

"Compass. Right," Maddie said, taking a few experimental flaps with her wings. "Except I don't have hands like I did before."

"I don't think you should even need hands. You didn't need the compass as an object, after all. It's merely a channel," Joss said. "It stands to reason that the only true compass is your heart."

"That's rather profound of you," Maddie said.

Joss added, "And thank you. It was a close one back there."

"You're welcome," she replied. "I didn't... well, I'm just glad your stunt landed us a ticket out of there, and not a journey to the depths. I guess that means, for now, we're playing by their rules."

"Oh?"

"They want me for one reason. Not because they like me, or because they want me in their club. But because I'm some important incarnation, right? Because I can find people. Because I have this compass."

"You may be right," Joss said.

Maddie sighed, considering the options. This was a wide, strange world, and she had only her heart to guide her. It sounded corny as hell, but it's all she held onto at that moment, staring out across the ocean, watching the stars blink to life on the horizon.

She closed her eyes, felt the wind blowing across her strange new body, and thought of her compass. Maddie saw it perfectly in her mind's eye and, with growing clarity, noted the dozens of points of light kindling on it. Not just Matilda and Randall and Alvin and the rest, but many more twains across many more worlds. Layers upon layers of them, with stories to tell and secrets to hide.

"Ready for takeoff?" she asked Joss.

"As much as I can be. And your compass?"

"Turns out I never lost it," she replied.

Time grew no more concrete, but Maddie was fairly certain about the span of a day passed before she felt Matilda's presence close enough to justify landing. They had spent half the day soaring over the water, but soon found land, crossing to verdant fields and forests inhabited mostly by birds. These strange flocks passed them on occasion, grey and white and brown-beaked, regarding Maddie with distant curiosity before following their route.

They never passed a city or a town, but they flew over many ruins, hints at the civilization that had once flourished on First World. Now and then, roads wound their way through mountain passes, or rocky hillsides suggested the outline of fences and farm boundaries. Seeing it made Maddie sad, and she wondered how long ago the godlings of First World had done away with humanity, and how they reconciled themselves with that decision. They had destroyed them, Dyas had said without so much as a shrug. Gone like mayflies in a hectic, hot summer.

It was a somber flight, but Maddie could not help but enjoy the feeling of the wind on her face, the thrill of it as it tickled through her feathers, the force of currents bolstering her up into the atmosphere. Flying was freedom and escape and joy, up in the clouds, and part of her regretted to have to sit down and give it up.

Someday, she decided, if she made it out of First World alive, she was going to fly somewhere remarkable. Alone, and free.

"This is familiar," Maddie said, scanning the landscape. She couldn't be certain, but it reminded her of where she had first touched down with Randall. The topography was nothing but rolling hills, streams, and trees, but she remembered it as if she had seen it from this distance before.

And the darkness. She remembered the feeling of Matilda lingering all too well.

"When did it happen?" she asked Joss as they started their descent. "With Matilda. When did she... break?"

Joss shuffled in his seat, clearing his throat. "She suffered the death of a child. Their child. Fifty years ago, perhaps. I don't recall. It's so rare for a twain to conceive..."

"It was Randall's?" Maddie asked, not wanting the answer necessarily.

"I highly doubt that. She cracked then, but she was never a faithful wife," Joss said, as softly as he could.

Maddie felt insulted, somehow, as if she, too, could never

be true to a husband. Not that she'd ever thought much on the subject.

Joss leaned over to get a better look at the landscape, chang-ing the subject. "Up there, to the north, that's where I met you. The composition of the stream is right. There's a dark copse of trees leading to the stream where we fought the green man."

It stood to reason that Matilda would be lurking in the shadows. Maddie could sense her, as surely as if they were sharing a body again. Her nerves fired, and her hackles rose as she made her descent. Instead of landing in the darker wood, Maddie set down gently at the edge of a small clearing. It was a better landing than her first, but still jarring. Joss tumbled off her back into the soft grass, coughing and winded.

"Sorry," she said. "I'm still getting the hang of things."

"No trouble," Joss said, standing and brushing himself off. He stared into the trees, frowning.

"She knows I'm here," Maddie whispered, falling down into a more protective stance. She dug her claws into the ground and lowered her head, letting out a growl. She didn't have any idea how such a noise could come from her, but it felt natural and somehow important. "It's like... it's almost like she's being scrambled, her broadcast. Something is in the way... She's an-gry, but I can't make sense of her words."

"It may be she is thinking in something much more an-cient than English," Joss said. "If she's as angry as I imagine she is... well, she has all the abilities you do, Maddie. She is dangerous."

"I think I can take care of her," Maddie said, but the words were not convincing her heart to stop pounding.

"There, I can hear something," Joss said, holding his mas-sive hands to the ground.

Maddie could feel Matilda's presence as surely as if she could see her. She was just behind the cover of the trees, and Maddie's stomach did backflips thinking of what it would be like to see her face-to-face.

"Why doesn't she just come out?" Joss asked. "We know she's in there."

"She's biding her time," said Maddie, just as she felt the air ripple slightly. Her hackles rose, and she wanted the taste of blood so strongly it almost frightened her. "Maybe she wants to come to a compromise?" she tried.

They were two sides of a coin, after all. Try as she might do otherwise, Maddie still pitied Matilda. She held onto the pity, let it keep her calm, prevent her strange new body from lunging into the trees and biting whatever moved, tasting its blood. Because that's what she wanted to do. Her face might have been human, but her heart was a lion's.

Joss was moving behind her, changing into something more useful, perhaps, when something black and limp flew out from the trees, rotating head over feet and making no effort to counter the force propelling it.

Randall.

His bird's body hit the ground with a whisper of feathers on grass, and Maddie pounced beside it before she could prevent herself. Her body came with a new set of rules, and she was finding it difficult to control. She had to protect him.

Bending down, Maddie sniffed at his poor little bird body. He was not dead, at least. Maddie could still sense his heart beating. But he was wounded by something that coiled around him like black vines, and his life was ebbing away.

"You!" shouted Maddie into the trees. "Come out where I can see you!"

"Madeline..." croaked Randall. "Don't... she's..."

Scooping up Randall's body in one of her great paws, Maddie took a few paces backward, finding a soft bed of moss on which to rest him. He would have to wait.

The battle was coming, and she could do nothing to stop it.

Fight

"Y ou've come a long way, I see," Matilda voice called out, her body still beyond Maddie's field of vision.

The trees moved, parting for Matilda as if she commanded them. But nothing was yet visible save the shadows. The whole world held its breath for her entrance. Indeed, some things did not change, even across worlds.

Maddie waited, keeping her breathing as even as possible; every muscle in her impressive new frame was rigid and simply waiting for the right moment to pounce.

"If you've hurt Randall, I'll kill you," Maddie growled.

"How quaint. You still think this is about him! Well, I see you've managed to figure out transfiguration, at the very least," Matilda cooed, amused, from the darkness. "It's a start."

"There's no need to keep hidden," Joss shouted, his voice full of echoes and odd resonances. The trees rustled back at him. Maddie spared a moment to look over her wings; Joss was keeping guard over Randall, as a horse again. He continued, stomping the ground, "We've found you. It's time we end this."

"Bold words from a turncoat," Matilda observed. "But

you have always been fickle, so I can't say I'm surprised."

"I gave you every chance," Maddie said. "I trusted you. I believed you–"

"How sweet. But that doesn't matter now." Matilda laughed her haunted laugh, and at last emerged into the dim light that was First World.

Maddie fell back, unable to take in the sight of her twain at first. What Matilda had become defied explanation. True, Maddie was now a sphinx, a transformation that was hardly Biology 101. But while Maddie was just learning the skill, Matilda was positively expert. She was a beautiful terror and perfect, gleaming as if carved in black glass.

Matilda stood the height of a draft horse, cloaked in dark, writhing tendrils of power. She was black, shadowed and strange, with a tapered nose more like that of a deer than a horse, and eyes of a vicious red. The wings that spouted from Matilda's back were covered in shiny black feathers, tinted red and sharp-tipped. When she shook her coat, flecks of blood–Maddie could tell by the smell–splattered upon the forest floor, hissing.

And when Matilda opened her mouth, Maddie cowered to see teeth sharp as razors, white needles against elegant lips. Yes, Maddie had seen this beast before, lingering on the edge of Matilda's consciousness. Had she allowed Maddie to see it? Or was it a rift in her defenses? Maddie desperately hoped for the latter.

Matilda moved, but her feet did not touch the ground. Instead, she shifted across the grass, smoke and blood and fear propelling her.

"I suppose in some strange way, I'm sorry to have to kill you now," Matilda said, flapping her wings.

Maddie squinted as shadows surrounded her. Whatever Matilda was doing was working, sending her into a panic. First World dimmed around her, and she felt her body struggling, losing her grasp on her stronger sphinx form.

"You put up more of a fight than I anticipated," Matilda continued, her voice taking on a simpering note.

"You just used me to get to M'ora," Maddie managed, straining to speak through her fear. She only wanted to lie down and curl into a ball, to give up, to die. It felt like the right thing to do. Matilda was right.

"I did," Matilda said. "I suspected Randall was conspiring to get you to Second World. Why would I let him have all the fun? You are surprisingly useful, if bogglingly dull-witted."

In the swirling dark, Maddie felt her body wasting away. Her feathers sunk back into her skin, her limbs withered. The strength she had possessed ebbed away from her, drifting away. And with the fading of her sphinx form, she sensed her weakness, her nakedness.

Matilda did, too. She circled Maddie, buffeting her wings, speaking her poisonous words through heinous teeth. The language was strange and sibilant, but Maddie was too terrified to understand more than its predominant theme: death.

Death and darkness surrounded Matilda, flocked to her and grew in number. It was like the darkness Maddie had experienced when Matilda had taken over their once-shared body; she knew the feeling, the pressing power, the utter hopelessness. It had been inevitable then; why not now? Maddie felt childish and ashamed for having ever thought she could rise up against her twain. She should have worshiped Matilda, she thought dimly, not fought against her.

"Remember what we share!"

The very earth seemed to speak, for just a moment, in Joss's voice. And Maddie remembered what she had said to him, why she trusted him. They shared love, after all. And it was the only thing that separated them from Matilda, and separated Maddie from ultimate despair.

So she bent down and concentrated, opening up her heart. And it was not Alvin she thought of as she cowered in Matilda's encroaching darkness. It was not Randall, or Mrs. Roth; it was not Ian, or Agnes, or any of the other people—twains and otherwise—she had encountered in her short life.

It was Randy, and Randy only. It was his eyes, his smile she knew so well. She remembered the smell of his wool sweater and their mutual love of junk food. She remembered the first time she saw him, and the last time. He was as near to her as if he had been in First World. For a brief moment, she thought she saw him standing at the corner of her vision, a light in the darkness.

Whatever power was in that love, it was enough. One spark of hope and Maddie held out her hands, her nails still long and clawed, and she closed her eyes, reaching deep inside herself.

Not her body; no, it was beyond that. Her body was inconsequential. She knew it was useless to fight by claw and nail. But she had to survive, somehow. And she had power. All the same power as Matilda. She could harness the power of transfiguration and transcorporeal travel.

"I can't win this. Not now. Not yet," Maddie said, mostly to herself.

Matilda pressed closer, sensing that something was happening. The energy ripping from her body became uneven, agitated.

"What are you doing?" Matilda demanded. "What game are you playing?"

"No game," Maddie said, looking up and into the darkness. "Just truth."

She thought of kissing Randy in Dr. Keats's sitting room, and it happened. A thousand memories flooded through her, and with them came power and pain. Maddie felt the very center of her open up, a warm ecstasy that only her most passionate moments had ever hinted at. Her arms flew wide, her head snapped back, and light radiated from the core of her being. It grew, it swelled, it finally crested, a fulfillment of something she had been waiting to show for her whole life, but had never known.

The light that came from her was as brilliant as sunlight, and it filled cold, dark First World with golden hues and brilliant greens. For a moment, the skies lit up, bright blue and clear. Nearby animals called out; plants strained toward the source, toward Maddie herself.

How long had they been lost in this sunless, sad world? Maddie would have wept to see it, but her heart was too full of power. She was lost to it.

When the beams of light hit Matilda's frightening exterior, she fell back, her darkness expelled. The creature that was Matilda ceased to exist, and only her human form persisted: small and sad and broken. Maddie had only a moment to look, though; she knew what she had done. The light coming from her was so intense it filled up the skies all around them, a beacon.

M'ora would come. They all would come. To judge, to punish...

Maddie fell back on the grass, spent. Back to her human self, perhaps, but different. Changed.

Joss was over her again, but though his lips moved, she could not hear him. Her ears whined, and she had the strange sensation that the earth was undulating under her feet.

"Apparently I'm an atom bomb, baby," she whispered, or tried to. Her throat was as raw as if she had screamed for hours on end. She tasted blood, but it was her own. "Matilda?"

Joss gestured off to his left. "She's out," he said. The words were distant, like talking under water.

"Can I go to sleep now?" Maddie asked.

"No, Maddie—they're here—Maddie, don't fall asleep!"

For a moment, Maddie thought Joss was cradling her in his hands, his fingers as broad as tree limbs. But that shouldn't be.

She sighed and the world went black again, but this time of her own volition.

"What a liar you must think me."

Maddie's eyes opened wide, and after another moment of disorientation, she rolled to her side awkwardly.

M'ora. It was M'ora's voice. But was it in her head, or was it coming from somewhere else?

The room Maddie awoke in was enormous, dark, and full of echoes. And no matter how Maddie moved, her arms were pinned behind her. Her whole body felt strange and out of place, and she felt dizzy when she tried to stand, falling over to her side.

"Hush, don't struggle so much, please," M'ora whispered. "You're breaking my heart."

Maddie tried to talk, but her mouth was hard and unwieldy. She fell to her side again and felt sick to her stomach; her heart was beating far too fast to be healthy.

Then she tried to think, think at M'ora the way she had with Matilda. But there was nothing. She heard her own thoughts: *I doubt you have a heart, M'ora.* But it was clear that M'ora did not hear them. Maddie knew the feeling when she was projecting; her thoughts felt fuzzy and heavy, louder in her head than they ought to be.

"We had to bind you. With a length of Matilda's hair," M'ora said, kneeling down. She stared down, far down at her. "You're in bird form, you see. And you will stay that way until you are freed."

Maddie struggled some more, for the first time truly regretting her inability to launch a stream of profanity at one of her twains, either aloud or in her mind. What was going on? Why couldn't she move? Had M'ora said something about Matilda's hair? Was this some strange take on Samson and Delilah?

"Right now, we cannot communicate as we can elsewhere. There is a place, here in First World, that my brothers and sisters and I have created, combining our magic to prevent most interference. Magical interference. Physical interference still works, however, and that is why we harvested Matilda's hair for your restraints. For now."

M'ora was lovely as she had been the last time Maddie had seen her, and yet there was a weariness in her voice. She had said she was old, and this time Maddie believed her. She could sense it, smell it.

Maddie tried to make a noise, but it was just a sad little chirrup.

"Not a dove," M'ora said standing, "but a skylark. So fitting for you, my dear. So fitting. I'm sorry it's come to this. Rest now, while you can. When we are all gathered, you will be allowed to speak again, and you will see how true godlings conduct themselves when rules are broken."

Drip. *Drip.* Drip. Water was dripping on Maddie's nose, and only when she raised her arm to wipe it away did she realize she was no longer a bird, and no longer bound. She glanced down at the stone and hay strewn floor to see two thin braids of hair chewed in half, pale against the rock. Pale and silvery. Since when was Matilda grey-haired?

"Down here."

Maddie startled, drawing her legs up under her chin. She was naked. Again. "Who...?" she whispered.

In the corner of the cell, head down and ducking into the shadows, was Randall. Still a raven. He looked up at her, his head twitching back and forth, his feet hopping over the cracks in the stone.

"And we could have made such a pair," Maddie said, stretching. Her whole body hurt. She didn't want to even consider what went into transfiguration on such a scale, and so so soon after her last transformation. Her back felt as if it had been stretched across a rack and stomped upon by clog-wearing goblins. "I'm glad to see you, Randall."

Randall didn't say anything more, but hopped over toward the cell door. Light kindled in the darkness, illuminating a set of stairs in the distance. And two figures approached, cloaked in pale fabric.

The source of the light, Maddie saw, was not a torch or a flashlight, but rather the face and hands of the second figure. She burned as she walked, as bright as a Coleman lantern.

M'ora walked with her, her head bowed as well, though she was significantly dimmed in the presence of this incandescent one.

"Not surprisingly," M'ora said as her eyes met Maddie's, "you've managed to free yourself of your bonds. You are unusual, Madeline."

"I had help," Maddie said, standing. Randall flew up to her shoulder, and picked at a lock of her hair as if it were a piece of straw. Maddie had half a mind to slap him, but she wanted to save face. All she had at the moment was a clever bird. "Thankfully."

Maddie could tell M'ora was alarmed by Randall's presence, but she was acting restrained. Her emotions came across loudly, regardless of what she said about their abilities being dampened in this place. "Yes. That bird has a habit of turning up," M'ora said.

Randall squawked.

"But that is not my concern. Madeline, this is... you may call her Pietá," Mora said. "I wanted her to speak with you a moment. Before we proceed."

"Pietá. Mary, then?" Maddie asked.

Pietá raised her head, and Maddie squinted against the light. It was warm, comforting. Like a candle during a power outage. Maddie felt the warmth of it all over her body, welcome and gentle over her skin.

Maddie couldn't help but sigh in relief. She hungered for light, for the sun.

Then Pietá nodded, bowed her head, and departed back up the steps, and Maddie shivered, once again in the dark.

M'ora lingered to watch Maddie until Pietá was gone.

"Well, you've been granted a boon," M'ora said. "Pietá has consented to let you walk free during the proceedings, so long as you stay in line. You will require no restraints or other measures as you walk our sacred grounds."

"How... how did you understand her?" Maddie asked. She felt the comfort of Pietá's presence ebb away from her, and she felt her eyes fill with tears. Anger, even affected anger, helped prevent her from breaking down. Because that's really what she wanted to do.

"She is my sister, and very old. We know you made a series of pure transfigurations," M'ora explained.

"Right," Maddie said. Her attitude was that of a fifteen-year-old rolling her eyes at her mother, and Randall pecked at her ear just for saying it. "So I can do tricks, what of it?"

M'ora was unshaken. "As acerbic and foul as that tongue of yours is," she said, "your abilities do not seem to stem from the same source as Matilda's. It was... a concern."

"And now it's not? Just like magic?" asked Maddie.

"Yes. Just like that," M'ora said. "I continually forget how young you are, and how unschooled in our ways. In time, I suppose, that will change. But for now, I'd like to take you to the proceedings. So long as you give your oath not to harm me."

"My oath?" Maddie almost laughed. "You'll take my word for it?"

M'ora took a deep breath and walked to the metal door of the cell, resting her all too familiar hands on the latch. "In some worlds, words have true meaning."

"Will I get to speak to Alvin?" Maddie asked. "I'm guessing you have him."

"We do. And yes: You will be given that opportunity."

"Then I give you my oath," Maddie said, holding out her hand.

To her surprise, as she said the words, the compass flared in her hand for a moment and then went out.

M'ora did not hide the wonder in her expression. "Come, now, I've got some suitable clothing for you. Then we must attend."

Maddie was given a long, brown tunic with a broad leather belt, soft boots, and a white, fur-lined cloak. It was sumptuous on her skin, and she reveled in its warmth. She had been so cold for such a long time, she'd forgotten what it was like to not be chilled. As a sphinx, she had not noticed it so much, what with all the fur. But now she felt smaller, at the mercy of the elements.

"And Joss?" Maddie asked, as she followed M'ora up the set of narrow stairs. "And Randall? He can't stay a bird forever."

"Randall is Ravel's business, but Joss has settled in rather well with Posis. You will see; the rest have all gathered at the amphitheater."

They emerged into snow flurries swirling down from a dusky sky. Maddie felt Randall tense on her shoulder, and she looked around through the mist and precipitation to get her bearings.

"This place was hidden to you before," M'ora said. "But now you may behold."

M'ora raised her hands, and the world parted; the snow lifted like a curtain, and a sun-dappled morning was revealed.

"It isn't warm, but at least it's not snowing," M'ora said, stepping through. "Come with me. You will see."

Randall started squeezing Maddie's shoulder with his talons, and she swatted at him, hoping he'd get the message. He was just as anxious as she. Together they walked into the place beyond the darkness of First World, turning their heads first toward the sun and then taking in the scene before them.

Maddie followed M'ora through a thin barrier of wispy willows and low clustered alders. On the other side stood an ancient amphitheater, crafted of wood and earth and shaped in a semi-circle around a stage area. The style was a heightened medieval look that would have been at home in Camelot. Colored banners draped the stands, and garlands of holly adorned the entryway; it was so pristine, it had the look of a new structure. Though there were no spectators, it was built for multitudes. Maddie caught a whiff of cedar and loamy earth as she entered, staring up to the sky above. It was dim here, still, and yet the contrast was sharp, as if she had night vision.

As impressive as the theater was from a design perspective, it was dominated by an unusual burnished bronze pillar, an obelisk, at the precise center of the stage, rising at least twelve feet high. It commanded attention, despite the relative simplicity of its design. It was etched with no hieroglyphs or pictographs, no strange runes or inscriptions. It exuded no light, but appeared to cast shadows from it. And around the middle, there were ropes, dark against the bright bronze, lashed in a crisscross pattern.

Figures stood around the obelisk, all cloaked in white and brown. Theirs were faces familiar and strange, known and unknown, changed by time and place, and altogether foreign. They were brothers and sisters, lost within the First World for a very long time. At first glance, they appeared small and very human-like, but Maddie noticed if she looked at them in her peripheral vision, they were as large and godlike as Dyas had been to her on the island when he had challenged her. Their greatness lingered just behind them.

"You know some of my kin. Daena. Amela. Dyas. Posis. Arthur. You recognize Ravel, I'm sure. And there's Pietá, of course," M'ora said, quickly making introductions as if this were some trans-dimensional tea party.

As Maddie approached the obelisk, she noticed someone else for the first time. Matilda stood just to the side of the obelisk, bound with long dark braids twining about her wrists and legs, her lips pressed together in fury, her eyes ablaze. She was dressed in her riding attire, and her hair was a complete mess; it was also white as snow. The beast she had been was gone, but still Matilda was wild. And furious. Maddie could no longer sense her twains as she had been able to before, and she found the sensation strange. She almost missed it.

"Well, here he is," Matilda said as Maddie caught her eye. "Aren't you going to save him now?" Her mockery was sharp as a dagger.

For there was Alvin himself, tied to the obelisk, on the opposite side from Matilda, slumped down at its base. Matilda had obscured him. Alvin looked far worse than he had in Charleston; his head lolled to one side, his eyes were closed. And worse, there was blood smeared all around the obelisk above him in strange symbols and letters. The edges of the blood glowed slightly against the metal, as if drawn in flame.

Maddie felt her stomach tighten, freeze. Something was wrong. Something was wicked.

"Come, child," M'ora said, her voice resonating with the skill of a trained actress. "Take your place among us."

Maddie took a step into the circle of earth, and as she did, Randall flew up into the branches of the trees, saying something too quietly for her to hear. His absence was sudden and painful. Her nerves jangled as if she'd been roused in the middle of the night by a barking dog.

Looking around at the theater and its occupants, Maddie felt her head swim again, then a pulse fired in the very center of her. A warning? The world was too bright, too detailed; her vision went hazy to accommodate everything at once.

"Yes, it's a bit much to take in, I know," M'ora said, her

voice almost compassionate. "There, now, see? Your friend Joss. Safe and sound."

M'ora gestured across to where a tall man stood; he was grizzled with age, but Maddie saw the familiar lines in his face. This was not Joss, but his twain.

Then she blinked, and could scarcely believe she had thought they were the same. It was not, she realized for the first time, that this new figure bore a resemblance to his twain in the flesh. It was beneath that, deeper under the surface. She was reminded of the bright lines beneath her skin, the ley lines of power she had discovered during her time with Joss on the island. John had said the twains could look as they wanted, and sometimes they did look alike. She realized that Matilda might have patterned her face to look like Maddie's own, to please Randall. And that Randall could have made himself look like Randy just to please her. Her stomach was sinking and she touched her face, finding her fingers cold and trembling.

It was making sense. Almost.

Posis's face was worn with a thousand lines, as if he had commanded a ship on the sea for a hundred years; his chest was barrel-shaped and broad. As he swept aside his robe, he revealed the form of Joss Raddick, crouching on the ground like a scolded child.

"Joss is recuperating," M'ora said. "When he is strong enough, we will send him home."

"You won't hurt him?" Maddie asked. Her heart fluttered in her chest, rattling against her ribs. To see Joss like that, reduced to quivering and cowering, Maddie felt her hope slipping away. To go from a sense of such power and surety to this? How long could she possibly last with these people if Joss had already fallen?

"I have given my oath," Posis said, though not without a hint of scorn. "As a peace offering. We do not wish strife with the other worlds."

"Yes, but first, we must attend to our own sorrows," said the twain who looked like Ian, the one Maddie had seen when she was first sent to be tested. He was much smaller, now, but he still carried with him an air of authority. Dyas. Zeus. Brahma. Odin.

All the twains nodded in reply, many turning their heads to get a better look at Maddie. In spite of the terror and worry growing in side of her, she held up her head. She had almost forgotten about the rest of them, she was so absorbed with thoughts of Alvin and Joss and Randall.

Well, they could look all they wanted. They had tested her and she had *survived.* Flourished. Transfigured. She had not fallen into despair with memories of Agnes; she had not wasted away on the island; she had not been maimed by Joss. She had even bested Matilda.

Maddie had the feeling they had no idea what to do with her.

While she watched the twains of First World arrange themselves, Maddie glanced up to the trees. She couldn't see Randall, but she got a better idea of the structure of the amphitheater. Absorbing the details was a good way to calm herself.

There were eight rows of seats surrounding the theater itself, which was circular and made of lacquered wood, inlaid with scrollwork of a style Maddie couldn't place. Although the stands were empty, she had the feeling she was being watched.

She tried not to look at Alvin as she passed him by, but her eyes were drawn to him regardless. He was completely unconscious, and his face was streaked with blood that had to have been applied with fingers; it looked like war paint, the pattern measured and intentional. His breath came infrequently, and very shallow.

Maddie was quite certain it was too late for Alvin. Surely, they were going to let Arthur destroy him—that's what they wanted. It was the only answer she could come up with. The godlings of First World had let Alvin do the dirty work, and now they'd have their own god. Young, gawky Arthur would inherit the power of chaos and discord, and Alvin would die knowing he had failed.

"You hurt him," Maddie said to M'ora, as she came closer.

"Yes," M'ora said. "We did."

"You had your... Arthur hurt him."

"Yes," M'ora replied, just as evenly as before. "He has been wounded, for now."

Maddie was ashamed to love Alvin. She still believed, on some delusional level, that Alvin simply needed time alone with her. That she could coax him out, connect with him, that he would see the error of his ways. Even now she considered the right words, the one thing she could say to him to change him back to the Alvin she knew before.

She looked over her shoulder, back to where she had emerged from the trees, to try and spy Randall one last time. The coward. He'd run away again. And she'd loved him, and trusted him.

Surely love didn't matter anymore.

Maddie closed her eyes a moment, wishing for a world where Randy would have been spared everything. Maybe in some other universe, some dim mirror of these eight worlds– Randall had said they were infinite, after all–maybe she and Randy were happy together. But no. No twain, no matter how powerful or magnificent, would ever be like Randy. Maddie knew that for sure.

At least he was safe. At least he was protected from all this madness. Maddie knew quite well she might not survive, but she was comforted to know she had at least kept Randy safe.

"We are delaying," said Ravel. His voice, similar to Randall's, was tinged with a raspiness that made him sound far older than his looks. "Shall we commence, now that we are all arrived and oathed?"

Maddie turned and looked at him more closely. Ravel's

eyes were deeper, his face more lined. He had a beard, close-cropped, and long hair that fell past his shoulders, braided at the ends. But the lines, the ley lines that made up his being, they were virtually the same as those that made Randall and Randy.

It was a deeply disconcerting sensation. Looking at him, Maddie felt her fingers crackle, then fade, her power interrupted. She knew him. She loved him, too, somehow...

Ravel smiled as he looked at Maddie, but the smile was cold and distant—a knowing, pompous smile. Not a human smile.

"Looking for a raven?" he asked, leaning forward.

"Don't you hurt him," warned Maddie.

Ravel was about to say something more, when M'ora shushed him with a wave of her hand. "Madeline. We must begin."

A shadow fell across her, and Maddie looked up to the top of the bronze obelisk, where black wings fluttered. So that's where Randall had gone. He was barely keeping his grip on the top of the structure with his talons, and adjusting himself by batting his wings now and again, but he was surveying the scene from there. His head went back and forth, nervous and calculating.

She felt such a profound feeling of relief at his arrival that she shivered.

Maddie's feet were burning, so she paced a little. She couldn't mistake M'ora's narrow-eyed gaze falling on her, but she tried to ignore it.

"Well, I'd like to know what Arthur thinks about all this," Maddie said, walking toward Alvin's twain. "Unless he is not as innocent as you'd have me believe."

Maddie approached Arthur, and as she did so, she noticed he was wavering slightly on his legs. Dyas, who was beside him, gently helped him stay upright, avoiding Maddie's gaze.

When Maddie finally got close enough to see, Arthur looked drugged, his eyes lazy and unfocused. He was pale, confused.

"Mother?" he asked as Maddie took a step back from him.

Before Maddie could ask, she felt M'ora's hand on her shoulder. "Before you judge us, Madeline, you must hear us out."

"We've already ruled on some matters," said Dyas. His attempt at a kind tone was almost believable, but like Ian, he was too lazy to be completely convincing at it. "Matilda and Alvin have been found guilty of conspiracy against their brethren, for breaking the pact set forth from the very beginning. And, in Alvin's case, for killing four of his own twains in worlds Three, Four, Six, and Eight."

Maddie gritted her teeth. "Then why do you need me here if you've already figured things out?"

"Because you will exact the punishment on Madam Roth here," said M'ora. "You were instrumental in helping us secure her, hinder her. You stood up to her, remarkably well, and prevented a further tragedy."

"You want me... to kill her?" Maddie asked. "With what, my bare hands?"

"No. With this."

M'ora held up a knife that she'd pulled out from her boot. Just looking at it made Maddie's blood run cold. The blade was silvery-white, serrated at the very end, and half as long as M'ora's arm. It was a marvel of craftsmanship, the pommel made to look like the face of a man, eyes wide, tongue lolling. Corkscrews and curls were etched into the blade, swirling up to the tip. As detailed and delicate as the weapon itself was, the overall design reminded Maddie more of Maya art than anything remotely Western. It was a blood-seeking blade.

Every impulse told Maddie to take the weapon, to hold it, to balance it in her hands. And more. She could see herself thrusting it into Matilda's soft belly, twisting, and feeling the hot blood run down her hands. She *wanted* to do it.

"Will you do it?" asked M'ora, the blade flashing as if in reply.

"No," she said, shoving her hands into the crooks of her elbows. Maddie indicated Alvin with a jerk of her head. "I guess you're hoping Arthur here's going to give Alvin the coup de grace, too. Convenient."

"Clever," M'ora chuckled. "But no."

"Dear Madeline," said Joss's twain, Posis. His voice was lower, rumbling. Like earthquakes and the churn of the sea, the thrumming low notes of Barber's Adagio for Strings, Opus 11. "Even if we do away with Alvin, it will not stop there. They have been doing this to themselves throughout the ages."

"They?" asked Maddie.

"Yes. So often they are reborn... difficult," Amela hissed. She pointed her spear toward Alvin and snarled, as if from personal experience. "And we are tired of the struggle."

"We can bind him," Daena said. "But it is no easy task. It is the binding that we disagree on." Maddie caught the look she gave Dyas; clearly the two had not come to the same conclusion on the matter.

"You're a bit of a tie-breaker," M'ora said. "At least, so long as we're not considering the bird..."

"Tell me, then," Maddie said. "Tell me what this binding is all about."

Posis said. "Have you ever heard of how Loki was bound?"

15

Dissolve

Maddie had gone rigid during the conversation, and now she was trembling. "You're going to bind Alvin—with Arthur's... with his..." She couldn't say it. It was too horrid. *With his entrails. With Arthur's entrails.*

"It has been done before, in other worlds, with success," said Dyas. "I believe we should perform a permanent binding; others disagree. Pietá and Daena, in particular, wish to rehabilitate Arthur, bring him up themselves, in hopes he will not turn out as troublesome as his predecessors. But I have lived longer than all of you, and I see no hope in that."

Pietá said nothing, but Maddie thought she caught her tilting her head, just so, as if listening to her name.

"But he's your son!" cried Maddie, desperate to make some kind of impact. If she had to start somewhere with M'ora, guilt was likely an easy way in. "You have a duty to him, as his mother."

The others exchanged glances, some curious, others irritated. No one had been speaking above a polite tone, and Maddie just shattered it.

M'ora withdrew the knife, which she had still been holding out. "That means nothing."

"It means nothing to you? That you raised this son, the reborn incarnation of a twain you knew, and probably loved?" Maddie asked. She could feel her hand flaring up, daring her to use the compass even in the magical dead zone. What the hell would it show her now? It just might explode. But she knew, without even asking, that M'ora's connection with Arthur—and his previous twain—was just as complex, if not more so, than that of Randall and Matilda.

M'ora frowned, averting her eyes. When she spoke, her voice was softer. "Had you seen what I have, you would understand. This must be done."

"What about love?" Maddie pressed, putting her hand to her chest; she could feel it burning.

"Love is an anomaly." M'ora said it, softly, and turned her face from Maddie.

"But you... we... we *are* love," Maddie tried, one last time. "I know that well enough, and hell, I'm just this baby twain. I know that being part of the goddess of love isn't just about beauty and sex and passion, it's about loving people without boundaries. Sometimes that love is dark, and I think the only person Matilda truly loves that way is herself... but it's something we can all understand. I don't believe you're so far gone, M'ora."

"You underestimate her," Matilda said, growling in her throat.

"I have hope in her," Maddie corrected. "I even still have hope in you, Matilda."

Matilda laughed a dry, desperate laugh and turned away, closing her eyes. "Don't you see, Maddie? You've already killed me. You might as well strike the final blow."

"Never," Maddie said, tears forming in her eyes. "I will never be Alvin."

Was this what it felt like to be part of a god? To hurt so

much? Maddie felt like a star ready to go supernova. Her fingertips were tender to the touch, as if she'd seared them on the
stovetop. Even her lips felt puffy and cracked, sunburned. But
there was no sun here, there was no escape, and the gods of the
First World had already made their decision.

They were frightened of what Alvin was and of what Arthur might become. Alvin and his kind had proved time and
time again, through the ages, that they were incapable of behaving. What started as tricks and games turned into blood and
destruction.

They were tired of tricks and war. That part, at least, she
could understand. But why they thought she must be involved
in their decisions was beyond her.

"Why not give the knife to Arthur, then?" Joss asked. He'd
regained some of his composure, and Maddie was pleased to
see the gleam in his eyes. It looked like he was getting ready
for a fight again. "You have him here, in the comfort of your
world; surely he can be watched, measured."

Posis replied. "We fear to unleash a full god in what would
be the end of our world. As it is, we are but fragments of gods,
and it is safer this way."

"Has there ever been a full god?" asked Joss. "Truly?"

"It is a matter of much debate..." Dyas answered.

The conversation ebbed away from her as Maddie stole
another glance toward Alvin. Anger and love flared at the same
time, and she looked back to Joss.

What could she do? She was no trickster; she could never
fool the whole pantheon into doing the opposite of what they
wanted—that's what Alvin would have done. She couldn't magic her way out of it, like Randall would try. She had only love,
and lust, beauty and passion. Aphrodite, the mighty lover.

She was about to say something, as Joss and Posis continued to discuss the ethical ramifications of what they were doing,
when she noticed Randall again, out of the corner of her eye.

Except... he was behaving very strangely.

Maddie had been so busy trying to make sense of the madness of First World and its ruthless godlings that she had failed to pay attention to Randall's hopping about. In fact, everyone else was just as distracted. Randall was pecking a circle around the top of the obelisk, over and over again. Hop, hop, flap, a bob of the head, then *cwurp, cwurp...* Weaving a pattern. Then he pecked on the obelisk with his beak: *tap-a-tap, tap-a-tap-tap.*

Just like Randy.

Just like...

Maddie almost fainted with the realization. She swayed on her feet, felt her stomach bottom out, and took a measured breath only out of sheer will. Even her vision swam for a moment before she gathered enough strength to shake it off.

The last comfort she held onto snapped like a dry twig.

None of them knew. None of them even *suspected*; the obelisk blotted out the mental connection and they thought themselves safe. But Randy had somehow come through with Randall and was watching everything. It was probably him who had freed her in the cell.

Damn Randall for not telling her!

The stakes were higher, now. Much, much higher. She had to get Randy home, safe, out of this mess. She had risked his life for her own demented need to see Alvin again. And now Randy was watching this from the top of a creepy obelisk in a world of forever dusk.

Randy still loved Alvin, as Randall did. They shared a common love, and it was worth fighting for. Even if the odds were pretty damned slim.

"Let me talk to Alvin," Maddie said, a little too fast. The voices of the rest of the pantheon quieted, and Matilda shot her a withering glance.

"I'm not sure that's..." Ravel began to say.

"Listen," Maddie said, rounding on him. "I understand

I'm far from the most seasoned twain here." She almost stumbled over the word twain. "But you all clearly want peace, even if you have to spill blood to get it. Why not at least let me try the way of peace, first?"

"We can rouse him," Pietá said, her voice like the whisper of windswept barley. The other godlings hadn't had a moment to reply. "It is a noble request. Her heart is right in this matter."

Ravel nodded to Maddie. Apparently Pietá had quite the pull.

Pietá held out her hand, small and luminescent white, and as she turned it, Maddie thought of pure moonlight on water. Pietá spoke in whispers. "You can speak to him, but not for long. We must make decisions. We are very busy."

"Pietá–" M'ora said, but the godling was not listening and had bowed her head again.

Maddie said, "Yes, please. Rouse him."

A sound like a sigh emanated from the strange glowing twain, and Pietá stretched out her hands, her fingers lengthening into streams of light. Like vines, they grew from her hands, finding their way to Alvin, and wrapping around him, encircling him. They entered his nose, his mouth, his ears, filling him with moonlight; his eyes glowed dully from under the eyelids, turning the flesh red.

Maddie had seen such a thing before after kissing Joss, and if she could, she would have spoken with Pietá about it. But now was not the time. Pietá let go and the healing tendrils retreated. She folded her hands, and dropped her head.

Alvin stirred, and Matilda was struggling in her bonds again. M'ora leveled the knife at her. She didn't need words to get her point across. But Maddie suspected Matilda was beyond the fear of death. She was as colorless as her hair, cold as a cinder gone dead in the fire.

Maddie walked slowly over to Alvin. She tried to suppress the feelings she still had from their last conversation, telling herself he had spoken out of anger. Deep down, she had to believe that Alvin—the one she knew, that her heart knew—was still in there.

So she thought of a day when they went walking together in Baltimore. He was attending a conference at Johns Hopkins, and she had come along to keep him company. They had been happy, then. Baltimore never held that much charm as in that April. The whole city was alive, full to bursting with pastel blossoms and heady fragrances. Everything was awash in pinks and yellows and brightest greens, new and alive. They'd hardly been able to keep their hands off of one another.

Maddie remembered how they found a little park, tucked away in a neighborhood full of gigantic Tudor-style manor houses, and the entire place was covered in tulips. They'd tickled each other, laughed until their sides ached, rolling in the grass like two love-sick fools. And she looked up at him, the sun behind his head, his eyes sparkling, dark and deep, and kissed him. It was the most perfect moment she could recall, a happiness so complete she could never let it go.

Yes, that was it. M'ora had said that Maddie's armor had been fear and sadness. Now it was memory and love, perhaps a little sorrow, still. But she felt stronger.

Kneeling down, Maddie stroked Alvin's face reflecting how she still knew every line. He'd been a lie, every bit of him, but he'd been a lie she loved. Sometimes she hated him, but she never would have done him harm. Maybe that was the difference between them.

Then she kissed him on his cracked lips, and she gave him the memory. She let it flow into him. She painted it into his mind, obelisk or no. It was hers to give, woven into her physical being. Flowers, fragrances, and all.

"Hey, Alvin," she said, softly, pulling away. "Honey. It's me."

Alvin tilted his head left and right, and Maddie squinted

up at the top of the obelisk again as his eyes fluttered open. Randy was still doing his hopping dance. She closed her eyes, wishing that Randall were still here, hoping that he hadn't simply run away and let Randy in. Why did she always assume the worst of him, and the best of Randy?

Alvin's mouth worked, but he didn't say anything coherent. Then he licked his lips and tried again. "Madeline," he said. "The tulips...."

"Hey babe," Maddie said, and she started to cry.

She didn't care that everyone was watching her. She was crying because she had loved Alvin, and because she didn't love him anymore. She cried because she knew what he really was, but wanted to remember what he had been. She cried for herself, for the weariness in her bones she'd carried around with her since she found out he'd vanished, pulling her down until the anger over his infidelity had burned it away. Maddie cried because she knew it was over, and because she knew it was just beginning. She cried because she would never be the same again and she would never really know him.

Even amidst the chaos, she could see the beauty in him, strangled and darkened as it was.

"You were so beautiful that day," Alvin said. "I almost told you... what you were."

"I won't ever forget it," she said.

Maddie took her hand away, and watched his gaze rise and take in the group about him. He smiled a little weakly. "Damn. I hoped I'd dreamed this part."

"Nope, you've still pissed off just about every demigod or deity in the multiverse," she said with a laugh. "And me. And Randall..."

"I guess I deserve it... what they're going to do," he said, looking over Maddie's shoulder to where Matilda and M'ora were. "Sorry, Mad. I just thought... if I *was* more, I could *know* more. I wanted to figure it out."

In a perfect world where love won and didn't hurt so much, Maddie would have said she loved him eternally, that all the moon and stars in the worlds wouldn't have prevented her from being together with him again. But there would be no happy ending, here. She knew it. Even if she could have had it, she no longer wanted it.

"I thought I came here because I loved you," she said, dropping her voice.

His eyes narrowed, half a wince, but he didn't say anything.

"But I don't love you enough to help you." She closed her eyes.

Alvin bit down on his lower lip. He looked disappointed, but not surprised.

"And I don't think I have any way to get you out of this," Maddie said, tasting her tears.

"I thought it would make a more peaceful world," Alvin said, after a moment's hesitation. "I thought I could bring that."

"No, you couldn't. God, Alvin. It's like you killed yourself, over and over again. I think that's worse than thinking you just jumped off a bridge. I could live with that."

The twains were all listening, transfixed. They had forgotten about the bird at the top of the obelisk, if they had ever known about him at all, but Maddie hadn't. Whatever he was doing, he needed time. That was the one thing she could give him, now.

Alvin searched her eyes back and forth. "I saw the whole fabric of the universe, and I set myself in the very middle. All I needed was a little more time; I was almost there."

"There is no middle," said Maddie. "None of this is even about you."

He sighed, and dropped his head.

She hesitated to speak the words, but they bubbled up from her throat. She had to know. "Are you sorry? Do you regret it?"

"Maddie..."

"Do you regret what you've done? To me? To Randy and Randall? To everyone here?" Maddie sobbed the words, and knew the answer even before he replied.

Alvin sighed, closing his eyes. "No. None of it. It was for my work; they didn't understand."

"Enough!" shouted M'ora, throwing up her hands.

But Randy had been waiting. He had been listening. He needed the answers to Maddie's questions, it seemed, just as much as she did.

With a screech, Randy flew down from the obelisk in a straight line, right into M'ora's face. As he reached her, wings flapping and beak clicking with a hideous noise, M'ora startled at the sight. With the black wings enveloping her field of vision, she lost her grip on the dagger.

M'ora was no war goddess, Maddie thought. She reacted as Maddie would have. And having put her faith in the obelisk, in First World, she never anticipated the bird.

The dagger... this was the shining gift that the bird wanted. Randy clutched it quickly in his talons and flew—up and up—straight to the top of the obelisk and higher. But why? Surely there was more than that! There had to be.

"Ravel! Control him!" shouted Dyas.

"Randy!" Maddie shouted. "Randy, come back!"

But it was too late. Ravel's face twisted in pain and something unwound here at the heart of First World. Even the obelisk itself shuddered. Then the ground joined in the trembling and Maddie felt her hand thrum, her heart soar. She could not communicate with M'ora or Matilda, but her power, new as it was, came rushing back to her. She felt, rather than saw, the compass, knowing immediately where everyone was standing around her without having to look. The rush was welcome, but dangerous.

She was not the only one that could tell. Randy had undone the spell, or at least Ravel's part of it. And the twains of First World were threatened.

They sprung into action. The power of the imperiled godlings exploded around Maddie in a thousand emotions, memories, and whispered spells, ready for action.

Attack. *Attack.* Maddie felt it in the air.

Alvin was behind her, weeping. But not with remorse—
with resignation.

Randy climbed higher, and the godlings' anger and fear
amplified.

"Maddie," Alvin said, but his mouth did not move. She
could hear him in her head. "I'm sorry about Randall."

Panic struck at Maddie's heart and she reached out to
hold Alvin's hand as the world spun around her, tilting and
undulating as if it were made of nothing but silk and ribbons. A
high, keening whine resounded in her temples, and she gasped,
pressing her free hand to her head.

"We can stop him!" came a voice. Randall. Ravel. Randy.

Stop who? Alvin? Randy? Maddie?

The world blurred to darkness, deeper than night. Deeper
than the places in between worlds Maddie had visited.

"Look," Alvin whispered. "Before he's gone."

Maddie strained her eyes toward where she had last seen
Randy.

"You are a wanderer, too," Alvin whispered, squeezing
her hand. "Be brave enough to watch this gift he is giving. I'll
see you … again."

The bird was outlined against the dark, rays of light emanating from him. And in that moment, Maddie slipped out of herself
for a moment, able to experience the world from a distance.

All at once the attack began. No command was given, but
the imperative was clear.

Daena loosed her arrow; Posis threw a stream of water;
Arthur shouted a battle cry; Dyas cast a thin bolt of crackling
lightning; Amela flung her spear, the shaft arcing in the air.
Pietá cast a pillar of fire so brilliant it brought the whole world

into vivid light, every color leaping to life, burning the images in Maddie's eyes.

"No!" Maddie screamed. "Stop!"

The ground undulated and trembled, and Maddie tumbled into Matilda, who hissed and screamed. Just being near her, Maddie felt the hatred rippling off, the searing power of such fury. It was poison. To have nothing left to live for, to be filled with such hatred—and to know that such a fate was possible, sent Maddie reeling.

Elbowing Matilda in the ribs, Maddie rolled to the side and watched as all the weapons and spells met in the air, striking Randy dead on. Colors and tendrils of energy flashed and flared around him, each absorbed in turn until he was just one black bird with a great and terrible knife.

Maddie screamed as Matilda kicked at her, but she gained enough ground to watch as the dagger in Randy's talons twisted upwards as if moved by invisible hands. He froze in midair.

"God... gods, no! Stop this!" Maddie shouted.

The sky above them flashed white and blue, and the body of the bird contorted, changed, elongated. Wings lengthened, talons swelled and reshaped themselves into feet. The head turned round and round, the body moving and writhing around the many wounds. The dagger pierced him again and again, Maddie knew it; she could feel the wounds as if she had given them to him herself. It was M'ora's dagger, after all, and in a way, her own. Saint Sebastian.

He knew. Goddamnit. He knew all along.

The face that turned toward Maddie had the same kind blue eyes she knew so well as Randy's, framed by the same short russet curls. And his smile. Sweet and knowing. Accepting.

A gift. A sacrifice. He had seven wounds. The last would be...

No, Randy... you could have told me... you tried to tell me... God, no...

Time suspended, but only for so long. Down, down Randy came, from an impossible height, limbs moving not by his own volition but by the wind and gravity, pulling him to the earth.

Randy fell, simply as that, impaling himself on the obelisk. Maddie tried to shriek, but she had no voice. It was worse than dying herself. Pain flooded her body and she gasped for air, reaching out but unable to do anything. Even Matilda was still.

Randy made no sound, but stared face up, legs and arms spread-eagle; he twitched, and was still. Blood dripped from his eyes, from his hands, from the gaping wound in the middle of him and those riddling his body.

His blood spilled down over Alvin, combining with the magic auras from the twains' collective power. The obelisk took on an awful green glow, an eldritch hue, and pulsed over and over, a network of power weaving around it, mingled with blood.

"Farewell, brothers," said Pietá, and she clapped her hands above her head. "May the fires purify you."

"Alvin!" Maddie shouted, but she could feel Matilda pulling at her, fingers digging into her arms again. "God, no..."

Matilda began clawing after Maddie, but her strength was waning. Maddie was bolstered by her own despair, and she hoisted her smaller, frailer twain up by the collar and punched her across the face. Immediately, she felt the impact of it, as if she'd hit herself, leaving her winded and sobbing. But Matilda crumpled in a heap, and Maddie was free of her for a moment. Free to mourn and watch the two men she had most loved in the world burn.

Pietá's fire blazed brilliant, consuming Alvin and Randy in but the beating of a heart. Immense flames, their fire so bright it warmed Maddie's face, scaled the sides of the obelisk and the brilliant bronze began to run to molten metal.

Maddie saw Alvin's hand outstretched, fingers searching before they were encased in bronze; then they vanished behind the flames as the obelisk began to sink down into the ground.

And she could do nothing.

The obelisk continued to blaze and melt down, flesh and blood and metal, burning with such fury that only magic could keep it going. Smoke rose from it, an offering to the skies, black and gray and terrible.

It burned right down to the ground, the flames abating slowly at first, then extinguishing all at once with a hiss and a giant plume of steam.

In moments—or hours, or years; it was impossible to tell in First World—all that remained was a molten pool, cooling on the ground. The fire had singed some of the wood on the stage, but caused little else in the way of damage. The bronze left behind was now blood-red, streaked with black; as it continued to solidify, it bowed in the middle, like a deep bowl or well. Steam and smoke still rose from it still, and it curled and twisted high in the air above it and around it.

The world was covered in fog. It came from the trees, snaking around trunks and through vines, slipping over rocks and streams, and it surrounded them all. The temperature dropped. The birds began to sing in the distance.

The world had responded to the offering.

Joss was the first to walk closer. Posis tried to stop him, but he held up his hand in a silent threat. Then he turned to where the bronze bowl was, and opened his hands, filling it with water, tempered with his own tears.

Maddie had nothing left in her. Emotion was eroded to the point of pain, and she closed her eyes. Then, as tendrils of fog curled through her legs, dampening her hair, caressing her skin, she began to recite the poem:

> *"Ethereal Minstrel! Pilgrim of the sky!*
> *Dost thou despise the earth where cares abound?*
> *Or while the wings aspire, are heart and eye*
> *Both with thy nest upon the dewy ground?*

Thy nest which thou canst drop into at will,
Those quivering wings composed, that music still!

To the last point of vision, and beyond
Mount, daring warbler!—that love-prompted strain
('Twixt thee and thine a never-failing bond)
Thrills not the less the bosom of the plain:
Yet mightst thou seem, proud privilege! to sing
All independent of the leafy Spring.

Leave to the nightingale her shady wood;
A privacy of glorious light is thine,
Whence thou dost pour upon the world a flood
Of harmony, with instinct more divine;
Type of the wise, who soar, but never roam—
True to the kindred points of Heaven and Home!"

The world was silent, white murky fog moving in, obscuring vision even a few feet away. Maddie let herself be lost to it, wrap herself in it. It was calm, it was silence.

Out of the white nothingness, she heard Arthur weeping. She saw him, then, bent over, kneeling on the ground where he had been standing so proud and tall before. M'ora rushed to his side, putting her arms around him, whispering gently to him.

Something had changed.

"He's... not gone, but he's... he's..." Arthur was saying, over and over again, unable to get the words out. As young as Maddie felt in the presence of these people, Arthur was still younger. "He's bound. He's quiet."

Maddie tried to stand, to speak, to welcome the one moment of joy. Alvin was bound, and Arthur was alive. But Matilda had recovered and came from behind her, charging like an enraged bull. There were words being said and even more being thought—Maddie could pick them out in her consciousness now that the obelisk was destroyed—but she couldn't make sense of it.

Then Maddie knew: Matilda had no more power but her physical self. She was trying to change herself into her creature, but it was gone from her. All that was left to her was fury.

Taken off-guard, Maddie fell back to the ground and felt Matilda's teeth break through the skin of her forearm. She shrieked, getting in a good kick, but was exhausted and overwhelmed quickly. Matilda's bonds had been loosed, somehow, in the fire. Burned away, perhaps. Maddie had noticed her fingers before, but had not put two and two together.

But there was no time.

"For one of love to love so little," M'ora said from behind them, her voice clear and terrible, "is a sin beyond what I can bear. This pains me more than you can know. But I am not without mercy. I will give you a chance to come home to us." Her voice was strange, echoing in the misty amphitheater, her head disembodied in the fog for a moment as her movement stilled. "Come back to us, sister."

M'ora held out her hand and Maddie shaded her eyes, squinting. She could see enormous wings behind M'ora, scaled and glinting red. A dragon. A real dragon.

In reply, Matilda spat at M'ora, her lips chapped and running with blood; she looked like a horse in a fire, her eyes rolling in her head with madness and anger and fear.

"Never. And when you kill me, I will haunt you in my next life," Matilda shrieked.

"In that case, I'll be ready," M'ora said.

In a movement quicker than in any martial arts movie Maddie had ever seen, M'ora reached out, one hand on top of Matilda's head, and another below. She twisted, and Matilda fell to the theater floor with a heavy thud and did not move again. Maddie saw her eyes, black and unseeing, before the fog swirled and consumed her, but not before Maddie was wracked with pains from the very center of her.

She curled up, and looked up at M'ora, who was bracing from pain, as well.

A breeze came, pushing some of the fog away. The pain dissipated, too. And Maddie could breathe again. When she looked up at M'ora, she saw how pale and spent she was.

Maddie staggered to a stand, trying to focus through the pain. Her arms were bleeding, and when Ravel approached her, at first she hesitated. But he gave her a look, and it was so like Randall that she consented.

Randy. Randall. Thoughts of them overwhelmed her, and she started sobbing again as Ravel drew his hands over Maddie's arms and neck, where Matilda had bitten her, and the wounds healed up, though faint scars remained.

The crushing pain abated, but Maddie felt no different. No stronger. Just that there was something missing, a gaping hole in the center of her where Randy and Alvin had once been. She mourned them in the deepest places of her being, and she mourned Matilda, too. For Matilda was a part of her, would always serve as a warning of what she could become.

Maddie breathed through the grief, and let Ravel know she was well enough, and let her gaze fall upon M'ora again. She was standing with her son, their heads bent together like willow branches, speaking to each other in low voices.

Posis walked forward to join Joss, looking down into the pool. Maddie tried to find any sign of the bird, or of Randy–of Randall–but all was gone. Just clear, pure water, in a blood-red bronze bowl, not unlike what M'ora had shown her.

"The bird... It was–" Maddie tried to say.

"Randy," said Pietá, who had drawn up next to the bowl. She knelt down, and drew a moonlit finger through the water. It rippled to her touch, like starlight. "We did not sense him here."

"The body that fell, that body was from my world, from the Sixth, so Randy is–" Maddie said, her lips hardly obeying through the tears.

"Gone," Ravel said, from behind her. "He is gone." His voice was so like theirs, Maddie shivered. "The obelisk was magic of my own making, inscribed with my own blood. As indirectly as it may have been, my hand was the one that made the final blow."

I'm sorry about Randall. That's what Alvin had said.

"And what about Randall?" Maddie asked, almost too afraid to voice the words. She wanted someone to hold. No, she wanted Randall to hold. She knew that now. Over and over, she had thought the worst of him.

Ravel closed his eyes, concentrated. "He may yet live. I did not sense his death."

It was not a sure hope, and Maddie was slow to accept it. But a poor hope was better than none, and welcoming it made her feel less afraid. It soothed some of the grief that kept creeping up to her. In the darkness of death, a light still lingered.

Joss must have sensed her struggle and came up to her, eyes swimming with tears. His voice was rough, and weary. "You look exhausted, kid."

"Exhausted doesn't even begin to describe it," she said, as Joss drew her up into his arms. She cried there as he held her, his warmth enveloping her, his breathing even and reliable. A friend. A true, true friend.

"I'm sorry I couldn't..."

"You stayed," she said into his shirt. "That's all that matters."

Joss wiped Maddie's hair out of her face and addressed M'ora. "And Alvin? You spoke with him, but I couldn't hear some of it..."

"He loved him," said Maddie. "Randy. He loved Alvin. More than I ever did. He saved him, and us... and Arthur, in the end."

"Perhaps it is that," M'ora said from behind Maddie. She

had been listening, no doubt, internally and externally. For once, though, Maddie felt as if she had nothing to hide. "Does love conquer all? I'd never believed it to be so. But now... I think we have all been conquered, and humbled. Our vanity laid bare by an uninitiated twain who we all underestimated."

By and by the members of the pantheon departed; Amela went first, her head down, tears still in her eyes. Maddie wished there was more to say about Agnes, but she felt she had made her peace. For her part, Amela said nothing, and didn't need to. M'ora was right; they had all been beaten that day, one way or another. Randy had shown them something ancient, powerful, forgotten. Even the twains of First World, so powerful and resolute, had been beaten at their own game.

Daena departed with Ravel, and they both expressed their gratitude to Maddie, however difficult it was for them to do so. Posis left with Dyas, and Maddie thought they might be laughing together as they vanished into the forest again. They had not lost as she had, no. Her sorrows were but small gnats in terms of their long existences.

"My cottage is not far," M'ora said, weariness breaking through. Her voice was almost a whisper. Maddie had no idea how much of her was flesh and blood, but it was enough. She had seen a glimpse of the dragon, and had no desire to truly wake her. "Will you walk with me, Madeline? Arthur would like to stay here a while and I think I owe him that."

"So the cottage is real?" Maddie asked, stumbling in her steps. She wiped her nose with the back of her sleeve. "I was beginning to think nothing you showed me was."

"Yes. An instance of truth in my less than stellar record," M'ora admitted.

Joss's strong arms held Maddie up as she was about to

lose her balance again. She could swear he had not been there a moment ago. "Looks like you need someone to help you up," Joss said. "Mind if I walk with you?" he asked.

"Well, I'm afraid without you to lean on, I might not make it," Maddie said. She almost laughed, but she looked over her shoulder at the remnants of the obelisk, and thought of Randy. Her stomach lurched and she squeezed Joss's hand for comfort.

Joss helped her, and Maddie walked by M'ora's side, their shadows and their strides in perfect unison. The trees gave way to a field, and then the cottage, just as Maddie had remembered it. They had been close, after all. But now it was spring, and tulips grew in their wake as they proceeded.

"I think I'll stay outside, if it's all the same," Maddie said, when M'ora offered to bring her in.

"You've become a wanderer, Madeline," said M'ora. "There are many other worlds left to you—you could go any-where you choose. You can navigate the worlds by the same principles you learned here, on the islands. It is no different."

"I just don't get any of it," Maddie said. "You really were ready to—with Arthur, I mean…"

"Yes." M'ora looked away, her lips trembling. "It was not an easy choice. And thankfully, one I was spared making in the end. He will understand, someday."

Maddie put her hand on M'ora's shoulder. The cloth of her cloak was rough-spun, so real to touch. Maddie could feel every fiber. "But maybe that's okay. Maybe we should just con-centrate on the stuff that's less difficult." She was tearing up again, thinking about Randy—wondering about Mrs. Roth, how she would get by now. Some companion Maddie was.

"You cannot be everywhere at once," M'ora said, reflect-ing Maddie's thoughts. "If you start blaming yourself for that, you will never find happiness."

"You think that's what Alvin wanted? To be everywhere

at once?"

"I think Alvin wanted power, and knowledge. But even we have limitations."

"He was a lot better at this than I am," Maddie said.

"But you... you have love. You have pinpoints of love, all along the way, to guide you. It is how I traveled, once. Our compass."

"*Our* compass?"

M'ora smiled, and held out her hand. It kindled into a compass of a thousand brilliant points, bright as a new star. Then she extinguished it. "But now, now I will stay here, and be with my son, and pray every day that he will be a good man."

"I might check in, if you don't mind," said Maddie.

"I wouldn't expect any less from you. And I thank you. I hope in time you might forgive me for my lies, for my deceptions. For such an old dragon, I am still learning."

Maddie nodded. "I think we're all a bunch of liars. But we're family. It sort of comes with the territory. In the end, Alvin had no remorse. You... you're different. I think."

"And Matilda?"

"She let darkness overwhelm her. And I trusted her because her darkness spoke to me, but it almost did me in, in the end," Maddie sighed. "I mistook her for a friend."

"Do you think *we* could be friends?"

"Who knows? "

M'ora smiled. "You won't stay a while?" she asked.

"No. I need to get home. Wherever that is, right now."

"Then fare you well, Madeline. May love light your way home."

16

Dragon

Someone was pounding on the oaken door with such violence that the hinges were rattling. Maddie startled awake, blinking in the complete darkness of the room. Wherever she was, it was the middle of the night.

"Just a sec!" she said, fumbling through the covers. They were soft, high quality, embroidered from corner to corner on the coverlet. A quality she'd never afforded in her own home. This could only be—

"Mrs. Roth?" came a voice. It was Mrs. Fitz. "The door's just about locked shut. I heard you come in last night, and I'm beside myself with worry. I'm about to break my shoulder opening it."

Shit, *shit.* How was she supposed to light the lamp, again? Maddie was clumsy, and a little giddy: She'd done it. The jump had been a bit more complicated than she'd thought, but she was fairly sure she had the right coordinates. She was still having a difficult time orienting herself when moving from place to place but...

Great, she was naked. Again.

Maddie fumbled for the switch on the gas-lamp beside

her bed, and after two clicks, it bathed the room in somber amber light. It was as she remembered it, and if Mrs. Fitz was yelling at her through the door, then the world had not gone on without her.

She grabbed one of the kimonos at the end of the bed, and wrapped it around herself hastily. The wobbling light around the door meant that Mrs. Fitz was still waiting, likely holding a lamp herself, tapping her foot impatiently.

Maddie opened the door, and Mrs. Fitz greeted her with a look of relief.

"I know you said not to disturb you for any reason, but it's been a hours and hours and hours and I'm about worried sick—"

"No, no. Mrs. Fitz, it's perfectly alright," Maddie said, in her best approximation of more refined speech. "Don't worry yourself. I'm better now."

Mrs. Fitz narrowed her eyes at Maddie. "I do say you look better... but that's not the half of it."

"What's the matter?" asked Maddie.

"There's been an accident. Aboard the *Faust*, in Charleston. They found Joss Raddick there with Mr. Roth, but poor Mr. Roth!"

Mrs. Fitz started weeping.

"He's... he's not—" Maddie knew he couldn't be dead. Not unless there was a twain about. The thought shook her into action.

"Stop crying and tell me what's happening," Maddie demanded, shaking off memories of Matilda in this place. It would take a long time to be rid of those shadows.

"We hear he got in a fight with someone, and don't know who but...it's so unlike him, ma'am! It must have been brigands, though Mother Mary knows I can't imagine why he'd be there in the first place!"

"Where is Randall?" Maddie asked firmly, taking the servant woman by the hands. "I just want to see him."

Mrs. Fitz's tears were as big as pearls, slipping down the curve of her cheek. "Oh, I'm sorry, I'm just so out of sorts. But the master is at the temple now, asking for you."

"... the temple?"

"One of the infirmaries at the Weeping Lady, yes," said Mrs. Fitz. "Shall I send Frank there to retrieve him? Surely we can call Dr. Halver here; there's no reason he should be kept at the–"

"No, no," Maddie said. "I'm coming..."

"You...are coming?"

"Yes, now, if you will help me into something appropriate–and quickly?"

Mrs. Fitz stared, then nodded enthusiastically.

The long corridor leading down to the infirmary of the Weeping Lady was lit with candles, casting lovely, flickering light on the beautiful frescoes on the walls, but Maddie did not linger to look. She walked ahead, Mrs. Fitz trailing behind her and barely keeping her breath, her boot-heels clicking every step. It was going to take some getting used to, all of this. Being here with *her* body was quite another experience. Second World was filled with more scents, good and bad, than she remembered, something she had never noticed with Matilda.

"This way," the priestess said, gesturing to a short wing off of the hallway. There was a door at the end of it. "He's been sleeping."

"Thank you–" Maddie said, faltering a little, unsure of how to reply.

"Sister Marsha," said the woman, bowing low. Maddie thought there might have been a knowing smile hidden in her eyes, but she did not take the time to seek it out. She'd had enough of secrets for a while.

The room was whitewashed stone, set with a bed and a dresser in high Victorian style: scrollwork, fluting, and inlay. There was a pleasant window, too, that likely had a good view somewhere. A good room, a room for someone of stature. There was water by the bedside, and a chair, too.

Joss Raddick sat in the chair, and Randall slept under the white covers, his head bandaged, and his eyes closed. He breathed softly, like a child, his mouth slightly ajar. This was the man she had come across worlds for. So much more than a man, though. He no longer looked so much like Randy when she gazed upon him, somehow.

Joss looked up immediately, surprised. "Mad—Madeline?" He squinted, then got to his feet. He came to her and embraced her, picking her up off the ground. "You made it back... thank heavens."

"Thank you for keeping an eye on him, Joss," Maddie said. "I just needed some time after all that. A little self-serving, I know."

"It was a big thing that happened, and you deserve any time you can get," Joss said, steadying his hand on her shoulder. "You know that, don't you? *Everything* is different."

"I know," she said.

"And you're staying here? In Second?"

"For now."

"Joss..." There was so much she wanted to say to him—to thank him, first and foremost. He was a friend, a true friend, and the knowledge of that sent a bubble to her throat and she almost sobbed. All her life she had been so lonely, but she no longer was. For all her loss, she had gained something new and remarkable.

"Not now. We'll have plenty of time for that later." He smiled, brushing a tear off of Maddie's cheek with the back of his hand. "Randall needs you now. Are you ready for that?

I think he's waking up. I couldn't take care of all his wounds. Our bodies can still be bruised, after all... but he's better than he was when I got here. I think the nurses were ready to give up on him at that point. As a twain, he would have healed, of course, but it would have taken a while without intervention."

She took a deep breath. "Thank you."

"You settled everything?"

She nodded. "I did."

Mrs. Fitz was at the door, staring at them. Maddie raised her voice and turned away her tear-stained face, remembering her manners. "Captain Raddick, if you don't mind attending to Mrs. Fitz while I spend some time with Mr. Roth?"

"Of course," he said, trying to suppress a smile; she really did sound just like Matilda when she tried. He gave Maddie one last smile, and left, promising to give Mrs. Fitz a grand tour of some of the more unknown areas of the Cathedral while they awaited word.

Maddie closed the heavy door, feeling the cold iron latches, and stood in the silence a few moments before turning to get a better look at Randall.

He was already stirring, and she fought back tears. Dawn was streaking the horizon pink, and Maddie almost laughed with the romantic atmosphere of it all. Sometimes life was like a fairy tale, and she figured she'd take it while the getting was good.

"Randall?" she asked, leaning forward. "You there?"

Randall opened his eyes, and they were bloodshot; he was squinting through sleep and swelling. He winced in pain as he adjusted himself on the bed.

"Did I get hit by a train?" he asked, focusing on Maddie next to him. She was wearing Matilda's clothing, so she had no idea if he would recognize her or not.

"Madeline?" he said, then, his voice breaking as he did. "You're really here? I'm not–"

"I'm here, Randall," Maddie said. She leaned over and

brushed his hair from his forehead, underneath the bandage. It didn't really help matters, but the gesture was comforting to her, at least. "For what it's worth."

"It's worth a great, great deal." His eyes welled with tears and he looked away, out the window, where light from the rising sun dappled the green grass of the cloister, casting long shadows from the pillars and arches.

"How much do you remember?" Maddie asked.

In between bouts of tears, and visits from some of the sisters bringing opium-laced tea to help his pain—he had, they indicated, broken three ribs and sprained his shoulder and left ankle—he told the story as he recalled it.

Yes, he had known Randy was present the moment they set foot on the First World, but he had promised to keep it secret. Randy had the reins most of the time, as it were, but he was allowing Randall through, letting him speak, because he knew Maddie would respond better to his presence. And, no doubt, would have been furious to know Randy had come along.

"He made me swear not to tell you he was there. And I felt as if I owed it to him, to give him that. He was enjoying the ride with the whole raven business, sitting with me, flying above. He knew so much about Alvin that I wondered if he hadn't been visiting me all along and I had just..." he trailed off, shaking his head. "I had just been an imbecile."

"I think Randy ran deeper than any of us could have suspected," Maddie said, fighting tears again. Someday it might not hurt so much, but now she was wounded deeply by his death. "I mean, I supposed he might have some capability, but now—"

"He told me he could see patterns in the First World, as we flew, said he understood the ley lines, the way that energy moved about. Every tree, every vine, every blade of green grass, he said was connected, and that we were moving toward a point of convergence. But he made me promise that, if he deemed it the right time, he could take over the body of the bird."

"He could see all that?" Maddie said, squeezing Randall's hand gently. She stroked the back of his knuckles, feeling the rise and roughness of the scabs there. "It's almost the same way that I can see the lines in people..."

Randall swallowed. "But when the obelisk came into view, he thrust me out of control entirely. He flew up and away. Then he started—"

"Dancing, I saw him," Maddie replied. "I figured it was him. But Ravel said the obelisk cancelled out our abilities to communicate," she remembered. "How did you do it, then?"

"I suspect that since we entered First together, we were able to circumvent that restriction, or that Randy figured his way around it. He was able to unravel the spells about the obelisk, after all. I may have hurt him in some ways, restrained some of his abilities, but he had other capabilities I can only dream of—capabilities that not even Ravel could predict or control." Randall squeezed her hand back, then put his other atop hers. "Randy knew what had to be done. He suspected there was an alternate way, a very old magic, on the tips of everyone's tongues. So many gathered, so much potential."

"And you didn't leave him? You could have. Your body was still here in Second."

"He needed someone with him. He was..." Randall nearly choked on the word, trying to suppress his emotion. "He was terrified. But he did it out of love—for you..."

Maddie couldn't speak; the tears made her throat too thick.

Randall continued. "I felt the piercing with him; the arrow, the fire, the water, the spear. It was pain nearly too much to bear—but I bore it with him, together. Until..."

"Until you fell."

"He pushed me out. If the magic had kept us together for that long, it could kill us together, and though there was a chance another of us was in one of the Eight Worlds, it could grant Ravel powers we did not wish to give him.

"He told me to love you. To help you. To keep you as I could, if I could. That part of him would always be here," Randall said, touching his heart.

Maddie let the tears get the better of her for a moment. Mourning Randy felt like thorns were growing in her heart.

She tweaked his chin gently. "You're a mess, Randall. Joss helped to improve matters, but he could only go so far. Alvin told me 'I'm sorry about Randall,' and I feared the worst. What did he do to you?"

"Alvin, yes," Randall said, his eyes unfocusing a moment as he lingered in memory. "He knew I'd go after you, and knew what happened to my body when I translated. So he locked me in a room on the *Faust* before I left, and told some of the brigands on the ship I'd cheated at cards." He shuddered. "Hence, the bruises. I wasn't dead, and I wasn't responsive, and I wager the criminals aboard decided to see how far they could go before they could wake me up. Joss found me, when he returned, and brought me here."

"You were brave," Maddie said.

"Not as brave as Randy."

"But Randy is dead, and you are not."

"And Matilda? And Alvin?"

Randall listened as Maddie recounted what had happened after Randy's impalement on the obelisk, how it had melted; "Then Matilda tried to kill me. Or bite my face off, I don't know which," she said with a shudder. "But M'ora did away with her... and Alvin..."

"Randy told me what might happen. He let me make the decision, and I told him if Alvin was beyond redemption, then he truly was a plague on our kind," Randall said softly.

"It's stupid, but I miss him. Even though he was dead to me for so long, now that he's..."

"I know." Randall squeezed her hand. "But you are here now. I didn't dare to dream you'd come back. *There's no place like home,* isn't that how it goes?"

"I did go back to Sixth World," Maddie admitted.

"And what did you find there?"

Maddie smiled a little. Her eyelids were so heavy, she could have just fallen asleep right there, next to Randall on the bed.

"Here," Maddie said. "Let me show you."

Maddie leaned over and gave Randall a kiss of memory.

Maddie opens the door to Dr. Keats's bathroom to find the house more or less in the same state she left it. She creeps through the house; it's nighttime, and she can hear a far-away snore from the opposite end of the house. It's got to be Dr. Keats, but she won't bother him.

Her coat is still by the door, hanging where she left it. Dr. Keats did not give up, apparently. She opens the door slowly, trying to minimize the squeaking of the hinges. They're in need of some WD-40.

Maddie thinks about writing Dr. Keats a note, thanking him, explaining things to him. But she thinks better of it. He'll know when her coat is gone. He'll know what to make of it; and if he's smart, he won't go looking for her. Why should he?

The car is parked alongside the house now, and she almost bursts into tears when she opens the door. It smells just like it always has, slightly stale with a citrus burst from the air freshener. There are many of her things inside: her purse, some books, half-finished knitting. But nothing feels like hers and everything reminds her of Randy.

The trip down the Masspike is uneventful, and the world is cast in shadows of night. The clock on the dash starts out at four in the morning, but by the time she enters Sunderland by way of Route 116, it's truly morning. Late enough that people are out walking already. It might be Sunday, but she really has no idea. She didn't look that closely at the calendar.

She's been rehearsing the speech in her head since she got into the car, trying to make a story that's worthy to tell Mrs. Roth. How does she say it? How can she tell her? That Randy saved her life... somewhere? That he was a bird and she was a sphinx? No, perhaps Maddie will say she had tried to jump a bridge, just as Agnes had, and...

It's easier than saying, "Mrs. Roth, your son was a personification of a deity, and he sacrificed himself to prevent your other son, Alvin, from pretty much destroying at least an entire world. Sooner or later, anyway. Oh, and by the way, Alvin wasn't dead, and technically isn't really dead now, but he's bound and..."

But when she pulls up by the big house on Main Street, the one that she has frequented so often in the last six years, she's surprised. There are two cars in the driveway, an SUV and a van, the kind that only soccer moms have. And, in fact, on the dashboard is the stick-figure representation of a husband and wife, and their children—three of them. Even a dog and a cat.

She parks across the street, and stares at the house. The lawn is covered in snow, but there are a hundred little footprints running across it.

When the door to the house opens up, Maddie ducks down behind her steering wheel, wishing the car wasn't so obviously hers.

But she doesn't need to worry because Mrs. Roth isn't looking across the street. She's looking at the trail of children coming out the front door in their winter best. They're about two years apart in age—two girls, and a younger boy, and they've still got their pajamas on, but they're wearing winter coats and boots over them. The ground is still wet, and though the buds on the trees are reluctant to come out, they're still tinged green. It's Easter Sunday.

Okay, so she was a little off the mark. But Easter is early this year.

The kids careen through the yard, picking up plastic eggs, diving into the bushes, and Mrs. Roth stands at the doorway watching them. A man emerges, tall and in his sixties, smiling through a white mustache. Then, later, carrying coffee, come the parents of the kids–presumably the mustached man's son, by the way he favors him so much. They all stand together on the stoop, watching the children hoot and holler through the yard, drinking cups of coffee, and chatting to one another.

Not much about Mrs. Roth has changed, except that she's smiling. She's smiling so brilliantly it makes her look ten years younger. The older man puts his arm around her shoulders, and squeezes, knowingly. And if there is sorrow in her eyes for something, for someone lost, she doesn't let it show. She is grinning too much.

Maybe with Randy gone, she doesn't remember. Maybe he's been erased from the world. Maddie doesn't know anything more than what her heart tells her.

All she knows is that Mrs. Roth has moved on.

"I never said anything to her," Maddie said, when the memory dissipated; she blushed slightly. "I drove away, picked up a Mountain Dew and a Twinkie, then went to the Bridge of Flowers in Shelburne Falls. To make my peace. With my ghosts. With myself. With Randy. The flowers weren't blooming yet, of course, but it felt right."

She took a deep breath, looking down at her hands. "And I decided that the only place left in the Eight Worlds I wanted to be was here. The wonder, the magic, the beauty of my world had just faded. Seeing Randy do what he did gave me a perspective on my life, the world, and my place in it."

"And you came back–so precisely?" he asked. "I mean, it's only been a handful of days, but there are so many variables to consider. Even erring slightly could cause you to lose time–centuries, even."

"Randall. You're sounding too much like a scientist, and not enough like a magician. Remember, some things just can't be explained. I learned that, sometimes, I can get where I need to go by just using my..." she laughed, because it sounded so corny, but she said it anyway, "my heart. Even time, when it comes down to it, is just relative. Sure, I overcompensated a little getting to First World, but not enough to make a difference. I came back here at the right time, and that's what matters."

Sinking down into his pillows, Randall closed his eyes and expelled a long breath. "I can scarcely believe it all," he said. "I feel myself to be, quite possibly, the most fortunate of my kind in all the Eight Worlds."

"Don't get all poetic. I'm still angry with you."

"Maddie–"

"It's going to take a while for me to forgive you. But I will. In time." She kissed him, gently and thoughtfully. "You're the last link I have to Randy, and he trusted you. I owe it to him to do the same. I know he'd want... he'd want me to be happy."

"You are a wonder, you know that?" he said, taking her hand and kissing it. "I'm not deserving of this..."

"Yeah, yeah. Just promise me we can take it easy for a while, okay?" she said, leaning down to kiss him on the cheek. "I hear there's a war brewing, thanks to Miriam and John. Chances are we should take a break while we can."

He chuckled. "Take it easy, eh? And after that?"

Maddie grinned in spite of herself. "There's at least five more worlds to explore. You don't think I'm going to settle for seeing just three of them, do you?"

Thanks:

To Karen Gadient, my soul-friend. You know why.

To Dorothy Walsh Sasso, who first followed Maddie through the looking glass.

To Mr. Warchol: Sorry about the talking animals. But thank you for encouraging me to write fantasy, anyway.

To my parents for never telling me my dreams were impossible.

To my husband, Michael, for the years we spent together here and in the Shire; to my son Liam for inspiring me to be more honest with myself as a writer and helping me see the world with new eyes every day.

To William Wordsworth and John Keats for never failing to inspire.

Special thanks are due, as well, to a few other people: to Samuel Montgomery-Blinn and the whole *Bull Spec* crew here in the Triangle for the support, community, and consistently amazing events. To the writers in my first writing online group: Michelle Muenzler, Paul Jessup, and Jonathan Wood, for encouragement, laughs, and general zaniness.

Special thanks, too, to Brigid Ashwood, whose work inspired me before I put pen to paper on this tale, and continues to do so.

And last, but certainly not least, to my editor, Kate Sullivan, for not just "getting" my odd little book but encouraging me to dig deeper and find more within the manuscript. You are my compass.

About the Author

Natania Barron has been traveling to other worlds from a very young age, and will be forever indebted to Lucy Pevensie and Meg Murry for inspiring her to go on her own adventures.

She currently resides in North Carolina with her family, and is, at heart, a hobbit–albeit it one with a Tookish streak a mile wide.

Follow the author online:

www.pilgrimofthesky.com

www.nataniabarron.com
Twitter: @nataniabarron

CPSIA information can be obtained at www.ICGtesting.com
Printed in the USA
BVOW041637060212

282242BV00001B/1/P